KU-258-536

MARGUERITE YOURCENAR

MEMOIRS OF HADRIAN

TRANSLATED FROM THE FRENCH BY
GRACE FRICK
IN COLLABORATION WITH
THE AUTHOR

THE
BRITISH
MUSEUM

WITHDRAWN

THE PAUL HAMLYN LIBRARY

843. 912219. YOU

A KING PENGUIN
PUBLISHED BY PENGUIN BOOKS
In association with MARTIN SECKER AND WARBURG

Penguin Books Ltd, Harmondsworth, Middlesex, England
Penguin Books, 40 West 23rd Street, New York, New York 10010, U.S.A.
Penguin Books Australia Ltd, Ringwood, Victoria, Australia
Penguin Books Canada Ltd, 2801 John Street, Markham, Ontario, Canada L3R 1B4
Penguin Books (N.Z.) Ltd, 182–190 Wairau Road, Auckland 10, New Zealand

—

Mémoires d'Hadrien first published 1951
First published in England by Martin Secker and Warburg 1955
Published in Penguin Books 1959
Reprinted 1978, 1982
Reprinted with 'Reflections on the Composition' 1983

—

Copyright © Marguerite Yourcenar, 1951, 1955
All rights reserved

—

Made and printed in Great Britain
by Hazell Watson & Viney Ltd,
Aylesbury, Bucks
Set in Monotype Plantin

12322

BM2
(YOU)

Except in the United States of America,
this book is sold subject to the condition
that it shall not, by way of trade or otherwise,
be lent, re-sold, hired out, or otherwise circulated
without the publisher's prior consent in any form of
binding or cover other than that in which it is
published and without a similar condition
including this condition being imposed
on the subsequent purchaser

CONTENTS

BRITISH MUSEUM

1 4 MAR 1984

EDUCATION SERVICE
LIBRARY

THE ROMAN EMPIRE
Under Hadrian
The Frontiers of Hadrian — Thus

A

SARMATIA

DACIA

Sarmizegethusa

DANUVIUS

PANNONIA
SUPERIOR
PANNONIA
INFERIOR

MOESIA
SUPERIOR

MOESIA INFERIOR

Odessus

PONTUS EUXINUS
(BLACK SEA)

Sinope

THRACIA

ET PONTUS

Hadrianopolis
Plotinopolis

Bosphorus

Byzantium

MACEDONIA

Propontis

Nicomedia

Claudiopolis

Satala

Brundisium

Hadrianopolis

Hadriantheræ

BYTHNIA

GALATEA

CAPPADOCIA

ARMENIA

EPIRUS

Dodona

MYSIA

Pergamum

MESOPOTAMIA

EUPHRATES

Chaeronea
Delphi

Smyrna

Ephesus

Laodicea

Edessa

ATHENS

Corinth
Arcadia
Mantinea

Delos

Aphrodisias

COMMAGENE

Doura

Sparta

ÆGÆUM

LYCIA

CILICIA

Solinus

Seleucia

ANTIOCH

Mons Cassius

PALMYRA

CRETE

Rhodes

CYPRUS

SYRIA

Luxufeu

INTERNUM

Sidon
Tyre

PALÆSTINA

PETRA

LIBYCUM

Gadara

CYRENE

ALEXANDRIA

Nicopolis

Canopus

Gaza

JERUSALEM
Ælia (capitolina)

ARABIA

CYRENAICA

LIBYA

Pelusium

Berenice

EGYPT

NILUS

ANTINOOPOLIS

GEO. MANSELL. 1955

ANIMULA VAGULA, BLANDULA,
HOSPES COMESQUE CORPORIS;
QUAE NUNC ABIBIS IN LOCA
PALLIDULA, RIGIDA, NUDULA,
NEC, UT SOLES, DABIS IOCOS . . .

P. AELIUS HADRIANUS, IMP.

ANIMULA VAGULA BLANDULA

MY DEAR MARK,

Today I went to see my physician Hermogenes, who has just returned to the Villa from a rather long·journey in Asia. No food could be taken before the examination, so we had made the appointment for the early morning hours. I took off my cloak and tunic and lay down on a couch. I spare you details which would be as disagreeable to you as to me, the description of the body of a man who is growing old, and is about to die of a dropsical heart. Let us say only that I coughed, inhaled, and held my breath according to Hermogenes' directions. He was alarmed, in spite of himself, by the rapid progress of the disease, and was inclined to throw the blame on young Iollas, who has attended me during his absence. It is difficult to remain an emperor in the presence of a physician, and difficult even to keep one's essential quality as man. The professional eye saw in me only a mass of humours, a sorry mixture of blood and lymph. This morning it occurred to me for the first time that my body, my faithful companion and friend, truer and better known to me than my own soul, may be after all only a sly beast who will end by devouring his master. But enough. . . . I like my body; it has served me well, and in every way, and I do not begrudge it the care it now needs. I have no faith, however, as Hermogenes still claims to have, in the miraculous virtues of herbs, or the specific mixture of mineral salts which he went to the Orient to get. Subtle though he is, he has nevertheless offered me vague formulas of reassurance too trite to deceive anyone; he knows how I hate this kind of pretence, but a man does not practise medicine for more than thirty years without some falsehood. I forgive this good servitor his endeavour to hide my death from me. Hermogenes is learned; he is even wise, and his integrity is well above that of the ordinary court physician. It will fall to my lot as a sick man to have the best of care. But no one can go beyond prescribed limits: my swollen limbs no longer sustain me through

9

the long Roman ceremonies; I fight for breath; and I am now sixty.

Do not mistake me; I am not yet weak enough to yield to fearful imaginings, which are almost as absurd as illusions of hope, and are certainly harder to bear. If I must deceive myself, I should prefer to stay on the side of confidence, for I shall lose no more there and shall suffer less. This approaching end is not necessarily immediate; I still retire each night with hope to see the morning. Within those absolute limits of which I was just now speaking I can defend my position step by step, and even regain a few inches of lost ground. I have nevertheless reached the age where life, for every man, is accepted defeat. To say that my days are numbered signifies nothing; they always were, and are so for us all. But uncertainty as to the place, the time, and the manner, which keeps us from distinguishing the goal toward which we continually advance, diminishes for me the progress of my fatal malady. A man may die at any hour, but a sick man knows that he will no longer be alive in ten years' time. My margin of doubt is a matter of months, not years. The chances of ending by a dagger thrust in the heart or by a fall from a horse are slight indeed; plague seems unlikely, and leprosy or cancer appear definitely left behind. I no longer run the risk of falling on the frontiers, struck down by a Caledonian axe or pierced by an arrow of the Parths; storms and tempests have failed to seize the occasions offered, and the soothsayer who told me that I should not drown seems to have been right. I shall die at Tibur or in Rome, or in Naples at the farthest, and a moment's suffocation will settle the matter. Shall I be carried off by the tenth of these crises, or the hundredth? That is the only question. Like a traveller sailing the Archipelago who sees the luminous mists lift toward evening, and little by little makes out the shore, I begin to discern the profile of my death.

Already certain portions of my life are like dismantled rooms of a palace too vast for an impoverished owner to occupy in its entirety. I can hunt no longer: if there were no one but me to disturb them in their ruminations and their play the deer in the Etrurian mountains would be at peace. With the Diana of the forests I have always maintained the swift-changing and passionate relations which are those of a man with the object of his love : the boar hunt gave me my first chance, as a boy, for command and for encounter with danger; I fairly threw myself into the sport, and my excesses in it brought reprimands from Trajan. The kill in a Spanish forest was my earliest acquaintance with death and with courage, with pity for living creatures and the tragic pleasure of seeing them suffer. Grown to manhood, I found in hunting release from many a secret struggle with adversaries too subtle or too stupid in turn, too weak or too strong for me; this evenly-matched battle between human intelligence and the wisdom of wild beasts seemed strangely clean compared to the snares set by men for men. My hunts in Tuscany have helped me as emperor to judge the courage or the resources of high officials; I have chosen or eliminated more than one statesman in this way. In later years, in Bithynia and Cappadocia, I made the great drives for game a pretext for festival, a kind of autumnal triumph in the woods of Asia. But the companion of my last hunts died young, and my taste for these violent pleasures has greatly abated since his departure. Even here in Tibur, however, the sudden bark of a stag in the brush is enough to set trembling within me an impulse deeper than all the rest, by virtue of which I feel myself leopard as well as emperor. Who knows? Possibly I have been so sparing of human blood only because I have shed so much of the blood of wild beasts, even if sometimes, privately, I have preferred beasts to mankind. However that may be, they are more in my thoughts, and it is hard not to let myself go into interminable tales of the chase which would try the patience of my supper guests. Surely the recollection of the day of my adoption has its charm, but the memory of lions killed in Mauretania is not bad either.

To give up riding is a greater sacrifice still : a wild beast is first of all an adversary, but my horse was a friend. If the choice of my condition had been left to me I would have decided for that of centaur. Between Borysthenes and me relations were of almost mathematical precision; he obeyed me as if I were his own brain, not his master. Have I ever obtained as much from a man? Such total authority comprises, as does any other power, its risk of error for the possessor, but the pleasure of attempting the impossible in jumping an obstacle was too strong for me to regret a dislocated shoulder or a broken rib. My horse knew me not by the thousand approximate notions of title, function, and name which complicate human friendships, but solely by my just weight as a man. He shared my every impetus; he knew perfectly, and perhaps better than I, the point at which my strength faltered under my will. But I no longer inflict upon Borysthenes' successor the burden of an invalid whose muscles are flabby, and who is too weak to heave himself unassisted upon a horse's back. My aide Celer is exercising him at this moment on the road to Praeneste; all my past experiments with swift motion help me now to share the pleasure of both horse and rider, and to judge the sensations of the man at full gallop on a day of sun and high wind. When Celer leaps down from his horse I too regain contact with the ground. It is the same with swimming: I have given it up, but I still share the swimmer's delight in water's caress. Running, even for the shortest distance, would today be as impossible for me as for a heavy statue, a Caesar of stone; but I recall my childhood races on the dry hills of Spain, and the game played with myself of pressing on to the last gasp, never doubting that the perfect heart and healthy lungs would re-establish their equilibrium; and with any athlete training for the stadium I have a common understanding which the intelligence alone would not have given me. Thus from each art practised in its time I derive a knowledge which compensates me in part for pleasures lost. I have supposed, and in my better moments think so still, that it would be possible in this manner to participate in the existence of everyone; such sympathy would be one of the least revocable kinds of immortality. There have been moments when that comprehension tried to go beyond human experience, passing from the swimmer to the wave. But in such a realm, since there is nothing exact left to guide me, I verge upon the world of dream and metamorphosis.

Overeating is a Roman vice, but moderation has always been my delight. Hermogenes has had to change nothing in my diet, except perhaps the impatience which made me devour the first thing served, no matter where or when, in order to satisfy the needs of hunger simply and at once. It is clear that a man of wealth, who has never known anything but voluntary privation, or has experienced it only provisionally as one of the more or less exciting incidents of war or travel, would have but ill grace to boast of undereating. Stuffing themselves on certain feast days has always been the ambition, joy, and natural pride of the poor. At army festivities I liked the aroma of roasted meats and the noisy scraping of kettles, and it pleased me to see that the army banquets (or what passes for a banquet in camp) were just what they always should be, a gay and hearty contrast to the deprivations of working days. I could stand well enough the smell of fried foods in the public squares at the Saturnalia, but the banquets of Rome filled me with such repugnance and boredom that if at times I have expected to die in the course of an exploration or a military expedition I have said to myself, by way of consolation, that at least I should not have to live through another dinner! Do not do me the injustice to take me for a mere ascetic; an operation which is performed two or three times a day, and the purpose of which is to sustain life, surely merits all our care. To eat a fruit is to welcome into oneself a fair living object, which is alien to us but is nourished and protected like us by the earth; it is to consume a sacrifice wherein we sustain ourselves at the expense of things. I have never bitten into a chunk of army bread without marvelling that this coarse and heavy concoction can transform itself into blood and warmth, and perhaps into courage. Alas, why does my mind, even on its best days, never possess but a particle of the assimilative powers of the body?

It was in Rome, during the long official repasts, that I began to think of the relatively recent origins of our riches, and of this nation of thrifty farmers and frugal soldiers formerly fed upon garlic and barley now suddenly enabled by our conquests to luxuriate in the culinary arts of Asia, bolting down those complicated viands with the greed of hungry peasants. We Romans cram ourselves with ortolans, drown ourselves in sauces, and poison ourselves with spices. An Apicius glories in the succession of courses and the sequence of sweet or sour, heavy or dainty foods which make up the exquisite order of his banquets; these dishes would perhaps be tolerable if each were served separately, and consumed for its own sake, learnedly savoured by an expert whose taste and appetite are both unspoiled. But presented pell-mell, in the midst of everyday vulgar profusion, they confound a man's palate and confuse his stomach with a detestable mixture of flavours, odours, and substances in which the true values are lost and the unique qualities disappear. My poor Lucius used to amuse himself by concocting delicacies for me; his pheasant pasties with their skilful blending of ham and spice bore witness to an art which is as exacting as that of a musician or painter, but I could not help regretting the unadulterated flesh of the fine bird. Greece knew better about such things: her resin-steeped wine, her bread sprinkled with sesame seed, fish grilled at the very edge of the sea and unevenly blackened by the fire or seasoned here and there by the grit of sand, all satisfied the appetite alone without surrounding by too many complications this simplest of our joys. In the merest hole of a place in Aegina or Phaleron I have tasted food so fresh that it remained divinely clean despite the dirty fingers of the tavern waiter; its quantity, though modest, was nevertheless so satisfying that it seemed to contain in the most reduced form possible some essence of immortality. Likewise meat cooked at night after a hunt had that same almost sacramental quality, taking us far back to the primitive origins of the races of men.

Wine initiates us into the volcanic mysteries of the soil and its hidden mineral riches; a cup of Samos drunk at noon in the heat of the sun or, on the contrary, absorbed of a winter evening when fatigue makes the warm current felt at once in the hollow of the diaphragm and the sure and burning dispersion spreads along our arteries, such a drink provides a sensation which is almost sacred, and is sometimes too strong for the human head. No feeling so pure comes from the vintage-numbered cellars of Rome; the pedantry of great connoisseurs of wine wearies me. Water drunk more reverently still, from the hands or from the spring itself, diffuses within us the most secret salt of earth and the rain of heaven. But even water is a delight which, sick man that I am, I may now consume only with strict restraint. No matter: in death's agony itself, and mingled with the bitterness of the last potions, I shall try still to taste on my lips its fresh simplicity.

In the schools of philosophy, where it is well to try once for all each mode of life, I have experimented briefly with abstention from meat; later, in Asia, I have seen the Indian Gymnosophists avert their eyes from smoking lamb quarters and gazelle meat served in the tent of Osroës. But this practice, in which your youthful love of austerity finds charm, calls for attentions more complicated than those of culinary refinement itself; and it separates us too much from the common run of men in a function which is nearly always public, and in which either friendship or formality presides. I should prefer to live all my life upon woodcock and fattened goose rather than be accused by my guests, at each meal, of a display of asceticism. As it is I have had some trouble to conceal from my friends, by the help of dried fruits or the contents of a glass sipped slowly, that the masterpieces of my chefs were made more for them than for me, and that my interest in these courses ended before theirs. A prince lacks the latitude afforded to the philosopher in this respect: he cannot allow himself to be different on too many points at a time; and the gods know that my points of difference were already too numerous, though I flattered myself that many were invisible. As to the religious scruples of the Gymnosophist and his disgust at the sight of bleeding flesh, I should be more affected thereby if I had not sometimes asked myself in what essentials the suffering of grass, when it is cut, differs from the suffering of slaughtered sheep, and if our horror in presence of murdered beasts does not arise from the fact that our sensations belong to the same physical order as theirs. But at certain times of life, for example in periods of ritual fasting or in the course of religious initiations, I have learned the advantage for the mind (and also the dangers) of different forms of abstinence, or even of voluntary starvation, those states approaching giddiness where the body, partly lightened of ballast, enters into a world for which it is not made, and which affords it a foretaste of the cold and emptiness of death. At other moments such experiences have given me the chance to toy with the idea of slow suicide, of decease by inanition which certain philosophers have employed, a kind of debauch in reverse, continued to the point of exhaustion of the human substance. But it never would have pleased me to adhere too closely to a system, and I should not have allowed a scruple to take away my right, say, to stuff myself with sausages, if by chance I so desired, or if that particular food were the only one at hand.

The cynics and the moralists agree in placing the pleasures of love among the enjoyments termed gross, that is, between the desire for drinking and the need for eating, though at the same time they call love less indispensable, since it is something which, they assert, one can go without. I expect almost anything from the moralist, but am astonished that the cynic should go thus astray. Probably both fear their own daemons, whether resisting or surrendering to them, and they oblige themselves to scorn their pleasure in order to reduce its almost terrifying power, which overwhelms them, and its strange mystery, wherein they feel lost. I shall never believe in the classification of love among the purely physical joys (supposing that any such things exist) until I see a gourmet sobbing with delight over his favourite dish like a lover gasping on a young shoulder. Of all our games, love's play is the only one which threatens to unsettle the soul, and is also the only one in which the player has to abandon himself to the body's ecstasy. To put reason aside is not indispensable for a drinker, but the lover who leaves reason in control does not follow his god to the end. In every act save that of love, abstinence and excess alike involve but one person; any step in the direction of sensuality, however, places us in the presence of the Other, and involves us in the demands and servitudes to which our choice binds us (except in the case of Diogenes, where both the limitations and the merits of reasonable expediency are self-evident). I know no decision which a man makes for simpler or more inevitable reasons, where the object chosen is weighed more exactly for its balance of sheer pleasure, or where the seeker after truth has a better chance to judge the naked human being. Each time, from a stripping down as absolute as that of death, and from a humility which surpasses that of defeat and of prayer, I marvel to see again reforming the complex web of experiences shared and refused, of mutual responsibilities, awkward avowals, transparent lies, and passionate compromises between my pleasures and those of the Other, so

·many bonds impossible to break but nevertheless so quickly loosened. That mysterious play which extends from love of a body to love of an entire person has seemed to me noble enough to consecrate to it one part of my life. Words for it are deceiving, since the word for pleasure covers contradictory realities comprising notions of warmth, sweetness, and intimacy of bodies, but also feelings of violence and agony, and the sound of a cry. The short and obscene sentence of Poseidonius about the rubbing together of two small pieces of flesh, which I have seen you copy in your exercise books with the application of a good schoolboy, does no more to define the phenomenon of love than the cord touched by the finger accounts for the infinite miracle of sounds. Such a dictum is less an insult to pleasure than to the flesh itself, that amazing instrument of muscles, blood, and skin, that red-tinged cloud whose lightning is the soul.

And I admit that the reason stands confounded in presence of the veritable prodigy that love is, and of the strange obsession which makes this same flesh (for which we care so little when it is that of our own body, and which concerns us only to wash and nourish it, and if possible to keep it from suffering) inspire us with such a passion of caresses simply because it is animated by an individuality different from our own, and because it presents certain lineaments of beauty, disputed though they may be by the best judges. Here human logic stops short, as before the revelations of the Mysteries. Popular tradition has not been wrong in regarding love always as a form of initiation, one of the points of encounter of the secret with the sacred. Sensual experience is further comparable to the Mysteries in that the first approach gives to the uninitiated the impression of a ritual which is more or less frightening, and shockingly far removed from the familiar functions of sleeping, eating, and drinking; it appears matter for jest and shame, or even terror. Quite as much as the dance of the Maenads or the frenzy of the Corybantes, love-making carries us into a different world, where at other times we are forbidden to enter, and where we cease to belong as soon as the ardour is spent, or the ecstasy subsides. Nailed to the beloved body like a slave to his cross, I have learned some secrets of life which are now dimmed in my memory by the operation of that same law which ordains that the convalescent, once cured, ceases to understand the mysterious truths laid bare by illness, and that the prisoner, set free, forgets his torture, or the returning hero, his triumph passed, forgets his glory.

I have sometimes thought of constructing a system of human knowledge which would be based on eroticism, a theory of contact wherein the mysterious value of each being is to offer to us just that point of perspective which another world affords. In such a philosophy pleasure would be a more complete but also more specialized form of approach to the Other, one more technique for getting to know what is not ourselves. In the least sensual encounters it is still in our contacts that emotion begins, or ends: the somewhat repugnant hand of the old woman who presents me her petition, the moist brow of my father in death's agony, the wound which I wash for an injured soldier. Even the most intellectual or the most neutral exchanges are made through this system of body-signals: the sudden enlightenment on the face of a tribune to whom a manoeuvre is explained on the morning of battle, the impersonal salute of a subordinate whom my passing fixes into an attitude of attention, the friendly glance of a slave at my thanks for the tray which he brings me, or the appreciative grimace of an old friend to whom a rare cameo is given. The slightest and most superficial of contacts are enough for us with most persons, or prove even too much. But when these contacts persist and multiply about one unique being, to the point of embracing him entirely, when each fraction of a body becomes laden for us with meaning as overpowering as that of the face itself, when this one creature haunts us like music and torments us like a problem (instead of inspiring in us, at most, mere irritation, amusement, or boredom), when he passes from the periphery of our universe to its centre and finally becomes for us more indispensable than ourselves, then the astonishing prodigy takes place wherein I see much more an invasion of the flesh by the spirit than a simple play of the body alone.

Such views on love might lead to the career of seducer. If I have not fulfilled that role it is doubtless because I have done something else, if no better. Short of genius, such a career de-

mands attentions and even stratagems for which I was little
suited. Those set traps, always the same, and the monotonous
routine of perpetual advances, leading no further than conquest
itself, have palled on me. The technique of a great seducer requires a facility and an indifference in passing from one object
of affection to another which I could never have; however that
may be, my loves have left me more often than I have left them,
for I have never been able to understand how one could have
enough of any beloved. The desire to count up exactly the riches
which each new love brings us, and to see it change, and perhaps
watch it grow old, accords ill with multiplicity of conquests. I
used once to believe that a certain feeling for beauty would serve
me in place of virtue, and would render me immune from
solicitations of the coarsest kind. But I was mistaken. The lover
of beauty ends by finding it everywhere about him, a vein of
gold in the basest of ores; by handling fragmentary masterpieces,
though stained or broken, he comes to know a collector's
pleasure in being the sole seeker after pottery which is commonly
passed by. A problem more serious (for a man of taste) is a
position of eminence in human affairs, with the risks from
adulation and lies which are inherent in the possession of almost
absolute power. The idea that anyone should sham in my
presence, even in the slightest degree, is enough to make me pity
and despise or even hate him. Indeed I have suffered from the
inconveniences of my fortune as a poor man does from those of
his privations. One step more and I might have accepted the
fiction of pretending that one is a seducer when one knows oneself to be merely the master. But that is the road to disgust, or
perhaps to fatuity.

One would end by preferring the plain truths of debauchery
to the outworn stratagems of seduction if there, too, lies did not
prevail. In principle I am ready to admit that prostitution is an
art like massage or hairdressing, but for my part I find it hard to
get much enjoyment from barbers or masseurs. There is nothing
more crude than an accomplice. The sidelong glance of the
tavern-keeper who would reserve the best wine for me (and con-
sequently deprive some other customer) sufficed even in my
younger days to dull my appetite for the amusements of Rome.

It displeases me to have some creature think that he can foresee and profit from my desire, automatically adapting himself to what he supposes to be my taste. At such moments the absurd and deformed reflection of myself which a human brain returns to me would almost make me prefer the ascetic's sorry state. If legend does not exaggerate the excesses of Nero and the erudite researches of Tiberius, those two great consumers of pleasure must have had inert senses indeed to put themselves to the expense of so complicated a machinery, and must have held mankind in singular disdain to let themselves in for such mockery and extortion. And yet, if I have virtually given up these too mechanical forms of pleasure, or have never indulged in them at too great length, I owe it more to chance than to impregnable virtue. I could well fall back into such habits in growing old, just as into any kind of confusion or fatigue, but sickness and approaching death will save me from monotonous repetition of the same procedures, like droning through a lesson too long known by note.

Of all the joys which are slowly abandoning me, sleep is one of the most precious, though one of the most common, too. A man who sleeps but little and poorly, propped on many a cushion, has ample time to meditate upon this particular delight. I grant that the most perfect repose is almost necessarily a complement to love, that profound rest which is reflected in two bodies. But what interests me here is the specific mystery of sleep partaken of for itself alone, the inevitable plunge risked each night by the naked man, solitary and unarmed, into an ocean where everything changes, the colours, the densities, and even the rhythm of breathing, and where we meet the dead. What reassures us about sleep is that we do come out of it, and come out of it unchanged, since some mysterious ban keeps us from bringing back with us in their true form even the remnants of our dreams. What also reassures us is that sleep heals us of fatigue, but heals us by the most radical of means in arranging that we cease temporarily to exist. There, as elsewhere, the pleasure and the art consist in conscious surrender to that blissful unconsciousness, and in accepting to be slightly less strong, less light, less heavy, and less definite than our waking selves.

I shall return later to the strange world of our dreams, for I prefer to speak here of certain experiences of pure sleep and pure awakening which border on death and resurrection. I am trying to recapture the exact sensation of such overpowering sleep as that of boyhood, where, still fully clad, one toppled over one's books, transported as if by lightning out of mathematics and the law into the midst of a deep and substantial sleep so filled with unused energy that one tasted, as it were, the very essence of being through the closed eyelids. I evoke the short, sudden snatches of slumber on the bare ground, in the forest after tiring days of hunts; the barking of the dogs would awaken me, or their paws planted on my chest. So total was the eclipse that each time I might have found myself to be someone else, and I was perplexed and often saddened by the strict law which brought me back from so far away to re-enter this narrow confine of humanity which is myself. What are those particularities upon which we lay most store, since they count so little for us when we are liberated in sleep, and since for one second before returning into the body of Hadrian I was about to savour almost consciously that new existence without content and without past?

On the other hand, sickness and age have also their prodigies and receive from sleep other forms of benediction. About a year ago, after a singularly exhausting day in Rome, I experienced one of these respites wherein the depletion of one's forces serves to work the same miracle as did the unexploited reserves of former days. I go but rarely to the City now; once there I try to accomplish as much as possible. The day had been disagreeably full: a meeting of the Senate had been followed by a session in court, and by an interminable discussion with one of the quaestors; then by a religious ceremony which could not be cut short, and upon which it steadily rained. I myself had fitted all these different activities closely together, crowding them in so as to leave between them the least time possible for importunate requests and useless flatteries. The return on horseback was one of my last trips of the kind. I reached the Villa sickened and chilled as we are only when the blood actually refuses, and no longer works in our veins. Celer and Chabrias rushed to my aid, but solicitude can be wearing even when it is sincere. Retiring to my apartment I swallowed a few spoonfuls of a hot broth which I prepare myself, not out of suspicion, as is surmised, but because I thus procure for myself the luxury of being alone. I lay down : sleep seemed as far removed from me as health itself, and as youth or vigour. I dozed off. The sand-glass proved to me that I had slept barely an hour, but a brief moment of complete repose, at my age, is equal to sleep which formerly lasted throughout half a revolution of the stars; my time is measured from now on in much smaller units. An hour had sufficed to accomplish the humble and unexpected prodigy : the heat of my blood was rewarming my hands; my heart and my lungs had begun to function with a kind of good will, and life was welling up like a spring which, though not abundant, is faithful. Sleep, in so short a time, had repaired my excesses of virtue with the same impartiality which it would have applied to the repair of my vices. For the divinity of the great restorer consists in bestowing his benefits upon the sleeper without concern for him, exactly as water charged with curative powers cares not at all who may drink from its source.

But if we think so little about a phenomenon which absorbs at least a third of every life it is because a certain modesty is needed to appreciate its gifts. Asleep, Gaius Caligula and Aristides the Just are alike; my important but empty privileges are forgotten, and nothing distinguishes me from the black porter who lies guard at my door. What is our insomnia but a mad obstinacy of our mind in manufacturing thoughts and trains of reasoning, syllogisms and definitions of its own, refusing to abdicate in favour of that divine stupidity of closed eyes, or the wise folly of dreams? The man who cannot sleep, and I have had only too many occasions for some months to establish the point for myself, refuses more or less consciously to entrust himself to the flow of things. Brother of Death. . . . Isocrates was wrong, and his sentence is a mere exercise in rhetoric. I begin to have some acquaintance with death; it has other secrets, more alien still to our present condition as men. And nevertheless, so intricate and so profound are these mysteries of absence and partial oblivion that we feel half assured that somewhere the white spring of sleep flows into the dark spring of death. I have never cared to gaze, as they slept, upon those I loved; they were resting from me, I know; they were escaping me, too. And every man feels some shame of his visage in the sully of sleep; how often, when I have risen early to read or to study, have I replaced the rumpled pillows myself, and the disordered covers, those almost obscene evidences of our encounters with nothingness, proofs that each night we have already ceased to be.

* * *

Little by little this letter, begun in order to tell you of the progress of my illness, has become the diversion of a man who no longer has the energy necessary for continued application to affairs of state; it has become, in fact, the written meditation of a sick man who holds audience with his memories. I propose now to do more than this: I have formed a project for telling you about my life. To be sure, last year I composed an official summary of my career, to which my secretary Phlegon gave his name. I told as few lies therein as possible; regard for public interest and decency nevertheless forced me to modify certain facts. The truth which I intend to set forth here is not particularly scandalous, or is so only to the degree that any truth creates a scandal. I do not expect your seventeen years to understand anything of it. I desire, all the same, to instruct you and to shock you as well. Your tutors, whom I have chosen myself, have given you this severe education, well supervised and too much protected, perhaps; from it I hope that eventually great benefit will accrue both to you and to the State. I offer you here, in guise of a corrective, a recital stripped of preconceived ideas of mere abstract principles; it is drawn wholly from the experience of one man, who is myself. I am trusting to this examination of facts to give me some definition of myself, and to judge myself, perhaps, or at the very least to know myself better before I die.

Like everyone else I have at my disposal only three means of evaluating human existence: the study of self, which is the most difficult and most dangerous method, but also the most fruitful; the observation of our fellow men, who usually arrange to hide their secrets from us, or to make us believe that they have secrets; and books, with the particular errors of perspective to which they inevitably give rise. I have read nearly everything that our historians and poets have written, and even our story-tellers, although the latter are considered frivolous; and to such reading I owe perhaps more instruction than I have gathered in the somewhat varied situations of my own life. The written word has taught me to listen to the human voice, much as the great unchanging statues have taught me to appreciate bodily motions. On the other hand, but more slowly, life has thrown light for me on the meaning of books.

But books lie, even those that are most sincere. The less adroit, for lack of words and phrases wherein they can enclose life, retain of it but a flat and feeble likeness. Some, like Lucan, make it heavy, and encumber it with a solemnity which it does not possess; others, on the contrary, like Petronius, make life lighter than it is, like a hollow, bouncing ball, easy to toss to and fro in a universe without weight. The poets transport us into a world which is vaster and more beautiful than our own, with more ardour and sweetness, different therefore, and in practice almost uninhabitable. The philosophers, in order to study reality pure, subject it to much the same transformation as fire or pestle make substance undergo: nothing that we have known of a person or of a fact seems to subsist in those ashes or those crystals to which they are reduced. Historians propose to us systems too perfect for explaining the past, with sequence of cause and effect much too exact and clear to have ever been entirely true; they rearrange that dead, unresisting material, but I know that even Plutarch will never recapture Alexander. The story-tellers and spinners of erotic tales are hardly more than butchers who hang up for sale morsels of meat attractive to flies. I should take little comfort in a world without books, but reality is not to be found in them because it is not there whole.

Direct observation of man is a method still less satisfactory, limited as it frequently is to the cheap reflections which human malice enjoys. Rank, position, all such hazards tend to restrict the field of vision for the student of mankind: my slave has totally different facilities for observing me from what I possess for observing him, but his means to do so are as limited as my own. Every morning for twenty years, old Euphorion has handed me my flask of oil and my sponge, but my knowledge of him ends with his acts of service, and his knowledge of me ends with my bath; any effort on the part of either emperor or slave to learn more straightway produces the effect of an indiscretion. Almost everything that we know about anyone else is second hand. If by chance a man does confess, he pleads his own cause and his apology is made in advance. If we are observing him, then he is not alone. They have reproached me for liking to read the police reports of Rome, but I learn from them, all the time, matter for amazement; whether friends or suspects, familiars or persons unknown, these people astound me; and their follies serve as excuse for mine. Nor do I tire of comparing the clothed and the unclothed man. But these reports, so artlessly detailed, add to my store of documents without aiding me in the least to render a final verdict. That this magistrate of austere appearance may have committed a crime in no way permits me to know him better. I am henceforth in the presence of two phenomena instead of one, the outer aspect of the magistrate *and* his crime.

As to self-observation, I make a rule of that, if only to come to terms with that individual with whom I must live up to my last day, but an intimacy of nearly sixty years' standing leaves still many chances for error. When I seek deep within me for knowledge of myself, what I find is obscure, internal, unformulated, and as secret as any complicity. A more impersonal approach yields information as cool and detached as the theories which I could develop on the science of numbers: I employ what intelligence I have to look from above and afar upon my life, which accordingly becomes the life of another. But these two procedures for gaining knowledge are difficult, and require, the one, a descent into oneself, the other, a departure from self. Out of inertia I tend, like everyone else, to substitute for such methods those of mere habit, thus conceiving of my life partly as the public sees it, with judgements ready-made, that is to say poorly made, like a set pattern to which an unskilful tailor laboriously fits the cloth which we bring him. All this is equipment of unequal value; the tools are more or less dulled; but I have no others: it is with them that I must fashion for myself as well as may be some conception of my destiny as man.

When I consider my life, I am appalled to find it a shapeless mass. A hero's existence, such as is described to us, is simple; it goes straight to the mark, like an arrow. Most men like to reduce their lives to a formula, whether in boast or lament, but almost always in recrimination; their memories obligingly construct for them a clear and comprehensible past. My life has contours less firm. As is often the case with other men, it is what I have not been which defines me, perhaps, most aptly: a good soldier, but not a great warrior; a lover of art, but not the artist which Nero thought himself to be at his death; capable of crime, but not laden with it. I have come to think that great men are characterized precisely by the extreme position which they take, and that their heroism consists in holding to that extremity throughout their lives. They are our poles, or antipodes. I have occupied each of the extremes in turn, but have not kept to any of them; life has always drawn me away. And nevertheless neither can I boast, like some ploughman or worthy carter, of a middle-of-the-road existence.

The landscape of my days appears to be composed, like mountainous regions, of varied materials heaped up pell-mell. There I see my nature, itself composite, made up of equal parts of instinct and training. Here and there protrude the granite peaks of the inevitable, but all about is rubble from the landslips of chance. I strive to retrace my life to find in it some plan, following a vein of lead, or of gold, or the course of some subterranean stream, but such devices are only tricks of perspective in the memory. From time to time, in an encounter, or an omen, or in a particular series of happenings, I think that I recognize the working of fate, but too many paths lead nowhere at all, and too many sums add up to nothing. To be sure, I perceive in this diversity and disorder the presence of a person; but his form seems nearly always to be shaped by the pressure of circumstances; his features are blurred, like a figure reflected in water. I am not of those who say that their actions bear no resemblance to them. Indeed, actions must do so, since they alone give my measure, and are the sole means of engraving me upon the memory of men, or even upon my own memory (and since perhaps the very possibility of continuing to express and modify oneself by action may constitute the real difference between the state of the living and of the dead). But there is between me and these acts which compose me an indefinable hiatus, and the proof of this separation is that I constantly feel the necessity of weighing and explaining what I do, and of giving account of it to myself. In such an evaluation certain works of short duration are surely negligible; yet occupations which have extended over a whole lifetime signify just as little. For example, it seems to me as I write this hardly important to have been emperor.

Besides, a good three-quarters of my life escapes this definition by acts: the mass of my wishes, my desires, and even my projects remains nebulous and fleeting as a phantom; the remainder, the palpable part, more or less authenticated by facts, is barely more distinct, and the sequence of events is as confused as that of dreams. I have a chronology of my own which is wholly unrelated to anything based on the founding of Rome, or on the era of the Olympiads. Fifteen years with the armies have lasted less long than a single morning at Athens; there are people whom I have seen much of throughout my life whom I shall not recognize in Hades. Planes in space overlap likewise: Egypt and the Vale of Tempe are near, indeed, nor am I always in Tibur when I am here. Sometimes my life seems to me so commonplace as to be unworthy even of careful contemplation, let alone writing about it, and is not at all more important, even in my own eyes, than the life of any other person. Sometimes it seems to me unique, and for that very reason of no value, and useless, because it cannot be reduced to the common experience of men. No one thing explains me: neither my vices nor my virtues serve for answer; my good fortune tells more, but only at intervals, without continuity, and above all, without logical reason. Still, the mind of man is reluctant to consider itself as the product of chance, or the passing result of destinies over which no god presides, least of all himself. A part of every life, even a life meriting very little regard, is spent in searching out the reasons for its existence, its starting point, and its source. My own failure to discover these things has sometimes inclined me towards magical explanations, and has led me to seek in the frenzies of the occult for what common sense has not taught me. When all the involved calculations prove false, and the philosophers themselves have nothing more to tell us, it is excusable to turn to the random twitter of birds, or toward the distant mechanism of the stars.

VARIUS MULTIPLEX MULTIFORMIS

Marullinus, my grandfather, believed in the stars. This tall old man, emaciated and sallow with age, conceded to me much the same degree of affection, without tenderness or visible sign, and almost without words, that he felt for the animals on his farm and for his lands, or for his collection of stones fallen from the sky. He was descended from a line of ancestors long established in Spain, from the period of the Scipios, and was third of our name to bear senatorial rank; before that time our family had belonged to the equestrian order. Under Titus he had taken some modest part in public affairs. Provincial that he was, he had never learned Greek, and he spoke Latin with a harsh Spanish accent which he passed on to me, and for which I was later ridiculed in Rome. His mind, however, was not wholly uncultivated; after his death they found in his house a trunk full of mathematical instruments and books untouched by him for twenty years. He was learned in his way, with a knowledge half scientific, half peasant, that same mixture of narrow prejudice and ancient wisdom which characterized the elder Cato. But Cato was a man of the Roman Senate all his life, and of the war with Carthage, a true representative of the stern Rome of the Republic. The almost impenetrable hardness of Marullinus came from farther back, and from more ancient times. He was a man of the tribe, the incarnation of a sacred and awe-inspiring world of which I have sometimes found vestiges among our Etruscan soothsayers. He always went bareheaded, as I was criticized for doing later on; his horny feet spurned all use of sandals, and his everyday clothing was hardly distinguishable from that of the aged beggars, or of the grave tenant farmers whom I used to see squatting in the sun. They said that he was a wizard, and the village folk tried to avoid his glance. But over animals he had singular powers. I have watched his grizzled head approaching cautiously, though in friendly wise, toward a nest of adders, and

before a lizard have seen his gnarled fingers execute a kind of
dance.

On summer nights he took me with him to study the sky from
the top of a barren hill. I used to fall asleep in a furrow, tired out
from counting meteors. He would stay sitting, gazing upward
and turning imperceptibly with the stars. He must have known
the systems of Philolaus and of Hipparchus, and that of Aris-
tarchus of Samos which was my choice in later years, but these
speculations had ceased to interest him. For him the stars were
fiery points in the heavens, objects akin to the stones and slow-
moving insects from which he also drew portents, constituent
parts of a magic universe in which were combined the will of the
gods, the influence of daemons, and the lot apportioned to men.
He had cast my horoscope. One night (I was eleven years old at
the time) he came and shook me from my sleep and announced,
with the same grumbling laconism that he would have employed
to predict a good harvest to his tenants, that I should rule the
world. Then, seized with mistrust, he went to fetch a brand from
the small fire of root ends kept going to warm us through the
colder hours, held it over my hand, and read in my solid, childish
palm I know not what confirmation of lines written in the sky.
The world for him was all of a piece; a hand served to confirm
the stars. His news affected me less than one might think; a child
is ready for anything. Later, I imagine, he forgot his own proph-
ecy in that indifference to both present and future which is
characteristic of advanced age. They found him one morning in
the chestnut woods on the far edge of his domain, dead and
already cold, and torn by birds of prey. Before his death he had
tried to teach me his art, but with no success; my natural curiosity
tended to jump at once to conclusions without burdening itself
under the complicated and somewhat repellent details of his
science. But the taste for certain dangerous experiments has remained with me, indeed only too much so.

My father, Aelius Hadrianus Afer, was a man weighed down
by his very virtues. His life was passed in the thankless duties
of civil administration; his voice hardly counted in the Senate.
Contrary to usual practice, his governorship of the province of
Africa had not made him richer. At home, in our Spanish town-

ship of Italica, he exhausted himself in the settlement of local disputes. Without ambitions and without joy, like many a man who from year to year thus effaces himself more and more, he had come to put a fanatic application into minor matters to which he limited himself. I have myself known these honourable temptations to meticulousness and scruple. Experience had produced in my father a scepticism toward all mankind in which he included me, as yet a child. My success, had he lived to see it, would not have impressed him in the least; family pride was so strong that it would not have been admitted that I could add anything to it. I was twelve when this overburdened man left us. My mother settled down, for the rest of her life, to an austere widowhood; I never saw her again from the day that I set out for Rome, summoned hither by my guardian. My memory of her face, elongated like those of most of our Spanish women and touched with melancholy sweetness, is confirmed by her image in wax on the Wall of Ancestors. She had the dainty feet of the women of Gades, in their close-fitting sandals; the gentle swaying of the hips which marks the dancers of that region was also visible in this virtuous young matron.

I have often reflected upon the error that we commit in supposing that a man or a family necessarily shares in the ideas or events of the century in which they happen to exist. The effect of intrigues in Rome barely reached my parents in that distant province of Spain, even though at the time of the revolt against Nero my grandfather had for one night offered hospitality to Galba. We lived on the memory of obscure heroes of archives without renown, of a certain Fabius Hadrianus who was burned alive by the Carthaginians in the siege of Utica, and of a second Fabius, an ill-starred soldier who pursued Mithridates on the roads of Asia Minor. Of the writers of the period my father knew practically nothing: Lucan and Seneca were strangers to him, although like us they were of Spanish origin. My great uncle Aelius, a scholar, confined his reading to the best-known authors of the time of Augustus. Such disdain for contemporary fashion spared them many a fault of taste; to this indifference they had owed their avoidance of all cheap rhetoric. Hellenism and the Orient were unknown, or at best regarded frowningly from afar;

there was not, I believe, a single good Greek statue in the whole peninsula. Thriftiness went hand in hand with wealth, and a certain rusticity was always present in our love of pompous ceremony. My sister Paulina was grave, silent, and sullen; she was married young to an old man. The standard of honesty was rigorous, but we were harsh to slaves. There was no curiosity about anything whatsoever; one was careful to think on all subjects what becomes a citizen of Rome. Of so many virtues, if indeed those are virtues, I shall have been the squanderer.

Officially a Roman emperor is said to be born in Rome, but it was in Italica that I was born; it was upon that dry but fertile country that I later superposed so many regions of the world. The official fiction has some merit: it proves that decisions of the mind and of the will do prevail over circumstance. The true birthplace is that wherein for the first time one looks intelligently upon oneself; my first homelands have been books, and to a lesser degree schools. The schools of Spain had suffered from the effects of provincial leisure. Terentius Scaurus' school, in Rome, gave mediocre instruction in the philosophers and the poets but afforded rather good preparation for the vicissitudes of human existence: teachers exercised a tyranny over pupils which it would shame me to impose upon men; enclosed within the narrow limits of his own learning, each one despised his colleagues, who, in turn, had equally narrow knowledge of something else. These pedants made themselves hoarse in mere verbal disputes. The quarrels over precedence, the intrigues and calumnies, gave me acquaintance with what I was to encounter thereafter in every society in which I have lived, and to such experiences was added the brutality of all childhood. And nevertheless I have loved certain of my masters, and those strangely intimate though elusive relations existing between student and teacher, and the Sirens singing somewhere within the cracked voice of him who is the first to reveal to you a masterpiece, or to unveil for you a new idea. The greatest seducer was not Alcibiades, after all; it was Socrates.

The methods of grammarians and rhetoricians are perhaps less absurd than I thought them to be during the years when I was subjected to them. Grammar, with its mixture of logical rule and arbitrary usage, proposes to a young mind a foretaste of what will be offered to him later on by law and ethics, those sciences of human conduct, and by all the systems wherein man has codified his instinctive experience. As for the rhetorical exercises in which we were successively Xerxes and Themistocles, Octavius and Mark Antony, they intoxicated me; I felt like Proteus. They taught me to enter into the thought of each man in turn, and to understand that each makes his own decisions, and lives and dies according to his own laws. The reading of the poets had still more overpowering effects; I am not sure that the discovery of love is necessarily more exquisite than the discovery of poetry. Poetry transformed me: initiation into death itself will not carry me farther along into another world than does a dusk of Virgil's. In later years I came to prefer the roughness of Ennius, so close to the sacred origins of our race, or Lucretius' bitter wisdom; or to Homer's noble ease the homely parsimony of Hesiod. The most complicated and most obscure poets have pleased me above all; they force my thoughts to strenuous exercise; I have sought, too, the newest and the oldest, those who open wholly new paths, or help me to find lost trails. But in those days I liked chiefly in the art of verse what fell most directly upon the senses, whether the polished metal of Horace, or Ovid's soft flesh. Scaurus cast me into despair in assuring me that I should never be more than a mediocre poet; that both the gift and the application were wanting. For a long time I thought he was mistaken; somewhere locked away are a volume or two of my love poems, most of them imitated from Catullus. But it is of little concern to me now whether my personal productions are worthless or not.

To my dying day I shall be grateful to Scaurus for having put me early to the study of Greek. I was still a child when for the first time I tried to trace on my tablets those characters of an unknown alphabet: here was a new world and the beginning of my great travels, and also the feeling of a choice as deliberate, but at the same time as involuntary, as that of love. I have loved the language for its flexibility, like that of a supple, perfect body, and for the richness of its vocabulary in which every word bespeaks direct and varied contact with reality; and because almost everything that men have said best has been said in Greek. There are, I know, other languages, but they are petrified, or have yet to be born. Egyptian priests have shown me their antique symbols; they are signs rather than words, ancient attempts at classification of the world and of things, the sepulchral speech of a dead race. During the Jewish War the rabbi Joshua translated literally for me some texts from Hebrew, that language of sectarians so obsessed by their god that they have neglected the human. In the armies I grew accustomed to the language of the Celtic auxiliaries, and remember above all certain of their songs. ... But barbarian jargons are chiefly important as a reserve for human expression, and for all the things which they will doubtless say in time to come. Greek, on the contrary, has its treasures of experience already behind it, experience both of man and of the State. From the Ionian tyrants to the Athenian demagogues, from the austere integrity of an Agesilaus to the excesses of a Dionysius or a Demetrius, from the treason of Demaratus to the fidelity of Philopoemen, everything that any one of us can do to help or hinder his fellow man has been done, at least once, by a Greek. It is the same with our personal decisions : from cynicism to idealism, from the scepticism of Pyrrho to the mystic dreams of Pythagoras, our refusals or our acceptances have already taken place; our very vices and virtues have Greek models. There is nothing to equal the beauty of a Latin votive or burial inscription : those few words graved on stone sum up with majestic impersonality all that the world need ever know of us. It is in Latin that I have administered the empire; my epitaph will be carved in Latin on the walls of my mausoleum beside the Tiber; but it is in Greek that I shall have thought and lived.

At sixteen I returned to Rome after a stretch of preliminary training in the Seventh Legion, then stationed well into the Pyrenees, in a wild region of Spain very different from the southern part of the peninsula where I had passed my childhood. Acilius Attianus, my guardian, thought it good that some serious study should counterbalance these months of rough living and violent hunting. He allowed himself, wisely, to be persuaded by Scaurus to send me to Athens to the sophist Isaeus, a brilliant man with a special gift for the art of improvisation. Athens won me straightway; the somewhat awkward student, a brooding but ardent youth, had his first taste of that subtle air, those swift conversations, the strolls in the long golden evenings, and that incomparable ease in which both discussions and pleasure are there pursued. Mathematics and the arts, as parallel studies, engaged me in turn; Athens afforded me also the good fortune to follow a course in medicine under Leotychides. The medical profession would have been congenial to me; its principles and methods are essentially the same as those by which I have tried to fulfil my function as emperor. I developed a passion for this science, which is too close to man ever to be absolute, but which, though subject to fad and to error, is constantly corrected by its contact with the immediate and the nude. Leotychides approached things from the most positive and practical point of view; he had developed an admirable system for reduction of fractures. We used to walk together at evening along the shore; this man of universal interests was curious about the structure of shells and the composition of sea mud. But he lacked facilities for experiment and regretted the Museum at Alexandria, where he had studied in his youth, with its laboratories and dissection rooms, its clash of opinions, and its competition between inventive minds. His was a clear, dry intelligence which taught me to value things above words, to mistrust mere formulas, and to observe rather than to judge. It was this bitter Greek who taught me method.

In spite of the legends surrounding me, I have cared little for youth, and for my own youth least of all. This much vaunted portion of existence, considered dispassionately, seems to me often a formless, opaque, and unpolished period, both fragile and unstable. Needless to say I have found a certain number of exquisite exceptions to the rule, and two or three were admirable; of these, Mark, you yourself will have been the most pure. As for me, I was at twenty much what I am today, but not consistently so. Not everything in me was bad, but it could have been: the good or the better parts served to support the worse. I look back with shame on my ignorance of the world, which I thought that I knew, and on my impatience, and on a kind of frivolous ambition and gross avidity which I then had. Must the truth be told? In the midst of the studious life of Athens, where all

pleasures, too, received their due, I regretted not Rome itself but
the atmosphere of the place where the business of the world is
continually done and undone, where are heard the pulleys and
gears in the machine of governmental power. The reign of
Domitian was drawing to a close; my cousin Trajan, who had
covered himself with glory on the Rhine frontier, ranked now as
a popular hero; the Spanish tribe was gaining hold in Rome.
Compared with that world of immediate action, the beloved
Greek province seemed to me to be slumbering in a haze of ideas
seldom stirred by change, and the political passivity of the
Hellenes appeared a somewhat spiritless form of renunciation.
My appetite for power, and for money (which is often with us a
first form of power) was undeniable, as was the craving for glory
(to give that beautiful and impassioned name to what is merely
our itch to hear ourselves spoken of). There was mingled con-
fusedly with these desires the feeling that Rome, though inferior
in many things, was after all superior in its demand that its
citizens should take part in public affairs, those citizens at least
who were of senatorial or equestrian rank. I had reached the point
where I felt that the most ordinary debate on such a subject as
importation of Egyptian wheat would have taught me more about
government than would the entire *Republic* of Plato. Even a few
years earlier, as a young Roman broken to military discipline, I
could see that I had a better understanding than my professors
of what it meant to be a Spartan soldier, or an athlete of Pindar's
time. I left the mellow light of Athens for the city where men
wrapped and hooded in heavy togas battle against February
winds, where luxury and debauch are barren of charm, but where
the slightest decision taken affects the fate of some quarter of the
world. There a young and eager provincial, not wholly obtuse
but pursuing at first only vulgar ambitions, was little by little to
lose such aspirations in the act of fulfilling them; he was to learn
to contend both with men and with things, to command, and
what is perhaps in the end slightly less futile, to serve.

Much was unsavoury in that accession to power of a virtuous
middle class which was hurrying to establish itself in anticipation
of a change of régime : political honesty was gaining the upper
hand by means of dubious stratagems. The Senate, by gradual

transfer of all administrative posts to the hands of its favoured
dependants, was completing the encirclement of the hard-pressed
Domitian; the newcomers, with whom all my family ties allied
me, were not perhaps so different from those whom they were
about to replace; they were chiefly less soiled by possession of
power. Provincial cousins and nephews hoped at least for
subaltern positions; still they were expected to fill such offices
with integrity. I had my share: I was named judge in the court
dealing with litigation over inheritances. It was from this modest
post that I witnessed the last thrusts in a duel to the death
between Domitian and Rome. The emperor had lost hold on the
City, where he could no longer maintain himself except by resort
to executions, which in turn hastened his own end; the whole
army joined in plotting his death. I grasped but little of this
fencing match, so much more deadly than those of the arena, and
felt only a somewhat arrogant disdain for the tyrant at bay,
philosopher's pupil that I then was. Wisely counselled by
Attianus, I kept to my work without meddling too much in
politics.

That first year in office differed little from the years of study.
I knew nothing of law but was fortunate in having Neratius
Priscus for colleague in the tribunal. He consented to instruct
me, and remained throughout his life my legal counsellor and
my friend. His was that rare type of mind which, though master
of a subject, and seeing it, as it were, from within (from a point of
view inaccessible to the uninitiated), nevertheless retains a sense
of its merely relative value in the general order of things, and
measures it in human terms. Better versed than any of his contemporaries in established procedures, he never hesitated when
useful innovations were proposed. It is with his help that I have
succeeded in my later years in putting certain reforms into effect.
There were other things to think of. My Spanish accent had
stayed with me; my first speech in the tribunal brought a burst
of laughter. Here I made good use of my intimacy with actors,
which had scandalized my family: lessons in elocution throughout long months proved the most arduous but most delightful of
my tasks, and were the best guarded of my life's secrets. In those
difficult years even dissipation was a kind of study: I was trying

to keep up with the young fashionables of Rome, but in that I never completely succeeded. With the cowardice typical of that age, when our courage is wholly physical, and is expended elsewhere, I seldom dared to be myself; in the hope of resembling the others I sometimes subdued and sometimes exaggerated my natural disposition.

I was not much liked. There was, in fact, no reason why I should have been. Certain traits, for example my taste for the arts, which went unnoticed in the student at Athens, and which was to be more or less generally accepted in the emperor, were disturbing in the officer and magistrate at his first stage of authority. My Hellenism was cause for amusement, the more so in that ineptly I alternated between dissimulating and displaying it. The senators referred to me as 'the Greekling'. I was beginning to have my legend, that strange flashing reflection made up partly of what we do, and partly of what the public thinks about us. Plaintiffs, on learning of my intrigue with a senator's wife, brazenly sent me their wives in their stead, or their sons when I had flaunted my passion for some young mime. There was a certain pleasure in confounding such folk by my indifference. The sorriest lot of all were those who tried to win me with talk about literature.

The technique which I was obliged to develop in those unimportant early posts has served me in later years for my imperial audiences : to give oneself totally to each person throughout the brief duration of a hearing; to reduce the world for a moment to this banker, that veteran, or that widow; to accord to these individuals, each so different though each confined naturally within the narrow limits of a type, all the polite attention which at the best moments one gives to oneself, and to see them, almost every time, make use of this opportunity to swell themselves out like the frog in the fable; and finally to devote seriously a few moments to thinking about their business or their problem. It was again the method of the physician; I uncovered old and festering hatreds, and the leprous sores of lies. Husbands against wives, fathers against children, collateral heirs against everyone : the small respect in which I personally hold the institution of the family has hardly held up under it all.

It is not that I despise men. If I did I should have no right, and no reason, to try to govern. I know them to be vain, ignorant, greedy, and timorous, capable of almost anything for the sake of success, or for raising themselves in esteem (even in their own eyes), or simply for avoidance of suffering. I know, for I am like them, at least from time to time, or could have been. Between another and myself the differences which I can recognize are too slight to count for much in the final total; I try therefore to maintain a position as far removed from the cold superiority of the philosopher as from the arrogance of a ruling Caesar. The most benighted of men are not without some glimmerings of the divine: that murderer plays passing well upon the flute; this overseer flaying the backs of his slaves is perhaps a dutiful son; this simpleton would share with me his last piece of bread. And there are few who cannot be made to learn at least something reasonably well. Our great mistake is to try to exact from each person virtues which he does not possess, and to neglect the cultivation of those which he has. I might apply here to the search for these partial virtues what I was saying earlier, in sensuous terms, about the search for beauty. I have known men infinitely nobler and more perfect than myself, like your father Antoninus, and have come across many a hero, and even a few sages. In most men I have found little consistency in adhering to the good, but no steadier adherence to evil; their mistrust and indifference, usually more or less hostile, gave way almost too soon, almost in shame, changing too readily into gratitude and respect, which in turn were equally short-lived; even their selfishness could be bent to useful ends. I am always surprised that so few have hated me; I have had only one or two bitter enemies, for whom I was, as is always the case, in part responsible. Some few have loved me: they have given me far more than I had the right to demand, or to hope for: their deaths, and sometimes their lives. And the god whom they bear within them is often revealed when they die.

There is but one thing in which I feel superior to most men: I am freer, and at the same time more compliant, than they dare to be. Nearly all of them fail to recognize their due liberty, and likewise their true servitude. They curse their fetters, but seem sometimes to find them matter for pride. Yet they pass their days in vain licence, and do not know how to fashion for themselves the lightest yoke. For my part I have sought liberty more than power, and power only because it can lead to freedom. What interested me was not a philosophy of the free man (all who try that have proved tiresome), but a technique: I hoped to discover the hinge where our will meets and moves with destiny, and where discipline strengthens, instead of restraining, our nature. Understand clearly that here is no question of harsh Stoic will, which you value too high, nor of some mere abstract choice or refusal, which grossly affronts the condition of our universe, this solid whole, compounded as it is of objects and bodies. No, I have dreamed of a more secret acquiescence, or of a more supple response. Life was to me a horse to whose motion one yields, but only after having trained the animal to the utmost. Since everything is finally a decision of the mind, however slowly and imperceptibly made, and involves also the body's assent, I strove to attain by degrees to that state of liberty, or of submission, which is almost pure. In this effort gymnastics helped, and dialectics aided me, too. I sought at first the simple liberty of leisure moments; each life well regulated has some such intervals, and he who cannot make way for them does not know how to live. A step further, and I conceived of a liberty of simultaneity, whereby two actions or two states would be possible at the same time; I learned, for example, by modelling myself upon Caesar to dictate more than one text at a time, and to speak while continuing to read. I invented a mode of life where the heaviest task could be accomplished perfectly without engaging myself wholly therein; in fact, I have sometimes gone so far as to propose to myself elimination of even the idea of physical fatigue.

At other moments I practised a liberty acquired by methods of alteration: feelings, thoughts, or work had all to be subject to interruption at any moment, and then resumed; the certainty of being able to summon or dismiss such preoccupations, like slaves, robbed them of all chance for tyranny, and freed me of all sense of servitude. I did a better thing: I organized the day's activities round some chosen train of thought and did not let it go; whatever would have distracted or discouraged me from it, such as projects or work of another kind, words of no import, or the thousand incidents of the day, were made to take their place around it as a vine is trained round the shaft of a column. Sometimes, on the contrary, I made infinite divisions of each thought and each fact under view, breaking and sectioning them into a vast number of smaller thoughts and facts, easier thus to keep in hand. By this method resolutions difficult to take were broken down into a veritable powder of minute decisions, to be adopted one by one, each leading to the next, and thereby becoming, as it were, easy and inevitable.

But it was still to the liberty of submission, the most difficult of all, that I applied myself most strenuously. I determined to make the best of whatever situation I was in; during my years of dependence my subjection lost its portion of bitterness, and even ignominy, if I learned to accept it as a useful exercise. Whatever I had I chose to have, obliging myself only to possess it totally, and to taste the experience to the full. Thus the most dreary tasks were accomplished with ease as long as I was willing to give myself to them. Whenever an object repelled me, I made it a subject of study, ingeniously compelling myself to extract from it a motive for enjoyment. If faced with something unforeseen or near cause for despair, like an ambush or a storm at sea, after all measures for the safety of others had been taken, I strove to welcome this hazard, to rejoice in whatever it brought me of the new and unexpected, and thus without shock the ambush or the tempest was incorporated into my plans, or my thoughts. Even in the throes of my worst disaster, I have seen a moment when sheer exhaustion reduced some part of the horror of the experience, and when I made the defeat a thing of my own in being willing to accept it. If ever I am to undergo torture (and illness will doubtless see to that) I cannot be sure of maintaining the impassiveness of a Thrasea, but I shall at least have the resource of resigning myself to my cries. And it is in such a way, with a mixture of reserve and of daring, of submission and revolt carefully concerted, of extreme demand and prudent concession, that I have finally learned to accept myself.

* * *

Had it been too greatly prolonged, this life in Rome would undoubtedly have embittered or corrupted me, or else would have worn me out. My return to the army saved me. Army life has its compromises too, but they are simpler. Departure this time meant travel, and I set out with exultation. I had been advanced to the rank of tribune in the Second Legion Adjutrix, and passed some months of a rainy autumn on the banks of the Upper Danube with no other companion than a newly published volume of Plutarch. In November I was transferred to the Fifth Legion Macedonia, stationed at that time (as it still is) at the mouth of the same river, on the frontiers of Lower Moesia. Snow blocked the roads and kept me from travelling by land. I embarked at Pola, but had barely time on the way to revisit Athens, where later I was so long to reside. News of the assassination of Domitian, announced a few days after my arrival in camp, surprised no one, and was cause for general rejoicing. Trajan was promptly adopted by Nerva; the advanced age of the new ruler made actual succession a matter of months at the most. The policy of conquest on which it was known that my cousin proposed to launch Rome, the regrouping of troops which began, and the progressive tightening of discipline, all served to keep the army in a state of excited expectancy. Those Danubian legions functioned with the precision of newly greased military machines; they bore no resemblance to the sleepy garrisons which I had known in Spain. Still more important, the army's attention had ceased to centre upon palace quarrels and was turned instead to the empire's external affairs; our troops no longer behaved like a band of lictors ready to acclaim or to murder no matter whom.

The most intelligent among the officers attempted to trace some general plan in these reorganizations in which they took part, hoping to foresee the future, and not their own prospects alone. There were, however, a goodly number of absurdities exchanged by way of comment upon these initial events, and strategic planning as idle as it was ill-founded smeared the surface of the tables at each evening meal. For these professionals, with their firm belief in the beneficence of our authority and in the mission of Rome to govern the world, Roman patriotism assumed brutal forms to which I was not yet accustomed. On the frontiers, just where, for the moment at least, address was needed to conciliate certain of the nomad chieftains, the soldier completely eclipsed the statesman; exaction of labour and requisitions in kind gave rise to abuses too generally condoned. Thanks to incessant divisions among the barbarians, the situation to the north-east was about as favourable as it ever could be; I doubt if even the wars which followed have improved matters there to any extent. Frontier incidents cost us few losses, and these were disquieting only because they were continuous. Let us admit that this perpetual vigilance was useful in any case for whetting the military spirit. All the same, I was convinced that a lesser expenditure, coupled with somewhat greater mental effort on our part, would have sufficed to subdue some chieftains and to win others to us. I decided to devote myself especially to this latter task, which everyone else was neglecting.

I was drawn the more to this aim by my love of things foreign; I liked to deal with the barbarians. This great country lying between the mouths of the Danube and the Borysthenes, a triangular area of which I have covered at least two sides, is one of the most remarkable regions of the world, at least for us who are born on the shores of the Interior Sea and are used to the clear, dry line of southern landscape, with its hills and promontories. At times there I worshipped the goddess Earth in the way that we here worship the goddess Rome; I am speaking not so much of Ceres as of a more ancient divinity, anterior even to the invention of the harvest. Our Greek and Latin lands, everywhere supported by their bones of rock, have the trim beauty of a male body; the heavy abundance of the Scythian earth was that of a reclining woman. The plain ended only where the sky began. My wonder never ceased in presence of the rivers : that vast empty land was but a slope and a bed for their waters. Our rivers are short; we never feel far from their sources; but the enormous flow which ended there in confused estuaries swept with it the mud of an unknown continent and the ice of uninhabitable regions. The cold of Spain's high plateaux is second to none, but this was the first time that I found myself face to face with true winter, which visits our countries but briefly. There it sets in

43

for a long period of months; farther north it must be unchanging, without beginning and without end. The evening of my arrival in camp the Danube was one immense roadway of ice, red at first and then blue, furrowed by the inner working of currents with tracks as deep as those of chariots. We made use of furs to protect ourselves from the cold. The presence of that enemy, so impersonal as to be almost abstract, produced an indescribable exaltation, and a feeling of energy accrued. One fought to conserve body heat as elsewhere one fights to keep one's courage. There were days when the snow effaced the few differences in level on the steppes; we galloped in a world of pure space and pure atoms. The frozen coating gave transparency to the most ordinary things, and the softest objects took on a celestial rigidity. Each broken reed was a flute of crystal. Assar, my Caucasian guide, chopped through the ice to water our horses at dusk. These animals were, by the way, one of our most useful points of contact with the barbarians: a kind of friendship grew up over the trading and endless bargaining, and out of the respect felt on each side for some act of prowess in horsemanship. At night the camp-fires lit up the extraordinary leaping of the slender-waisted dancers and their extravagant bracelets of gold.

Many a time in spring, when the melting snows let me venture farther into the interior, I would turn my back on the southern horizon, which enclosed the seas and islands that we know, and on the western horizon likewise, where at some point the sun was setting on Rome, and would dream of pushing still farther into the steppes or beyond the ramparts of the Caucasus, toward the north or to uttermost Asia. What climates, what fauna, what races of men should I have discovered, what empires ignorant of us as we are of them, or knowing us at most through some few wares transmitted by a long succession of merchants, and as rare for them as the pepper of India or the amber of Baltic regions is for us? At Odessos a trader returning from a voyage of several years' time made me a present of a green stone, of translucent substance held sacred, it seems, in an immense kingdom of which he had at least skirted the edges, but where he had noted neither customs nor gods, grossly centred upon his profit as he was. This exotic gem was to me like a stone fallen from the heavens, a

meteor from another world. We know but little as yet of the con-
figuration of the earth, though I fail to understand resignation to
such ignorance. I envy those who will succeed in circling the two
hundred and fifty thousand Greek stadia so ably calculated by
Eratosthenes, the round of which would bring us back to our
point of departure. In fancy I took the simple decision of going
on, this time on the mere trail to which our roads had now given
way. I played with the idea. . . . To be alone, without possessions,
without renown, with none of the advantages of a civilization,
to expose oneself among new men and amid fresh hazards. . . .
Needless to say it was only a dream, and the briefest dream of
all. This liberty that I was inventing ceased to exist upon closer
view; I should quickly have rebuilt for myself everything that I
had renounced. Furthermore, wherever I went I should only have
been a Roman away from Rome. A kind of umbilical cord
attached me to the City. Perhaps at that time, in my rank of
tribune, I felt still more closely bound to the empire than later as
emperor, for the same reason that the thumb-joint is less free
than the brain. Nevertheless I did have that outlandish dream, at
which our ancestors, soberly confined within their Latian fields,
would have shuddered; to have harboured the thought, even for
a moment, makes me for ever different from them.

*   *   *

Trajan was in command of the troops in Lower Germany; the
army of the Danube sent me there to convey its felicitations to
him as the new heir to the empire. I was three days' march from
Cologne, in mid-Gaul, when at the evening halt the death of
Nerva was announced. I was tempted to push on ahead of the
imperial post, and to be the first to bring to my cousin the news of
his accession. I set off at a gallop and continued without stop,
except at Treves where my brother-in-law Servianus resided in
his capacity as governor. We supped together. The feeble head
of Servianus was full of imperial vapours. This tortuous man,
who sought to harm me or at least to prevent me from pleasing,
thought to forestall me by sending his own courier to Trajan.
Two hours later I was attacked at the ford of a river; the assail-
ants wounded my orderly and killed our horses. We managed,

however, to lay hold on one of the attacking party, a former slave of my brother-in-law, who told the whole story. Servianus ought to have realized that a resolute man is not so easily turned from his course, at least not by any means short of murder, but before such an act his cowardice recoiled. I had to cover some three miles on foot before coming upon a peasant who sold me his horse. I reached Cologne that night, beating my brother-in-law's courier by only a few lengths. This kind of adventure met with success; I was the better received for it by the army. The emperor retained me there with him as tribune in the Second Legion Fidelis.

Trajan had taken the news of his accession with admirable composure. He had long expected it, and it left his plans unchanged. He remained what he had always been, and what he was to be up to his death, a commander-in-chief; but his virtue was to have acquired, by means of his wholly military conception of discipline, an idea of order in government. Around that idea everything else was organized, in the beginning at least, even his plans for war and his designs for conquest. A soldierly emperor, but not at all a military adventurer. He altered nothing in his way of living; his modesty left room neither for affection nor for arrogance. While the army was rejoicing he accepted his new responsibilities as a part of the day's ordinary work, and very simply made evident his contentment to his intimates.

He had but little confidence in me. We were cousins, but he was twenty-four years my senior, and had been my co-guardian since my father's death. He fulfilled his family obligations with provincial seriousness, and was ready to do the impossible to advance me, if I proved worthy; if incompetent, to treat me with more severity than anyone else. He had taken my youthful follies with an indignation which was not wholly unjustified, but which is seldom encountered outside the bosom of the family; my debts, in any case, shocked him more than my misdoings. Other things in me disturbed him. Though his learning was limited, he had a touching respect for philosophers and scholars; but it is one thing to admire the great philosophers from afar, and quite another to have at one's side a young lieutenant who dabbles in letters. Not knowing where my principles lay, or my safeguards or restraints, he supposed me to have none, and to be without resource against my own nature. I had, at least, never committed the error of neglecting my duties. My reputation as an officer reassured him, but in his eyes I was no more than a young and promising tribune, who would bear close watching.

An incident of our personal lives soon threatened to be my undoing. A handsome face was my conqueror. I became passionately attached to a youth whom the emperor also fancied. The adventure was dangerous, and was relished as such. A certain secretary Gallus, who had long taken it upon himself to report each of my debts to Trajan, denounced us to the emperor. His irritation knew no bounds; things were bad enough for a while. Some friends, Acilius Attianus among others, did their best to keep him from settling into a permanent and rather ridiculous resentment. He ended by yielding to their entreaties, and the reconciliation, though at first barely sincere on either side, was more humiliating for me than the scenes of anger had been. I admit to having harboured for this Gallus a hatred beyond compare. Many years later he was found guilty of embezzlement of the public funds, and it was with utter satisfaction that I saw myself avenged.

The first expedition against the Dacians got under way the following year. By preference and by political conviction I have always been opposed to a policy based on war, but I should have been either more or less than a man if these great enterprises of Trajan had not intoxicated me. Viewed as a whole, and from afar, those years of war count among my happy years. They were hard at the start, or seemed to me so. At first I held only secondary posts, since Trajan's good will was not yet fully won. But I knew the country, and knew that I was useful. Although barely aware of what was growing within me, winter by winter, encampment after encampment, battle after battle, I began to feel objections to the emperor's policy, objections which at this period it was not my duty, or even my right, to voice; furthermore, nobody would have listened to me. Placed more or less to one side, in fifth or tenth rank, I knew my troops the better for my position; I shared more of their life. I still retained a certain liberty of action, or rather a certain detachment toward action itself, which cannot readily be indulged in once one has attained power, and has passed the age of thirty. There were also advantages special to me: my liking for this harsh land, and my passion for all voluntary (though of course intermittent) forms of privation and discipline. I was perhaps the only one of the young officers who did not regret Rome. The longer the campaign years extended into the mud and the snow the more they brough forth my resources.

There I lived through an entire epoch of extraordinary exaltation, due in part to the influence of a small group of lieutenants around me who had brought back strange gods from the garrisons deep in Asia. The cult of Mithra, less widespread then than it has become since our expedition in Parthia, won me over temporarily by the rigours of its stark asceticism, which drew taut the bowstring of the will, and by its obsession with death, blood, and iron, which elevated the routine harshness of our military lives to the level of a symbol of universal struggle. Nothing could have been more in contradiction to the views which I was beginning to hold about war, but those barbarous rites creating bonds of life and death between the affiliates all served to flatter the most secret aspirations of a young man impatient of the present, uncertain as to the future, and thereby open to the gods. My initiation took place in a turret constructed of wood and reeds on the banks of the Danube, with Marcius Turbo, my fellow officer, for sponsor. I remember that the weight of the bull in its death throes nearly brought down the latticed floor beneath which I lay to receive the bloody aspersion. In recent years I have reflected upon the dangers which this sort of near-secret society might entail for the State under a weak ruler, and I have finally restricted them, but I admit that in presence of an enemy they give their followers a strength which is almost godlike. Each of us believed that he was escaping from the narrow limits of his human state, feeling himself to be at the same time himself and his own adversary, at one with the god who seems to be both the animal victim and the human slayer. Such fantastic dreams, which sometimes terrify me now, were not so very different from the theories of Heraclitus upon the identity of the mark and the bow. They helped me in those days to endure life. Victory and defeat were inextricably mixed, like rays of the same sun. These Dacian footsoldiers whom I crushed under my horse's hoofs, those Sarmatian cavalrymen overthrown in the close combat of later years when our rearing horses tore at each other's chests, were all struck down the more easily if I identified myself with them. Had my body been abandoned on the battlefield, stripped of its attire, it would not have differed greatly from theirs. The shock of the final sword thrust would have been the same. I am confessing to you here some extraordinary thoughts, among the most secret of my life, and a strange intoxication which I have never again experienced under that same form.

A certain number of deeds of daring, which would have passed unnoticed, perhaps, if performed by a simple soldier, won me a reputation in Rome and a sort of renown in the army. But most of my so-called acts of prowess were little more than idle bravado; I see now with some shame that, mingled with that almost sacred exaltation of which I was just speaking, there was still my ignoble desire to please at any price, and to draw attention upon myself. It was thus that one autumn day when the Danube was swollen by floods I crossed the river on horseback, wearing the full heavy equipment of our Bavarian auxiliaries. For this feat of arms, if it was a feat, my horse deserved credit more than I. But that period of heroic foolhardiness taught me to distinguish between the different aspects of courage. The kind of courage which I should like always to possess would be cool and detached, free from all physical excitement and impassive as the calm of a god. I do not flatter myself that I have ever attained it. The semblance of such courage which I later employed was, in my worst days, only a cynical recklessness toward life; in my best days it was only a sense of duty to which I clung. When confronted with the danger itself, however, that cynicism or that sense of duty quickly gave place to a mad intrepidity, a kind of strange orgasm of a man mated with his destiny. At the age which I then was this drunken courage persisted without cessation. A being afire with life cannot foresee death; in fact, by each of his deeds he denies that death exists. If death takes him, he is probably unaware of the fact; it is no more for him than a shock

49

or a spasm. I smile with some bitterness at the realization that now out of any two thoughts I devote one to my own death, as if so much ceremony were needed to decide this worn body for the inevitable. At that time, on the contrary, a young man who would have lost much in not living a few years longer was daily risking his future with complete unconcern.

It would be easy to construe what I have just told as the story of a too scholarly soldier who wishes to be forgiven his love for books. But such simplified perspectives are false. Different persons ruled in me in turn, though no one of them for long; each fallen tyrant was quick to regain power. Thus have I played host successively to the meticulous officer, fanatic in discipline, but gaily sharing with his men the privations of war; to the melancholy dreamer intent on the gods; the lover ready to risk all for a moment's rapture; the haughty young lieutenant retiring to his tent to study his maps by lamplight, making clear to his friends his disdain for the way the world goes; and finally the future statesman. But let us not forget, either, the base opportunist who in fear of displeasing succumbed to drunkenness at the emperor's table; the young fellow pronouncing upon all questions with ridiculous assurance; the frivolous wit, ready to lose a friend for the sake of a bright remark; the soldier exercising with mechanical precision his vile gladiatorial trade. And we should include also that vacant figure, nameless and unplaced in history, though as much myself as all the others, the simple toy of circumstance, no more and no less than a body, lying on a camp bed, distracted by an aroma, aroused by a breath of wind, vaguely attentive to some eternal hum of a bee. But little by little a newcomer was taking hold, a stage director and manager. I was beginning to know the names of my actors, and could arrange plausible entrances for them, or exits; I cut short superfluous lines, and came gradually to avoid the most obvious effects. Last, I learned not to indulge too much in monologue. Little by little my acts were forming me.

My military successes might have earned me enmity from a lesser man than Trajan. But courage was the only language which he grasped at once; its words went straight to his heart. He came to see in me a kind of second-in-command, almost a son, and nothing of what happened later could wholly separate us. On my side, certain of my newly conceived objections to his views were, at least momentarily, put aside or forgotten in presence of the admirable genius which he displayed with the armies. I have always liked to see a great specialist at work; the emperor, in his own field, had a skill and sureness of hand second to none. Placed at the head of the First Legion Minerva, most glorious of them all, I was assigned to wipe out the last enemy entrenchments in the region of the Iron Gates. After we had surrounded and taken the citadel of Sarmizegethusa, I followed the emperor into that subterranean hall where the councillors of King Decebalus had just ended their last banquet by swallowing poison; Trajan gave me the order to set fire to that weird heap of dead men. The same evening, on the steep heights of the battlefield, he transferred to my finger the diamond ring which Nerva had given him, and which had come to be almost a token of imperial succession. That night I fell asleep content.

*   *   *

My newly won popularity diffused over my second stay in Rome something of the feeling of euphoria which I was to know again, but to a much stronger degree, during my years of felicity. Trajan had given me two million sesterces to distribute in public bounty; naturally it was not enough, but by that time I was administering my own estate, which was considerable, and money difficulties no longer troubled me. I had lost most of my ignoble fear of displeasing. A scar on my chin provided a pretext for wearing the short beard of the Greek philosophers. In my attire I adopted a simplicity which I carried to greater extremes after becoming emperor; my time of bracelets and perfumes had passed. That this simplicity was itself still an attitude is of little importance. Slowly I accustomed myself to plainness for its own sake, and to that contrast, which I was later to value, between a collection of gems and the unadorned hands of the collector. To speak further of attire, an incident from which omens were drawn occurred during the year of my tribuneship in Rome. One day of appallingly bad weather, when I was to deliver a public address, I had mislaid my mantle of heavy Gallic wool. Protected only by my toga, which caught the water in its gutter-like folds, I had continually to wipe the rain from my eyes as I pronounced my discourse. Catching cold is an emperor's privilege in Rome, since he is forbidden, regardless of weather, to put anything over the toga; from that day on, every huckster and melon seller believed in my approaching good fortune.

We talk much of the dreams of youth. Too often we forget its scheming. That, too, is a form of dream, and is no less extravagant than the others. I was not the only one to indulge in such calculations throughout that period of Roman festivities; the whole army rushed into the race for honours. I broke gaily enough into the role of ambitious politician, but I have never been able to play it for long with conviction, or without need of constant help from a prompter. I was willing to carry out with utmost conscientiousness the tiresome duty of recorder of senatorial proceedings; I knew what services would count most. The laconic style of the emperor, though admirable for the armies, did not suffice for Rome; the empress, whose literary tastes were akin to mine, persuaded him to let me compose his speeches. This was the first of the good offices of Plotina. I succeeded all the better for having had practice in that kind of accommodation: in the difficult period of my apprenticeship I had often written harangues for senators who were short of ideas or turns of phrase; they ended by thinking themselves the authors of these pieces. In working thus for Trajan, I found exactly the same delight as that afforded by the rhetorical exercises of my youth; alone in my room, trying out my effects before a mirror, I felt myself an emperor. In truth I was learning to be one; audacities of which I should not have dreamed myself capable became easy when someone else would have to shoulder them. The emperor's thinking was simple but inarticulate, and therefore obscure; it became quite familiar to me, and I flattered myself that I knew it somewhat better than he did. I enjoyed aping the military style of the commander-in-chief, and hearing him thereafter in the Senate pronounce phrases which seemed typical, but for which I was responsible. On other days, when Trajan kept to his room, I was entrusted with the actual delivery of these discourses, which he no longer even read, and my enunciation, by this time above reproach, did honour to the lessons of the tragic actor Olympus.

Such personal services brought me into intimacy with the emperor, and even into his confidence, but the ancient antipathy went on. It had momentarily given way to the pleasure which an ageing ruler feels on seeing a young man of his blood begin a career which the elder imagines, rather naïvely, is to continue his own. But perhaps that enthusiasm had mounted so high on the battlefield at Sarmizegethusa only because it had come to the surface through so many superposed layers of mistrust. I think still that there was something more there than ineradicable animosity arising from quarrels painfully patched up, from differences of temperament, or merely from habits of mind in a man already growing old. By instinct the emperor detested all indispensable subordinates. He would have understood better on my part a mixture of irregularity and devotion to duty; I seemed to him almost suspect by reason of being technically irreproachable. The fact was apparent when the empress thought to advance my career in arranging for me a marriage with his grandniece. Trajan opposed himself obstinately to the project, adducing my lack of domestic virtues, the extreme youth of the girl, and even the old story of my debt. The empress persisted with like stubbornness; I warmed to the game myself; Sabina, at that age, was not wholly without charm. This marriage, though tempered by almost continuous absence, became for me subsequently a source of such irritation and annoyance that it is hard now to recall it as a triumph at the time for an ambitious young man of twenty-eight.

I was more than ever a member of the family, and was more or less forced to live in it. But everything in that circle displeased me, except for the handsome face of Plotina. Innumerable Spanish cousins were always present at the imperial table, just as later on I was to find them at my wife's dinners during my rare visits to Rome; nor would I even say that later I found them grown older, for from the beginning all those people seemed like centenarians. From them emanated a kind of stale propriety and ponderous wisdom. The emperor had passed almost his whole life with the armies; he knew Rome infinitely less well than I

myself. With incomparable earnestness he endeavoured to surround himself with the best that the City had to offer, or with
what had been presented to him as such. The official set was
made up of men wholly admirable for their decency and respect-
ability, but learning did not rest easily upon them, and their
philosophy lacked the vigour to go below the surface of things.
I have never greatly relished the pompous affability of Pliny,
and the sublime rigidity of Tacitus seemed to me to enclose a
Republican reactionary's view of the world, unchanged since the
death of Caesar. The unofficial circle was unpleasantly vulgar, a
deterrent which kept me for the moment from running new risks
in that quarter. I nevertheless constrained myself to the utmost
politeness toward all these folk, diverse as they were. I was
deferent toward some, compliant to others, dissipated when
necessary, clever but not too clever. I had need of my versatility;
I was many-sided by intention, and made it a game to be incal-
culable. I walked a tight-rope, and could have used lessons not
only from an actor, but from an acrobat.

*   *   *

I was reproached at this period for adulterous relations with
women of high rank. Two or three of these much criticized
liaisons endured more or less up to the beginning of my principate. Although Rome is rather indulgent toward debauchery, it
has never favoured the loves of its rulers. Mark Antony and Titus
had a taste of this. My adventures were more modest than theirs,
but I fail to see how, according to our customs, a man who could
never stomach courtesans and who was already bored to death
with marriage might otherwise have come to know the varied
world of women. My elderly brother-in-law, the impossible
Servianus, whose thirty years' seniority allowed him to stand
over me both as schoolmaster and spy, led my enemies in giving
out that curiosity and ambition played a greater part in these
affairs than love itself; that intimacy with the wives introduced
me gradually into the political secrets of the husbands, and that
the confidences of my mistresses were as valuable to me as the
police reports with which I regaled myself in later years. It is
true that each attachment of any duration did procure for me,

almost inevitably, the friendship of the fat or feeble husband, a pompous or timid fellow, and usually blind, but I seldom gained pleasure from such a connexion, and profited even less. I must admit that certain indiscreet stories whispered in my ear by my mistresses served to awaken in me some sympathy for these much mocked and little understood spouses. Such liaisons, agreeable when the women were expert in love, became truly moving when these women were beautiful. It was a study of the arts for me; I came to know statues, and to appreciate at close range a Cnidian Venus or a Leda trembling under the weight of the swan. It was the world of Tibullus and Propertius: a melancholy, an ardour somewhat feigned but intoxicating as a melody in the Phrygian mode, kisses on back stairways, scarves floating across a breast, departures at dawn, and wreaths of flowers left on doorsteps.

I knew almost nothing of these women; the part of their lives which they conceded to me was narrowly confined between two half-opened doors; their love, of which they never ceased talking, seemed to me sometimes as light as one of their garlands; it was like a fashionable jewel, or a fragile and costly fillet, and I suspected them of putting on their passion with their necklaces and their rouge. My own life was not less mysterious to them; they hardly desired to know it, preferring to dream vaguely, and mistakenly, about it; I came to understand that the spirit of the game demanded these perpetual disguises, these exaggerated avowals and complaints, this pleasure sometimes simulated and sometimes concealed, these meetings contrived like the figures of a dance. Even in our quarrels they expected a conventional response from me, and the weeping beauty would wring her hands as if on the stage.

I have often thought that men who care passionately for women attach themselves at least as much to the temple and to the accessories of the cult as to their goddess herself: they delight in fingers reddened with henna, in perfumes rubbed on the skin, and in the thousand devices which enhance that beauty and sometimes fabricate it entirely. These tender idols differed in every respect from the tall females of the barbarians, or from our grave and heavy peasant women; they were born from the golden volutes of great cities, from the vats of the dyers or the baths' damp vapour, like Venus from the foam of Greek seas. They hardly seemed separable from the feverish sweetness of certain evenings in Antioch, from the excited stir of mornings in Rome, from the famous names which they bore, or from that luxury amid which their last secret was to show themselves nude, but never without ornament. I should have desired more: to see the human creature unadorned, alone with herself as she indeed must have been at least sometimes, in illness or after the death of a first-born child, or when a wrinkle began to show in her mirror. A man who reads, reflects, or plans belongs to his species rather than to his sex; in his best moments he rises even above the human. But my fair loves seemed to glory in thinking only as women: the mind, or perhaps the soul, that I searched for was never more than a perfume.

There must have been more to it than that: hidden behind a curtain like a character of comedy awaiting the auspicious moment, I would listen intently to the sounds of an unknown interior, the particular tone of women's chatter, a burst of anger or of laughter, intimate murmurings; all this would cease the moment they knew I was there. The children, and the perpetual preoccupation with clothing or money matters, must again have taken first place once I was gone, though their importance was never mentioned in my presence; even the scorned husband would become essential, and perhaps an object for love. I compared my mistresses with the ill-humoured faces of the women of my family, those whose concerns were chiefly domestic, interminably at work on the household accounts, and those who, steeped in family pride, were for ever directing the care and repainting of ancestral busts; I wondered if these frigid matrons would also be embracing a lover in some garden recess, and if my pliant beauties were not waiting merely for my departure to plunge again into some interrupted quarrel with a housekeeper. I tried as best I could to fit together these two aspects of the world of women.

Last year, shortly after the conspiracy in which Servianus came to his end, one of my mistresses of yore chose to travel all the way to the Villa in order to inform against one of her sons-in-law. I took no action upon the denunciation, which could have been inspired as much by a mother-in-law's hatred as by a desire of being useful to me. But the conversation interested me : just as in the inheritance court of old, it was wholly about wills, darkest machinations between relatives, unforeseen or unfortunate marriages. Here again was the narrow domain of women, their hard practical sense and their horizon turned grey the moment that love ceased to illumine it. A certain acerbity and a kind of harsh loyalty brought to mind my vexatious Sabina. My visitor's features seemed flattened out, melted, as it were, as if the hand of time had passed brutally back and forth over a mask of softened wax; what I had consented, for a moment, to take for beauty had never been more than a fragile flower of youth. But artifice reigned there still : the wrinkled face played awkwardly at smiles. Voluptuous memories, if ever there had been any, were completely effaced for me; this was no more than a pleasant exchange with a creature marked like me by sickness or age; I felt the same slightly irritated sympathy that I would have had for an elderly cousin from Spain, or a distant relative coming from Narbonne.

For a moment I try to recapture the curls of smoke, or the iridescent bubbles of some childish game. But it is easy to forget. . . . So many things have happened since the days of those ephemeral loves that doubtless I no longer recognize their flavour; above all I am pleased to deny that they ever made me suffer. And yet among those mistresses there is one, at least, who was a delight to love. She was both more delicate and more firm than the others, gentler but harder, too; her slender body was rounded like a reed. I have always warmed to the beauty of human hair, that silken and undulating part of a body, but the headdresses of most of our women are towers, labyrinths, ships, or nests of adders. Hers was simply what I like them to be : the cluster of harvest grapes, or the bird's spread wing. Lying beside me and resting her small proud head against mine, she used to speak with admirable candour of her loves. I liked her intensity and her detachment in loving, her exacting taste in pleasure, and her consuming passion for harrowing her very soul. I have known her to take dozens of lovers, more than she could keep count of; I was only a passer-by who made no demands of fidelity.

She fell in love with a dancer named Bathyllus, so handsome that all follies for his sake were justified in advance. She sobbed out his name in my arms, and my approbation gave her courage. At other times we laughed a great deal together. She died young, on a fever-ridden island to which her family had exiled her after a scandalous divorce. She had feared old age, so I could only rejoice for her, but that is a feeling we never have for those whom we have truly loved. Her need for money was fantastic. One day she asked me to lend her a hundred thousand sesterces. I brought them to her the next morning. She sat down on the floor like some small, trim figure playing at knucklebones, emptied the sack on the marble paving, and began to divide the gleaming pile into heaps. I knew that for her, as for all us prodigals, those pieces of gold were not true-ringing specie marked with the head of a Caesar, but a magic substance, a personal currency stamped with the effigy of a chimera and the likeness of the dancer Bathyllus. I had ceased to exist for her; she was alone. Almost plain for the moment, and puckering her brow with delightful indifference to her own beauty, like a pouting schoolboy she counted and re-counted upon her fingers those difficult additions. To my eyes she was never more charming.

* * *

The news of the Sarmatian incursions reached Rome during the celebration of Trajan's Dacian triumph. These long-delayed festivities lasted eight days. It had taken nearly a year to bring from Africa and from Asia wild animals destined for slaughter in the arena; the massacre of twelve thousand such beasts and the systematic destruction of ten thousand gladiators turned Rome into an evil resort of death. On that particular evening I was on the roof of Attianus' house, with Marcius Turbo and our host. The illuminated city was hideous with riotous rejoicing: that bitter war, to which Marcius and I had devoted four years of our youth, served the populace only as pretext for drunken festival, a brutal, vicarious triumph. It was not the time to announce publicly that these much vaunted victories were not final, and that a new enemy was at our frontiers. The emperor, already absorbed in his projects for Asia, took less and less interest in the situation in the north-east, which he preferred to consider as settled once and for all. That first Sarmatian war was represented as a simple punitive expedition. I was sent out to it with the title of governor of Pannonia, and with full military powers.

The war lasted eleven months, and was atrocious. I still believe the annihilation of the Dacians to have been almost justified; no chief of state can willingly assent to the presence of an organized enemy established at his very gates. But the collapse of the kingdom of Decebalus had created a void in those regions upon which the Sarmatians swooped down; bands starting up from no one knew where infested a country already devastated by years of war and burned time and again by us, thus affording no base for our troops, whose numbers were in any case inadequate; new enemies teemed like worms in the corpse of our Dacian victories. Our recent successes had sapped our discipline: at the advance posts I found something of the gross heedlessness evinced in the feasting at Rome. Certain tribunes gave proof of foolish over-confidence in the face of danger: perilously isolated in a region where the only part we knew well was our former frontier, they were depending for continued victories upon our armament, which I knew to be daily diminishing from loss and from wear, and upon reinforcements which I had no hope to see, knowing that all our resources would thereafter be concentrated upon Asia.

Another danger began to threaten: four years of official requisitioning had ruined the villages to our rear; from the time of the first Dacian campaigns, for each herd of oxen or flock of sheep so ostentatiously captured from the enemy I had seen innumerable droves of cattle seized from the inhabitants. If that state of things continued, the moment was approaching when our peasant population, tired of supporting our burdensome military machine, would end by preferring the barbarians. Pillage by our soldiery presented a less important problem, perhaps, but one which was far more conspicuous. My popularity was such that I could risk imposition of the most rigorous restrictions upon the troops; I made current an austerity which I practised myself, inventing the cult of the Imperial Discipline, which later I succeeded in extending throughout the army. The rash and the ambitious, who were complicating my task, were sent back to Rome; in their stead I summoned technicians, of whom we had too few. It was essential to repair the defensive works which proud elation over our recent victories had left singularly neglected; I abandoned entirely whatever would have been too costly to maintain. Civil administrators, solidly installed in the disorder which follows every war, were rising by degrees to the level of semi-independent chieftains, capable of all kinds of extortion from our subjects and of every possible treachery toward us. On that score, as well, I could see in the more or less immediate future the beginning of revolts and divisions to come. I do not believe that we can avoid these disasters, any more than we can escape death, but it depends upon us to postpone them for a few centuries. I got rid of incompetent officials; I had the worst executed. I was discovering myself to be inexorable.

A humid summer gave way to a misty autumn, and then to a cold winter. I had need of my knowledge of medicine, and needed it first of all to treat myself. That life on the frontiers brought me little by little down to the level of the Sarmatian tribesmen: the philosopher's beard changed to that of the barbarian chieftain. I again went through what we had already seen, to the point of revulsion, during the Dacian campaigns. Our enemies burned their prisoners alive; we began to slaughter ours, for lack of means to transport them to slave markets in Rome or in Asia. The stakes of our palisades bristled with severed heads. The enemy tortured their hostages; several of my friends perished in this way. One of them dragged himself on his bleeding limbs as far as the camp; he had been so disfigured that I was never able, thereafter, to recall his former aspect. The winter took its toll of victims: groups of horsemen caught in the ice or carried off by the river floods, the sick racked by coughs, groaning feebly in their tents, wounded men with frozen extremities. Some admirable spirits gathered round me; this small, closely bound company whose devotion I held had the highest form of virtue, and the only one in which I still believe, namely, the firm determination to be of service. A Sarmatian fugitive whom I had made my interpreter risked his life to return to his people, there to foment revolts or treason; I suceeded in coming to an understanding with this tribe, and from that time on its men fought to protect our advance posts. A few bold strokes, imprudent in themselves but skilfully contrived, demonstrated to the enemy the absurdity of attacking the Roman State. One of the Sarmatian chieftains followed the example of Decebalus: he was found dead in his tent of felt; beside him lay his wives, who had been strangled, and a horrible bundle which contained the bodies of their children. That day my disgust for waste and futility extended to the barbarian losses themselves; I regretted these dead whom Rome might have absorbed and employed one day as allies against hordes more savage still. Our scattered attackers disappeared as they had come, into that obscure region from which no doubt many another storm will break forth. The war had not ended. I was obliged to take it up again and finish it some months after my accession. Order reigned for the moment, at least, on that frontier. I returned to Rome covered with honours. But I had aged.

*　*　*

My first consulate proved also to be a year of campaign, but this time the struggle was secret, though incessant, and was waged on behalf of peace. It was not, however, a struggle carried on alone. Before my return a change of attitude parallel to my own had taken place in Licinius Sura, Attianus, and Turbo alike, as if, in spite of the severe censorship which I exercised over my letters, these friends had already understood, and were either following me or had gone on ahead. Formerly the ups and downs of my fortunes worried me chiefly because of my friends' solicitude; fears or impatience which I should have borne lightly, if alone, grew oppressive when they had to be concealed from others or, on the contrary revealed, to their distress. I resented the fact that in their affection they felt more concern for me than I did for myself, and that they failed to see beneath the surface agitation that more tranquil being to whom no one thing is wholly important, and who can therefore endure anything. But there was no time thereafter to think about myself, or not to think either. My person began to count less precisely because my point of view was beginning to matter. What was important was that someone should be in opposition to the policy of conquest, envisaging its consequences and the final aim, and should prepare himself, if possible, to repair its errors.

My post on the frontiers had shown me an aspect of victory which does not appear on Trajan's Column. My return to civil administration gave me the chance to accumulate against the military party evidence still more decisive than all the proofs which I had amassed in the army. The ranking personnel of the legions and the entire Praetorian Guard are formed exclusively of native Italian stock; these distant wars were draining off the reserves of a country already underpopulated. Those who survived were as much a loss for this country as the others, since they were forced to settle in the newly conquered lands. Even in the provinces the system of recruiting caused some serious uprisings at about that time. A journey in Spain undertaken somewhat later on in order to inspect the operation of copper mines on my family estates convinced me of the disorder introduced by war into all branches of the economy; I confirmed my belief in the justice of the protestations of business men whom I knew in Rome. I was not so sanguine as to think that it would always lie within our power to avoid all wars, but I wished them to be no more than defensive; I dreamed of an army trained to maintain order on frontiers less extended, if necessary, but secure. Every new increase in the vast imperial organism seemed to me an unsound growth, like a cancer or dropsical oedema which would eventually cause our death.

Not one of these ideas could be presented to the emperor. He had reached that moment in life, different for each one of us, when a man abandons himself to his daemon or to his genius, following a mysterious law which bids him either to destroy or outdo himself. On the whole, the achievements of his principate had been admirable, but the labours of peace to which the best of his advisers had ingeniously directed him, those great projects of the architects and legists of his reign, had always counted less for him than a single victory. This man, so nobly parsimonious for his personal needs, was now seized by a passion for expenditure. Barbarian gold raised from the bed of the Danube, the five hundred thousand ingots of King Decebalus, had sufficed to defray the cost of a public bounty and donations to the army, of which I had had my part, as well as the wild luxury of the games and the initial outlay for the tremendous venture in Asia. These baneful riches falsified the true state of the finances. The fruits of war were food for new wars.

Licinius Sura died at about that time. He was the most liberal of the emperor's private councillors. His death was a battle lost for our side. He had always been like a father in his solicitude for me; for some years illness had left him too little strength to fulfil any of his personal ambitions, but he had always enough energy to aid a man whose views appeared to him sane. The conquest of Arabia had been undertaken against his advice; he alone, had he lived, would have been able to save the State the gigantic strain and expense of the Parthian campaign. Ridden by fever, he employed his hours of insomnia in discussing with me plans for reform; they exhausted him, but their success was more important to him than a few more hours of life. At his bedside I lived in advance, and to the last administrative detail, certain of the future phases of my reign. This dying man spared the emperor in his criticisms, but he knew that he was carrying with him to the tomb what reason was left in the régime. Had he lived two or three years longer, I might perhaps have avoided some tortuous devices which marked my accession to power; he would have succeeded in persuading the emperor to adopt me sooner, and openly. But even so the last words of that statesman in bequeathing his task to me were one part of my imperial investiture.

If the group of my followers was increasing, so was that of my enemies. The most dangerous of my adversaries was Lusius Quietus, a Roman with some Arab blood, whose Numidian squadrons had played an important part in the second Dacian campaign, and who was pressing fiercely for the Asiatic war. I detested everything about him, his barbarous luxury, the pretentious swirl of his white headgear bound with cord of gold, his false, arrogant pride, and his unbelievable cruelty toward the conquered and to those who had offered their submission. The leaders of the military party were destroying themselves in internal strife, but those who remained were thereby only the more entrenched in power, and I was only the more exposed to the mistrust of Palma or to the hatred of Celsus. My own position, happily, was almost impregnable. The civil administration was coming increasingly into my hands, since the emperor now occuped himself exclusively with his plans for war. My friends, who would have been the only persons capable of supplanting me because of their ability or their knowledge in affairs, with noble self-effacement yielded me first place. Neratius Priscus, whom the emperor trusted, daily confined his activities more deliberately within his legal speciality. Attianus organized his life with a view to serving me, and I had the prudent approbation of Plotina. A year before the war I was promoted to the governorship of Syria; later was added the post of military legate. Ordered to organize and supervise our bases, I became one of the levers of command in an undertaking which I knew to be out of all reason. I hesitated for some time, and then accepted. To refuse would have been tantamount to closing the roads to power at a moment when power was more vital to me than ever. It would also have deprived me of the one chance to act as moderator.

During these few years which preceded the great crises for the State, I had taken a decision which left me for ever exposed to the accusation of frivolity by my enemies, and which was in part calculated for that effect, to parry thus all chance of attack. I had gone to spend some months in Greece. Political considerations were no part of this voyage, in appearance at least. It was an excursion for pleasure and for study : I brought back some graven cups, and some books which I shared with Plotina. Of all my official honours, it was there that I received the one accepted with purest joy. I was named archon of Athens. I allowed myself some months of effortless work and delights, walks in spring on hillsides strewn with anemones, friendly contact with bare marble. At Chaeronea, where I went to muse upon the heroic friendships of the Sacred Battalion, I spent two days as the guest of Plutarch. I had had my own Sacred Battalion, but, as is often the case with me, my life was less moving to me than history itself. I had some hunting in Arcadia, and went to Delphi to pray. At Sparta, on the edge of the Eurotas, some shepherds taught me an ancient air on the flute, a strange bird-song. Near Megara there was a peasant wedding which lasted the night long; my companions and I joined in the dances, as we should not have dared do in custom-bound Rome.

The traces of Roman crimes were visible on all sides: the walls of Corinth, left in ruins by Mummius, and the spaces within the sanctuaries left empty by Nero's organized theft of statues during his scandalous voyage. Impoverished Greece lived on in an atmosphere of pensive grace, with a kind of lucid subtlety and sober delight. Nothing had changed since the period when the pupil of the rhetorician Isaeus had breathed in for the first time that odour of warm honey, salt, and resin; nothing, in short, had changed for centuries. The sands of the palaestrae were as golden as before; Phidias and Socrates no longer frequented them, but the young men who exercised there still resembled the exquisite Charmides. It seemed to me sometimes that the Greek spirit had not carried the premises of its own genius through to their ultimate conclusions : the harvests were still to be reaped; the grain ripened in the sun and already cut was but little in comparison with the Eleusinian promise of riches hidden in that fair soil. Even among my savage enemies, the Sarmatians, I had found vases of perfect form and a mirror decorated with Apollo's image, gleams from Greece like a pale sun on snow. I could see possibilities of Hellenizing the barbarians and Atticizing Rome, thus imposing upon the world by degrees the only culture which has once for all separated itself from the monstrous, the shapeless, and the inert, the only one to have invented a definition of method, a system of politics, and a theory of beauty. The light disdain of the Greeks, which I have never ceased to feel under their most ardent homage, did not offend me; I found it natural. Whatever virtues may have distinguished me from them, I knew that I should always be less subtle than an Aegean sailor, less wise than a herb vendor of the Agora. I accepted without irritation the slightly haughty condescension of that proud race, according to an entire nation the privileges which I have always so readily conceded to those I loved. But to give the Greeks time to continue and perfect their work some centuries of peace were needed, with those calm leisures and discreet liberties which peace allows. Greece was depending upon us to be her protector, since after all we say that we are her master. I promised myself to stand watch over the defenceless god.

*   *   *

I had held my post as governor of Syria for a year when Trajan joined me in Antioch. He came to inspect the final preparations for the Armenian expedition, which was preliminary in his thoughts to the attack upon the Parthians. Plotina accompanied him as always, and his niece Matidia, my accommodating mother-in-law, who for some years had gone with him in camp as the head of his household. Celsus, Palma, and Nigrinus, my old enemies, still sat in the Council and dominated the general staff. All these people packed themselves into the palace while awaiting the opening of the campaign. Court intrigues flourished as never before. Everyone was laying his bets in expectation of the first throws of the dice of war.

The army moved off almost immediately in a northerly direction. With it departed the vast swarm of high officials, office-seekers, and hangers-on. The emperor and his suite paused for a few days in Commagene for festivals which were already triumphal; the lesser kings of the Orient, gathered at Satala, outdid each other in protestations of loyalty upon which, had I been in Trajan's place, I should have counted little for the future. Lusius Quietus, my dangerous rival, placed in charge of the advance posts, took possession of the shores of Lake Van in the course of a sweeping but absurdly easy conquest; the northern part of Mesopotamia, vacated by the Parthians, was annexed without difficulty; Abgar, king of Osroëne, surrendered in Edessa. The emperor came back to Antioch to take up his winter quarters, postponing till spring the invasion of the Parthian Empire itself, but already determined to accept no overture for peace. Everything had gone according to his plans. The joy of plunging into this adventure, so long delayed, restored a kind of youth to this man of sixty-four.

My views of the outcome remained sombre. The Jewish and

the Arabian elements were more and more hostile to the war; the great provincial landowners were angered at having to defray costs of troops passing through; the cities objected strenuously to the imposition of new taxes. Just after the emperor's return, a first catastrophe occurred which served as forerunner to all the rest: in the middle of a December night an earthquake laid a fourth of the city of Antioch in ruins within a few seconds. Trajan was bruised by a falling beam, but heroically went on tending the wounded; his immediate following numbered several dead. The Syrian mobs straightway sought to place the blame for the disaster on someone, and the emperor, for once putting aside his principles of tolerance, committed the error of allowing a group of Christians to be massacred. I have little enough sympathy for that sect myself, but the spectacle of old men flogged and children tortured all contributed to the general agitation of spirit and rendered that sinister winter more odious still. There was no money for prompt repair of the effects of the earthquake; thousands of shelterless people camped at night in the squares. My rounds of inspection revealed to me the existence of a hidden discontent and a secret hatred which the dignitaries who thronged the palace did not even suspect. In the midst of the ruins the emperor was pursuing his preparations for the next campaign: an entire forest was used up in the construction of movable bridges and rafts for the crossing of the Tigris. He had received with joy a whole series of new titles conferred upon him by the Senate, and was impatient to finish with the Orient in order to return to his triumph in Rome. The slightest delay would loose furies which shook him like an access of fever.

The man who restlessly paced the vast halls of that palace built long ago by the Seleucids, and which I had myself embellished (what a spiritless task that was!) with eulogistic inscriptions in his honour and with panoplies of the Dacian war, was no longer the man who had welcomed me to the camp in Cologne nearly twenty years earlier. Even his virtues had aged. His somewhat heavy joviality, which formerly disguised genuine kindness, was now no more than vulgar habit; his firmness had changed to obstinacy; his aptitude for the immediate and the practical had led to a total refusal to think. The tender respect which he felt

for the empress and the grumbling affection manifested for his
niece Matidia had changed into a senile dependence upon these
women, whose counsels, nevertheless, he resisted more and
more. His attacks of liver disorder disturbed his physician Crito,
though he himself took no thought for it. His pleasures had
always lacked art, and they fell still lower as he grew older. It was
of little importance that the emperor, when his day's work was
over, chose to abandon himself to barrack-room debaucheries in
company with youths whom he found agreeable, or handsome. It
was, on the contrary, rather serious that he could hardly stand
wine, and took too much of it; and that this small court of increasingly mediocre subalterns, selected and manipulated by
freedmen of dubious character, was so placed as to be present at
all my conversations with him, and could report them to my
adversaries. In daytime I saw him only at staff meetings, which
were wholly given over to details of planning, and where the
moment never came to express an independent opinion. At all
other times he avoided private talks. Wine provided this man of
little subtlety with a veritable arsenal of clumsy ruses. His sus-
ceptibilities of other years had indeed given way : he insisted that
I should join him in his pleasures; the noise, the laughter, the
feeblest jokes of the young men were always welcomed·as so
many ways of signifying to me that this was no time for serious
business. He waited for the moment when one more glass would
deprive me of my reason. Everything reeled about me in this hall
where barbaric trophies of wild ox heads seemed to laugh in my
face. The wine jars followed in steady succession; a vinous song
would spurt forth here and there, or the insolent, beguiling laugh
of a page; the emperor, resting an ever more trembling hand
upon the table, immured in a drunkenness possibly half feigned,
lost far away upon the roads of Asia, sank heavily into his
dreams. . . .

Unfortunately these dreams had beauty. They were the same
as those which had formerly made me think of giving up everything for the sake of following northern routes beyond the
Caucasus toward Asia. This fascination, to which the elderly
emperor was yielding as if entranced, had lured Alexander before him. That prince had almost made a reality of these same

dreams, and had died because of them at thirty. But the gravest danger in these mighty projects lay still more in their apparent soundness: as always, practical reasons abounded for justification of the absurd and for being carried away by the impossible. The problem of the Orient had preoccupied us for centuries; it seemed natural to rid ourselves of it once and for all. Our exchanges of wares with India and the mysterious Land of Silks depended entirely upon Jewish merchants and Arabian exporters who held the franchise for Parthian roads and ports. Once the vast and loosely jointed empire of the Arsacid horsemen had been reduced to nothingness we should touch directly upon those rich extremities of the world; Asia once unified would become but a province more for Rome. The port of Alexandria-in-Egypt was the only one of our outlets toward India which did not depend upon Parthian good will; there, too, we were continually confronted with the troublesome demands and revolts of the Jewish communities. Success on the part of Trajan's expedition would have allowed us to disregard that untrustworthy city. But such array of reasoning had never persuaded me. Sound commercial treaties would have pleased me more, and I could already foresee the possibility of reducing the role of Alexandria by creating a second Greek metropolis near the Red Sea, as I did later on in founding Antinoöpolis. I was beginning to know this complicated world of Asia. The simple plan of total extermination which had worked for Dacia was not the right thing in this country of much more abundant and settled population, upon which, besides, the wealth of the world depended. Beyond the Euphrates began for us the land of mirage and danger, the sands where one helplessly sank, and the roads which ended in nothing. The slightest reversal would have resulted in a jolt to our prestige giving rise to all kinds of catastrophe; the problem was not only to conquer but to conquer again and again, perpetually; our forces would be drained off in the attempt. We had tried it already: I thought with horror of the head of Crassus, tossed from hand to hand like a ball in the course of a performance of Euripides' *Bacchae* which a barbarian king with a smattering of Greek learning had presented on the afternoon of a victory over Rome. Trajan thought to avenge this ancient defeat; I hoped chiefly to keep it from happening again. I could foretell the future with some accuracy, a thing quite possible, after all, when one is informed on a fair number of the elements which make up the present: a few meaningless victories would draw our armies too far on, leaving other frontiers perilously exposed; the dying emperor would cover himself with glory, and we who must go on living would have to resolve all the problems and remedy all the evils.

Caesar was right to prefer the first place in a village to the second in Rome. Not by ambition, nor by vain glory, but because a man in second place has only the choice between the dangers of obedience and those of revolt, or those still more serious dangers of compromise. I was not even second in Rome. The emperor, though about to set forth upon a hazardous expedition, had not yet designated his successor; each step taken to advance his projects offered some opportunity to the chiefs of the general staff. This man, though almost naïve, seemed to me now more complicated than myself. Only his rough manner reassured me; in his gruffness he treated me like a son. At other moments I expected to be supplanted by Palma or cut off by Quietus as soon as my services could be dispensed with. I had no real power: I did not even manage to obtain an audience for the influential members of the Sanhedrin of Antioch, who were as fearful as we of the surprise moves of the Jewish agitators, and who would have enlightened Trajan as to the contrivings of their fellow Jews. My friend Latinius Alexander, who was descended from one of the ancient royal families of Asia Minor, and whose name and wealth had great weight, was heeded no more than I. Pliny, sent out four years before to Bithynia, died there without having had time to inform the emperor of the exact state of public opinion and finances, even supposing that his incurable optimism would have allowed him to do so. The secret reports of the Lycian merchant Opramoas, who knew Asian affairs thoroughly, were derided by Palma. The freedmen took advantage of the morning headaches which followed the drunken evenings to keep me out of the imperial bedchamber; the emperor's orderly, a man named Phoedimus, an honest but stupid fellow, and set against me, twice refused me entry. On the contrary, my enemy,

Celsus, of consular rank, locked himself in one evening with Trajan for a conference which lasted for hours, and at the end of which I thought myself lost. I sought allies where I could; for a price, in gold, I corrupted former slaves whom I would otherwise have willingly sent to the galleys; I caressed more than one curly-headed darling. Nerva's diamond had lost its fire.

And it was then that the wisest of my good geniuses came to my aid: Plotina. I had known the empress for nearly twenty years. We were of the same circle and of about the same age. I had seen her living calmly through almost as constrained an existence as my own, and one more deprived of future. She had taken my part, without appearing to notice that she did so, in my difficult moments. But it was during the evil days at Antioch that her presence became indispensable to me, as was always her esteem in after times, an esteem which I kept till her death. I grew accustomed to that white-clad figure, in garments as simple as a woman's can be, and to her silences, or to words so measured as to be never more than replies, and these as succinct as possible. Nothing in her appearance or bearing was out of keeping with that palace more ancient than the splendours of Rome: this daughter of a race newly come to power was in no way inferior to the Seleucids. We two were in accord on almost everything. Both of us had a passion for adorning, then laying bare, our souls, and for testing our minds on every touchstone. She leaned toward Epicurean philosophy, that narrow but clean bed whereon I have sometimes rested my thought. The mystery of gods, which haunted me, did not trouble her, nor had she my passionate desire for the human body. She was chaste by reason of her disgust with the merely facile, generous by determination rather than by nature, wisely mistrustful but ready to accept anything from a friend, even his inevitable errors. Friendship was a choice to which she devoted her whole being; she gave herself to it utterly, and as I have done only to my loves. She has known me better than anyone has; I have let her see what I carefully concealed from everyone else: for example, my secret lapses into cowardice. I like to think that on her side she has kept almost nothing from me. No bodily intimacy ever existed between us; in its place was this contact of two minds closely intermingled.

Our accord dispensed with explanations and avowals, or reti-
cences: facts themselves sufficed. She observed them more
closely than I; under the heavy braids which the fashion demanded her smooth brow was that of a judge. Her memory retained the exact impression of the minutest objects; therefore,
unlike me, she never had occasion to hesitate too long or to decide too quickly. She could detect at a glance my most secret
adversaries, and evaluated my followers with cool detachment. In
truth, we were accomplices, but the most trained ear would
hardly have been able to catch the tones of a secret accord between us. She never committed the gross error of complaining
to me about the emperor, nor the more subtle one of excusing or
praising him. On my side, my loyalty was not questioned.
Attianus, who had just come from Rome, joined in these discussions, which sometimes lasted all night; but nothing seemed
to tire this imperturbable, yet frail, woman. She had managed to
have my former guardian named privy councillor, thus elimin-
ating my enemy Celsus. Trajan's mistrust of me, or else the im-
possibility of finding someone to fill my post in the rear, would
keep me in Antioch: I was counting upon these friends to inform
me about everything not revealed in the official dispatches. In
case of disaster they would know how to rally round me the
fidelity of a part of the army. My adversaries would have to
reckon with the presence of this aged sufferer from gout, who
was setting forth only in order to serve me, and with this woman
who could exact of herself the long endurance of a soldier.

I watched them depart, the emperor on horseback, firm and
admirably placid, the patient group of women borne in litters,
Praetorian guards mingled with the Numidian scouts of the re-
doubtable Lusius Quietus. The army, which had passed the
winter on the banks of the Euphrates, moved forward as soon as
its chief arrived; the Parthian campaign was beginning in earnest.
First reports were magnificent: Babylon conquered, the Tigris
crossed, Ctesiphon fallen. Everything, as always, gave way before the astonishing mastery of this man. The prince of Chara-
cene Arabia declared his allegiance, opening thus the entire
course of the Tigris to the Roman barges. The emperor embarked for the port of Charax at the head of the Persian Gulf.

He was nearing the fabled shores. My fears persisted, but I hid them like something criminal; to be right too soon is to be in the wrong. Worse still, I was beginning to doubt my judgement; had I been guilty of that base incredulity which keeps us from recognizing the grandeur of a man whom we know too well? I had forgotten that certain beings shift the boundaries of destiny and alter history thereby. I had uttered blasphemy against the Genius of the emperor. I was consumed with anxiety at my post. If by chance the impossible were to take place, was I to play no part? Since everything is always easier than to exercise common sense, the desire seized me to don once more the coat of mail of the Sarmatian wars, using Plotina's influence to get myself recalled to the army. I envied the least of our soldiers their lot on the dusty roadways of Asia and the shock of their encounter with Persia's mailed battalions. This time the Senate voted the emperor the right to celebrate not one triumph but a succession of triumphs which would last as long as he lived. I myself did what the occasion demanded: I ordered festivities and went to offer sacrifice on the summit of Mount Casius.

Suddenly the fire which was smouldering in that land of the Orient burst forth everywhere at one time. The Jewish merchants refused to pay tax at Seleucia; Cyrene straightway revolted, and the Oriental element of the city massacred the Greek element; the roads by which Egyptian grain was brought to our troops were cut by a band of Zealots from Jerusalem; at Cyprus the Greek and Roman residents were seized by the Jewish populace, who forced them to slay each other in gladiatorial combats. I succeeded in maintaining order in Syria, but could see flame in the eyes of beggars sitting at the doors of the synagogues, and mute sneers on the heavy lips of the camel drivers, a hatred which after all we did not merit. The Jews and Arabs had made common cause from the beginning against a war which threatened to ruin their commerce; but Israel took advantage of the times to throw itself against a world from which it was excluded by its religious frenzies, its strange rites, and the intransigence of its god. The emperor returned with all speed to Babylon, delegated Quietus to chastise the rebel cities: Cyrene, Edessa, Seleucia, great Greek centres of the Orient, were set on fire as punishment for treason planned at mere caravan stops or contrived and directed from jewries. Some time later, in visiting these cities for reconstruction, I passed beneath colonnades in ruins and between rows of broken statues. The emperor Osroës, who had subsidized these revolts, immediately took the offensive: Abgar rose up in resistance to re-enter demolished Edessa; our Armenian allies, on whom Trajan had thought he could depend, lent a helping hand to the Persian war lords. Without warning, the emperor found himself at the centre of an immense field of battle where he had to face the enemy on all sides.

He wasted the winter in the siege of Hatra, a virtually impregnable eagle's nest situated in the heart of a desert; it cost our army some thousands of deaths. His stubbornness became more and more a form of personal courage: this ailing man would not let go. I knew from Plotina that Trajan still refused to name his heir, in spite of the admonition of a brief attack of paralysis. If this imitator of Alexander were to die, in his turn, of fever or intemperance in some unhealthy corner of Asia this foreign war would be complicated by civil war; a struggle to the death would break out between my supporters and those of Celsus or of Palma. Suddenly reports ceased almost completely; the thin line of communication between the emperor and me was maintained only by the Numidian bands of my worst enemy. It was at this period that I ordered my physician for the first time to mark with red ink on my chest the position of my heart; if it came to the worst, I did not intend to fall, alive, into Lusius Quietus' hands. The difficult task of pacifying the adjacent islands and provinces was now added to the other duties of my office, but the exhausting work of daytime was nothing in comparison with the length of the restless nights. All the problems of the empire weighed upon me at once, but my own plight was matter for still graver concern. I desired the supreme power. I desired it that I might put my own plans into effect, try my remedies, and restore peace. I wanted it above all in order to become my full self before I died.

I was in my fortieth year. If I were to die at that time, nothing more of me would survive than a name in a series of high functionaries, and an inscription in Greek in honour of an archon of Athens. Ever since that anxious period, each time that I have witnessed the disappearance of a man just at middle age, whose successes and reverses the public thinks it can judge exactly, I have recalled that at the same age I still figured only in my own eyes, and in those of a few friends, who must sometimes have doubted my abilities as I doubted them myself. I have come to the realization that few men fulfil themselves before death, and I have judged their interrupted work with the more pity. This obsession with the possibility of a life frustrated immobilized my thought at one point, drawing everything to it like an abscess. My hunger for power was like the craving for love, which keeps the lover from eating or sleeping, from thinking, or even from loving so long as certain rites remain unperformed. The most urgent tasks seemed vain when I was not the free master over decisions affecting the future; I needed to be assured of reigning in order to recapture the desire to serve. That palace of Antioch, where I was to live some years later on in a virtual frenzy of delight, was for me then but a prison, and perhaps my death cell. I sent messages to the oracles, to Jupiter Ammon, to Castalia, and to Zeus Dolichenus. I summoned Persian Magi; I went so far as to send to the dungeons of Antioch for a criminal intended for crucifixion, those throat was slit in my presence by a sorcerer in the hope that the soul, floating for an instant between life and death, would reveal the future. The wretch gained thereby escape from a slower death, but the questions put remained unanswered. At night I trailed from one window recess to another, from balcony to balcony through the rooms of that palace where the walls were still cracked from the earthquake, here and there tracing my astrological calculations upon the stones, and questioning the trembling stars. But it is on earth that the signs of the future have to be sought.

At last the emperor raised the siege of Hatra and decided to come back over the Euphrates, which never should have been crossed at all. The heat, which was already torrid, and harassing from the Parthian archers rendered that bitter return more disastrous still. On a burning evening in May I rode out beyond the city gates along the banks of the Orontes to meet the small group so worn by anxiety, fever, and fatigue : the ailing emperor, Attianus, and the women. Trajan determinedly kept to his horse as far as the palace door. He could hardly stand; this man once so full of vitality seemed more changed than others are by the approach of death. Crito and Matidia helped him to climb the steps, induced him to lie down, and thereafter established themselves at his bedside. Attianus and Plotina recounted to me those incidents of the campaign which they had not been able to include in their brief dispatches. One of these episodes so moved me as to become for ever a personal remembrance, a symbol of my own. As soon as the weary emperor had reached Charax he had gone to sit upon the shore, looking out over the brackish waters of the Persian Gulf. This was still the period when he felt no doubt of victory, but for the first time the immensity of the world overwhelmed him, and the feeling of age, and those limits which circumscribe us all. Great tears rolled down the cheeks of the man ever deemed incapable of weeping. The supreme commander who had borne the Roman eagles to hitherto unexplored shores knew now that he would never embark upon that sea so long in his thoughts : India, Bactria, the whole of that vague East which had intoxicated him from afar, would continue to be for him only names and dreams. On the very next day bad news forced him to turn back. Each time, in my turn, that destiny has denied me my wish I have remembered those tears shed that evening on a distant shore by an old man who, perhaps for the first time, was confronting his own life face to face.

I went the following morning to the emperor's room. I felt filial toward him, perhaps fraternal. The man who had prided himself on living and thinking in every respect like any ordinary soldier of his army was ending his life in complete solitude; lying abed he continued to build up grandiose plans in which no one was any longer interested. As always, his cut and dried speech served to disfigure his thought; forming his words now with utmost difficulty he talked to me of the triumph which they were preparing for him in Rome. He was denying defeat just as he was denying death. Two days later he had a second attack. My anxious consultations were renewed with Attianus, and with Plotina. The foresight of the empress had just effected the elevation of my old friend to the all-powerful position of commander of the Praetorian cohorts, bringing the imperial guard thus under our control. Happily Matidia, who never left the invalid's chamber, was wholly on our side; in any case, this simple, affectionate woman was like wax in Plotina's hands. But not one of us dared to remind the emperor that the question of the succession was still pendent. Perhaps like Alexander he had decided not to name his heir himself; perhaps, known to himself alone, he had commitments toward the party of Quietus. More likely, he was refusing to face his end. One sees thus in families many an obstinate old man dying intestate. For them it is less a matter of keeping their treasure to the last (or their empire), from which their numbed fingers are already half detached, than of avoiding too early an entry into that posthumous state where one no longer has decisions to take, surprises to give, or threats or promises to make to the living. I pitied him; we were too different for him to find in me what most people who have wielded total authority seek desperately on their deathbeds, a docile successor pledged in advance to the same methods, and even to the same errors. But the world about him was void of statesmen : I was the only one whom he could choose without failing in his obligations as a good executive and great prince; this chief so accustomed to evaluate records of service was almost forced to accept me. That was, moreover, an excellent reason to hate me. Little by little his health was restored just enough to allow him to leave his room. He spoke of undertaking a new campaign; he did not believe in it himself. His physician Crito, who feared for him the effects of midsummer heat, succeeded at last in persuading him to reembark for Rome. The evening before his departure he summoned me on board the ship which was to take him back to Italy and named me commander-in-chief in his place. He committed himself thus far. But the essential was not done.

Contrary to the orders given me I began negotiations immediately, but in secret, for peace with Osroës. I was banking on the fact that I should probably no longer have to render an accounting to the emperor. Less than ten days later I was awakened in the middle of the night by the arrival of a messenger; at once I recognized a confidential envoy of Plotina. He brought two missives. One, official, informed me that Trajan, unable to stand the sea voyage, had been put down at Selinus-in-Cilicia, where he lay gravely ill in the house of a merchant. A second letter, this one secret, told me of his death, which Plotina promised to keep hidden as long as possible, thus giving me the advantage of being the first one warned. I set off immediately for Selinus, after having taken all necessary precautions to assure myself of the loyalty of the Syrian garrisons. I was barely on the way when a new courier brought me official announcement that the emperor was dead. His will, which designated me as his heir, had just been sent to Rome in safe hands. Everything which for ten years' time had been feverishly dreamed of, schemed, discussed, or kept silent, was here reduced to a message of two lines, traced in Greek in a small, firm, feminine hand. Attianus, who awaited me on the pier at Selinus, was the first to salute me with the title of emperor.

And it is here, in that interval between the disembarkation of the invalid and the moment of his death, that occurs one of those series of events which will for ever be impossible for me to reconstruct, and upon which nevertheless my destiny has been built. Those few days passed by Attianus and the women in that merchant's house determined my life for ever after, but concerning them, as later on concerning a certain afternoon on the Nile, I shall never know anything precisely because it would be of utmost importance to me to know all. Any idler in Rome has his views about these episodes of my life, but I am the least informed of men on that score. My enemies have accused Plotina of taking advantage of the emperor's last moments to make the dying man pen the few words which bequeathed me the power. Calumniators more lurid-minded still have described a curtained bed, the uncertain gleam of a lamp, the physician Crito dictating the last wishes of Trajan in a voice which counterfeited that of the dead man. They have pointed out that the orderly Phoedimus, who hated me, and whose silence could not have been bought by my friends, very opportunely died of a malignant fever the day after the death of his master. There is something in those pictures of violence and intrigue to strike the popular imagination, and even my own. It would not displease me that a handful of reasonable people should have proved capable of verging upon crime in my behalf, nor that the devotion of the empress should have carried her so far. She was well aware of the dangers which a decision *not* taken portended for the State; I respect her enough to believe that she would have agreed to commit a necessary fraud if discretion, common sense, public interest, and friendship had all impelled her to it. Subsequently to these events I have seen this document, so violently contested by my adversaries; I am unable to pronounce either for or against the authenticity of this last dictation of a sick man. Certainly I prefer to think that Trajan himself, relinquishing his personal prejudices before he died, did of his own free will leave the empire to him whom he judged on the whole most worthy. But it must be admitted that the end, in this case, was of more concern to me than the means; the essential is that the man invested with power should have proved thereafter that he deserved to wield it.

The body was burned on the shore, not long after my arrival, as a preliminary to the triumphal rites which would be solemnized in Rome. Almost no one was present at the very simple ceremony, which took place at dawn and was only a last episode in the prolonged domestic service rendered by the women to the person of Trajan. Matidia wept unrestrainedly; Plotina's features seemed blurred in the wavering air round the heat of the funeral pyre. Calm, detached, slightly hollow from fever, she remained, as always, coolly impenetrable. Attianus and Crito watched until everything had been dully consumed; the faint smoke faded away in the pale air of unshadowed morning. None of my friends referred to the incidents of those few days which had preceeded the emperor's death. Their rule was evidently to keep silent; mine was to ask no dangerous questions.

That same day the widowed empress and her companions reembarked for Rome. I returned to Antioch, accompanied along the way by the acclamations of the legions. An extraordinary calm had come over me: ambition and fear alike seemed a nightmare of the past. Whatever happened, I had always been determined to defend my chance of empire to the end, but the act of adoption simplified everything. My own life no longer preoccupied me; I could once more think of the rest of mankind.

TELLUS STABILITA

Oᴿᴅᴇʀ was restored in my life, but not in the empire. The world which I had inherited resembled a man in full vigour of maturity who was still robust (though already revealing, to a physician's eyes, some barely perceptible signs of wear), but who had just passed through the convulsions of a serious illness. Negotiations were resumed, this time openly; I let it be generally understood that Trajan himself had told me to do so before he died. With one stroke of the pen I erased all conquests which might have proved dangerous : not only Mesopotamia, where we could not have maintained ourselves, but Armenia, which was too far away and too removed from our sphere, and which I retained only as a vassal state. Two or three difficulties, which would have made a peace conference drag on for years if the principals concerned had had any advantage in lengthening it out, were smoothed over by the skilful mediation of the merchant Opramoas, who was in the confidence of the Satraps. I tried to put into these diplomatic conversations the same ardour that others reserve for the field of battle; I forced a peace. Osroës, moreover, desired peace at least as much as I : the Parthians were concerned only to reopen their trade routes between us and India. A few months after the great crisis I had the joy of seeing the line of caravans re-form on the banks of the Orontes; the oases were again the resort of merchants exchanging news in the glow of their evening fires, each morning repacking along with their goods for transportation to lands unknown a certain number of thoughts, words, and customs genuinely our own, which little by little would take possession of the globe more securely than can advancing legions. The circulation of gold and the passage of ideas (as subtle as that of vital air in the arteries) were beginning again within the world's great body; earth's pulse began to beat once more.

The fever of rebellion subsided in its turn. In Egypt it had been so violent that they had been obliged to levy peasant militia at the utmost speed while awaiting reinforcements. Immediately I sent my comrade Marcius Turbo to re-establish order there, a task which he accomplished with judicious firmness. But order in the streets was hardly enough for me; I desired to restore order in the public consciousness, if it were possible, or rather to make order rule there for the first time. A stay of a week in Pelusium was given over entirely to adjusting differences between those internal incompatibles, Greeks and Jews. I saw nothing of what I should have wished to see: neither the banks of the Nile nor the Museum of Alexandria, nor the temple statues; I barely found time to devote a night to the agreeable debauches of Canopus. Six interminable days were passed in the steaming vat of a court-room, protected from the heat without by long slatted blinds which slapped to and fro in the wind. At night enormous mosquitoes swarmed round the lamps. I tried to point out to the Greeks that they were not always the wisest of peoples, and to the Jews that they were by no means the most pure. The satiric songs with which these low-class Hellenes were wont to antagonize their adversaries were scarcely less stupid than the grotesque imprecations from the jewries. These races who had lived side by side for centuries had never had the curiosity to get to know each other, nor the decency to accept each other. The exhausted litigants who did not give way till late into the night would find me on my bench at dawn, still engaged in sorting over the rubbish of false testimony; the stabbed corpses which they offered me as evidence for conviction were frequently those of invalids who had died in their beds and had been stolen from the embalmers. But each hour of calm was a victory gained, though precarious, like all victories; each dispute arbitrated served as precedent and pledge for the future. It mattered little to me that the accord obtained was external, imposed from without and perhaps temporary; I knew that good like bad becomes a routine, that the temporary tends to endure, that what is external permeates to the inside, and that the mask, given time, comes to be the face itself. Since hatred, stupidity, and delirium have lasting effects, I saw no reason why good will, clarity of mind, and just practice should not have their effects, too. Order on the frontiers was nothing if I could not persuade a Jewish pedlar and a Greek grocer to live peaceably side by side.

Peace was my aim, but not at all my idol; even to call it my ideal would displease me as too remote from reality. I had considered going so far in my refusal of conquests as to abandon Dacia, and would have done so had it been prudent to break openly with the policy of my predecessor; but it was better to utilize as wisely as possible those gains acquired before my accession and already recorded by history. The admirable Julius Bassus, first governor of that newly organized province, had died in his labours there, as I myself had almost succumbed in my year on the Sarmatian frontiers, exhausted by the thankless task of endless pacification in a country which had supposedly been subdued. I ordered a funeral triumph for him in Rome, an honour reserved ordinarily only for emperors; this homage to a good servitor sacrificed in obscurity was my last, and indirect, protest against the policy of conquest; nor had I need to denounce it publicly from the time that I was empowered to cut it short. On the other hand, military measures had to be taken in Mauretania, where agents of Lusius Quietus were fomenting revolt; nothing, however, required my immediate presence there. It was the same in Britain, where the Caledonians had taken advantage of the withdrawal of troops for the war in Asia to decimate the reduced garrisons left on the frontiers. Julius Severus saw to what was most urgent there while awaiting the time when restoration of order in Roman affairs would permit me to undertake that long voyage. But I greatly desired to take charge myself in the Sarmatian war, which had been left inconclusive, and this time to throw in the number of troops requisite to make an end of barbarian depredations. For I refused, here as everywhere, to subject myself to a system. I accepted war as a means toward peace where negotiations proved useless, in the manner of a physician who decides to cauterize only after having tried simples. Everything is so complicated in human affairs that my rule, even if pacific, would also have periods of war, just as the life of a great captain has, whether he likes it or not, its interludes of peace.

Before heading north for the final settlement of the Sarmatian conflict, I saw Quietus once more. The butcher of Cyrene remained formidable. My first move had been to disband his columns of Numidian scouts, but he still had his place in the Senate, his post in the regular army, and that immense domain of western sands which he could convert at will into either a springboard or a hiding-place. He invited me to a hunt in Mysia, deep in the forests, and skilfully engineered an accident in which with a little less luck or less bodily agility I should certainly have lost my life. It seemed best to appear unsuspecting, to be patient, and to wait. Shortly thereafter, in Lower Moesia, at a time when the capitulation of the Sarmatian princes allowed me to think of an early return to Italy, an exchange of dispatches in code with my former guardian warned me that Quietus had come back abruptly to Rome and had just conferred there with Palma. Our enemies were strengthening their positions and realigning their troops. No security was possible so long as we had these two men against us. I wrote to Attianus to act quickly. The old man struck like lightning. He overstepped his orders and with a single stroke freed me of the last of my avowed foes : on the same day, a few hours apart, Celsus was killed at Baiae, Palma in his villa at Terracina, and Nigrinus at Faventia on the threshold of his summer house. Quietus met his end on the road, on departing from a conference with his fellow conspirators, struck down on the step of the carriage which was bringing him back to the City. A wave of terror broke over Rome. Servianus, my aged brother-in-law, who had seemed resigned to my success but who was avidly anticipating my errors to come, must have felt an impulse of joy more nearly akin to ecstasy than any experience of his whole life. All the sinister rumours which circulated about me found credence anew.

I received this news aboard the ship which was bringing me back to Italy. I was appalled. One is always content to be relieved of one's adversaries, but my guardian had proceeded with the indifference of age for the far-reaching consequences of his act : he had forgotten that I should have to live with the after-effects of these murders for more than twenty years. I thought of the proscriptions of Octavius, which had for ever stained the memory of Augustus; of the first crimes of Nero, which had been followed by other crimes. I recalled the last years of Domitian, of that merely average man, no worse than another, whom fear had gradually destroyed (his own fear and the fears he caused), dying in his palace like a beast tracked down in the woods. My public life was already getting out of hand: the first line of the inscription bore in letters deeply incised a few words which I could no longer erase. The Senate, that great, weak body, powerful only when persecuted, would never forget that four of its members had been summarily executed by my order; three intriguing scoundrels and a brute would thus live on as martyrs. I notified Attianus at once that he was to meet me at Brundisium to answer for his action.

He was awaiting me near the harbour in one of the rooms of that inn facing toward the East where Virgil died long ago. He came limping to receive me on the threshold, for he was suffering from an attack of gout. The moment that I was alone with him, I burst into upbraiding: a reign which I intended to be moderate, and even exemplary, was beginning with four executions, only one of which was indispensable and for all of which too little precaution had been taken in the way of legal formalities. Such abuse of power would be cause for the more reproach to me whenever I strove thereafter to be clement, scrupulous, and just; it would serve as a pretext for proving that my so-called virtues were only a series of masks, and for building about me a trite legend of tyranny which would cling to me perhaps to the end of history. I admitted my fear; I felt no more exempt from cruelty than from any other human fault; I accepted the commonplace that crime breeds crime, and the example of the animal which had once tasted blood. An old friend whose loyalty had seemed wholly assured was already taking liberties, profiting by the weaknesses which he thought that he saw in me; under the guise of serving me he had arranged to settle a personal score against Nigrinus and Palma. He was compromising my work of pacification, and was preparing for me a grim return to Rome, indeed.

The old man asked leave to sit down, and rested his leg, swathed in flannel, upon a stool. While speaking I arranged the coverlet over his ailing foot. He let me run on, smiling meanwhile like a grammarian who listens to his pupil making his way through a difficult recitation. When I had finished, he asked me calmly what I had planned to do with the enemies of the régime. It could be proved, if need were, that these four men had plotted my death; it was to their interest, in any case, to do so. Every transition from one reign to another involved its operations of mopping up; he had taken this task upon himself in order to leave my hands clean. If public opinion demanded a victim, nothing was simpler than to deprive him of his post of Praetorian prefect. He had envisaged such a measure; he was advising me to take it. And if more were needed to conciliate the Senate, he would approve my going as far as relegation to the provinces, or exile.

Attianus had been the guardian from whom money could be wheedled, the counsellor of my difficult days, the faithful agent; but this was the first time I had ever looked attentively at that face with its carefully shaven jowls, at those crippled hands tranquilly clasped over the handle of his ebony cane. I knew well enough the different elements of his life as a prosperous citizen: his wife, whom he loved, and whose health was frail; his married daughters and their children, for whom he was modest but tenacious in his ambitions, as he had been for himself; his love of choice dishes; his decided taste for Greek cameos and for young dancing girls. He had given me precedence over all these things: for thirty years his first care had been to protect me, and next to serve me. To me, who had not yet given first place to anything except to ideas or projects, or at the most to a future image of myself, this simple devotion of man to man seemed prodigious and unfathomable. No one is worthy of it, and I am still unable to account for it. I followed his counsel: he lost his post. His faint smile showed me that he expected to be taken at his word. He knew well that no untimely solicitude toward an old friend would ever keep me from adopting the more prudent course; this subtle politician would not have wished me otherwise. Let us not exaggerate the extent of his disgrace: after some months of eclipse, I succeeded in having him admitted to the Senate. It was the greatest honour that I could afford to this man of equestrian rank. He lived to enjoy the easy old age of a wealthy Roman knight, much sought after for his perfect knowledge of families

and public affairs; I have often been his guest at his villa in the
Alban Hills. Nevertheless, like Alexander on the eve of a battle,
I had made a sacrifice to Fear before entering into Rome: I
sometimes count Attianus among my human victims.

*　*　*

Attianus had been right in his conjectures: the virgin gold of
respect would be too soft without some alloy of fear. The murder
of four men of consular rank was received as was the story of
the forged will: the honest and pure of heart refused to believe
that I was implicated; the cynics supposed the worst, but admired me only the more. As soon as it was known that my resentment had suddenly come to an end, Rome grew calm; each
person's joy in his own security caused the dead to be promptly
forgotten. My clemency was a matter for astonishment because
it was deemed deliberate and voluntary, chosen each morning in
preference to a violence which would have been equally natural to
me; my simplicity was praised because it was thought that
calculation figured therein. Trajan had had most of the virtues of
the average man, but my qualities were more unexpected; one
step further and they would have been regarded as a refinement
of vice itself. I was the same man as before, but what had
previously been despised now passed for sublime: my extreme
courtesy, considered by the unsubtle a form of weakness, or even
of cowardice, seemed now the smooth and polished sheath of
force. They extolled my patience with petitioners, my frequent
visits to the sick in the military hospitals, and my friendly famil-
iarity with the discharged veterans. Nothing in all that differed
from the manner in which I had treated my servants and tenant
farmers my whole life long. Each of us has more virtues than he
is credited with, but success alone brings them to view, perhaps
because then we may be expected to cease practising them.
Human beings beray their worst failings when they marvel to find
that a world ruler is neither foolishly indolent, presumptous, nor
cruel.

I had refused all titles. In the first months of my reign the
Senate had adorned me, before I could know of it, with that
long series of honorary appellations which is draped like a

fringed shawl round the necks of certain emperors. Dacicus, Parthicus, Germanicus: Trajan had loved these brave blasts of martial music, like the cymbals and drums of the Parthian regiments; what had roused echoes and responses in him only irritated or bewildered me. I got rid of all that, and also postponed, for the time, the admirable title of Father of the Country; Augustus accepted that honour only late in life, and I esteemed myself not yet worthy. It was the same with a triumph; it would have been ridiculous to consent to one for a war in which my sole merit had been to force a conclusion. Those who saw modesty in these refusals were as much mistaken as they who reproached me for pride. My motives related less to the effect produced on others than to advantages for myself. I desired that my prestige should be my own, inseparable from my person, and directly measurable in terms of mental agility, strength, and achievements. Titles, if they were to come, would come later on; but they would be other titles, evidences of more secret victories to which I dared not yet lay claim. For the moment I had enough to do to become, or merely to be, Hadrian to the utmost.

They accuse me of caring little for Rome. It had beauty, though, during those two years when the State and I were feeling our way with each other, the city of narrow streets, crowded Forums, and ancient, flesh-coloured brick. Rome revisited, after the Orient and Greece, was clothed with a strangeness which a Roman born and bred wholly in the City would not find there. I accustomed myself once more to its damp and soot-grimed winters; to the African heat of its summers, tempered by the refreshing cascades of Tibur and by the Alban lakes; to its almost rustic population, bound with provincial attachment to the Seven Hills, but gradually exposed to the influx of all races of the world, driven thither by ambition, enticements to gain, and the hazards of conquest and servitude, the tattooed black, the hairy German, the slender Greek, and the heavy Oriental. I freed myself of certain fastidious restraints. I no longer avoided the public baths at popular hours; I learned to endure the Games, where hitherto I had seen only brutal and stupid waste. My opinion had not changed; I detested these massacres where the beast had not one chance, but little by little I came to feel their ritual value, their effect of tragic purification upon the ignorant multitude. I wanted my festivities to equal those of Trajan in splendour, though with more art and decorum. I forced myself to derive pleasure from the perfect fencing of the gladiators, but only on the condition that no one should be compelled to practise this profession against his will. In the Circus I learned to parley with the crowd from the height of the tribune, speaking through heralds, and not to impose silence upon the throngs save with deference (which they repaid me a hundred-fold); likewise never to accord them anything but what they had reasonably the right to expect, nor to refuse anything without explaining my refusal. I did not take my books with me, as you do, into the imperial box; it is insulting to others to seem to disdain their joys. If the spectacle revolted me, the effort to bear it out was for me a more valuable exercise than the study of Epictetus.

Morals are a matter of private agreement; decency is of public concern. Any conspicuous licence has always struck me as a tawdry display. I forbade use of the baths by both sexes at the same time, a custom which had given rise to almost continual brawling; I returned to the State treasury the colossal service of silver dishes, melted down by my order, which had been wrought for the hoggish appetite of Vitellius. Our early Caesars have acquired an odious reputation for courting inheritances; I made it a rule to refuse both for myself and for the State any legacy to which direct heirs might think themselves entitled. I tried to reduce the exorbitant number of slaves in the imperial household, and especially to curb their arrogance, which leads them to rival the upper classes and sometimes to terrorize them. One day one of my servants had the impertinence to address a senator; I had the man slapped. My hatred of disorder went so far as to decree flogging in the Circus for spendthrifts sunk in debt. To preserve distinction of rank I insisted that the toga and senatorial robe be worn at all times in public, even though these garments are inconvenient, like everything honorific, and I feel no obligation to wear them myself except when in Rome. I made a practice of rising to receive my friends and of standing through-out my audiences, in reaction against the negligence of a sitting or reclining posture. I reduced the insolent crowd of carriages which cumber our streets, for this luxury of speed destroys its own aim; a pedestrian makes more headway than a hundred conveyances jammed end to end along the twists and turns of the Sacred Way. For visits to private homes I took the habit of being carried inside by litter, thus sparing my host the irksome duty of awaiting me without, or of accompanying me back to the street in the heat of the sun, or in the churlish wind of Rome.

I was again among my own people: I have always had some affection for my sister Paulina, and Servianus himself seemed less obnoxious than before. My mother-in-law Matidia had come back from the Orient already revealing the first symptoms of a mortal disease; to distract her from her suffering I devised simple dinners, and contrived to inebriate this modest and naïve matron with a harmless drop of wine. The absence of my wife, who had retreated to the country in a fit of ill humour, in no way detracted from these family pleasures. Of all persons she is probably the one whom I have least succeeded in pleasing; to be sure, I have made little effort to do so. I went often to the small house where the widowed empress now gave herself over to the serious delights of meditation and books; there I found unchanged the perfect silence of Plotina. She was withdrawing gently from life; that garden and those light rooms were daily becoming more the enclosure of a Muse, the temple of an empress already among the gods. Her friendship, however, remained exacting; but all things considered, her demands were only reasonable and wise.

I saw my friends again, and felt the subtle pleasure of renewed contact after long absence, of reappraising and of being reappraised. My companion in former pleasures and literary pursuits, Victor Voconius, had died; I made up some sort of funeral oration, provoking smiles in mentioning among the virtues of the deceased a chastity which his poems belied, as did the presence at the funeral of that very Thestylis, him of the honey-coloured curls, whom Victor used to call his 'fair torment'. My hypocrisy was less blatant than might appear: every pleasure enjoyed with art seemed to me chaste. I rearranged Rome like a house which the master intends to leave safe in his absence; new collaborators proved their worth, and adversaries now reconciled supped together at the Palatine with my supporters in former trials. At my table Neratius Priscus sketched his legislative plans; there the architect Apollodorus explained his designs; Ceionius Commodus, a wealthy patrician of Etruscan origin, descended from an ancient family of almost royal blood, was the friend who helped me work out my next moves in the Senate; he knew men, as well as wines.

His son Lucius Ceionius, barely eighteen at the time, brought the gay grace of a young prince to these banquets, which I had kept austere. He was already addicted to certain delightful follies: a passion for concocting rare dishes for his friends, an exquisite mania for arranging flowers, a wild love of travesty, and also of gambling. Martial was his Virgil; he recited these wanton poems with charming effrontory. I made promises which have cost me some trouble since; this dancing young fawn filled six months of my life.

I have so often lost sight of Lucius, then found him anew in the course of the years which followed, that perhaps I retain an image of him which is made up of memories superposed, a composite which corresponds to no one phase of his brief existence. The somewhat arrogant arbiter of Roman fashion, the budding orator timidly dependent upon models of style and seeking my advice on a difficult passage, the anxious young officer twisting his thin beard, the invalid exhausted by coughing whom I watched over to his death, none of these existed till much later on. The picture of Lucius the boy is confined to more secret recesses of my memory: a face, a body, a complexion with the pale flush of alabaster, the exact equivalent of an amorous epigram of Callimachus or of certain perfectly turned, unadorned lines of Strato.

But I was eager to leave Rome. My predecessors, up to this time, had absented themselves chiefly for war; for me the great undertaking, the activities of peace, and my life itself began outside Rome's bounds.

There was one last service to perform, the duty of giving to Trajan, that triumph which had obsessed his dying dreams. Actually a triumph becomes only the dead. When we are living there is always someone to reproach us for our failings; thus once they mocked Caesar for his baldness and his loves. But the dead are entitled to such inauguration into the tomb, to those few hours of noisy pomp before the centuries of glory and the millenniums of oblivion. Their fortune is safe from all reverses, and even their defeats acquire the splendour of victories. The last triumph of Trajan commemorated not his more or less dubious success over Parthia, but the honourable effort which his whole life had been. We had come together to celebrate the best emperor that Rome had known since the later years of Augustus, the hardest working, the most honest, and the least unjust. His very defects were no more than those distinguishing traits which prove the perfect resemblance between the marble portrait and the face. The emperor's soul ascended to the heavens, borne up along the still spiral of the Trajan Column. My adoptive father became a god: he had taken his place in that series of soldierly incarnations of the eternal Mars who come from century to century to shake and to change the world. As I stood upon the balcony of the Palatine I weighed the differences between us; I was directing myself toward calmer ends. I began to dream of truly Olympian rule.

*　　*　　*

Rome is no longer confined to Rome: henceforth she must identify herself with half the globe, or must perish. Our homes and terraced roofs of tiles, turned by the setting sun to rose and gold, are no longer enclosed, as in the times of our kings, within city walls. Our true ramparts now are thousands of leagues from Rome. I have constructed a good part of these defences myself along edges of Germanic forest and British moor. Each time that I have looked from afar, at the bend of some sunny road, toward a Greek acropolis with its perfect city fixed to the hill like a flower to its stem, I could not but feel that the incomparable plant was limited by its very perfection, achieved on one point of space and in one segment of time. Its sole chance of expansion, as for that of a plant, was in its seed: with the pollen of its ideas Greece has fertilized the world. But Rome, less light and less shapely, sprawling to the plain at her river's edge, was moving towards vaster growth: the city has become the State. I should have wished the State to expand still more, likening itself to the order of the universe, to the divine nature of things. Virtues which had sufficed for the small city of the Seven Hills would have to grow less rigid and more varied if they were to meet the needs of all the earth. Rome, which I was first to venture to call 'eternal', would come to be more and more like the mother deities of the cults of Asia, bearer of youths and of harvests, sheltering at her breast both the lions and the hives of bees.

But anything made by man which aspires to eternity must adapt itself to the changing rhythm of nature's great bodies, to accord with celestial time. Our Rome is no longer the village of the days of Evander, big with a future which has already partly passed by; the plundering Rome of the time of the Republic has performed its role; the mad capital of the first Caesars inclines now to greater sobriety; other Romes will come, whose forms I see but dimly, but whom I shall have helped to mould. When I was visiting ancient cities, sacred but wholly dead, and without present value for the human race, I promised myself to save this Rome of mine from the petrifaction of a Thebes, a Babylon, or a Tyre. She would no longer be bound by her body of stone, but would compose for herself from the words *State, citizenry* and *republic* a surer immortality. In the countries as yet untouched by our culture, on the banks of the Rhine and the Danube, or the shores of the Batavian Sea, each village enclosed within its wooden palisade brought to mind the reed hut and dunghill where our Roman twins had slept content, fed by the milk of the wolf; these cities-to-be would follow the pattern of Rome. Over separate nations and races, with their accidents of geography and history and the disparate demands of their gods and their ancestors, we should have superimposed for ever a unity of human conduct and the empiricism of sober experience, but should have done so without destruction of what had preceded us. Rome would be perpetuating herself in the least of the towns where magistrates strive to demand just weight from the merchants, to clean and light the streets, to combat disorder, slackness, superstition, and injustice, and to give broader and fairer interpretation to the laws. She would endure to the end of the last city built by man.

Humanitas, Libertas, Felicitas: those noble words which grace the coins of my reign were not of my invention. Any Greek philosopher, almost every cultured Roman, conceives of the world as I do. I have heard Trajan exclaim, when confronted by a law which was unjust because it was too rigorous, that to continue its enforcement was to run counter to the spirit of the times. I shall have been the first, perhaps, to subordinate all my actions to this 'spirit of the times', to make of it something other than the inflated dream of a philosopher, or the slightly vague aspirings of some good prince. And I was thankful to the gods, for they had allowed me to live in a period when my allotted task consisted of prudent reorganization of a world, and not of extracting matter, still unformed, from chaos, or of lying upon a corpse in the effort to revive it. I enjoyed the thought that our past was long enough to provide us with great examples but not so heavy as to crush us under their weight; that our technical developments had advanced to the point of facilitating hygiene in the cities and prosperity for the population, though not to the degree of encumbering man with useless acquisitions; that our arts, like trees grown weary with the abundance of their bearing, were still able to produce a few choice fruits. I was glad that our venerable, almost formless religions, drained of all intransigence and purged of savage rites, linked us mysteriously to the most ancient secrets of man and of earth, not forbidding us, however, a secular explanation of facts and a rational view of human conduct. It was, in sum, pleasing to me that even these words *Humanity, Liberty, Happiness,* had not yet lost their value by too much misuse.

I see an objection to every effort toward ameliorating man's condition on earth, namely that mankind is perhaps not worthy of such exertion. But I meet the objection easily enough: so long as Caligula's dream remains impossible of fulfilment, and the entire human race is not reduced to a single head destined for the axe, we shall have to bear with humanity, keeping it within bounds by utilizing it to the utmost; our interest, in the best sense of the term, will be to serve it. My procedure was based on a series of observations made upon myself over a long period; any lucid explanation has always convinced me, all courtesy has won me over, every moment of felicity has almost always left me wise. I lent only half an ear to those well-meaning folk who say that happiness is enervating, liberty too relaxing, and that kindness is a corruption for those upon whom it is practised. That may be; but, in the world as it is, such reasoning amounts to refusal to nourish a starving man decently for fear that in a few years he may suffer from over-feeding. When useless servitude has been alleviated as far as possible, and unnecessary misfortune avoided, there will still remain as a test of man's fortitude that long series of veritable ills, death, old age, and incurable sickness, love unrequited and friendship rejected or betrayed, the mediocrity of a life less vast than our projects and duller than our dreams; in short, all the woes caused by the divine nature of things.

I should say outright that I have little faith in laws. If too severe, they are broken, and with good reason. If too complicated, human ingenuity finds means to slip easily between the meshes of this trailing but fragile net. Respect for ancient laws answers to what is deepest rooted in human piety, but it serves also to pillow the inertia of judges. The oldest codes are a part of that very savagery which they were striving to correct; even the most venerable among them are the product of force. Most of our punitive laws fail, perhaps happily, to reach the greater part of the culprits; our civil laws will never be supple enough to fit the immense and changing diversity of facts. Laws change more slowly than custom, and though dangerous when they fall behind the times are more dangerous still when they presume to anticipate custom. And nevertheless from that mass of outworn routines and perilous innovations a few useful formulas have emerged here and there, just as they have in medicine. The Greek philosophers have taught us to know something more of the nature of man; our best jurists have worked for generations along lines of common sense. I have myself effected a few of those partial reforms which are the only reforms that endure. Any law too often subject to infraction is bad; it is the duty of the legislator to repeal or to change it, lest the contempt into which that rash ruling has fallen should extend to other, more just legislation. I proposed as my aim a prudent avoidance of superfluous decrees, and the firm promulgation, instead, of a small group of well-weighed decisions. The time seemed to have come to evaluate anew all the ancient prescriptions in the interest of mankind.

One day in Spain, in the vicinity of Tarragona, when I was visiting alone a half-abandoned mine, a slave attacked me with a knife. He had passed most of his forty-three years in those subterranean corridors, and not without logic was taking revenge upon the emperor for his long servitude. I managed to disarm him easily enough; under the care of my physician his violence subsided, and he changed into what he really was, a being not less sensible than others, and more loyal than many. Had the law been applied with savage rigour, he would have been promptly executed; as it was, he became my useful servant. Most men are like this slave: they are only too submissive; their long periods of torpor are interspersed with a few revolts as brutal as they are ineffectual. I wanted to see if well-regulated liberty would not have produced better results, and I am astonished that a similar experiment has not tempted more princes. This barbarian condemned to the mines became a symbol to me of all our slaves and all our barbarians. It seemed to me not impossible to treat them as I had treated this man, rendering them harmless simply by kindness, provided that first of all they understand that the hand which disarms them is sure. All nations which have perished up to this time have done so for lack of generosity; Sparta would have survived longer had she given her Helots some interest in that survival; there is always a day when Atlas ceases to support the weight of the heavens, and his revolt shakes the earth. I wished to postpone as long as possible, and to avoid, if it could be done, the moment when the barbarians from without and the slaves within would fall upon a world which they have been forced to respect from afar, or to serve from below, but the profits of which are not for them. I was determined that even the most wretched, from the slaves who clean the city sewers to the famished barbarians who hover along the frontiers, should have an interest in seeing Rome endure.

I doubt if all the philosophy in the world can succeed in suppressing slavery; it will, at most, change the name. I can well imagine forms of servitude worse than our own, because more insidious, whether they transform men into stupid, complacent machines, who believe themselves free just when they are most subjugated, or whether to the exclusion of leisure and pleasures essential to man they develop a passion for work as violent as the passion for war among barbarous races. To such bondage for the human mind and imagination I prefer even our avowed slavery. However that may be, the horrible condition which puts one man at the mercy of another ought to be carefully regulated by law. I saw to it that a slave should no longer be anonymous merchandise sold without regard for the family ties which he has formed, or a contemptible object whom a judge submits to torture before taking his testimony, instead of accepting it upon oath. I prohibited forced entry of slaves into disreputable or dangerous occupations, forbidding their sale to brothel keepers, or to schools of gladiators. Let only those who like such professions practise them; the professions will but gain thereby. On farms, where overseers exploit the strength of slaves, I have replaced the latter, wherever possible, by free shareholders. Our collections of anecdotes abound in stories of gourmets who feed their household servants to their fish, but scandalous crimes are readily punishable, and are insignificant in comparison with the thousands of routine atrocities perpetrated daily by correct but heartless people whom no one would think of questioning. There was a great outcry when I banished from Rome a rich and highly esteemed patrician woman who maltreated her aged slaves; any bad son who neglects his old parents shocks the public conscience more, but I see little difference between their two forms of inhumanity.

The condition of women is fixed by strange customs: they are at one and the same time subjected and protected, weak and powerful, too much despised and too much respected. In this chaos of contradictory usage, the practices of society are superimposed upon the facts of nature, but it is not easy to distinguish between the two. This confused state of things is in every respect more stable than might appear: on the whole, women want to be just as they are; they resist change, or they utilize it for their one and only aim. The freedom of the women of today, which is greater, or at least more visible, than that of earlier times, is but an aspect of the easier life of a prosperous period; the principles and even the prejudices of old have not been seriously disturbed. Whether sincere or not, the official eulogies and epitaphs continue to attribute to our matrons those same virtues of industry, chastity, and sobriety which were demanded of them under the Republic. These real or supposed changes have in no respect modified the eternal freedom of morals in the humbler classes, nor the perpetual prudery of the bourgeoisie; time alone will prove which of these changes will last. The weakness of women, like that of slaves, lies in their legal status; they take their revenge by their strength in little things, where the power which they wield is almost unlimited. I have rarely seen a household where women do not rule; I have often seen also ruling with them the steward, the cook, or the enfranchised slave. In financial matters they remain legally subject to some form of guardianship, but in practice it is otherwise. In each small shop of the Suburra it is ordinarily the poulterer's or fruiterer's wife who is firmly ensconced in command of the counter. The wife of Attianus directed the family estate with the acumen of a true man of business. The law should differ as little as possible from accustomed practice, so I have granted women greater liberty to administer or to bequeath their fortunes, and to inherit. I have insisted that no woman should be married without her consent; this form of legalized rape is as offensive as any other. Marriage is their great venture; it is only fair that they should not engage upon it against their will.

One part of our ills comes from the fact that too many men are shamefully rich and too many desperately poor. Happily in our days we tend toward a balance between these two extremes; the colossal fortunes of emperors and freedmen are things of the past: Trimalchio and Nero are dead. But everything is still to be done for the intelligent reorganization of world economy. On coming to power I renounced the voluntary contributions made by the cities to the emperor; they are only a form of theft. I advise you to refuse them in your turn. My wholesale cancellation of private debts to the State was a more hazardous measure, but there was need to start afresh after ten years of wartime financing. Our currency had been dangerously depressed for a century; it is nevertheless by the exchange rate of our gold pieces that Rome's eternity is appraised; it behoves us to give them solid weight and true value in terms of commodities. Our lands are cultivated without plan: only the more fortunate regions, like Egypt, Africa, Tuscany, and a few others, have known how to create peasant communities carefully trained in the culture of vineyards or grain. One of my chief cares has been to promote that class, and to draw instructors from it for more primitive or conservative rural populations with less skill. I have put an end to the scandal of untilled fields neglected by great landowners too little concerned for the public good; any field not cultivated for five years' time belongs hereafter to the farmer who proposes to put it to use. It is much the same with the mines. Most of our rich men make enormous gifts to the State, and to public institutions and the emperor; many do this for their own interest, a few act unselfishly, but nearly all gain thereby in the end. I should have preferred to see their generosity take other forms than that of ostentation in alms, and to teach them to augment their possessions wisely in the interest of the community as they had done hitherto only for the enrichment of their children. With this intention I myself took over the direction of the imperial domains; no one has the right to treat the earth so unproductively as the miser does his pot of gold.

Our merchants are sometimes our best geographers, our best astronomers, and our most learned naturalists. Our bankers number among our ablest judges of men. I made use of these special capacities, but fought with all my strength against their possibilities for encroachment. Subsidies given to shipbuilders had multiplied tenfold our trade with foreign nations; thus I succeeded in reinforcing our costly imperial fleet with but slight expense. So far as imports from the Orient and Africa are concerned, Italy might as well be an island, dependent upon grain dealers for its subsistence, since it no longer supplies itself; the only means of coping with the dangers of this situation is to treat these indispensable men of business as functionaries to be watched over closely. In recent years our older provinces have attained to a state of prosperity which can still perhaps be increased, but it is important that that prosperity should serve for all, and not alone for the bank of Herod Atticus, or for the small speculator who buys up all the oil of a Greek village. No law is too strict which makes for reduction of the countless intermediaries who swarm in our cities, an obscene, fat, and paunchy race, whispering in every tavern, leaning on every counter, ready to undermine any policy which is not to their immediate advantage. In time of shortage a judicious distribution from the State granaries helps to check the scandalous inflation of prices, but I was counting most of all on the organization of the producers themselves, the vineyard owners in Gaul and the fishermen of the Black Sea (whose miserable pittance is devoured by importers of caviare and salt fish who batten on the produce of those dangerous labours). One of my best days was the one on which I persuaded a group of seamen from the Archipelago to join in a single corporation in order to deal directly with retailers in the towns. I have never felt myself more usefully employed as a ruler.

For the army, peace is too often only a period of turbulent idleness between two periods of combat: the alternative to inaction or to disorder is first, preparation for a war already determined upon, and then the war itself. I broke with these routines; my perpetual visits to the advance posts were only one means among many of maintaining that peacetime army in a state of useful activity. Everywhere, on level ground as in the mountains, on the edge of the forest and in the desert, the legions spread or concentrate their buildings, always the same, their drill fields, their barracks, constructed at Cologne to resist the snow, at Lambaesis for shelter from sand storms; likewise their storehouses, from which I ordered all useless materials to be sold, and their officers' clubs, presided over by a statue of the emperor.

But that uniformity is no more than apparent: those interchangeable quarters house throngs of auxiliary troops who are never the same; each race contributes to the army its particular strength and its characteristic weapons, the genius of its foot soldiers, horsemen, or archers. There I found, in the rough, that diversity in unity which I sought for the empire as a whole. I authorized the use of native speech for commands, and encouraged the soldiers in their national war cries; I sanctioned unions between veterans and barbarian women, and gave legal status to their children, trying thus to mitigate the harshness of camp life, and to treat these simple and ignorant men as men. At the risk of rendering them less effectively mobile I intended to attach them to whatever territory they were expected to defend; I did not hesitate to regionalize the army. On an imperial scale I was hoping to re-establish the equivalent of the militias of the early Republic, where each man was wont to defend his field or his farm.

I worked above all to develop the technical efficiency of the legions; my aim was to make use of these military centres as levers of civilization, as wedges strong enough to enter in little by little just where the more delicate instruments of civil life would have been blunted. The army was becoming a connecting link between the forest dwellers, the inhabitants of steppes and marshes, and the more refined urban populations; it offered primary schooling to the barbarians and a school of endurance and responsibilities for the educated Greeks or the young knights accustomed to the comforts of Rome. The arduous elements of that life were known to me at first hand, as well as its easier side, with its subterfuges. I abolished special privileges, forbidding too frequent leaves for the officers and ordering the camps to be cleared of costly gardens, pleasure pavilions, and banquet halls. These useless buildings were turned into infirmaries and veterans' homes. We were recruiting our soldiers at too tender an age and keeping them too old, a practice which was both uneconomic and cruel. I changed all that. The August Discipline ought to reflect the humane tendencies of our times.

We emperors are not Caesars; we are functionaries of the State. That plaintiff whom I refused one day to hear out was right when she exclaimed that if I had no time to listen to her, I had no time to rule. The excuses which I offered her were not merely a matter of form. And nevertheless time *is* lacking: the more the empire enlarges the more the different aspects of authority tend to be concentrated in the hands of the chief of State; this man so pressed for time has necessarily to delegate some part of his tasks to others; his genius will consist in surrounding himself more and more with trustworthy personnel. The great crime of Claudius or of Nero was that they indolently allowed their slaves and freedmen to take on the roles of agents, counsellors, and representatives for their masters. One portion of my life and my travels has been passed in choosing the administrative heads of a new bureaucracy, in training them, in matching as judiciously as I could the talents to the posts, and in opening possibilities of useful employment to that middle class upon whom the State depends.

I recognize the danger of these armies of civilians; it is comprised in a word, the danger of establishing routines. This mechanism, wound up for centuries to come, will run awry if we do not keep watch; the master must constantly regulate its movements, foreseeing and repairing the effects of wear. But experience shows that in spite of our infinite care in choosing our successors the mediocre emperors will always outnumber the wise, and that at least one fool will reign per century. In time of crisis these bureaux, if well organized, will go on with what must be done, filling the interim (sometimes very long) between two good rulers. Some emperors like to parade behind them whole lines of barbarians, bound at the neck, those interminable processions of the conquered. My cortège will be different; the best of those officials whom I have attempted to train will compose it. Thanks to the members of the imperial council I have been able to leave Rome for years at a time, coming back for only brief stays. I communicated with them by the swiftest of couriers, and in time of danger by semaphore. They have in their turn trained other useful auxiliaries. Their competence is of my making; their efficient activity has left me free to employ myself elsewhere. It is going to let me depart, without too much concern, to death itself.

In my twenty years of rule I have passed twelve without fixed abode. In succession I occupied palatial homes of Asiatic merchants, sober Greek houses, handsome villas in Roman Gaul provided with baths and hot-air heating, or mere huts and farms. My preference was still for the light tent, that architecture of canvas and cords. Lodgings at sea were no less diversified than those on land: I had my own ship, equipped with gymnasium and library, but I was too distrustful of all fixity to attach myself to any one dwelling, even to one in motion. Whether the pleasure bark of a Syrian millionaire, the great galleys of the fleet, or the light skiff of a Greek fisherman, all suited my needs. The one luxury was speed, and all that favoured it, the finest horses, the best swung carriages, the least cumbersome luggage, the clothing and accessories most fitted to the climate. But my greatest asset of all was perfect health: a forced march of twenty leagues was nothing; a night without sleep was no more than a chance to think in peace. Few men like prolonged travel; it disrupts all habit and endlessly jolts each prejudice. But I was striving to have no prejudices and few habits. I welcomed the delight of a soft bed, but liked also the touch and smell of bare earth, some contact with the rough or smooth segments of the world's circumference. I was well inured to all kinds of foods, from British gruel to African water melon. Once I tasted that delicacy of certain Germanic tribes, tainted game; it made me vomit, but the experiment had been tried. Though decided in my tastes in love, even there I feared routines. My attendants, reduced in number to the indispensable, or to the exquisite, separated me but little from other people; I took special care to be free in my movements, and to leave access to me easy. The provinces, those great official units for which I myself had chosen the emblems (Britannia on her throne of rocks, or Dacia with her scimitar) were entities for me composed of distinct parts, forests where I had sought shade, wells where I had slaked my thirst, chance encounters at halts, faces known and sometimes loved. I began to know each mile of our roads, Rome's finest gift, perhaps, to the world. But what was unforgettable was the moment when a road came to an end on the mountainside, and we hoisted ourselves from crevice to crevice, from boulder to boulder, to catch the dawn from an Alpine peak or a height of the Pyrenees.

A few men before me had travelled over the earth: Pythagoras, Plato, some dozen scholars, and a fair number of adventurers. For the first time the traveller was also the master, free both to see and to reform or create anew. That was my good

fortune; I reflected that centuries, perhaps, would pass before
there might be another such happy accord between an office, a
temperament, and a world. And it was then that I felt the
advantage of being a newcomer, a man alone, scarcely bound
even by marriage, childless and practically without ancestors, a
Ulysses with no external Ithaca. I must here admit what I have
told no one else: I have never had a feeling of belonging wholly
to any one place, not even to my beloved Athens, nor even to
Rome. Though a foreigner in every land, in no place did I feel
myself a stranger. The different professions which make up the
trade of emperor were practised along the way: I resumed
military life like a garment grown comfortable with use, and fell
back readily into the jargon of the camps, that Latin deformed
by the pressure of barbaric languages and sprinkled with the
usual profanity and obvious jokes; I again grew used to the heavy
equipment of the days of manoeuvres, and to that change in
equilibrium in the whole body which the weight of a shield on
the left arm can produce. More arduous were the interminable
duties of accountant, wherever I went, whether for auditing the
records of the Province of Asia or those of a small British town
in debt for the construction of public baths. I have already
spoken of my function as judge. Comparisons drawn from other
employments came to mind: I thought of the itinerant doctor
going from door to door to care for the sick, of the street department employee called to repair a pavement or to solder a water
main; of the overseer running back and forth on the ship, en-
couraging the oarsmen but sparing his whip as he could. And
today, on the Villa's terrace, watching the slaves treat the orchard
trees or weed the flower beds, I think most of all of the coming
and going of a watchful gardener.

The craftsmen whom I took with me on my rounds caused
me little concern: their love of travel was as strong as my own.
But I had trouble with the writers and scholars. The indispensable Phlegon fusses like an old woman, but he is the only
secretary who has held up under the years: he is still with me.
The poet Florus, to whom I proposed a Latin secretaryship,
proclaimed right and left that he would not have wished to be
Caesar, forced to battle with the cold of Scythia, or British rain.

The long excursions on foot did not appeal to him either. On my side, I gladly left to him the delights of Rome's literary life, the taverns where the same witticisms are exchanged each night and the same mosquitoes are endured in common. To Suetonius I had given the post of curator of archives, thus granting him access to secret documents which he needed for his biographies of the Caesars. This clever man so well named Tranquillus was hardly to be imagined outside a library; he remained in Rome, where he became one of my wife's intimates, a member of that small circle of discontented conservatives who gathered around her to criticize the ways of the world. This group was little to my liking; I had Tranquillus pensioned off, and he retired to his cottage in the Sabine Hills there to mull undisturbed over the vices of Tiberius. A Greek secretariat was held for some time by Favorinus of Arles. That dwarf with the high treble voice was not devoid of subtlety but his mind was the most given to false deductions of any that I have encountered. We were always disputing, but his erudition charmed me. I was amused at his hypochondria; he dwelt upon his health like a lover attending a cherished mistress. His Hindu servant prepared his rice, imported from the Orient at great expense; unfortunately, this exotic cook spoke Greek badly, and said but little in any language, so he taught me nothing about the marvels of his native land. Favorinus flattered himself on having accomplished three rather rare things in his life: though a Gaul, he had Hellenized himself better than anyone else; though of humble origin, he was constantly quarrelling with the emperor and coming off none the worse for it, a remarkable fact which was, however, entirely to my credit; though impotent, he was continually paying fines for seduction of married women. And it is true that his lady admirers in provincial literary circles caused him difficulties from which I had more than once to extricate him. I wearied of that, and Eudemo took his place. But on the whole I have been unaccountably well served. The respect of that little group of friends and employees has survived, the gods only know how, through the rough intimacies of travel; their discretion has been still more astonishing, if possible, than their fidelity. The Suetoniuses of the future will have few anecdotes to harvest concerning me.

What the public knows of my life I have revealed. My friends have kept my secrets, political and otherwise; it is fair to say that I often did the same for them.

To build is to collaborate with earth, to put a human mark upon a landscape, modifying it for ever thereby; the process also contributes to that slow change which makes up the history of cities. What thought and care to determine the exact site for a bridge, or for a fountain, and to give a mountain road that perfect curve which is at the same time the shortest. . . . The widening of the road to Megara transformed the shore along the Scironian Cliffs; the two thousand odd stadia of paved way, provided with cisterns and military posts, which connected Antinoöpolis with the Red Sea brought an era of security to the desert following an era of danger. For the construction of a system of aqueducts in Troas all the revenue from five hundred cities of the Province of Asia was not too high a price; an aqueduct for Carthage atoned in some part for the rigours of the Punic Wars. The erecting of fortifications was much like constructing dykes : the object was to find the line on which a shore, or an empire, could be defended, the point where the assault of waves (or barbarians) would be held back, stopped, or utterly broken. The beauty of the gulfs bore fruit with the opening of harbours. The founding of libraries was like constructing more public granaries, amassing reserves against a spiritual winter which by certain signs, in spite of myself, I see ahead.

I have done much rebuilding. To reconstruct is to collaborate with time gone by, penetrating or modifying its spirit, and carrying it toward a longer future. Thus beneath the stones we find the secret of the springs.

Our life is brief : we are always referring to centuries which precede or follow our own as if they were totally alien to us, but I have come close to them in my play with stone. These walls which I reinforce are still warm from contact with vanished bodies; hands yet unborn will caress the shafts of these columns. The more I have meditated upon my death, and especially upon that of another, the more I have tried to add to our lives these virtually indestructible extensions. At Rome I preferred to use our enduring brick; it returns but slowly to the earth, from which it comes, and its imperceptible settling and crumbling leave a mountainous mass even when the edifice has ceased to be visibly what it was built for, a fortress, a circus, or a tomb. In Greece and in Asia I chose the native marble, that fair substance which, once cut, stays so faithful to human measurements and proportions that the plan of an entire temple survives in each fragment of a broken column.

Architecture is rich in possibilities more varied than Vitruvius' four orders would seem to allow; our great stone blocks, like our tones in music, are amenable to endless regrouping. For the Pantheon I turned to the ancient Etruria of augurs and soothsayers; the sunny temple of Venus, on the contrary, is a round of Ionic forms, a profusion of white and pale rose columns clustered about the voluptuous goddess whence sprang the race of Caesar. The Olympieion of Athens, built on the plain, had to be in exact counterpoise to the Parthenon on its hill, vastness opposed to perfection, ardour kneeling before calm, splendour at the feet of beauty. The chapels of Antinous and his temples were magic chambers, commemorating a mysterious passage between life and death; these shrines to an overpowering joy and grief were places of prayer and evocation of the dead; there I gave myself over to my sorrow. My tomb on the bank of the Tiber reproduces on a gigantic scale the ancient vaults of the Appian Way, but its very proportions transform it, recalling Ctesiphon and Babylon with their terraces and towers by which man seeks to climb nearer the stars. Sepulchral Egypt provided the plan for the obelisks and rows of sphinxes of that cenotaph which forces upon a vaguely hostile Rome the memory of the friend for ever mourned.

The Villa was the tomb of my travels, the last encampment of the nomad, the equivalent, though in marble, of the tents and pavilions of the princes of Asia. Almost everything that appeals to our taste has already been tried in the world of forms; I turned toward the realm of colour : jasper as green as the depths of the sea, porphyry dense as flesh, basalt and sombre obsidian. The crimson of the hangings was adorned with more and more intricate embroideries; the mosaics of the walls or pavements were never too golden, too white, or too dark. Each building-stone was the strange concretion of a will, a memory, and sometimes a challenge. Each structure was the chart of a dream.

Plotinopolis, Hadrianopolis, Antinoöpolis, Hadrianotherae. . . . I have multiplied these human beehives as much as possible. Plumber and mason, engineer and architect preside at the births of cities; the operation also requires certain magical gifts. In a world still largely made up of woods, desert, and uncultivated plain, a city is indeed a fine sight, with its paved streets, its temple to some god or other, its public baths and latrines, a shop where the barber discusses with his clients the news from Rome, its pastry shop, cobblers' and perhaps a bookshop, its doctor's sign, and a theatre, where from time to time a comedy of Terence is played. Our men of fashion complain of the uniformity of our cities; they suffer in seeing everywhere the same statue of the emperor, and the same water pipes. They are wrong: the beauty of Nîmes is wholly different from that of Arles. But that very uniformity, to be found now on three continents, reassures the traveller as does the sight of a milestone; even the dullest of our towns have their comforting significance as shelters and posting stops. A city: that framework constructed by men for men, monotonous if you will, but only as are wax cells laden with honey, a place of meeting and exchange, where peasants come to sell their produce, and linger to gape and stare at the paintings of a portico. . . .

My cities were born of encounters, both my own encounters with given corners of the earth and the conjunction of my plans as emperor with the incidents of my personal life. Plotinopolis grew from the need to establish new market towns in Thrace, but also from the tender desire to honour Plotina. Hadrian-otherae is designed to serve as a trading town for the forest dwellers of Asia Minor: at first it had been for me a summer retreat, with its forest of wild game, its hunting lodge of rough hewn logs below the hill of the god Attys, and its headlong stream where we bathed each morning. Hadrianopolis in Epirus reopened an urban centre in the heart of an impoverished province: it owes its start to a visit which I made to the oracle of Dodona. Hadrianopolis in Thrace, an agricultural and military outpost strategically placed on the edge of barbarian lands, is

populated by veterans of the Sarmatian wars: I know at first
hand the strength and the weakness of each one of those men,
their names, the number of their years of service, and of their
wounds. Antinoöpolis, dearest of all, born on the site of sorrow,
is confined to a narrow band of arid soil between the river and
the cliffs. I was only the more desirous, therefore, to enrich it
with other resources, trade with India, river traffic, and the
learned graces of a Greek metropolis. There is not a place on
earth that I care less to revisit, but there are few to which I have
devoted more pains. It is a veritable city of columns, a perpetual
peristyle. I exchange dispatches with its governor, Fidus Aquila,
about the propylaea of its temple and the statues of its triumphal
arch; I have chosen the names of its district divisions and
religious and administrative units, symbolic names both obvious
and secret which catalogue all my memories. I myself drew the
plan of its Corinthian colonnades and the corresponding align-
ment of palm trees spaced regularly along the river banks. Countless times have I walked in thought that almost perfect quadri-
lateral, cut by parallel streets and divided in two by the broad
avenue which leads from a Greek theatre to a tomb.

We are crowded with statues and cloyed with the exquisite in
painting and sculpture, but this abundance is an illusion, for we
reproduce over and over some dozen masterpieces which are now
beyond our power to invent. Like other collectors I have had
copied for the Villa the Hermaphrodite and the Centaur, the
Niobid and the Venus. I have wanted to live as much as possible
in the midst of this music of forms. I have encouraged experi-
mentation with the thought and methods of the past, a learned
archaism which might recapture lost intentions and lost techniques. I tried those variations which consist of transcribing in
red marble a flayed Marsyas, portrayed heretofore only in white,
going back thus into the world of painted figures; or of trans-
posing to the pallor of Parian marble the black grain of Egypt's
statues, changing the idol to a ghost. Our art is perfect, that is to
say, completed, but its perfection can be modulated as finely as
can a pure voice: we have still the chance to play that skilful
game of perpetual approach to, or withdrawal from that solution
found once for all; we may go to the limit of control, or excess,

and enclose within that beauteous sphere innumerable new constructions.

There is advantage in having behind us multiple points of comparison, in being free to follow Scopas intelligently, or to diverge, voluptuously, from Praxiteles. My contacts with the arts of barbarians have led me to believe that each race limits itself to certain subjects and to certain modes among those conceivable; each period, too, makes a selection among the possibilities offered to each race. In Egypt I have seen colossal gods, and kings; on the wrists of Sarmatian prisoners I have found bracelets which endlessly repeat the same galloping horse, or the same serpents devouring each other. But our art (I mean that of the Greeks) has chosen man as its centre. We alone have known how to show latent strength and agility in bodies in repose; we alone have made a smooth brow the symbol of wise reflection. I am like our sculptors: the human contents me; I find everything there, even what is eternal. The image of the Centaur sums up for me all forests, so greatly loved, and storm winds never breathe better than in a sea goddess' billowing scarf. Natural objects and sacred emblems have value for me only as they are weighted with human associations: the phallic and funeral pine cone, the vase with doves which suggests siesta beside a fountain, the gryphon which carries the beloved to the sky.

The art of portraiture was of slight interest to me. Our Roman busts have value only as records, faces copied to the last wrinkle, with every single wart, stencils of figures with whom we brush elbows in life and whom we forgot as soon as they die. The Greeks, on the contrary, have loved human perfection to the point of caring but little for the varied visages of men. I tend merely to glance at my own likeness, that dark face so changed by the whiteness of marble, those wide-opened eyes, that thin though sensuous mouth, controlled to the point of quivering. But I have been more preoccupied by the face of another. As soon as he began to count in my life art ceased to be a luxury and became a resource, a form of succour. I have forced this image upon the world: there are today more portraits of that youth than of any illustrious man whatsoever, or of any queen. At first my desire was to have recorded in sculpture the successive beauties of a changing form; but later, art became a kind of magical operation, capable of evoking a countenance lost. Colossal effigies seemed to offer one means of expressing the true proportions which love gives to those we cherish; I wanted those images to be enormous, like a face seen at close range, tall and solemn figures, like visions and apparitions in a terrifying dream, and as overwhelming as the memory itself has remained. I demanded a perfect finish, an utter perfection; in short, that god who every boy dying at twenty is for those who have loved him; but I sought also an exact resemblance, the familiar presence and each irregularity of a face dearer than beauty itself. How many discussions it cost to keep intact the heavy line of an eyebrow, that slightly swollen curve of the lip.... I was counting desperately on the eternity of stone and the fidelity of bronze to perpetuate a body which is perishable, or already destroyed, but I also insisted that the marble, rubbed daily with a mixture of acid and oil, should take on the shimmer, and almost the softness, of youthful flesh.

The face was unique, still I found it everywhere; I amalgamated divinities, sexes, and eternal attributes, the hardy Diana of the forests with the melancholy Bacchus, the vigorous Hermes of the palaestrae with the twofold god who sleeps, head on arm, like a fallen flower. I remarked how much a thoughtful young man resembles a virile Athena.

My sculptors went slightly astray; the less able fell into the error of too soft a line, or too obvious; all, however, were more or less caught up in the dream. There are statues and paintings of the youth alive, reflecting that immense and changing landscape which extends from the fifteenth to the twentieth year: the serious profile of the obedient child; that statue where a sculptor of Corinth has ventured to retain the careless ease of a young boy with lounging posture and sloping shoulders, one hand on his hip, as if he were watching a game of dice at some street corner. There is that marble where Papias of Aphrodisias has outlined a body tenderly nude, with the fragile bloom of narcissus. And Aristeas has carved under my direction, in rather rough stonework, that young head so imperious and proud. There are the posthumous portraits, where death has left his mark, those great faces with the knowing lips, laden with secrets which I no longer share, because they are no longer those of the living. There is the bas-relief where the Carian Antonianos has transposed to a divine and melancholy shade the vintager clothed in a tunic of raw silk, his friendly dog nuzzling against his bare leg. And that almost intolerable mask, the work of a sculptor of Cyrene, where pleasure and pain meet on the same face, and seem to break against each other like two waves on the same rock. And those small clay figures sold for a penny which have served as a part of the imperial propaganda: *Tellus Stabilita*, the Genius of the Pacified Earth in the guise of a reclining youth who holds fruits and flowers.

Trahit sua quemque voluptas. Each to his own bent; likewise each to his aim or his ambition, if you will, or his most secret desire and his highest ideal. My ideal was contained within the word *beauty*, so difficult to define despite all the evidence of our senses. I felt responsible for sustaining and increasing the beauty of the world. I wanted the cities to be splendid, spacious, and airy, their streets sprayed with clean water, their inhabitants all human beings whose bodies were neither degraded by marks of misery or servitude nor bloated by vulgar riches; I desired that the schoolboys should recite correctly some useful lessons; that the women presiding in their households should move with maternal dignity, expressing both vigour and calm; that the gymnasiums should be used by youths not unversed in arts and in sports; that the orchards should bear the finest fruits and the fields the richest harvests. I desired that the might and majesty of the Roman Peace should extend to all, insensibly present like the music of the revolving skies; that the most humble traveller might wander from one country, or one continent, to another without vexatious formalities, and without danger, assured everywhere of a minimum of legal protection and culture; that our soldiers should continue their eternal pyrrhic dance on the frontiers; that everything should go smoothly, whether work-shops or temples; that the sea should be furrowed by brave ships, and the roads resounding to frequent carriages; that, in a world well ordered, the philosophers should have their place, and the dancers also. This ideal, modest on the whole, would be often

enough approached if men would devote to it one part of the
energy which they expend on stupid or cruel activities; great
good fortune has allowed me a partial realization of my aims
during the last quarter of a century. Arrian of Nicomedia, one of
the best minds of our time, likes to recall to me the beautiful lines
of ancient Terpander, defining in three words the Spartan ideal
(that perfect mode of life to which Lacedaemon aspired without
ever attaining it): *Strength, Justice, the Muses.* Strength was
the basis, discipline without which there is no beauty and firmness without which there is no justice. Justice was the balance of
the parts, that whole so harmoniously composed which no excess
should be permitted to endanger. Strength and Justice together
were but one instrument, well tuned, in the hands of the Muses.
All forms of dire poverty and brutality were things to forbid as
insults to the fair body of mankind, every injustice a false note
to avoid in the harmony of the spheres.

*   *   *

In Germany construction or renovation of camps, fortifications,
and roads detained me for nearly a year; new bastions, erected
over a distance of seventy leagues, reinforced our frontiers along
the Rhine. This country of vineyards and rushing streams was
wholly familiar to me: there I recrossed the path of the young
tribune who had borne news to Trajan of his accession to power.
There, too, beyond our farthest fort, built of logs from the spruce
forests, lay the same dark, monotonous horizon, the same world
which had been closed to us from the time of the imprudent
offensive launched by Augustus' legions, the ocean of trees and
that vast reserve of fair-haired men. When the task of reorganization was finished, I descended to the mouth of the Rhine along
the Belgian and Batavian plains. Desolate dunes cut by stiff
grasses made up the northern landscape; at the port of Novio-
magus the houses raised on piles stood abreast ships moored at
their doors; seabirds perched on their roofs. I liked those forlorn
places, though they seemed hideous to my aides, the overcast sky
and the muddy rivers channelling their way through a land
without form or visible spark, where no god has yet shaped the
clay.

I crossed to the Isle of Britain in a ship which was flat as a barge. More than once the wind threw us back toward the coast from which we had sailed: that difficult passage afforded some wonderfully vacant hours. Gigantic clouds rose out of a heavy sea muddied by sand and incessantly stirred in its bed. As formerly in the land of the Dacians and the Sarmatians I had venerated the goddess Earth, I had here a feeling for the first time of a Neptune more chaotic than our own, of an infinite world of waters. In Plutarch I had read a mariner's legend concerning an island in those regions which border the Arctic Sea, where centuries ago the victorious Olympians are said to have exiled the vanquished Titans. There those great captives of rock and wave, eternally lashed by a tireless ocean, never at rest, for ever consumed by dreams, continue to defy the Olympian rule with their violence, their anguish, and their burning but perpetually crucified desire. In this myth which is set on the remote edges of the world I came again upon philosophical theories which I had already adopted as my own: each of us has to choose, in the course of his brief life, between endless striving and wise resignation, between the delights of disorder and those of stability, between the Titan and the Olympian. . . . To choose between them, or to succeed, at last, in bringing them into accord.

The civil reforms effected in Britain are part of my administrative work of which I have spoken elsewhere. What imports here is that I was the first emperor to settle pacifically in that island situated on the boundaries of the known world, where before me only Claudius had ventured for several days' time in his capacity as commander-in-chief. For an entire winter Londinium became, by my choice, what Antioch had been by necessity at the time of the Parthian war, the virtual centre of the world. Thus each of my voyages changed the centre of gravity for imperial power, placing it for some time along the Rhine, or on the banks of the Thames, and permitting me to estimate what would have been the strength and the weakness of such a capital. That stay in Britain made me envisage a hypothetical empire governed from the West, an Atlantic world. Such imaginary perspectives have no practical value; they cease, however, to be

absurd as soon as the calculator extends his computations sufficiently far into the future.

Barely three months before my arrival the Sixth Legion
Victrix had been transferred to British territory. It replaced the
unhappy Ninth Legion, cut to pieces by the Caledonians during
the uprisings which made the grim aftermath, in Britain, of our
Parthian expedition. Two measures were necessary to prevent
the return of a like disaster. Our troops were reinforced by
creation of a native auxiliary corps at Eboracum. From the top
of a green knoll, I watched the first manoeuvres of this newly
formed British army. At the same time the erection of a wall
cutting the island in two in its narrowest part served to protect
the fertile, guarded areas of the south from the attacks of
northern tribes. I myself inspected a substantial part of those
constructions begun everywhere at the same time along an
earthwork eighty-four miles in length; it was my chance to try
out on that carefully defined space running from coast to coast
a system of defence which could afterward be applied anywhere
else. But already that purely military project was proving an aid
to peace and to development of prosperity in that part of Britain;
villages sprang up, and there was a general movement of settlers
toward our frontiers. The trench-diggers of the legion were aided
in their task by native crews; the building of the wall was for
many of these mountain dwellers, so newly subdued, the first
irrefutable proof of the protective power of Rome; their pay was
the first Roman money to pass through their hands. This rampart
became the emblem of my renunciation of the policy of conquest: below the northernmost bastion I ordered the erection of
a temple to the god Terminus.

Everything enchanted me in that rainy land: the shreds of
mist on the hillsides, the lakes consecrated to nymphs wilder
than ours, the melancholy grey-eyed inhabitants. I took as a
guide a young tribune of the British auxiliary corps, a fair-haired
god who had learned Latin and who spoke some halting Greek;
he even attempted timidly to compose love verses in that tongue.
One cold autumn night he served as interpreter between me and
a Sibyl. We were sitting in the smoky hut of a Celtic woodcutter,
warming our legs clad in clumsy, heavy trousers of rough wool,

when we saw creeping toward us an ancient creature drenched and dishevelled by rain and wind, wild and furtive as an animal of the wood. She fell upon the small oaten loaves which lay baking on the hearth. My guide coaxed this prophetess, and she consented to examine for me the smoke rings, the sudden sparks, and those fragile structures of embers and ashes. She saw cities a-building, and joyous throngs, but also cities in flames, with bitter lines of captives, who belied my dreams for peace; there was a young and gentle visage which she took for the face of a woman and in which I refused to believe; then a white spectre, which was perhaps only a statue, since that would be an object far stranger than any phantom for this denizen of forest and heath. And vaguely, at a distance of some years, she saw my death, which I could well have predicted without her.

There was less need for my presence in prosperous Gaul and wealthy Spain than in Britain. Narbonensian Gaul was again like Greece, which had been wafted thus far, the same fine schools of eloquence, the same porticoes under a cloudless sky. I stopped in Nîmes to plan a basilica dedicated to Plotina and destined one day to become her temple. Some family ties endeared this city to the empress and made its clear, sunwarmed landscape the dearer to me.

But the revolt in Mauretania was flaming still. I cut short my journey through Spain, with no stop between Corduba and the sea even for a moment in Italica, the city of my childhood and my ancestors. At Gades I embarked for Africa.

The handsome tattooed warriors of the Atlas mountains were still molesting the African coastal cities. For a very few days there I went through the Numidian equivalent of the Sarmatian battles; I again saw tribes subdued one by one and the surrender of haughty chiefs, prostrating themselves in the open desert in a chaos of women and packs and kneeling beasts. But this time the sand took the place of snow.

It would have been good, for once, to pass the spring in Rome, to find there the Villa begun, to have capricious Lucius and his caresses again, and the friendship of Plotina. But that stay in town was broken almost at once by alarming rumours of war. Peace with the Parthians had been concluded scarcely three years before, but already some grave incidents were occurring on the Euphrates. I set forth at once for the East.

* * *

I had made up my mind to settle these frontier disturbances by a method less commonplace than that of sending in the legions. A meeting was arranged with Osroës. I took with me his daughter, who had been captured in infancy, at the time of Trajan's occupation of Babylon, and held thereafter in Rome as a hostage. She was a thin child with enormous eyes. Her presence, and that of her women attendants, was something of an encumbrance on a journey which had above all to be made with speed. This cluster of creatures in veils was jolted along on camel-back across the Syrian desert. The curtains of their canopy were kept severely closed, but each evening at the halt I sent to inquire if the princess had need of anything.

In Lycia I stopped for an hour to persuade Opramoas, the merchant, who had already demonstrated his capacities for negotiation, to go with me into Parthia. The urgency of the moment restricted his customary display. Wealth and luxury had left him soft, but he was none the less admirable as a travelling companion, for he knew the desert and all its dangers.

The meeting was to take place on the left bank of the Euphrates, not far from Doura. We crossed the river on a raft. Along the bank the soldiers of the Parthian guard formed a dazzling line; their armour was of gold, and was matched in splendour by their horses' trappings. My ever-attendant Phlegon was decidedly pale, and even the officers who accompanied me were in some fear; this meeting might prove a trap. But Opramoas, accustomed to sniff the air of Asia, was wholly at ease in this mingling of silence and tumult, immobility and sudden gallop, and in all this magnificence thrown on the desert like a carpet on the sand. As for me, I was wondrous free from concern; like Caesar on his bark, I was entrusting myself to those planks which carried my Fortune. I gave proof of this confidence by restoring the Parthian princess immediately to her father, instead of holding her in our lines until my departure. I promised also to give back the golden throne of the Arsacid dynasty, which Trajan had taken as spoil. We had no use for the thing, but Oriental superstition held it in great esteem.

The high ceremony of these sessions with Osroës was purely external. In substance they differed little from talks between two neighbours who were trying to arrive at some peaceable settlement over a boundary dispute. I had to do with a sophisticated Greek-speaking barbarian, not at all obtuse, not necessarily more perfidious than I, but vacillating to the point of seeming untrustworthy. My peculiar mental disciplines helped me to grasp this elusive intelligence: seated facing the Parthian emperor, I learned to anticipate, and soon to direct, his replies; I entered into his game; last, I imagined myself as Osroës bargaining with Hadrian. I detest futile discussions where each party knows in advance that he will, or will not, give way; truth in business appeals to me most of all as a means of simplifying and advancing matters. The Parthians feared us; we, in turn, held them in dread, and from the mating of our two fears would come war. The Satraps were pressing toward this war for ends of their own; I could see at once that Osroës, like me, had his Quietus and his Palma. Pharasmanes, the most turbulent of those semi-independent border princes, was even more a danger for the Parthian Empire than for us. It had been charged against me that I kept those base and corruptible lords in hand by resort to subsidies; the money was well spent. For I was too confident of the superiority of our forces to be governed by false pride, so was ready for any concession of mere prestige, but for nothing else. The greatest difficulty was to persuade Osroës that if my promises were few it was because I meant to keep them. But he did believe me, in the end, or acted as if he did. The accord concluded between us in the course of that visit has endured; for fifteen years nothing has troubled the peace on the frontiers for either side. May I count on you, Marcus, to continue this state of things after my death.

One evening in Orsoës' tent, during a feast given in my honour, I observed among the women and long-eyelashed pages a naked, emaciated man who sat utterly motionless. His eyes were wide open, but he seemed to see nothing of that confusion of acrobats and dancers, or those dishes laden with viands. I addressed him through my interpreter, but he deigned no reply, for this was indeed a sage. His disciples, however, were more loquacious; these pious beggars came from India, and their master belonged to the powerful caste of Brahmans. I gathered that his meditations led him to believe that the whole universe is only a tissue of illusion and error; for him self-denial, renunciation, death were the sole means of escape from this changing flood of forms whereon, on the contrary, our Heraclitus had willingly been borne along. Beyond the world of the senses he hoped to rejoin the sphere of the purely divine, that unmoving firmament of which Plato, too, had dreamed.

I got some inkling, therefore, in spite of the bungling of my interpreters, of conceptions not unlike those of certain of our philosophers, but expressed by this Indian with more absolute finality. He had reached the state where nothing was left, except his body, to separate him from intangible diety, without substance or form, and with which he would unite; he had resolved to burn himself alive that next morning. Osroës invited me to the solemnity. A pyre of fragrant woods was prepared; the man leaped into it and disappeared without one cry. His disciples gave no sign of sorrow; for them it was not a funeral ceremony.

I pondered these things far into the night which followed. There I lay on the carpet of finest wool on the floor of a tent hung with gleaming brocades. A page massaged my feet. From without came the few sounds of that Asiatic night: the whispering of slaves at my door; the soft rustle of a palm, and Opramoas' snores behind a curtain; the stamp of a horse's hoof; from farther away, in the women's quarters, the melancholy murmur of a song. All of that had left the Brahman unmoved. In his veritable passion of refusal he had given himself to the flames as a lover to a bed. He had cast off everything and everyone, and finally himself, like so many garments which served to conceal from him that unique presence, the invisible void which was his all.

I felt myself to be different, and ready for wider choice. Austerity, renunciation, negation were not wholly new to me; I had been drawn to them young, as is almost always the case, at the age of twenty. I was even younger when a friend in Rome took me to see the aged Epictetus in his hovel in the Suburra, shortly before Domitian ordered his exile. As in his slave days, when a brutal master failed to extract from him even one cry, though the beating broke his leg, so now grown old and frail he was patiently bearing the slow torments of gravel; yet he seemed to me to enjoy a liberty which was almost divine. His crutches, his pallet, his earthenware lamp and wooden spoon in its vessel of clay were objects of admiration to me, the simple tools of a pure life.

But Epictetus gave up too many things, and I had been quick to observe that nothing was more dangerously easy for me than mere renunciation. This Indian, more logically, was rejecting life itself. There was much to learn from such pure-hearted fanatics, but on the condition of turning the lesson from the meaning originally intended. These sages were trying to rediscover their god above and beyond the ocean of forms, and to reduce him to that quality of the unique, intangible, and incorporeal which he had forgone in the very act of becoming universal. I perceived differently my relations with the divine. I could see myself as seconding the deity in his effort to give form and order to a world, to develop and multiply its convolutions, extensions, and complexities. I was one of the segments of the wheel, an aspect of that unique force caught up in the multiplicity of things; I was eagle and bull, man and swan, phallus and brain all together, Proteus who is also Jupiter.

And it was about this time that I began to feel myself divine. Don't misunderstand me: I was still, and more than ever, the same man, fed by the fruits and flesh of earth, and giving back to the soil their unconsumed residue, surrendering to sleep with each revolution of the stars, and nearly beside myself when too long deprived of the warming presence of love. My strength and agility, both of mind and of body, had been carefully maintained by purely human disciplines. What more can I say except that all that was lived as god-like experience? The dangerous experiments of youth were over, and its haste to seize the passing hour. At forty-eight I felt free of impatience, assured of myself, and as near perfection as my nature would permit, in fact, eternal. Please realize that all this was wholly on the plane of the intellect;

the delirium, if I must use the term, came later on. I was god, to put it simply, because I was man. The titles of divinity which Greece conferred upon me thereafter served only to proclaim what I had long since ascertained for myself. I even believe that I could have felt myself god had I been thrown into one of Domitian's prisons, or confined to the pits of a mine. If I make bold to such pretensions, it is because the feeling seems to me hardly extraordinary, and in no way unique. Others besides me have felt it, or will do so in time to come.

I have already mentioned that my titles added virtually nothing to this astonishing certitude; on the contrary, the feeling was confirmed in performing the simplest routines of my function as emperor. If Jupiter is brain to the world, then the man who organizes and presides over human affairs can logically consider himself as a part of that all-governing mind. Humanity, rightly or not, has almost always conceived of its god in terms of Providence; my duties forced me to serve as the incarnation of this Providence for one part of mankind. The more the State increases in size and power, extending its strict, cold links from man to man, the more does human faith aspire to exalt the image of a human protector at the end of this mighty chain. Whether I wished it or not, the Eastern populations of the empire already considered me a god. Even in the West, and even in Rome, where we are not officially declared divine till after death, the instinctive piety of the common people tends more and more to deify us while we are still alive. The Parthians, in gratitude to the Roman who had established and maintained peace, were soon to erect temples in my honour; even at Vologasia, in the very heart of that vast world beyond our frontiers, I had my sanctuary. Far from reading in this adoration a risk of arrogant presumption, or madness, for the man who accepts it, I found therein a restraint, and indeed an obligation to model myself upon something eternal, trying to add to my human capacity some part of supreme wisdom. To be god demands more virtues, all things considered, than to be emperor.

I was initiated at Eleusis eighteen months later. In one sense this visit to Osroës had been a turning point in my life. Instead of going back to Rome, I had decided to devote some years to.

the Greek and Oriental provinces of the empire; Athens was coming more and more to be the centre of my thought, and my home. I wished to please the Greeks, and also to Hellenize myself as much as possible, but though my motives for this initiation were in part political, it proved nevertheless to be a religious experience without equal. These ancient rites serve only to symbolize what happens in human life, but the symbol has a deeper purport than the act, explaining each of our motions in terms of celestial mechanism. What is taught at Eleusis must remain secret; it has, besides, the less danger of being divulged in that its nature is ineffable. If formulated, it would result only in commonplaces; therein lies its real profundity. The higher degrees which were later conferred upon me in the course of private talks with the Hierophant added almost nothing to that first emotion which I shared in common with the least of the pilgrims who made the same ritual ablutions and drank at the spring. I had heard the discords resolving into harmonies; for one moment I had stood on another sphere and contemplated from afar, but also from close by, that procession which is both human and divine, wherein I, too, had my place, this world where suffering exists still, but error is no more. Human destiny, that vague design in which the least practised eye can trace so many flaws, gleamed bright like the patterns of the heavens.

And it is here that I can best speak of a habit which led me throughout my life along paths less secret than those of Eleusis, but after all parallel to them, namely, the study of the stars. I have always been friend to astronomers and client to astrologers. The science of the latter is questionable, but if false in its details it is perhaps true in the total implication; for if man is part and parcel of the universe, and is ruled by the same laws as govern the sky, it is not unreasonable to search the heavens for the patterns of our lives, and for those impersonal attractions which induce our successes and our errors. On autumn evenings I seldom fail to greet Aquarius to the south, that heavenly Cup Bearer and Giver of Gifts under whose sign I was born. Nor did I forget to note in each of their passages Jupiter and Venus, who govern my life, nor to measure the influence of dangerous Saturn.

But if this strange refraction of human affairs upon the stellar vault preoccupied many of my waking hours, I was still more deeply absorbed in celestial mathematics, the abstract speculations to which those flaming spheres give rise. I was inclined to believe, along with certain of our more daring philosophers, that earth, too, takes part in that daily and nightly round which the sacred processions of Eleusis try, at best, to reproduce in human terms. In a world which is only a vortex of forces and whirl of atoms, where there is neither high nor low, periphery nor centre, I could ill conceive of a globe without motion, or a fixed point which would not move.

At other times I was haunted in my nightly vigils by the problem of the precession of the equinoxes, as calculated long ago by Hipparchus of Alexandria. I could see in this passage and return the mathematical demonstration of those same mysteries which Eleusis represents in mere fable and symbol. In our times the Spike of Virgo is no longer at the point of the map where Hipparchus marked it, but such variation itself completes a cycle, and serves to confirm the astronomer's hypotheses. Slowly, ineluctably, this firmament will become again what it was in Hipparchus' time; it will be again what it is in the time of Hadrian. Disorder is absorbed in order, and change becomes part of a plan which the astronomer can know in advance; thus the human mind reveals its participation in the universe by establishing such exact theorems about it, just as it does at Eleusis by ritual shout and dance. Both the man and the stars which are the objects of his gaze roll inevitably toward their ends, marked somewhere in the sky; but each moment of that descent is a pause, a guide mark, and a segment of a curve itself as solid as a chain of gold. Each movement in space brings us back to a point which, because we happen to be on it, seems to us a centre.

From the nights of my childhood, when Marullinus first pointed out to me the constellations above, my curiosity for the world of the spheres has not abated. In the watches of camp life I looked with wonder at the moon as it raced through the clouds of barbarian skies; in later years, in the clear nights of Attica, I listened while Theron of Rhodes, the astronomer, explained his

system of the world. In mid-Aegean, lying flat on the deck of a
ship, I have followed the slow oscillation of the mast as it moved
among the stars, swaying first from the red eye of Taurus to the
tears of the Pleiades, then from Pegasus to the Swan. I answered
as well as I could the naïve questions so gravely put by the youth
gazing with me at that same sky. Here at the Villa I have built an
observatory, but I can no longer climb its steps. Once in my life
I did a rarer thing. I made sacrifice to the constellations of an
entire night. It was after my visit to Osroës, coming back
through the Syrian desert: lying on my back, wide awake but
abandoning for some hours every human concern, I gave myself
up from nightfall to dawn to this world of crystal and flame.
That was the most glorious of all my voyages. Overhead shone
the great star of the constellation of Lyra, destined to be the polar
star for men who will live tens of thousands of years after we
have ceased to be. In the last light of the horizon Castor and
Pollux gleamed faintly; the Serpent gave way to the Archer;
next the Eagle mounted toward the zenith, wings widespread,
and beneath him appeared the constellation at that time un-
named by astronomers, but to which I have since given that
most cherished of names.

The night, which is never so black as people think who live
and sleep indoors, was at first more dark, and then grew lighter.
The fires, left burning to frighten the jackals, went out; their
dying coals made me think of my grandfather warming himself
as he stood in his vineyard, and of his prophecies, which by
then had become the present, and were soon to be the past. I
have tried under many a form to join the divine, and have known
more than one ecstasy; some of these have been atrocious, others
overpoweringly sweet, but the one of the Syrian night was
strangely lucid. It inscribed within me the heavenly motions with
greater precision that any partial observation would ever have
allowed me to attain. I know exactly, at the hour of this writing,
what stars are passing here at Tibur above this stuccoed and
painted ceiling; and elsewhere, far away, over a tomb. Some
years later it was death which was to become the object of my
constant contemplation, the thought to which I was to give every
faculty of my mind not absorbed by the State. And who speaks

of death speaks also of that mysterious world to which, perhaps, we gain access by death. After such long reflection, and so many experiments, some of them reprehensible, I still know nothing of what goes on behind death's dark curtain. But the Syrian night remains as my conscious experience of immortality.

SAECULUM AUREUM

THE summer following my meeting with Osroës was passed in Asia Minor: I made a stop in Bithynia in order to supervise in person the annual felling in the State forests there. At Nicomedia, that lustrous and learned city, I stayed with the procurator of the province, Cneius Pompeius Proculus, who lived in the ancient palace of Bithynia's last king, Nicomedes, where voluptuous memories of the young Julius Caesar abound. Breezes from the Propontis fanned those cool, shaded rooms. Proculus was a man of taste; he arranged some readings for my pleasure. Some visiting sophists and small groups of students and poetry-lovers met together in the gardens beside a spring consecrated to Pan. From time to time a servant filled a great jar of porous clay in the cooling water; the most limpid verses seemed halting compared to that pure stream.

One late afternoon we were reading an abstruse work of Lycophron, whom I enjoy for his daring juxtaposition of sounds, figures and allusions, a complex system of echoes and reflections. A little apart from the others a young boy was listening, half attentive, half in dream, to those difficult strophes; I thought at once of some shepherd, deep in the woods, vaguely aware of a strange bird's cry. He had brought neither tablet nor style. Seated on the edge of the water's basin he trailed a hand idly over the fair, placid surface. His father, I learned, had held a small post in the administration of the vast imperial domains; left young to a grandfather's care the boy had been sent to study in Nicomedia, and to reside there with a former guest of his parents, a shipowner and builder of the town who seemed rich to that modest family.

I kept him on after the others had gone. He had read little, and knew almost nothing of the world; though childishly trusting, he was also disposed to reflection. I had seen Claudiopolis, his native city, so I led him to speak of his home on the edge of the great pine forests which furnish masts for our ships; of the hilltop temple of Atys, whose strident music he loved; of the superb horses of his country and its strange gods. His voice was low, and his Greek had the accent of Asia. Suddenly aware of my attention, or of my gaze, perhaps, he grew confused, flushed, and fell back into one of those stubborn silences to which I was soon to become accustoméd. An intimacy gradually developed. He accompanied me thereafter in all my voyages, and the fabulous years began.

Antinous was Greek; I traced the story of this ancient but little-known family back to the time of the first Arcadian settlers along the shores of the Propontis. But Asia had produced its effect upon that rude blood, like the drop of honey which clouds and perfumes a pure wine. I could detect in him mystic super-stitions like those of a disciple of Apollonius, and the religious adoration, as well, of an Oriental subject for his monarch. His presence was extraordinarily silent: he followed me like some animal, or a familiar spirit. He had the infinite capacity of a young dog for play and for swift repose, and the same fierceness and trust. This graceful hound, avid both for caresses and com-mands, took his post at my feet.

I admired his almost haughty indifference for all that was not his delight or his cult; it served him in place of disinterestedness and scruple, and of all virtues painfully acquired. I marvelled at his gentleness, which had aspects of hardness, too, and the sombre devotion to which he gave his whole being. And yet this submission was not blind; those lids so often lowered in acquiescence or in dream were not always so; the most attentive eyes in the world would sometimes look me straight in the face, and I felt myself judged. But I was judged as is a god by his adorer: my harshness and sudden suspicions (for I had them later on) were patiently and gravely accepted. I have been abso-lute master but once in my life, and over but one being.

If I have said nothing yet of a beauty so apparent it is not merely because of the reticence of a man too completely con-quered. But the faces which we try so desperately to recall escape us; it is only for a moment. ... I see a head bending under its dark mass of hair, eyes which seemed slanting, so long were the lids, a young face broadly formed, as if for repose. This tender body varied all the time, like a plant, and some of its alterations were those of growth. The boy changed; he grew tall. A week of indolence sufficed to soften him completely; a single afternoon at the hunt made the young athlete firm again, and fleet; an hour's sun turned him from jasmine to the colour of honey. The boyish limbs lengthened out; the face lost its delicate childish round and hollowed slightly under the high cheekbones; the full chest of a young runner took on the smooth, gleaming curves of a Bacchante's breast; the brooding lips bespoke a bitter, sad satiety. In truth this visage changed as if I had moulded it night and day.

When I think back on these years I seem to return to the Age of Gold. Trouble was no more: past efforts were repaid by an ease which was almost divine. Travel was play, a pleasure well known, controlled, and skilfully planned. Work, though incessant, was only a form of delight. My life, where everything came late, power and happiness, too, now acquired the splendour of high noon, the luminous glow of siesta time when everything, the objects of the room and the figure lying beside one, bathes in golden shade. Passion satisfied has its innocence, almost as fragile as any other: the remainder of human beauty was relegated to the rank of mere spectacle, and ceased to be game for my pursuit. This adventure, though begun like any other, served to enrich but also to simplify my life: the future was matter for slight concern; I ceased to question the oracles; the stars were no longer anything more than admirable patterns upon the vault of heaven. Never before had I noted with such delight the glimmer of dawn on the distant islands, the coolness of caves sacred to nymphs and haunted by birds of passage, the low flight of quail at dusk. I re-read the poets; some seemed better to me than before, but most of them worse. I wrote verses myself which appeared less inadequate than usual.

There was the ocean of trees, the forests of cork-oak and pine in Bithynia; the hunting lodge with latticed galleries where the boy again idly at ease in his native land scattered at random his arrows, dagger, and belt of gold to tussle with the dogs on the leather divan. The plains had stored up the long summer's heat, and haze rose from the meadows along the Sangarius where

herds of wild horses ran. At break of day we would go down to
the river to bathe, brushing tall grass in our path still wet with
dew, while above us hung the thin crescent moon which is
Bithynia's emblem. This country received every privilege and
even added my name to its own.

Winter overtook us at Sinope; there, in almost Scythian cold,
I officially inaugurated the work of enlarging the port, already
begun at my order by the navy's men. On our way to Byzantium,
outside each village the local officials had enormous fires built up
for my guards to warm themselves. We crossed the Bosphorus in
full beauty of storm and snow. Then came long rides in the
Thracian Forest, with stinging wind swelling the folds of our
cloaks; the steady beat of rain on the leaves and the tent top; the
halt at the workers' camp where Hadrianopolis was to be built;
the ovations there from veterans of Dacian wars; the soft, wet
earth out of which walls and towers soon would rise. In spring an
inspection of the Danube garrisons took me back to Sarmizegethusa, which today is no more than a prosperous village; a bracelet
of King Decebalus now graced the wrist of the young Bithynian.

The return to Greece was made from the north: I lingered
in the valley of Tempe, all splashed as it is with streams; then
on to blond Euboea, and Attica's wine-rose hills. Athens was
but touched in passing; at Eleusis, for my initiation into the
Mysteries, I passed three days and three nights mingled with the
pilgrims attending the autumn feast; the only precaution taken
for me was to forbid the men to wear their daggers.

I took Antinous to his ancestral Arcadia: its forests were still
as impenetrable as in the days of those wolf hunters of old.
Sometimes, with a crack of the whip, a horseman would startle
a viper; on stony heights the sun burned hot as in summer;
against the boulders the lad slept, head bowed low and his hair
lightly blown by the breeze, almost a daylight Endymion. A
hare which my young hunter had tamed with great effort was
caught and torn by the hounds; that was the sole woe of shadow-
less days. The people of Mantinea uncovered some traces of
kinship with that family of Bithynian colonists, hitherto unknown; the city, where the boy was later to have his temples, was
enriched by me and adorned. Its immemorial sanctuary of

Neptune, though in ruins, was so venerable that all entrance whatsoever had been forbidden: mysteries more ancient than mankind itself were perpetuated behind those never-opening doors. I built a new temple, far more vast than the old and wholly enclosing the ancient edifice, which will lie hereafter within like the stone at the heart of a fruit. On the road not far from Mantinea I restored the tomb where Epaminondas, slain in the heat of battle, is laid to rest with the young companion struck down at his side; a column whereon a poem is inscribed was erected by my order to commemorate a time when everything, viewed at a distance, seems to have been noble, and simple too, whether tenderness, glory, or death.

In the Isthmus the Games were celebrated with a splendour unparalleled since ancient times; my hope, in reviving these Hellenic festivals, was to make Greece a living unity once more. We were drawn by the hunt to the valley of the Helicon, then in its last bronzed red of autumn; at the spring of Narcissus we paused, near the Sanctuary of Love; there we offered a trophy, the pelt of a young she-bear fixed by nails of gold to the temple wall, to Eros, that god who is wisest of all.

The ship lent me by Erastos, the merchant of Ephesus, to sail the Archipelago, idled at anchor in Phaleron Bay; I had come back to Athens like a man coming home. I ventured to add to the beauty of this city, trying to perfect what was already admirable. For the first time Athens was growing again, taking on new life after a long decline. I doubled the city in extent: along the Ilissus I planned a new Athens, the city of Hadrian joined to the city of Theseus. Everything had to be rearranged, or constructed anew. Six centuries earlier the great temple consecrated to the Olympian Zeus had been left abandoned almost as soon as the structure was started. My workmen took up the task and Athens again felt the joy of activity such as she had not known since the days of Pericles. I was completing what one of the Seleucids had aspired in vain to finish, and was making amends in kind for the depredations of our Sulla. To inspect the work I went daily in and out of a labyrinth of machines and intricate pulleys, of half-dressed columns and marble blocks haphazardly piled, gleaming white against the blue sky. There was something of the excitement of the naval shipyards; a mighty vessel had been salvaged and was being fitted out for the future.

In the evenings the art of building gave way to that of music, which is architecture, too, though invisible. I am somewhat practised in all the arts, but music is the only one to which I have steadily kept and in which I profess to some skill. At Rome I had to dissemble this taste, but could indulge it with discretion in Athens. The musicians used to gather in a court where a cypress grew, near a statue of Hermes. There were only six or seven of them, an orchestra of reeds and lyres; to these we sometimes added a professional with a cithara. My instrument was chiefly the long flute. We played ancient tunes, some almost forgotten, and newer works as well, composed for me. I liked the hard vigour of the Dorian airs, but certainly had no aversion to voluptuous or passionate melodies, or to the poignant, subtly broken rhythms which sober, fearful folk reject as intoxicating for the senses and the soul. Across the strings I could see the profile of my young companion, gravely absorbed in his part in the group, his fingers moving with care along the taut cords.

That perfect winter was rich in friendly intercourse: the opulent Atticus, whose bank was financing my constructions (though not without profit therefrom), invited me to his gardens in Kephissia where he lived surrounded by a court of lecturers and writers then in fashion; his son, young Herod, a subtle wit, proved indispensable at my Athenian suppers. He had certainly lost the timidity which once left him speechless before me, on the occasion of his embassy to the Sarmatian frontiers on behalf of the youth of Athens to congratulate me on my accession; but his growing vanity now seemed to me no more than mildly ridiculous. Herod's rival in eloquence, and in wealth, was the rhetorician Polemo, glory of Laodicea, who beguiled me by his Oriental style, shimmering and full as the gold-bearing waves of Pactolus; this clever craftsman in words lived as he discoursed, with splendour.

But the most precious of all these encounters was with Arrian of Nicomedia, the best of my friends. Younger than I by some twelve years, he had already begun that outstanding political

and military career in which he continues to distinguish himself
and to serve the State. His experience in government, his knowledge of hunting, horses, and dogs, and of all bodily exercise,
raised him infinitely above the mere word-mongers of the time.
In his youth he had been prey to one of those strange passions of
the soul without which, perhaps, there can be no true wisdom,
nor true greatness : two years of his life had been passed at
Nicopolis in Epirus in the cold, bare room where Epictetus lay
dying; he had set himself the task of gathering and transcribing,
word for word, the last sayings of that aged and ailing philosopher. That period of enthusiasm had left its mark upon him;
from it he retained certain admirable moral disciplines, and a kind
of grave simplicity. In secret he practised austerities which no
one even suspected. But his long apprenticeship to Stoic duty had
not hardened him into self-righteousness; he was too intelligent
not to realize that the heights of virtue, like those of love, owe
their special value to their very rarity, to their quality of unique
achievement and sublime excess. Now he was striving to model
himself upon the calm good sense and perfect honesty of
Xenophon. He was writing the history of his country, Bithynia; I
had placed this province, so long ill governed by proconsuls,
under my personal jurisdiction; Arrian advised me in my plans
for reform. This assiduous reader of Socratic dialogue treated my
young favourite with tender deference, for he knew full well the
long accumulated tradition of heroism, devotion, and even
wisdom, with which Greece has ennobled love between friends.
These two Bithynians spoke the soft speech of Ionia, where word
endings are almost Homeric in form. I later persuaded Arrian
to employ this dialect in his writings.

At that period Athens had its philosopher of the frugal life:
in a cabin of the village of Colonus, Demonax was leading an
exemplary but merry existence. He was no Socrates, for he lacked
both subtlety and intensity, but I relished his waggish good
humour. Another of these goodhearted friends was the actor
Arstomenes, a spirited performer of ancient Attic comedy. I used
to call him my Greek partridge; short, fat, happy as a child (or a
bird), he was better informed than anyone else on religious
rituals, poetry, and cookery of former days. He was long a source

of amusement and instruction to me. At about that time Antinous chose as his tutor the philosopher Charbrias, a Platonist with leanings toward Orphic teachings, and the most innocent of men; he developed a kind of watchdog fidelity to the boy which was later transferred to me. Eleven years of court life have not changed him; he is still the same honest, pious creature, chastely absorbed in his dreams, blind to all intrigue and deaf to rumour. He annoys me at times, but I shall part with him only at my death.

My relations with the Stoic philosopher Euphrates were of shorter duration. He had retired to Athens after brilliant successes at Rome. I engaged him as my reader, but the suffering which he had long endured from a liver abscess, and the resulting weakness, convinced him that his life no longer offered him anything worth the living. He asked my permission to quit my service by suicide. I have never been opposed to voluntary departure from life, and had considered it as a possible end in my hour of crisis before Trajan's death. The problem of suicide which has obsessed me since seemed then of easy solution. Euphrates received the authorization which he sought; I had it carried to him by my young Bithynian, perhaps because it would have pleased me myself to receive from the hands of such a messenger this final response. The philosopher came to the palace that same evening for a conversation which differed in no respect from all preceding visits; he killed himself the next day. We talked over the incident several times; the boy remained sombre for some days thereafter. This ardent young creature held death in horror; I had not observed that he already gave it much thought. For my part I could ill conceive that anyone would willingly leave a world which seemed to me so fair, or fail to exhaust to the end, despite all its evils, its utmost possibility of thought and of contact, and even of seeing. I have indeed changed since that time.

The years merge: my memory forms but a single fresco whereon are crowded the events and travels of several seasons. The luxuriously fitted bark of the merchant Erastos turned its prow first toward the Orient, then to the south, and only at last toward Italy, which was fast becoming for me the Occident. We twice touched Rhodes; Delos, blinding white, was visited on an April morning, and later on under the full moon of the summer solstice; storms on the coast of Epirus allowed me to prolong a stay in Dodona. In Sicily we delayed a few days to explore the mystery of Syracusan springs, Arethusa and Cyane, fair nymphs of the blue water. There I thought again of Licinus Sura, the statesman devoting his scant leisure to study of the marvels of hydraulics. They had told me much of the curious colours of dawn on the Ionian Sea, when beheld from the heights of Aetna. I decided to make the ascent of the mountain; we passed from the region of vines to the beds of lava, and on to the snow. The agile youth fairly ran on those steep slopes; the scientists who went with me rode up on muleback. At the summit a shelter had been built for us to await the dawn. It came: an immense rainbow arched from horizon to horizon; on the icy crest strange fires blazed; earth and sea spread out to view as far as Africa, within sight, and Greece, which we merely guessed at. That was truly an Olympian height in my life. All was there, the golden fringe of cloud, the eagles, and the cupbearer of immortality.

Halcyon seasons, solstice of my days. . . . Far from embellishing my former happiness, I must struggle against too weak a portrayal; even now the recollection overpowers me. More sincere than most men, I can freely admit the secret causes of this felicity: that calm so propitious for work and for discipline of the mind seems to me one of the richest results of love. And it puzzles me that these joys, so precarious at best, and so rarely perfect in the course of human life, however we may have sought or received them, should be regarded with such mistrust by the so-called wise, who denounce the danger of habit and excess in sensuous delight, instead of fearing its absence or its loss; in tyrannizing over their senses they pass time which would be better occupied in putting their souls to rights, or embellishing them. At that period I paid as constant attention to the greater securing of my happiness, to enjoying and judging it, too, as I had always done for the smallest details of my acts; and what is the act of love, itself, if not a moment of passionate attention on the part of the body? Every bliss achieved is a masterpiece; the slightest error turns it awry, and it alters with one touch of doubt; any heaviness detracts from its charm, the least stupidity renders it dull. My own felicity was in no way responsible for those of my imprudences which shattered it later on; in so far as I have acted in harmony with it I have been wise. I think still that someone wiser than I might well have remained happy till his death.

It was some time later, in Phrygia, on the borderlands where Greece melts into Asia, that I formed the clearest and most complete idea of the nature of this happiness. We were camping in a wild and desert place, on the site of the tomb of Alcibiades, who died there a victim of machinations of the Satraps. His grave had been neglected for several centuries; I ordered a statue of Parian marble for the effigy of that man so beloved by Greece. I also arranged for commemorative rites to be celebrated annually there. The neighbouring villagers joined with the members of my escort for the first of these ceremonies; a young bull was sacrificed, and part of its flesh put aside for the night's feast. A horse race was improvised upon the plain and dances likewise. The Bithynian took part with a kind of fiery grace, and later that evening beside the last fire he sang. The upraised head showed the curve of the fine, strong throat.

I like to measure myself alongside the dead; that night I compared my life with the life of that great artist in pleasure, no longer young, who fell pierced by arrows on this spot, defended to the end by a beloved companion and wept over by an Athenian courtesan. My young years made no pretension to the prestige of Alcibiades' youth, but my versatility equalled or surpassed his own. I had tasted as many delights, and reflected more, and had done far more work; I knew, like him, the strange felicity of being loved. Alcibiades had seduced everyone and everything, even History herself; and nevertheless he left behind him mounds of Athenian dead, abandoned in the quarries of Syracuse, his own country on the verge of collapse, and the gods of the crossroads drunkenly mutilated by his hands. I had governed a world infinitely larger than that of his time, and had kept peace therein; I had rigged it like a fair ship made ready for a voyage which might last for centuries; I had striven my utmost to encourage in man the sense of divine, but without at the same time sacrificing to it what is essentially human. My bliss was my reward.

* * *

There was Rome still. But I was no longer obliged to feel my way there, to reassure and to please. The achievements of my administration were not to be denied; the gates of the temple of Janus, open in time of war, remained closed; my plans were bearing fruit: the prosperity of the provinces flowed back upon the capital. I no longer refused the title which they had proposed to me at the time of my accession, Father of the Country.

Plotina was no more. On a previous sojourn in the City I had seen her for the last time, this woman with the tired smile whom official nomenclature named my mother, and who was so much more, my sole friend among women. This time there was only her funeral urn, placed in the chamber below Trajan's Column. I attended in person the ceremonies for her apotheosis, and contrary to imperial custom wore mourning for nine days' time. But death made little change in an intimacy which for years had dispensed with mere presence; the empress remained for me what she always had been, a mind and a spirit with which mine had united.

Some of the great works of construction were nearing completion: the Colosseum, restored and cleansed of reminders of Nero which still haunted its site, was no longer adorned with the image of that emperor, but with a colossal statue of the Sun, Helios the King, in allusion to my family name of Aelius. They were putting the last touches to the Temple of Venus and Rome, erected likewise on the site of the scandalous Golden House, where Nero had grossly displayed a luxury ill acquired. *Roma, Amor:* the divinity of the Eternal City was now for the first time identified with the Mother of Love, inspirer of every joy. It was a basic concept in my life. The Roman power was thus taking on that cosmic and sacred character, that pacific, protective form which I aspired to give it. At times it occurred to me to identify the late empress with that wise Venus, my heavenly counsellor.

More and more the different gods seemed to me merged mysteriously in one Whole, emanations infinitely varied, but all equally manifesting the same force; their contradictions were only expressions of an underlying accord. The construction of a temple for All Gods, a Pantheon, seemed increasingly desirable to me. I had chosen a site on the ruins of the ancient public baths given by Agrippa, Augustus' son-in-law, to the people of Rome. Nothing remained of the old structure except a porch and a marble plaque bearing his dedication to the Roman citizens; this inscription was carefully replaced, just as before, on the front of the new temple. It mattered little to me to have my name recorded on this monument, which was the product of my very thought. On the contrary, it pleased me that a text of more than a century ago should link this new edifice to the beginning of our empire, to that reign which Augustus had brought to peaceful conclusion. Even in my innovations I liked to feel that I was, above all, a continuator. Farther back, beyond Trajan and Nerva, now become officially my father and my grandfather, I looked for example even to those twelve Caesars so mistreated by Suetonius; the clearsightedness of Tiberius, without his harshness; the learning of Claudius, without his weakness; Nero's taste for the arts, but stripped of all foolish vanity; the kindness of Titus, stopping short of his sentimentality; Vespasian's thrift, but not his arbsurd miserliness. These princes had played their part in human affairs; it devolved upon me to choose hereafter from among their acts what should be continued, consolidating the best things, correcting the worst, until the day when other men, either more or less qualified than I, but charged with equal responsibility, would undertake to review my acts likewise.

The dedication of the Temple of Venus and Rome was a kind of triumph, celebrated by chariot races, public spectacles, and distribution of spices and perfumes. The twenty-four elephants which had transported the enormous blocks of building stone, reducing thereby the forced labour of slaves, figured in the procession, great living monoliths themselves. The date chosen for this festival was the anniversary of Rome's birth, the eighth day following the Ides of April in the eight hundred and eighty-second year after the founding of the City. Never had a Roman spring been so overwhelmingly sweet and so blue.

On the same day, with graver solemnity, as if muted, a dedicatory ceremony took place inside the Pantheon. I myself had revised its architectural plans, drawn with too little daring by Apollodorus: utilizing the arts of Greece only as ornamentation, like an added luxury, I had gone back for the basic form of the structure to the primitive, fabled times of Rome and to the round temples of ancient Etruria. My intention had been that this sanctuary of All Gods should reproduce the likeness of the terrestrial globe and of the stellar sphere, that globe wherein are enclosed the seeds of eternal fire, and that hollow sphere containing all. Such was also the form of our ancestors' huts where the smoke of man's earliest hearths escaped through an orifice at the top. The cupola, constructed of hard but lightweight volcanic stone, which seemed still to share in the upward movement of flames, revealed the sky through a great hole at the centre showing alternately dark and blue. This temple, both open and mysteriously enclosed, was conceived as a solar quadrant. The hours would make their round on that caissoned ceiling, so carefully polished by Greek artisans; the disk of daylight would rest suspended there like a shield of gold; rain would form its clear pool on the pavement below; prayers would rise like smoke toward that void where we place the gods.

This solemnity was for me one of those moments when all things converge. Standing beside me in that well of daylight was my entire administrative staff; these men were the materials which composed my destiny, by then already more than half completed and in its maturity. I could discern the austere vigour of Marcius Turbo, faithful servitor of the State; the frowning dignity of Servianus, whose grumblings, whispered ever lower, no longer reached my ears; the regal elegance of Lucius Ceionius; and slightly to one side, in that luminous shade which is best for divine apparitions, the dreamy visage of the young Greek in whom I had embodied my Fortune. My wife, present there also, had just received the title of empress.

For a long time, already, I had been more inclined toward the fables of love and quarrels of the gods than to the clumsy commentaries of philosophers upon the nature of divinity; I was willing to be the terrestrial image of Jupiter, who is the more god in that he is also man, who supports the world, incarnating justice and giving order to the universe, but who is at the same time the lover of Ganymedes and Europas, the negligent husband of a bitter Juno. Disposed that day to see everything without shadow, in fancy I likened the empress to that goddess in whose honour, during a recent visit to Argos, I had consecrated a golden peacock adorned with precious stones. I could have freed myself by divorce from this unloved woman; had I been a private citizen I should not have hesitated to do so. But she troubled me very little, and nothing in her conduct justified so public an insult. As a young wife she had taken offence at my ways, but only in much the same manner as her uncle had been irked by my debts. She was now confronted with manifestations of a passion which promised to endure, but she seemed not to notice them. Like many a woman little sensitive to love she poorly divined its power; such ignorance precluded the possibilities of benevolence and jealousy alike. She took umbrage only if her titles or her security were threatened, and such was not the case.

Nothing was left of that youthful charm which had briefly attracted me to her in former days; this Spanish woman grown prematurely old was grave and hard. I owed it to her natural coldness that she never took a lover, and was pleased that she wore her matronly veils with dignity; they were almost the veils of a widow. I rather liked to have the profile of an empress on the Roman coins, with an inscription on the reverse, sometimes to Matronly Virtue, sometimes to Tranquillity. Often now I thought of that symbolical marriage which takes place on the night of the Eleusinian festivities between the high priestess and the hierophant, and which is neither union nor contact, but is a rite, and is sacred as such.

From the top of a terrace on the night following these celebrations I watched Rome ablaze. These festive bonfires were surely as brilliant as the disastrous conflagrations lighted by Nero; they were almost as terrifying, too. Rome the crucible, but also the furnace, the boiling metal, the hammer, and the anvil as well, visible proof of the changes and repetitions of history, one place in the world where man will have most passionately lived. The great fire of Troy from which a fugitive had escaped, taking with him his aged father, his young son, and his household gods, had passed down to us that night in this flaming festival. I thought also, with something like awe, of conflagrations to come. These millions of lives past, present, and future, these structures newly arisen from ancient edifices and followed themselves by structures yet to be born, seemed to me to succeed each other in time like waves; by chance it was at my feet that night that this great surf swept to shore. I say nothing of those moments of rapture when the sacred cloth, the imperial purple, which I so seldom consented to wear, was thrown over the shoulders of the youth who was fast becoming for me my Genius; it pleased me, certainly, to place that rich red against the pale gold of a body, but I wanted above all to compel my Fortune and my Bliss, those uncertain, intangible entities, to assume this visible, earthly form, to acquire the warmth and reassuring weight of flesh. The solid walls of the Palatine Palace, which I occupied so little, but which I had just rebuilt, seemed to sway like a ship at sea; the curtains drawn back to admit the night air were like those of a cabin aft, and the cries of the crowd were the sound of wind in the sails. The massive reef in the distance, perceptible in the dark, that gigantic base of my tomb newly begun on the banks of the Tiber, suggested to me no regret, no terror, no vain meditation upon the brevity of life.

*　　*　　*

Little by little the light changed. For two years and more the very passage of time had been marked in the progress of a young life perfecting itself, growing radiant, and mounting to its zenith: the grave voice accustoming itself to cry orders to pilots and to masters of the hunt; the lengthened stride of the runner; the limbs of the horseman more expertly mastering his mount. The schoolboy of Claudiopolis who had learned by heart long fragments of Homer was now enamoured of voluptuous, abstruse poems, or infatuated with certain passages of Plato. My young shepherd was turning into a young prince. He was no longer a mere boy, eager to jump down from his horse at the halts to offer spring water cupped in his hands: the donor now knew the immense worth of his gifts. At the hunts organized in Lucius' domains in Tuscany it had pleased me to place this perfect visage in among the heavy and care-laden faces of high officials, or alongside the sharp Oriental profiles and the broad, hairy faces of barbarian huntsmen, thus obliging the beloved to maintain also the difficult role of friend. In Rome intrigues had been woven around that young head, and low devices used to secure his influence, or to supplant it. He had known enough to despise all that, or ignore it; absorption in his one thought endowed this youth of eighteen with a capacity for indifference which the wisest of men might envy. But the beautiful lips had taken on a bitter line already observed by the sculptors.

Here I give the moralists occasion for easy triumph. My critics are ready to point out the consequences of aberration and excess in what befell me; it is the harder for me to refute them in that I fail to see what the error is, or where the excess lies. I try to review my crime, if it is one, in its true proportions. I tell myself that suicide is not rare, and that it is common to die at twenty; that the death of Antinous is a problem and a catastrophe for me alone. It is possible that such a disaster was inseparable from too exuberant joy and from a plenitude of experience which I would have refused to forgo either for myself or for my young companion in danger. Even my remorse has gradually become a form of possession, though bitter, and a way of assuring myself that, to the end, I have been the sorry master of his destiny. But I am well aware that other factors exist, namely, the will and decision of that fair stranger who each loved one is, and remains for us, in spite of everything. In taking upon myself the entire fault I reduce the young figure to the proportions of a wax statuette which I might have shaped, and crushed, in my hands. I have no right to detract from the extraordinary masterpiece which he made of his departure; I must leave to the boy the credit for his own death.

It goes without saying that I lay no blame upon the physical desire, ordinary enough, which determined my choice in love. Similar passions had often occurred in my life; these frequent adventures so far had cost no more than a minimum of pledges, troubles, or lies. My brief fancy for Lucius had involved me in only a few follies easy to mend. There was nothing to keep this supreme affection from following the same course, nothing except precisely that unique quality which distinguished it from the others. Mere habit would have led us to that inglorious but safe ending which life brings to all who accept its slow dulling from wear. I should have seen passion change into friendship, as the moralists would have it do, or into indifference, as is more often the case. A young person would have grown away from me at about the time that our bonds would have begun to weigh me down; other sensual routines, or the same under other forms, would have been established in his life; the future would have held a marriage neither worse nor better than many another, a post in provincial administration, or the direction of some rural domain in Bithynia. Or otherwise, there would have been simple inertia, and court life continued in some subaltern position; to put it at the worst, one of those careers of fallen favourites who turn into confidants or panders. Wisdom, if I understand it at all, consists of admitting each of such possibilities and dangers, which make up life itself, while trying to ward off the worst. But we were not wise, neither the boy nor I.

I had not awaited the coming of Antinous to feel myself a god, but success was multiplying around me the sense of vertiginous heights. The seasons seemed to collaborate with the poets and musicians of my escort to make our existence one continuous Olympian festival. The day of my arrival in Carthage, a five-year drought came to an end; the crowds, wild with joy at the downpour, acclaimed me as dispenser of blessings from above; great works of public construction for Africa thereafter were only a means of channelling such celestial prodigality. A short time before, in the course of a stop in Sardinia, we took refuge in a peasant's hut during a storm; Antinous helped our host broil a few slices of tuna over the coals, and I felt like Zeus visiting Philemon in company with Hermes. The youth half reclining on a couch was that same Hermes untying his sandals; it was Bacchus who gathered grapes or tasted for me the cup of red wine; the fingers hardened by the bowstring were those of Eros. Amid so many fantasies, and surrounded by such wonders, I sometimes forgot the purely human, the boy who vainly strove to learn Latin, who begged the engineer Decrianus for lessons in mathematics, then quickly gave up, and who at the slightest reproach used to take himself off to the prow of the ship to gaze broodingly at the sea.

The African journey culminated in the full sun of July at the newly completed camp at Lambaesis; my companion donned cuirass and military tunic with boyish delight; for these few days I was the nude but helmeted Mars taking part in the camp sports, the athletic Hercules revelling in the feeling of still youthful vigour. In spite of the heat and the long labours of digging and grading completed before my arrival, the army functioned like everything else with divine facility: it would have been impossible to force a runner to one more hurdle, to demand of a horseman a single new jump without spoiling the value of the manoeuvres themselves, and breaking into that exact equilibrium which constitutes their beauty. I had to point out to the officers only one slight error, a group of horses left without cover during a feigned attack on open ground; my prefect Cornelianus satisfied me in every respect. Intelligent order governed these masses of men and beasts of burden, of barbarian women with their sturdy children who crowded round the headquarters to kiss my hands. This was not servile obedience; that wild energy was applied to the support of my programme for security; nothing had cost too much, and nothing had been neglected. I thought of making Arrian compose as perfect a treatise on tactics as is a body well-formed.

In Athens, three months later, the dedication of the Olympieion was occasion for festivals which recalled the Roman solemnities, but what in Rome had been celebrated on earth seemed there to occur in the heavens. Late on a luminous day of autumn I took my station in that portico which had been conceived on the superhuman scale of Zeus himself; the marble temple, built on the spot where Deucalion had watched the Deluge recede, seemed to lose its weight and float like a great white cloud; my ritual dress was in tone with the evening colours on nearby Hymettus. I had entrusted Polemo with the inaugural discourse. It was at this time that Greece granted me those divine appellations wherein I could recognize both a source of prestige and the most secret aim of my life's work: Evergetes, Olympian, Epiphanios, Master of All. And the most beautiful of these titles, and most difficult to merit, Ionian and Friend of Greece. There was much of the actor in Polemo, but the play of features in a great performer sometimes translates the emotion shared by a whole people, and a whole century. He raised his eyes to the heavens and gathered himself together before his exordium, seeming to assemble within him all gifts held in that moment of time: I had collaborated with the ages, and with Greek life itself; the authority which I wielded was less a power than a mysterious force, superior to man but operating effectively only through the intermediary of a human person; the marriage of Rome with Athens had been accomplished; the future once more held the hope of the past; Greece was stirring again like a vessel, long becalmed, caught anew in the current of the wind. Just then a moment's melancholy came over me: I could not but reflect that these words of completion and perfection contained within them the very word *end*; perhaps I had offered only one more object as prey to Time the Devourer.

We were taken next inside the temple where the sculptors were still at work; the immense, half-assembled statue of Zeus in ivory and gold seemed to lighten somewhat that dim shade; at the foot of the scaffolding lay the great python which I had sent for to India to be consecrated in this Greek sanctuary. Already reposing in its filigree basket, the divine snake embodied the spirit of Earth, a creature emblem long associated with the nude youth who symbolizes the emperor's Genius. Antinous, entering more and more into that role, himself fed the monster its ration of wing-clipped wrens. Then, raising his arms, he prayed. I knew that this prayer, made for me, was addressed to no one but myself, though I was not god enough to grasp its sense, nor to know if it would some day be answered. There was comfort in leaving that silence and pale twilight to regain the city streets, where lamps were alight, to feel the friendliness of the crowd and hear the vendors' cries in the dusty evening air. The young face which was soon to adorn so many coins of the Greek world was becoming a familiar presence for the people, and a sign.

I did not love less; indeed I loved more. But the weight of love, like that of an arm thrown tenderly across the chest, becomes little by little too heavy to bear. Passing interests reappeared: I remember the hard, elegant youth who was with me during a stay in Miletus, but whom I gave up. I recall that evening in Sardis when the poet Strato escorted us from brothel to brothel, and we surrounded ourselves with conquests of doubtful value. This same Strato, who had preferred obscurity in the freedom of Asia's taverns to life in my court, was a man of exquisite sensibility, a mocking wit quick to assert the vanity of all that is not pleasure itself, in order perhaps to excuse himself for having sacrificed to it everything else. And there was that night in Smyrna when I forced the beloved one to endure the presence of a courtesan. His conception of love had remained austere because it was centred on but one being; his disgust now verged on nausea. Later on he got used to that sort of thing. Such idle experiments on my part are explained well enough by a taste for dissipation; there was also mingled therein the thought of inventing a new kind of intimacy in which the companion in pleasure would not cease to be the beloved and the friend; there was the desire to instruct him, too, giving him some of the experiences which had been those of my own youth. And possibly, though less clearly avowed, there was some intention of lowering him slowly to the level of routine pleasures which involve no commitments.

An element of anguish lay in my need to wound this umbrageous affection which threatened to encumber my life. In the course of a journey in Troas we visited the plain of the Scamander under skies dark with catastrophe: the flood, which I had come to estimate at first hand for its damage, was changing the mounds of the ancient tombs to islets. I found time for a few moments' reflection at the tomb of Hector; Antinous went to dream over Patroclus' grave. I failed to recognize in the young fawn who accompanied me an emulator of Achilles' friend: when I derided those passionate loyalties which abound chiefly in books the handsome boy was insulted, and flushed crimson. More and more the only virtue to which I then constrained myself was frankness; I was beginning to realize that the heroic code which Greece had built around the attachment of a mature man for a younger companion is often no more for us in our time than hypocritical affectation. More sensitive to Rome's pre-

judices than I was aware, I recalled that although they grant
sensuality a role they see only shameful folly in love; I was again
seized by a mania for avoiding exclusive dependence on any one
being. Shortcomings which were merely those of youth, and as
such were inseparable from my choice, began to exasperate me.
In this passion of a wholly different order I was finally rein-
stating all that had irritated me in my Roman mistresses; perfumes, elaborate attire, and the cool luxury of jewels took their
place again in my life. Fears almost without justification had
entered that brooding heart; I have seen the boy anxious at the
thought of soon becoming nineteen. Dangerous whims and
sudden anger shaking the Medusa-like curls above the stubborn
brow alternated with a melancholy which was close to stupor,
and with a gentleness more and more broken. Once I struck him;
I shall remember for ever those horrified eyes. But the offended
idol remained an idol, and my expiatory sacrifices began.

All the sacred Mysteries of Asia, with their strident music,
served now to add to this voluptuous unrest. The period of
Eleusis had indeed gone by. Initiations into strange or secret
cults (practices tolerated rather than approved, and which the
legislator in me regarded with distrust) appealed at that moment
of life when dance leaves us reeling and song ends in outcry.
In Samothrace I had been initiated into the Mysteries of the
Cabiri, ancient and obscene rites, sacred as flesh and blood; at
the Cave of Trophonius milk-fed serpents glided about my ankles;
the Thracian feasts of Orpheus taught me savage brotherhood
rites. The statesman who had imposed severe penalties upon all
forms of mutilation now consented to attend the orgies of
Cybele: I witnessed the hideous whirling of bleeding dancers;
fascinated as a kid in presence of a snake, my young companion
watched with terror these men who were choosing to answer the
demands of age and of sex with a response as final as that of death
itself, and perhaps more dreadful.

But the height of horror was reached during a stay in Palmyra,
where the Arab merchant, Meles Agrippa, entertained us for
three weeks in the lap of splendid and barbaric luxury. One day
in the midst of the drinking, this Meles, who was a high official
in the Mithraic cult but who took somewhat lightly his priestly

duties, proposed to Antinous that he should share in the blood
baptism. The youth knew that I had formerly been inducted in
a ceremony of the same kind; he offered himself with fervour as
a candidate. I saw no reason to object to this fantasy; only a
minimum of purificatory rites and abstinence was required. I
agreed to serve myself as sponsor, together with Marcus Ulpius
Castoras, my secretary for the Arabian language. We descended
into the sacred cave at the appointed hour; the Bithynian lay
down to receive the bloody aspersion. But when I saw his body,
streaked with red, emerging from the ditch, his hair matted
with sticky mud and his face spattered with stains which could
not be washed away but had to be left to wear off themselves, I
felt only disgust and abhorrence for all such subterranean and
sinister cults. Some days later I forbade access to the black
Mithraeum for all troops stationed at Emesa.

Warnings there were: like Mark Antony before his last battle,
I heard receding into the night the music of the change of guard
as the protecting gods withdrew. . . . I heard, but paid no heed.
My assurance was like that of a horseman whom some talisman
protects from every fall. At Samosata an assembly of lesser kings
of the Orient were held under my auspices; during the mountain
hunts, Abgar himself, king of Osroëne, taught me the art of
falconry; great beats engineered like scenes on a stage drove
whole herds of antelope into nets of purple; Antinous had to pull
back with all his strength to hold in two panthers straining at
their heavy yoke of gold. Under cover of all these splendours
negotiations were concluded; the bargaining invariably ended in
my favour; I continued to be the player who wins at every
throw.

The winter was passed in that palace of Antioch where in
other days I had besought soothsayers to enlighten me as to
the future. But from now on the future had nothing to bring
me, nothing at least which could count as a gift. My harvests
were in; life's heady wine filled the vats to overflowing. I had
ceased to control my own destiny, it is true, but the disciplines
so carefully worked out in earlier years seemed now to me no
more than the first stage of a man's vocation; they were like those
chains which a dancer makes himself wear in order to leap the

higher after casting them off. On certain points austerity was still the rule: I continued to forbid the serving of wine before the second watch at night; I remembered the sight of Trajan's trembling hand on those same tables of polished wood. But there are other forms of inebriation. Though no shadow was cast on my days, whether death, defeat, or that subtle undoing which is self-inflicted, or age (which nevertheless would surely come), yet I was hurrying, as if each one of those hours was the most beautiful, but also the last of all.

My frequent sojourns in Asia Minor had put me in touch with a small group of scholars seriously concerned with the study of magic arts. Each century has its particular daring: the boldest minds of our time, weary of a philosophy which grows more and more academic, are venturing to explore those frontiers forbidden to mankind. In Tyre, Philo of Byblus had revealed to me certain secrets of ancient Phoenician magic; he continued in my suite to Antioch. There Numenius was giving a new interpretation to Plato's myths on the nature of the soul; his theories remained somewhat timid, but they would have led far a hardier intelligence than his own. His disciples could summon spirits; that was a game for us like any other. Strange faces which seemed made of the very marrow of my dreams appeared to me in the smoke of the incense, then wavered and dissolved, leaving me only the feeling that they resembled some known, living visage. All that was no more, perhaps, than a juggler's trick, but in this case the juggler knew his trade.

I went back to the study of anatomy, barely approached in my youth, but now it was no longer a question of sober consideration of the body's structure. I was seized with curiosity to investigate those intermediate regions where the soul and the flesh intermingle, where dream echoes reality, or sometimes even precedes it, where life and death exchange attributes and masks. My physician Hermogenes disapproved of such experiments, but nevertheless he acquainted me with a few practitioners who worked along these lines. I tried with them to find the exact seat of the soul and the bonds which attach it to the body, and to measure the time which it takes to detach itself. Some animals were sacrificed to this research. The surgeon Satyrus took me into his hospital to witness death agonies. We speculated together: is the soul only the supreme development of the body, the fragile evidence of the pain and pleasure of existing? Is it on the contrary more ancient than the body, which is modelled on its image and which serves it momentarily, more or less well, as instrument? Can it be called back inside the flesh, re-establishing with the body that close union and mutual combustion which we name life? If souls possess an identity of their own, can they be interchanged, going from one being to another like a segment of fruit or the sip of wine which two lovers exchange in a kiss? Every philosopher changes his opinion about these things some twenty times a year; in my case scepticism contended with desire to know, and enthusiasm with irony. But I had convinced myself that our brain allows only the merest residue of facts to filter through to us: I was more and more interested in the obscure world of sensation, that dark night where blinding suns flashed and revolved.

Near this same period Phlegon, who was a collector of ghost stories, told us one evening the tale of *The Bride of Corinth*, vouching for its authenticity. That adventure, wherein love brings a soul back to earth and temporarily grants it a body, moved each one of us, though at different depths. Several tried to set up a similar experiment: Satyrus attempted to evoke his master Aspasius, with whom he had made one of those pacts (never kept) according to which those who die promise to give information to the living. Antinous made me a promise of the same nature, which I took lightly, having no reason to believe that the boy would not survive me. Philo sought to bring back his dead wife. I permitted the names of my father and my mother to be pronounced, but a certain delicacy kept me from evoking Plotina. Not one of these attempts succeeded. But some strange doors had been opened.

A few days before the departure from Antioch I went to offer sacrifice, as in other years, on the summit of Mount Casius. The ascent was made by night; as for Aetna, I took with me only a small number of friends used to climbing. My purpose was not simply to accomplish a propitiatory rite in that very sacred sanctuary; I wished to see from its height the phenomenon of dawn, that daily miracle which I never have contemplated without a secret cry of joy. At the topmost point the sun brightens the copper ornaments of the temple and the faces smiling in full light while Asia's plans and the sea are still plunged in darkness; for the briefest moment the man who prays on that peak is sole beneficiary of the morning.

Everything was prepared for a sacrifice; we climbed with horses at first, and then on foot, along perilous paths bordered with broom and shrubs which we knew at night by their pungent perfumes. The air was heavy; that spring was as burning as summer elsewhere. For the first time while ascending a mountain I had trouble in breathing; I was obliged to lean for a moment on the shoulder of my young favourite. We were a hundred steps from the summit when a storm broke which Hermogenes had expected for some time, for he was expert in meteorology. The priests came out to receive us under flashes of lightning; the small band, drenched to the skin, crowded around the altar laid for the sacrifice. Just as it was to take place a thunderbolt bursting upon us killed both victim and officiating sacrificer in a single stroke. When the first moment of horror had passed, Hermogenes bent with a physician's curiosity over the stricken group; Chabrias and the high priest cried out in admiration that the man and fawn thus sacrificed by this divine sword were uniting with the eternity of my Genius; that these lives were prolonging mine in their substitution. Antinous, gripping fast to my arm was trembling, not from terror, as I then thought, but under the impact of a thought which I was to understand later on. A being terrified of decline, that is to say, of growing old, must have promised himself long ago to die at the first sign of change, or even before. I have come to think now that that promise, which so many of us have made to ourselves but without holding to it, went far back for him, to the period of Nicomedia and the encounter at the edge of the spring. It explained his indolence, his ardour in pleasure, his sadness, and his total indifference to all future. But it was still essential that this departure should have no air of revolt, and should contain no complaint. The lightning of Mount Casius had revealed to him a way out: death could become a last form of service, a final gift, and the only one which

seemed left for him to give. The illumination of dawn was as
nothing compared with the smile which arose on that overwhelmed countenance.

Some days later I saw that same smile again, but more hidden,
and ambiguously veiled; at supper, Polemo, who dabbled in
cheiromancy, wished to examine the hand of the youth, that
palm which alarmed even me by its astonishing fall of stars. But
the boy withdrew it and closed it gently, almost chastely. He
intended to keep the secret of his game, and that of his end.

*　　*　　*

We made a stop at Jerusalem. There I took occasion to study
the plan for a new capital which I proposed to construct on the
site of the Jewish city ruined by Titus. Good administration in
Judaea and greater commerce with the Orient showed the need
for developing a great metropolis at this intersection of routes.
I had in mind the usual Roman capital: Aelia Capitolina would
have its temples, its markets, it public baths, and its sanctuary
of the Roman Venus. My recent absorption in passionate and
tender cults led me to choose a grotto on Mount Moriah as best
suited for celebrating the rites of Adonis. These projects roused
indignation in the Jewish masses: the wretched creatures
actually preferred their ruins to a great city which would afford
them the chance of gain, of knowledge, and of pleasure. The
first workmen to touch those crumbling walls with pickaxes were
attacked by the mob. I went ahead notwithstanding; Fidus
Aquila, who was soon to employ his genius for planning in the
construction of Antinoöpolis, took up the work at Jerusalem. I
refused to see in those heaps of rubble the rapid growth of hatred.

A month later we arrived at Pelusium. I arranged to restore
the tomb of Pompey there: the deeper I delved into affairs of
the Orient the more I admired the political genius of that conquered but undying opponent of the great Julius. Pompey, in
endeavouring to bring order to this uncertain world of Asia,
sometimes seemed to me to have worked more effectively for
Rome than Caesar himself. That reconstruction was one of my
last offerings to History's dead; I was soon to be forced to busy
myself with other tombs.

Our arrival at Alexandria was kept discreetly quiet. The triumphal entry was postponed until the empress should come. Though she travelled little she had been persuaded to pass the winter in the milder climate of Egypt; Lucius, but poorly recovered from a persistent cough, was to try the same remedy. A small fleet of vessels was assembled for a voyage on the Nile with a programme comprising official inspections, festivals, and banquets which promised to be as tiring as those of a season at the Palatine. I myself had organized all that: the luxury and display of a court were not without political value in this ancient country accustomed to royal pomp.

But I had therefore the more desire to devote these few days which would precede the arrival of my guests to hunting. In Palmyra, Meles Agrippa had arranged some parties for us in the desert, but we had not gone far enough to see lions. Two years earlier Africa had provided the chance for some marvellous wild animal hunts; Antinous, then too young and inexperienced, had had no permission to take a significant part. In that respect I lacked courage for him in a way that I should not have dreamed for myself. Yielding, as always, I promised him now the chief role in this lion hunt. The time had passed for treating him as a child, and I was proud of his young strength.

We set off for the oasis of Ammon, some days' journey from Alexandria, that same place where long ago Alexander had learned from the priests of his divine birth. The natives were reporting the presence in the area of a particularly dangerous animal which often attacked men as well as beasts. At night around the camp fire we gaily compared our exploits-to-be with those of Hercules. But the first days brought us only a few gazelles. Then we decided to take up a position, the two of us, near a sandy pool all overgrown with rushes. The lion was supposed to come there at dusk to drink. The negroes were instructed to drive him toward us with the noise of conch horns, cymbals, and cries; the rest of our escort had been left some distance away. The air was heavy and still; there was no need even to consider the direction of the wind. We could hardly have passed the tenth hour of the day, for Antinous called my attention to the red water lilies still wide open on the pond.

Suddenly the royal beast appeared in a turmoil of trampled reeds and turned his handsome head toward us, one of the most god-like faces that danger can assume. Placed somewhat behind, I had no time to restrain the boy; he imprudently spurred his horse and hurled first his spear and then his two javelins, with skill, but from too close range. Pierced in the neck, the animal fell to earth, lashing the ground with his tail; the whirl of sand kept us from distinguishing more than a reddening, confused mass. At last the lion regained his feet and mustered his strength to spring upon horse and rider, now disarmed. I had foreseen this danger: happily Antinous' mount did not stir: our horses had been admirably trained for this sort of game. I interposed my horse, exposing the right flank; I was used to such action and it was not very difficult for me to dispatch the beast, already mortally stricken. He collapsed for the second time; the muzzle rolled in the mire and a stream of dark blood ran into the water. The mighty cat, colour of the desert, of honey, of the sun itself, expired with a majesty greater than man's. Antinous leaped down from his horse, which was covered with foam and trembling still; our companions rejoined us and the negroes dragged the immense prey back to the camp.

A feast was improvised; lying flat on his stomach before a platter of copper, the youth handed us our portions of lamb cooked under the coals. In his honour we drank palm wine. His exultation mounted like song. Perhaps he exaggerated the significance of the aid which I had given him, forgetting that I would have done as much for any hunter in danger; we felt, nevertheless, that we had gone back into that heroic world where lovers die for each other. Pride and gratitude alternated in his joy like the strophes of an ode. The blacks did wonders: soon under the starry sky the skin was swinging suspended on two stakes at the entrance of my tent. Despite the aromatics applied to it, its wild odour haunted us all night long. The next morning, after a meal of fruits, we left the camp; at the moment of departure we observed in a ditch what was left of the royal beast of the day before: it was no more than a red carcass surmounted by a cloud of flies.

Some days later we returned to Alexandria. The poet Pan-

crates arranged a special entertainment for me at the Museum;
in a music room was assembled a collection of fine and rare
instruments. Old Dorian lyres, heavier and more complicated
than ours today, stood side by side with curved citharas of
Persia and Egypt; there were Phrygian pipes shrill as eunuchs'
voices, and delicate Indian flutes, the name of which I do not
know. For a long time an Ethiopian beat upon some African
drums. A woman played a triangular harp of melancholy tone;
her cool beauty would have won me had I not already decided
to simplify my life by reducing it to what was for me the essential. My favourite musician, Mesomedes of Crete, used the water
organ to accompany the recitation of his poem *The Sphinx*, a
disturbing, undulating work, as elusive as the sand before the
wind. The concert hall gave on an inner court where some water-
lilies were growing in the fountain's basin; they lay wide open in
the almost furious heat of a late August afternoon. During an
interlude, Pancrates urged us to inspect more closely these
flowers of rare type, red as blood, which bloomed only at the
end of summer. At once we recognized our scarlet lilies of the
oasis of Ammon; Pancrates was suddenly fired by the idea of the
wounded beast expiring among the flowers. He proposed to me
that he should versify this episode of our hunt; the lion's blood
would be represented as tinting the lilies. The formula is not
new: I nevertheless gave the order. This Pancrates, who was
completely the court poet, improvised on the spot a few pleasant
verses in Antinous' honour: the rose, the hyacinth, and the
celandine were valued less in his hexameters than those scarlet
cups which would hereafter bear the name of the chosen one.
A slave was ordered to wade into the water to gather an armful
of the blossoms. The youth accustomed to homage gravely
accepted the waxlike flowers with the limp, snaky stems; the
petals closed like eyelids when night fell.

* * *

In the midst of these pleasures the empress arrived. The long
crossing had told on her: she was growing frail without ceasing
to be hard. Her political associations no longer caused me annoyance, as in the period when she had foolishly encouraged

Suetonius; she now had only inoffensive women writers about her. The confidante of the moment was a certain Julia Balbilla, whose Greek verse was fairly good. The empress and her suite established themselves in the Lyceum, from which they rarely went out. Lucius, on the contrary, was as always avid for all delights, including alike those of the mind and of the eye.

At twenty-six he had lost almost nothing of that arresting beauty which aroused acclamations from the youth in the streets of Rome. He was still absurd, ironic, and gay. His caprices of other days had now turned to manias: he made no move without his head cook; his gardeners composed astonishing flower plantings for him even aboard ship; he took his bed with him wherever he went, modelled on his own design of four mattresses stuffed with four special kinds of aromatics, on top of which he lay surrounded by his young mistresses like so many cushions. His pages, painted, powdered, and attired like Zephyrs and Eros, complied as well as they could with mad whims which were sometimes cruel: I had to intervene to keep the young Boreas, whose slenderness Lucius admired, from letting himself die of hunger. All that was more exasperating than charming. We visited together everything to be visited in Alexandria: the Lighthouse, the Mausoleum of Alexander and that of Mark Antony, where Cleopatra triumphs eternally over Octavia, the temples, the workshops and factories, and even the quarter of the embalmers. From a reputable sculptor I purchased an entire lot of Venuses, Dianas, and Hermes for Italica, my native city, which I had in mind to modernize and adorn. The priest of the temple of Serapis offered me a service of opaline glass, but I sent it to Servianus, with whom, out of regard for my sister Paulina, I tried to keep passable relations, at least at a distance. Great building projects took shape in the course of all these somewhat tedious rounds.

The religions in Alexandria are as varied as the trades; the quality of the product, however, is more doubtful. The Christians especially distinguish themselves there by a multiplication of sects which is, to say the least, useless. Two charlatans, Valentinus and Basilides, were intriguing against each other, closely watched over by the Roman police. As for the Egyptian populace, the dregs took advantage of each of their own ritual festivities to throw themselves, cudgel in hand, upon foreigners; the death of the bull Apis provokes more uprisings in Alexandria than an imperial succession in Rome. Fashionable people change gods there as elsewhere they change doctors, and with about as much success. But gold is their only idol : nowhere have I seen more shameless importuning. Grandiose inscriptions were displayed all about to commemorate my benefactions, but my refusal to exempt the inhabitants from a tax which they were quite able to pay soon alienated that rabble from me. The two young men who accompanied me were insulted more than once : Lucius was reproached for his lavish expenditure, which, it must be admitted, was excessive, and Antinous for his obscure origin, on the subject of which ran absurd rumours; both were blamed for the ascendancy which they were supposed to have over me. The last assumption was ridiculous : Lucius, whose judgement in public affairs was surprisingly acute, nevertheless had no political influence whatsoever; Antinous did not aspire to it. The young patrician, knowing the ways of the world, merely laughed at the jibes, but they were cause for suffering to Antinous.

The Jews of Alexandria, egged on by their co-religionists in Judaea, did their best to aggravate a situation already bad. The synagogue of Jerusalem sent me Akiba, its most venerable member, as delegate; almost a nonagenarian, and knowing no Greek, he came with the mission of winning me to renounce projects already under way at Jerusalem. Aided by my interpreters I held several colloquies with him which, on his part, were mere pretext for monologue. In less than an hour I felt able to define his thought exactly, though not subscribing to it; he made no corresponding effort concerning my own. This fanatic did not even suspect any reasoning possible on premises other than those he set forth. I offered his despised people a place among the others in the Roman community; Jerusalem however, speaking through Akiba, signified its intention of remaining, to the end, the fortress of a race and of a god isolated from human kind. That savage determination was expressed with tiresome deviousness: I had to listen to a long line of argument, subtly deduced step to step, proving Israel's superiority. At the end of eight days even this obstinate negotiator became aware that he was pursuing the wrong course, so he announced his departure. I abhor defeat, even for others, and it moves me the more when the vanquished is an old man. The ignorance of Akiba, and his refusal to accept anything outside his sacred books or his own people, endued him with a kind of narrow innocence. But it was difficult to feel sympathy for this bigot. Longevity seemed to have bereft him of all human suppleness: that gaunt body and dried mind had the locust's hard vigour. It seems that he died a hero later on for the cause of his people, or rather, for his law. Each of us dedicates himself to his own gods.

The distractions of Alexandria began to wane. Phlegon, who knew the local curiosities everywhere, whether procuress or famous hermaphrodite, proposed to take us to a local magician. This go-between for two worlds, the invisible and our own, lived in Canopus. We went there at night by boat along the torpid waters of the canal, a dismal ride. A silent hostility reigned, as always, between the two young men: the intimacy into which I was forcing them augmented their aversion for each other. Lucius hid this feeling under a mocking condescension; my young Greek enclosed himself in one of his dark moods. I happened to be rather tired; a few days before, on coming back from a race in full sun, I had had a brief fainting fit which only Antinous and the black Euphorion had witnessed. They had been unduly alarmed, and I had forbidden them to disclose the matter.

Canopus is no more than a tawdry stage-setting; the magician's house was situated in the most sordid part of that pleasure resort. We disembarked at a tumble-down terrace. The sorceress awaited us inside her house, surrounded by the dubious tools of her trade. She seemed competent; there was nothing of the stage witch about her; she was not even old.

Her predictions were sinister. For some time the oracles everywhere had been foretelling annoyances for me of every sort, political troubles, palace intrigues, and serious illness. I now believe that some decidedly human influences were at work upon those voices from below, sometimes to warn me, more

often to frighten me. The true condition of one part of the
Orient was more clearly explained therein than in the reports of
our proconsuls. I took these so-called revelations with calm, since
my respect for the invisible world did not go so far as to give
credence to such divine claptrap: ten years before, soon after
my accession to power, I had ordered the closing of the oracle
of Daphne, near Antioch, which had foretold my rule, for fear
that it might do the same for the first pretender who should
appear. But it is always annoying to hear talk of trouble.

After having disturbed us to the best of her ability the
prophetess offered her aid: one of those magical sacrifices in
which Egyptian sorcerers specialize would suffice to put everything right with destiny. My explorations in Phoenician magic
had already shown me that the horror of these forbidden practices lies less in what is revealed to us than in what they hide
from our sight; if my abomination of human sacrifice had not
been well known this practitioner would probably have advised
the immolation of a slave. As it was she contented herself with
speaking of some pet animal.

If it had been at all possible the sacrificial victim should have
belonged to me; it could not be a dog, which is an animal considered unclean in Egyptian superstition; a bird would have
done, but I do not travel with an aviary. My young master proposed his falcon. The conditions would be fulfilled thereby: I
had given him this beautiful bird after I had myself received it
from the king of Osroëne. The boy fed it himself; it was one of
the rare possessions to which he was attached. At first I refused;
he insisted, gravely; I gathered that he attributed some extraordinary significance to the offer, so I accepted, out of affection.
Provided with the most detailed instructions, my courier Menecrates went to fetch the bird from our apartments in the Serapeion. Even at a gallop the errand would take, in all, more than
two hours. There was no question of passing the interval in the
dirty hole of the magician, and Lucius complained of the damp-
ness aboard the boat. Phlegon found an expedient: we installed
ourselves as well as we could in the house of a procuress after
the inmates of the place had been disposed of. Lucius decided
to sleep; I made use of the time to dictate some dispatches, and

Antinous stretched out at my feet. Phlegon's reed-pen scratched away under the lamp. The last watch of the night was beginning when Menecrates brought back the bird, the glove, the hood, and the chain.

We returned to the house of the magician. Antinous removed the falcon's hood and for some moments caressed its little head, so sleepy and so wild, then handed it to the enchantress, who began with a series of magic passes. The bird, fascinated, fell asleep again. It was important that the victim should not struggle, and that the death should appear voluntary. Rubbed over with ritual honey and attar of roses, the animal, now inert, was placed in the bottom of a tub filled with Nile water; in drowning thus it was to be assimilated to Osiris borne along on the river's currents; the bird's earthly years were added to mine, and the little soul, issue of the sun, was united with the Genius of him for whom the sacrifice was made; the invisible Genius could hereafter appear to me and serve me under this form. The long manipulations which followed were no more interesting that some preparation for cooking. Lucius began to yawn. The ceremonies imitated human funerals in every detail : the fumigations and the psalm singing dragged on until dawn. The bird was finally enclosed in a casket lined with aromatic substances and the magician buried it in our presence at the edge of the canal, in an abandoned cemetery. When she had finished she crouched under a tree to count one by one the gold pieces which Phlegon paid her.

We returned to the boat. An unusually cold wind was blowing. Lucius, seated near me, drew closer the embroidered cotton coverlets with the tips of his slender fingers; for politeness' sake we continued to exchange remarks at broken intervals about business and scandal in Rome. Antinous, lying in the bottom of the boat, had leaned his head on my knees, pretending to sleep in order to keep apart from a conversation which did not include him. My hand passed over his neck, under his heavy hair; thus even in the dullest or most futile moments I kept some feeling of contact with the great objects of nature, the thick growth of the forests, the muscular back of the panther, the regular pulsation of springs; but no caress goes so deep as the soul. The sun was shining when we reached the Serapeion, and the melon merchants were crying their wares in the streets. I slept until it was time for the session of the local Council, which I attended. I learned later that Antinous took advantage of my absence to persuade Chabrias to go with him to Canopus. He went back to the house of the magician.

*　*　*

The first of the month of Athyr, the second year of the two hundred and twenty-sixth Olympiad. . . . That is the anniversary of the death of Osiris, the god of the dying; along the river piercing cries of lamentation had resounded from all the villages for three days' time. My Roman guests, less accustomed than I to the mysteries of the East, showed a certain curiosity for those ceremonies of another race. For me, on the contrary, they were tiring and irritating to the extreme. I had ordered my boat to be anchored at some distance from the others, far from any habitation; but a half-abandoned temple of the time of the Pharaohs stood near the river bank and had still its school of priests, so I did not entirely escape the sound of wailing.

On the preceding evening Lucius invited me to supper on his boat. I went there at sunset. Antinous refused to go with me, so I left him alone in my stern deck cabin lying on his lion skin, playing at knucklebones with Chabrias. Half an hour later, just as night fell, he changed his mind and called for a boat. Aided by a single oarsman, and pulling against the current, he rowed the considerable distance which separated us from the other boats. His entry into the deck tent where the supper was given interrupted the applause for the contortions of a dancing girl. He had arrayed himself in a long Syrian robe, sheer as the skin of a fruit and strewn over with flowers and chimeras. In order to row more easily he had freed his right arm from its sleeves; sweat was trembling on the smooth chest. Lucius tossed him a garland which he caught in mid-air: his gaiety, almost strident, did not abate for one moment, though hardly sustained by a single cup of Greek wine. We returned together in my boat with six oarsmen, followed by the cutting 'good night' of Lucius from above. The wild gay mood persisted. But in the morning

I happened by chance to touch a face wet with tears. I asked him impatiently the cause for such crying; he replied humbly, excusing himself on the ground of fatigue. I accepted the lie and fell back to sleep. His true agony took place in that bed, there beside me.

The mail from Rome had just come, and the day went by in reading and answering it. As usual Antinous went silently about the room; I know not at what moment that fair creature passed out of my life. Toward the twelfth hour Chabrias entered, in great agitation. Contrary to all regulations the youth had left the boat without stating his purpose or the length of his intended absence; two hours at least had gone by since his departure. Chabrias recalled some strange things said the evening before, and a recommendation made that very morning, concerning me. He voiced his fears. We descended in haste to the river bank. As if by instinct the old tutor made for a chapel on the water's edge, a small structure apart which was one of the outbuildings of the temple, and which he and Antinous had visited together. On an offering table lay ashes still warm from a sacrifice; turning them with his fingers, Chabrias drew forth a lock of hair, almost intact.

There was no longer anything for us to do but to search the shore. A series of reservoirs which must once have served for sacred ceremonies extended to a bend of the river; on the edge of the last basin Chabrias perceived in the rapidly lowering dusk a folded garment and sandals. I descended the slippery steps; he was lying at the bottom, already sunk in the river's mud. With Chabrias' aid I managed to lift the body, which had suddenly taken on the weight of stone. Chabrias hailed some boatmen who improvised a stretcher from sail cloth. Hermogenes, called in haste, could only pronounce him dead. That body, once so responsive, refused to be warmed again or revived. We took him aboard. Everything gave way; everything seemed extinguished. The Olympian Zeus, Master of All, Saviour of the World – all toppled together, and there was only a man with greying hair sobbing on the deck of a boat.

Two days went by before Hermogenes could make me even think of the funeral. The sacrificial rites with which Antinous had chosen to surround his death showed us the course to follow: it would not be for nothing that the day and hour of that end had coincided with the moment when Osiris descends into the tomb. I crossed the river to Hermopolis, to its quarter of embalmers. I had seen their work in Alexandria and knew to what outrages I was submitting this body; but fire is horrible too, searing and charring the beloved flesh; and in the earth it rots. The crossing was brief; squatting in a corner of the stern cabin Euphorion chanted in a low voice I know not what African dirge; this hoarse, half-muffled song seemed to me almost my own cry. We transferred the beloved dead into a room cleanly flushed with water which reminded me of the clinic of Satyrus; I aided the cast-maker to oil the face before the wax was applied. All the metaphors took on meaning: I held that heart in my hands. When I left the empty body it was no more than an embalmer's preparation, the first stage of a frightful masterpiece, a precious substance treated with salt and gum of myrrh, and never again to be touched by sun or air.

On the return I visited the temple near which the sacrifice had been consummated; I spoke with the priest. Their sanctuary would be renovated to become a place of pilgrimage for all Egypt; their college, enriched and augmented, would be consecrated hereafter to the service of my god. Even in my most obtuse moments I had never doubted that that young presence was divine. Greece and Asia would worship him in our manner, with games and dances, and with ritual offerings placed at the feet of a nude, white statue. Egypt, who had witnessed the death agony, would have also her part in the apotheosis: it would be the most secret and sombre part, and the harshest, for this country would play the eternal role of embalmer to his body. For centuries to come priests with shaven heads would recite litanies repeating that name which for them had no value, but for me held all. Each year the sacred barge would bear that effigy along the river; on the first of the month of Athyr mourners would walk on that shore where I had walked.

Every hour has its immediate duty, its special injunction which dominates all others: the problem of the moment was to defend from death the little that was left to me. Phlegon had assembled on the shore the architects and engineers of my suite, as I had ordered; sustained by a kind of clear-sighted frenzy I made them follow me along the stony hills; I explained my plan, the development of forty-five stadia of encircling wall, and I marked in the sand the position of the triumphal arch and that of the tomb. Antinoöpolis was to be born; that would already be a check to death to impose upon such a sinister land a city wholly Greek, a bastion which would hold off the nomads of Erythrea, a new market on the route to India. Alexander had celebrated the funeral of Hephaestion with devastation and mass slaughter of prisoners. It seemed to me finer to offer to the chosen one a city where his cult would be for ever mingled with the coming and going on the public square, where his name would be repeated in the casual talk of evening, where youths would toss crowns to each other at the banqueting hour. But on one point my thought fluctuated : it seemed impossible to abandon this body to foreign soil. Like a man uncertain of his next stop who reserves lodgings in several hostelries at a time, I ordered a monument for him at Rome, on the banks of the Tiber near my own tomb, but thought also of the Egyptian chapels which I had had built at the Villa by caprice, and which were suddenly proving tragically useful. A date was set for the funeral at the end of the two months demanded by the embalmers. I entrusted Mesomedes with the composition of funeral choruses. Late into the night I went back aboard; Hermogenes prepared me a sleeping potion.

* * *

The journey up the river continued, but my course lay on the Styx. In prisoners' camps on the banks of the Danube I had once seen wretches continually beating their heads against a wall with a wild motion, both mad and tender, endlessly repeating the same name. In the underground chambers of the Colosseum I had been shown lions pining away because the dog with which their keepers had accustomed them to live had been taken away. I tried to collect my thoughts : Antinous was dead. As a child I had wept and wailed over the corpse of Marullinus torn to shreds by crows, but had cried as does a mere animal, in the night. My father had died, but a boy orphaned at the age of twelve noticed no more than disorder in the house, his mother's tears, and his own terror; he knew nothing of the anguish which the dying man had experienced. My mother had died much later, about the time of my mission in Pannonia; I do not recall the exact date. Trajan had been only a sick man who must be made to make a will. I had not seen Plotina die. Attianus had died; he was old. During the Dacian wars I had lost comrades whom I believed that I loved ardently; but we were young, life and death were equally intoxicating and easy. Antinous was dead. I remembered platitudes frequently heard: 'One can die at any age', or 'They who die young are beloved by the gods'. I myself had shared in that loathsome misuse of words; I had talked of dying of sleep and dying of boredom. I had used the word *agony*, the word *mourning*, the word *loss*. Antinous was dead.

Love, wisest of gods.... But love had not been to blame for that negligence, for the harshness and indifference mingled with passion like sand with the gold borne along by a stream, for that blind self-content of a man too completely happy, and who is growing old. Could I have been so grossly satisfied? Antinous was dead. Far from loving too much, as doubtless Servianus was proclaiming at that moment in Rome, I had not been loving enough to force the boy to live on. Chabrias as a member of an Orphic cult held suicide a crime, so he tended to insist upon the sacrificial aspect of that ending; I myself felt a kind of terrible joy at the thought that that death was a gift. But I was the only one to measure how much bitter fermentation there is at the bottom of all sweetness, or what degree of despair is hidden under abnegation, what hatred is mingled with love. A being deeply wounded had thrown his proof of devotion in my very face; a boy fearful of losing all had found this means of binding me to him for ever. Had he hoped to protect me by such a sacrifice he must have deemed himself unloved indeed not to have realized that the worst of ills would be to lose him.

The tears ceased; the dignitaries who approached me were no longer obliged to avoid glancing at me (as if weeping were a thing obscene). Visits to model farms and irrigation canals were renewed; it mattered little how the hours were spent. Countless wild rumours were already afoot with regard to my disaster; I let them talk, the truth being not of the kind to cry in the streets. Then, too, the most malicious lies were accurate in their way; they accused me of having sacrificed him and, in a sense, I had done so. Hermogenes, who faithfully relayed these echoes to me from without, transmitted some messages from the empress; she behaved decently (people usually do in the presence of death). But such compassion was based on a misapprehension: I was to be pitied provided that I consoled myself rather promptly. Even I thought that I was somewhat calmed, and was almost embarrassed by the fact. Little did I know what strange labyrinths grief contains, or that I had yet to walk therein.

They tried to divert me. Some days after we reached Thebes I learned that the empress and her suite had gone twice to the base of the colossal statue of Memnon, hoping to hear the mysterious sound emitted from the stone at dawn, a well-known phenomenon which all travellers wish to witness. The prodigy had not occurred, but with superstitious awe they imagined that it would take place if I were present, so I agreed to accompany the women the next day; any means would do to shorten those interminable nights of autumn. Early that morning, at about the eleventh hour, Euphorion came to my cabin to relight the lamp and help me to put on my clothes. I stepped on deck; the sky, still wholly dark, was truly the iron sky of Homer's poems, indifferent to man's woes and joys alike. More than twenty days had passed since this thing had happened. I descended to the rowboat for the short trip, which did not pass without exclamations of fright from the women.

They landed us near the Colossus. A strip of dull rose extended along the East; still another day was beginning. The mysterious sound occurred three times, resembling the snap of a breaking bowstring. The inexhaustible Julia Balbilla produced on the spot a whole series of poems. The women undertook to visit the temples, but I accompanied them only part of the way, along walls monotonously covered with hieroglyphs. I had had enough of those colossal figures of kings all alike, sitting side by side, their long flattened feet planted straight before them; in such inert blocks of stone there is nothing which signifies life for us,

neither grief nor sensuous delight, nor movement which gives
limbs their freedom, nor that capacity which composes a world
round a pensive head. The priests who guided me seemed almost
as ill-informed as myself about those extinguished lives, though
from time to time some discussion arose over a name. They knew
vaguely that each of these monarchs had inherited a kingdom,
governed over his people, and begotten a successor; nothing besides remained. Those obscure dynasties extended farther back
than Rome, farther back than Athens, back beyond the day when
Achilles died before the walls of Troy, earlier than the astron-
omic cycle of five thousand years calculated by Meno for Julius
Caesar.

Feeling tired, I dismissed the priests and rested for a while
in the shade of the Colossus before returning to the boat. The
massive legs were covered to the knees with inscriptions traced
in Greek by sightseers : names, dates, a prayer, a certain Servius
Suavis, a certain Eumenius who had been in that same place six
centuries before me, a certain Panion who had visited Thebes
just six months ago.... Six months ago.... A fancy seized me
which I had not known since childhood days, when I used to
carve my name in the bark of chestnut trees on the Spanish
estate; the emperor who steadily refused to have his appellations
and titles inscribed upon the buildings and monuments of his
own construction now took his dagger to scratch a few Greek
letters on that hard stone, an abridged and familiar form of his
name, AΔPIANO .... It was one more thrust against time : a
name, a life sum (of which the innumerable elements would
never be known), a mere mark left by a man wholly lost in that
succession of centuries. Suddenly I remembered that it was the
twenty-seventh day of the month of Athyr, the fifth day before
our kalends of December. It was the birthday of Antinous; the
boy who would have been twenty that day had he been still
alive.

I went back aboard; the wound closed too quickly had opened
again; I stifled my cries in the cushion which Euphorion slipped
under my head. That corpse and I were drifting apart, carried
in different directions by two currents of time. The fifth day
before the kalends of December, the first day of the month of

Athyr: with each passing moment that body was sinking deeper, that death was more imbedded. Once more I climbed the treacherous ascent; with my very nails I strove to exhume that day dead and gone. Phlegon had sat facing the door, but remembered the successive entries and departures in the cabin only for the ray of light which had disturbed him each time that a hand pushed the blind. Like a man accused of a crime I strove to account for each hour: some dictation, a reply to the Senate of Ephesus; at which of those phrases did that agony take place? I tried to gauge the play of the footbridge under his tread, to reconstitute the dry bank and the flat paving stones; then the knife cutting the curl at the edge of his temple, the inclined body and knee bent to allow the hand to untie the sandal; the unique manner of opening the lips as he closed his eyes. It must have cost a desperate resolution indeed for so fine a swimmer to smother in that black silt. In my thoughts I tried to go as far as that revulsion through which we all shall pass, when the heart gives out and the brain stops short as the lungs cease to draw in life. I shall undergo a similar convulsion; I too shall die. But each passing is different; my attempts to picture his last agony came to no more than mere fabrication, for he had died alone.

I fought against my grief, battling as if it were gangrene: I recalled his occasional stubbornness and lies; I told myself that he would have changed, growing older and heavy. Such efforts proved futile; instead, like some painstaking workman who toils to copy a masterpiece, I exhausted myself in tasking my memory for fanatical exactitude, evoking that smooth chest, high and rounded as a shield. Sometimes the image leaped to mind of itself, and a flood of tenderness swept over me: once again I caught sight of an orchard in Tibur, and the youth gathering autumn fruits in his tunic, for lack of a basket. I had lost everything at once, the companion of the night's delights and the young friend squatting low to his heels to help Euphorion with the folds of my toga. If one were to believe the priests, the shade was also in torment, regretting the warm shelter of its body and haunting its familiar habitations with many a moan, so far and yet so near, but for the time too weak to signify the presence to me. If that were true my deafness was worse than death itself. But after all had I so well understood, on that morning, the living boy who sobbed at my side?

One evening Chabrias called me to show me a star, till then hardly visible, in the constellation of the Eagle; it flashed like a gem and pulsated like a heart. I chose it for his star and his sign. Each night I would follow its course until utterly wearied; in that part of the sky I have seen strange radiance. Folk thought me mad, but that was of little consequence.

Death is hideous, but life is too. Everything seemed awry. The founding of Antinoöpolis was a game, at best, just one more city to shelter fraudulent trading, official extortion, prostitution, disorder, and those cowards who weep for a while over their dead before forgetting them. Apotheosis was but an empty ceremony: such public honours would serve only to make of the boy a pretext for adulation or irony, a posthumous object of cheap desire, or of scandal, one of those legends already tainted which encumber the recesses of history. Perhaps my grief itself was only a form of licence, a vulgar debauch: I was still the one who profited from the experience and tasted it to the full, for the beloved one was giving me even his death for my indulgence. A man frustrated was weeping over himself.

Ideas jarred upon each other; words ground on without meaning; voices rasped and buzzed like locusts in the desert or flies on a dung pile; our ships with sails swelled out like doves' breasts were carriers for intrigue and lies; on the human countenance stupidity reigned. Death, in its aspect of weakness or decay, came to the surface everywhere: the bad spot on a fruit, some imperceptible rent at the edge of a hanging, a carrion body on the shore, the pustules of a face, the mark of scourges on a bargeman's back. My hands seemed always somewhat soiled. At the hour of the bath, as I extended my legs for the slaves to shave, I looked with disgust upon this solid body, this almost indestructible machine which absorbed food, walked, and managed to sleep, and would, I knew, re-accustom itself one day or another to the routines of love. I could no longer bear the presence of any but those few servants who remembered the departed one; in their way they had loved him. My sorrow found an echo in the rather foolish mourning of a masseur, or of the old negro who tended the lamps. But their grief did not keep them from laughing softly amongst themselves as they took the evening air along the river bank. One morning, leaning on the boat rail, I noticed a slave at work in the quarters reserved for the kitchens; he was cleaning one of those chickens which Egypt hatches by the thousands in its dirty incubators, and he gathered the slimy entrails into his hands to throw them into the water. I had barely time to turn away to vomit. At our stop in Philae, during a reception offered us by the governor, a child of three met with an accident: the son of a Nubian porter and dark as bronze, he had crept into the balconies to watch the dancing, and fell from that height. They did the best they could to hide the thing; the porter held back his sobs for fear of disturbing his master's guests, and was led out with the body through the kitchen doors; in spite of such precautions I caught a glimpse of his shoulders rising and falling convulsively, as under the blows of a whip. I had the feeling of taking that father's grief to myself as I had taken the sorrow of Hercules, of Alexander, of Plato, each of whom wept for a dead friend. I sent a few gold pieces to this poor fellow; what more could one do? Two or three days later I saw him again; he was contentedly picking at lice as he lay in the sun at the doorway.

Messages flooded in; Pancrates sent me his poems, finished at last; it was only a mediocre assemblage of Homeric hexameters, but the name which figured in almost every line made it more moving for me than many a masterpiece. Numenius sent me a *Consolation* written according to the usual formulas for such works; I passed a night reading it, though it contained every possible platitude. These feeble defences raised by man against death were developed along two lines: the first consisted in presenting death to us as an inevitable evil, and in reminding us that neither beauty, youth, nor love escapes decay; life and its train of ills are thus proved even more horrible than death itself, and it is better, accordingly, to die than to grow old. Such truths are cited to incline us toward resignation, but they justify chiefly despair. The second line of argument contradicts the first, but our philosophers care little for such niceties: the theme was no longer resignation to death but negation of it. Only the soul

was important, they said, arrogantly positing as a fact the immortality of that vague entity which we have never seen function
in the absence of the body, and the existence of which they had
not yet taken the trouble to prove. I was not so certain: since
the smile, the expression of the eyes, the voice, these imponder-
able realities, had ceased to be, then why not the soul, too? Was
it necessarily more immaterial than the body's heat? They
attached no importance to those remains wherein the soul no
longer dwelt; that body, however, was the only thing left to me,
my sole proof that the living boy had existed. The immortality
of the race was supposed to make up in some way for each
individual death, but it was hardly consoling to me that whole
generations of Bithynians would succeed each other to the end
of time along the banks of the Sangarius. We speak of glory,
that fine word which swells the heart, but there is wilful confusion between it and immortality, as if the mere trace of a
person were the same thing as his presence. They would have
had me see the resplendent god in place of the corpse, but I had
created that god; I believed in him, in my way, but a brilliant
posthumous destiny in the midst of the stellar spheres failed to
compensate for so brief a life; the god did not take the place of
the living one I had lost.

I was incensed by man's mania for clinging to hypotheses at
the expense of facts, for mistaking his dreams for more than
dreams. I felt otherwise about my obligations as the survivor.
That death would be in vain if I lacked the courage to look
straight at it, keeping in mind those qualities of cold and silence,
of coagulated blood and inert members which men cover up so
quickly with earth, and with hypocrisy; I chose to grope my way
in the dark without recourse to such weak lamps. I could feel
that those around me began to take offence at a grief of such
duration; furthermore, the violence of my sorrow scandalized
them more than its cause. If I had given way to the same tears
for the death of a brother or a son I should have been equally
reproached for crying like a woman. The memory of most men
is an abandoned cemetery where lie, unsung and unhonoured,
the dead whom they have ceased to cherish. Any lasting grief is
reproof to their neglect.

We came back down the river to the point where Antinoöpolis was beginning to rise. There were fewer boats in our party than before; Lucius, whom I had seen but little again, had returned to Rome, where his young wife was newly delivered of a son. His departure freed me of a good number of curious and troublesome onlookers. The work already started was altering the line of the shore; the plan of buildings-to-be became visible in the clearings between mounds of earth dug up everywhere for foundations; but I no longer recognized the exact place of the sacrifice. The embalmers delivered their handiwork; the slender coffin of cedar was placed inside a porphyry sarcophagus standing upright within the innermost room of the temple. I approached the dead boy timidly. He seemed as if costumed: the stiff Egyptian headdress covered his hair. His legs tightly bound in strips of linen were now only a long white bundle, but the profile of the young falcon had not changed; the lashes cast a shadow which I knew on the painted cheeks. Before they finished the wrapping of the hands I was urged to admire the gold fingernails.

The litanies began; the departed one, speaking through the priests, declared himself to have been perpetually truthful, perpetually chaste, perpetually compassionate and just, and boasted of virtues which, had he practised them as described, would have set him for ever apart from the living. The stale odour of incense filled the room, and through the smoky cloud I tried to give myself the illusion of a smile on those lips; the beautiful, immobile features seemed to tremble. I watched the magic passes whereby the priests force the soul of the dead to incarnate some portion of itself inside the statues which are to conserve his memory; there were other injunctions, stranger still. When all was over, the gold mask cast from the wax funeral mould was laid in place, perfectly fitting the features. That fair, incorruptible surface was soon to absorb within itself its own possibilities for radiance and warmth; it was to lie for ever in that case hermetically closed, like some inert symbol of immortality. A sprig of acacia was placed on his chest, and some dozen men lifted the heavy cover into position.

But I hesitated still about where to place the tomb. I recalled that in ordering rites of apotheosis everywhere, with funeral

games, issues of coins, and statues in the public squares, I had
made an exception for Rome, fearing to augment that animosity
which more or less surrounds any foreign favourite. I told myself
that I should not always be there to protect that sepulchre. The
monument envisaged at the gates of Antinoöpolis seemed too
public also, and far from safe. I followed the priests' advice. On a
mountain-side in the Arabic range, some three leagues from the
new city, they indicated to me one of those caverns formerly
intended by Egypt's kings to serve as their funeral vaults. A team
of oxen drew the sarcophagus up the slope; it was lowered with
ropes to those subterranean corridors, and was then slid into position to lean against a wall of rock. The youth from Claudiopolis
was descending into the tomb like a Pharaoh, or a Ptolemy. There
we left him, alone. He was entering upon that endless tenure,
without air, without light, without change of season, compared
with which every life seems short; such was the stability to which
he had attained, such perhaps was the peace. Centuries as yet
unborn within the dark womb of time would pass by thousands
over that tomb without restoring life to him, but likewise without
adding to his death, and without changing the fact that he had
been.

Hermogenes took my arm to help me go up again to the open
air; it was almost a joy to be above ground once more, to catch
sight of the cold blue sky between two slabs of tawny rock. The
remainder of the voyage was brief. At Alexandria the empress
re-embarked for Rome.

DISCIPLINA AUGUSTA

I RETURNED to Greece by the land route. The journey was long. I had reason to think that this would be my last official tour in the Orient, and I was the more anxious, therefore, to see everything for myself. Antioch, where I stopped for some weeks, appeared to me under a new light; I was less impressed than before by the spell of its theatres and festivals, by the delights of the pleasure gardens of Daphne, and by the brilliant colour in its passing crowds. I was increasingly aware of the eternal frivolity of the populace, mocking and malicious like the people of Alexandria, and of the stupidity of their so-called intellectual activities; likewise of the vulgar display of luxury on the part of the rich. Hardly one of these leading citizens grasped in its entirety my programme for public works and reforms in Asia; they were satisfied to profit by them for their city, and above all for themselves. For a short time I considered advancing Smyrna or Pergamum to the detriment of the arrogant Syrian capital, but the faults of Antioch are those inherent in any metropolis; no great city can escape them. My disgust with urban life made me apply myself even more, if possible, to agrarian reform; I put the finishing touches to the long and complex reorganization of the imperial domains in Asia Minor; the peasants were the better off for it, and the State, too. Crossing Thrace, I went to revisit Hadrianopolis, where veterans of the Dacian and Sarmatian campaigns had settled in great numbers, attracted by land grants and reductions in taxes. The same plan was to be put into operation in Antinoöpolis. I had long since made comparable exemptions everywhere for doctors and professors in the hope of favouring the survival and development of a serious, well-educated middle class. I know the deficiences of this class, but only through it does a State endure.

Athens remained the stop of my choice; I marvelled that its beauty depended so little upon memories, whether my own or those of history; that city seemed new with each new day. I stayed this time with Arrian. He had been initiated like me at Eleusis, so was accordingly adopted by one of the great priestly families of Attica, the Kerykes, as I had been by the family of the Eumolpides. He had married into the Kerykes family; his wife was a proud and elegant young Athenian. The two of them gave me every care. Their house was only a few steps from the new library with which I had just endowed Athens, and which offered every aid to meditation, or to the repose which must precede it: comfortable chairs and adequate heating for winters which are often so sharp; stairways giving ready access to the galleries where books are kept; a luxury of alabaster and gold, quiet and subdued. Particular attention had been paid to the choice of lamps, and to their placing. I felt more and more the need to gather together and conserve our ancient books, and to entrust the making of new copies to conscientious scribes. This noble task seemed to me no less urgent than aid to veterans or subsidies to prolific families of the poor; I warned myself that it would take only a few wars, and the misery that follows them, or a single period of brutality or savagery under a few bad rulers to destroy for ever the ideas passed down with the help of these frail objects in fibre and ink. Each man fortunate enough to benefit to some degree from this legacy of culture seemed to me responsible for protecting it and holding it in trust for the human race.

During that period I read a great deal. I had encouraged Phlegon to compose a series of chronicles, under the name of *Olympiads*, which would continue Xenophon's *Hellenica*, and which would come down to my reign, a bold plan in that it reduced Rome's vast history to a mere sequel of that of Greece. Phlegon's style is annoyingly dry, but it would already be something done to have untangled and assembled the facts. The project inspired me to re-read the historians of other days; their work, judged in the light of my own experience, filled me with sombre thoughts; the energy and good intentions of each statesman seemed of slight avail before this flood so fortuitous and so fatal, this torrent of happenings too confused to be foreseen or directed, or even appraised. The poets, too, engaged me; I liked to conjure those few clear, full voices out of a distant past.

Theognis became a friend, the aristocrat, the exile, observing human activities without illusion and without indulgence, ever ready to denounce the faults and errors which we call our woes. This clear-sighted man had known love's poignant delights; his liaison with Cyrnus, in spite of suspicions, jealousies, and mutual grievances, had endured into the old age of the one and the mature years of the other : the immortality which he was wont to promise to that youth of Megara was more than an empty assurance, since their two memories have come down to me through a space of more than six centuries. But among the ancient poets Antimachus especially won me : I liked his rich but abstruse style, his ample though highly concentrated phrases, like great bronze cups filled with a heavy wine. I preferred his account of Jason's expedition to the more romantic *Argonautica* of Apollonius : Antimachus understood better the mystery of voyages and horizons, and how ephemeral a shadow man throws on this abiding earth. He had wept passionately over the death of his wife, Lydia, and had given her name to a long poem made up of all manners of legends of grief and mourning. That Lydia, whom perhaps I should have taken no notice of as a living being, became a familiar figure for me, dearer than many a feminine face in my own existence. Such poems, though almost forgotten, were little by little restoring to me my faith in immortality.

I revised my own works, the love poems, the occasional pieces, and the ode to the memory of Plotina. One day, perhaps, someone would wish to read all that. A group of obscene verses were matter for hesitation, but I ended, after all, by including them. Our best and most cultivated men write such things. They make a game of it; I should have preferred mine to be more than that, to reflect exactly the naked truth. But there as elsewhere the commonplace entraps us; I was beginning to understand that it takes more than audacity of mind to free us from banality, and that the poet triumphs over routines or imposes his thought upon words only by efforts as long and as persevering as my work of emperor. For my part I could only aspire to the rare good, luck of the amateur : it would already be considerable if from all this rubble two or three verses were to survive. At about this time, however, I outlined a rather ambitious work, half in prose, half in verse, wherein I intended to include the curious facts observed in the course of my life, together with my meditations and certain dreams, mingling the serious and the ironic; all this would have been bound together by the merest thread, a sort of *Satyricon*, but harsher. In it I should have set forth a philosophy which had become my own, the Heraclitean idea of change and return. But I have put aside that project as far too vast.

In that same year I had several conversations with the priestess who had formerly initiated me at Eleusis (and whose name must remain secret) in order to discuss and establish details of the cult of Antinous, one by one. The great Eleusiac symbols continued to exert upon me their calming effect; the world has no meaning, perhaps, but if it does have one, that meaning is expressed at Eleusis more wisely and nobly than anywhere else. It was under this woman's influence that I undertook to plan the administrative divisions of Antinoöpolis, its demes, its streets, its city blocks, on the model of the world of the gods, and at the same time to include there a reflection of my own life. All the deities were to be represented, Hestia and Bacchus, divinities of the hearth and of the orgy, the gods of the heavens, and those of the underworld. I placed my imperial ancestors there, too, Trajan and Nerva, now an integral part of that system of symbols. Plotinia figured; the good Matidia was there, in the likeness of Demeter; my wife herself, with whom at the time my relations were cordial enough, made one of that procession of divinities. Some months later I bestowed the name of my sister Paulina upon a district of Antinoöpolis; I had finally broken off with her as the wife of Servianus, but she had now died and thus had regained her unique position of sister in that city of memories. The site of sorrow was becoming the ideal centre for reunions and recollections, the Elysian Fields of a life, the place where contradictions are resolved and where everything, within its rank, is equally sacred.

Standing at a window in Arrian's house, under night skies alive with stars, I thought of those words which the Egyptian priests had had carved on Antinous' tomb : *He has obeyed the command of heaven.* Can it be that the sky intimates its orders to us, and that only the best among us hear them while the remainder of mankind is aware of no more than oppressive silence? The priestesses of Eleusis and Chabrias both thought so. I should have liked them to be right. In my mind I could see the palm of that hand again, smoothed by death, as I had looked on it for the last time that morning at the embalmers'; the lines which had previously disquieted me in it were no longer visible; the surface was like a wax tablet from which an instruction, once carried out, had been erased. But such lofty affirmations enlighten without re-warming us, like the light of stars, and the night all around us is darker still. If the sacrifice of Antinous had been thrown into the balance in my favour in some divine scale, the results of that terrible gift of self were not yet manifest; the benefits were neither those of life nor even those of immortality. I hardly dared seek a name for them. Sometimes, at rare intervals, a feeble gleam pulsed without warmth on my sky's horizon; but it served to improve neither the world nor myself; I continued to feel more deteriorated than saved.

It was near this period that Quadratus, a bishop of the Christians, sent me a defence of his faith. I had made it a principle to maintain towards that sect the strictly equitable line of conduct which had been Trajan's in his better days: I had just reminded the provincial governors that the protection of the law extends to all citizens, and that defamers of Christians would be punished if they levelled accusations against that group without proof. But any tolerance shown to fanatics is immediately mistaken by them for sympathy with their cause; though I can hardly imagine that Quadratus was hoping to make a Christian of me, he assuredly strove to convince me of the excellence of his doctrine, and to prove, above all, that it offered no harm to the State. I read his work, and was even enough interested to make Phlegon collect some information about the life of the young prophet named Jesus who had founded the sect, but who died a victim of Jewish intolerance about a hundred years ago. This young sage seems to have left behind him some teachings not unlike those of Orpheus, to whom at times his disciples compare him. In spite of Quadratus' singularly flat prose I could discern through it the appealing charm of virtues of simple folk, their kindness, their ingenuousness, and their devotion to each other. All that strongly resembled the fraternities which slaves or poor citizens found almost everywhere in honour of our gods in the crowded quarters of our cities. Within a world which remains, despite all our efforts, hard and indifferent to men's hopes and trials, these small societies for mutual aid offer the unfortunate a source of comfort and support.

But I was aware, too, of certain dangers. Such glorification of virtues befitting children and slaves was made at the expense of more virile and more intellectual qualities; under that narrow, vapid innocence I could detect the fierce intransigence of the sectarian in presence of forms of life and of thought which are not his own, the insolent pride which makes him value himself above other men, and his voluntarily circumscribed vision. I speedily tired of Quadratus' captious arguments, and of those scraps of wisdom ineptly borrowed from the writings of our philosophers. Chabrias, ever preoccupied to offer the gods the worship due them, was disturbed by the progress of sects of this kind among the populace of large cities; he feared for the welfare of our ancient religions, which yoke men to no dogma whatsoever, but lend themselves, on the contrary, to interpretations as varied as nature itself; they allow austere spirits who desire to invent for themselves a higher morality to do so, but they do not bind the masses by precepts so strict as to engender immediate constraint and hypocrisy. Arrian shared these views. I passed a whole evening discussing with him the injunction which consists in loving another as oneself; it is too foreign to the nature of man to be followed with sincerity by the average person, who will never love anyone but himself, and it is not at all suited to the philosopher, who is little given to self-love.

On many points, however, the thinking of our philosophers also seemed to be limited and confused, if not sterile. Three-quarters of our intellectual performances are no more than decorations upon a void; I wondered if that increasing vacuity was due to the lowering of intelligence or to moral decline; whatever the cause, mediocrity of mind was matched almost everywhere by shocking selfishness and dishonesty. I had directed Herod Atticus to supervise the construction of a chain of aqueducts in the Troad; he made use of that trust to squander public funds in shameful fashion, and when called to render an accounting sent back the insolent reply that he was rich enough to cover all deficits; such wealth was itself a scandal. His father, who had but recently died, had made a discreet arrangement to disinherit him by multiplying bounties to the Athenian citizenry; young Herod refused outright to pay the paternal legacy, and a law suit ensued which is still going on. In Smyrna my erstwhile intimate, Polemo, had the effrontery to oust a deputation of senators from Rome who had thought it reasonable to count on his hospitality. Your father Antoninus, the gentlest of men, was enraged; statesman and sophist finally came to blows over the matter; such pugilism, if unworthy of an emperor-to-be, was still more disgraceful for a Greek philosopher. Favorinus, that greedy dwarf whom I had showered with money and honours, was peddling witticisms on all sides at my expense: the thirty legions which I commanded were, according to him, my only strong arguments in the philosophical bouts wherein I had the vanity to indulge, and wherein, he explained, he took care to leave the last word to the emperor. That was to tax me with both presumption and stupidity, but it amounted, above all, to admission of singular cowardice on his part. Pedants are always annoyed when others know their narrow speciality as well as they do themselves, and everything now served as pretext for their ugly remarks: because I had added the much neglected works of Hesiod and Ennius to the school curriculum, those routine minds promptly attributed to me the desire to dethrone Homer, and the gentle Virgil as well (whom nevertheless I was always quoting). There was nothing to be done with people of that sort.

Arrian was better than that. I liked to talk with him on all subjects. He had retained a fervent and profoundly serious memory of the Bithynian youth; I was grateful to him for ranking that love, which he had witnessed, with the famous mutual attachments of antiquity; from time to time we spoke of it, but although no lie was uttered I frequently had the impression of a certain falsity in our words; the truth was being covered beneath the sublime. I was almost as much disappointed by Chabrias: his blind devotion to Antinous had been like that of an aged slave for a young master, but, absorbed as he was in the worship of the new god, he seemed to have lost all remembrance of the living boy. My black Euphorion had at least observed our life at closer range. Arrian and Chabrias were dear to me, and I felt myself in no way superior to those two decent men, but sometimes it seemed to me that I was the only person struggling to keep his eyes wholly open.

Yes, Athens remained exquisite, and I did not regret the choice of Greek disciplines for my life. Everything in us which is human, or well-ordered and clearly thought out comes to us from them. But I was beginning to feel that Rome's seriousness, even if somewhat heavy, and its sense of continuity and love of the concrete, had all been needed for the full realization of what was for Greece still only an admirable idea, a splendid impulse of the soul. Plato had written the *Republic* and glorified the Just, but we were the ones who were striving, warned by our own errors, to make the State a machine fit to serve man, with the least possible risk of crushing him. The word *philanthropy* is Greek, but the legist Salvius Julianus and I are the ones who are working to change the wretched condition of the slaves. Rome had taught me prudence and assiduous application to detail, those virtues which temper the boldness of broad general views.

There were times, too, when deep within myself I would come upon those vast, melancholy landscapes of Virgil, and his twilights veiled by tears; if I searched deeper still I would encounter the burning sadness of Spain and its barren violence; I reflected upon the varied blood, Celtic, Iberian, Punic perhaps, which must have infiltrated into the veins of those Roman colonists in Italica: I recalled that my father had been surnamed 'the African'. Greece had helped me evaluate those elements in my nature which were not Greek. Likewise for Antinous: I had made him the very image and symbol of that country so passionate for beauty, and he would be, perhaps, the last of its gods; yet the refinements of Persia and the savagery of Thrace had met in Bithynia with the shepherds of ancient Arcadia; that slightly arched nose recalled profiles of Osröes' pages; the broad visage and high cheekbones were those of the Thracian horsemen who gallop along the shores of the Bosphorus, and who burst forth at night into wild, sad song. No formula is so complete as to contain all.

That year I completed the revision of the Athenian constitution, which I had begun long before. For the new instrument I went back, in so far as possible, to Cleisthenes' ancient democratic laws. Governmental costs were lightened by reducing the number of officials; I tried, too, to put a stop to the farming of taxes, a disastrous system unfortunately still employed here and there by local administrations. University endowments, established at about the same period, helped Athens to become once more an important centre of learning. Beauty lovers who flocked to that city before my time had been content to admire its monuments without concern for the growing poverty of the inhabitants. On the contrary, I had done my utmost to increase the resources of that poor land. One of the great projects of my reign was realized shortly before my departure: the establishment of annual assemblies in Athens, wherein delegates from all the Greek world would hereafter transact all affairs for Greece, restored this small, perfect city to its due rank of metropolis. The plan had taken shape only after delicate negotiations with cities jealous of Athens' supremacy and still nursing ancient resentments against her; little by little, however, common sense and even enthusiasm carried the day. The first of those assemblies coincided with the opening of the Olympieion for public worship; that temple was becoming more than ever the symbol of a reawakened Greece.

On that occasion a series of spectacles was given, with marked success, in the theatre of Dionysos; my seat there was beside that of the Hierophant, and only slightly higher; thereafter the priest of Antinous had his place, too, among the notables and the clergy. I had had the stage of the theatre enlarged and ornamented with new bas-reliefs; on one of these friezes my young Bithynian was receiving a kind of eternal freedom of the city from the Eleusinian goddesses. In the Panathenaic stadium, transformed for a few hours into a forest of mythology, I staged a hunt in which some thousand wild animals figured; thus was revived for the brief space of the festival that primitive and rustic town of Hippolytus, servitor of Diana, and Theseus, companion of Hercules.

A few days later I left Athens. Nor have I returned there since.

* * *

The governing of Italy, left for centuries wholly in the hands of the praetors, had never been definitely codified. The *Perpetual Edict*, which controls administration once and for all, dates from this period of my life. For years I had been corresponding with Salvius Julianus about these reforms, and my return to Rome served to hasten their completion. The Italian cities were not to be deprived of their civil liberties; on the contrary, we had everything to gain, in that respect, as in others, if we did not forcibly impose upon them a factitious unity. I am even surprised that such townships, many of which are older than Rome, should be so ready to renounce their customs (some of them wise, indeed) in order to follow the capital in every respect. My purpose was simply to diminish the mass of contradictions and abuses which eventually turn legal procedure into a wilderness where decent people hardly dare venture and where bandits abound. Such endeavours obliged me to travel frequently from one place to another about the country. I made several stays in Baiae, in the former villa of Cicero which I had purchased early in my reign; this province of Campania interested me, for it reminded me of Greece. On the edge of the Adriatic, in the small city of Hadria whence my ancestors had emigrated to Spain nearly four centuries earlier, I was honoured with the highest municipal offices. Near the stormy sea whose name I bear, I came upon some of my family urns in a ruined cemetery. There I meditated on those men, of whom I knew almost nothing but from whom I sprang, and whose race would end with me.

In Rome they were enlarging my mausoleum, since Decrianus had cleverly redrawn the plans; they are still at work upon it, even now. The idea for those circular galleries came from Egypt, and likewise the ramps descending to underground chambers; I had conceived of a colossal tomb to be reserved not for myself alone, or for my immediate successors, but as the eventual resting-place of future emperors for centuries to come; princes yet to be born have thus their places already marked in this palace of death. I saw also to the ornamentation of the cenotaph erected on the Field of Mars in memory of Antinous; a barge from Alexandria had already discharged its load of sphinxes and obelisks for this work. A new project long occupied me, and has not ceased to do so, namely, the construction of the Odeon, a model library provided with halls for courses and lectures and serving as a centre of Greek culture in Rome. I made it less splendid than the new library at Ephesus, built three or four years ago, and graced it with less elegance than the library of Athens, but I intend to make this foundation a close second to, if not the equal of, the Museum of Alexandria; its further development will rest with you. In working upon it I often think of that noble inscription which Plotina had had placed over the door of the library established by her efforts in Trajan's Forum: *Dispensary to the Soul.*

The Villa was near enough completion to have my collections transported to it, my musical instruments and the several thousand books bought here and there in the course of my travels. I gave a series of banquets where everything was assembled with care, both the menu for the repasts and the somewhat restricted list of my guests. My goal was to have all in harmony with the calm beauty of these gardens and these halls, to have fruits as exquisite as the music, and the sequence of courses as perfect as the chasing on the silver plates. For the first time I took an interest in the choice of foods, giving orders that the oysters must come from Lucrinus and the crayfish be taken from the rivers of Gaul. My dislike of the combined pomposity and negligence which too often characterize an emperor's table led me to rule that all viands be shown to me before they were presented to any of my guests, even to the least of them. I insisted upon verifying the accounts of cooks and caterers myself; there were times when I recalled that my grandfather had been miserly.

Neither the small Greek theatre of the Villa, nor the Latin theatre, hardly larger, had been completed, but I had a few plays produced in them nevertheless, tragedies, pantomimes, musical dramas, and old, local farces. I delighted above all in the subtle gymnastics of the dance, and discovered a weakness for women with castanets, who reminded me of the region of Gades and the first spectacles which I had attended as a child. I liked the brittle sound, those uplifted arms, the furling and unfurling of veils, the dancer who changed now from woman to cloud, and then to bird, who became sometimes the boat and sometimes the wave. For one of these creatures I even took a fancy, though briefly enough. Nor had the kennels and studs been neglected in my absence; I came back to the rough coats of the hounds, the silken horses, the fair pack of the pages. I arranged a few hunting parties in Umbria, on the shore of Lake Trasimene, or nearer Rome, in the Alban woods.

Pleasure had regained its place in my life; my secretary Onesimus served me as purveyor. He knew when to avoid certain resemblances, or when, just the reverse, it was better to seek them out. But such a hurried and half attentive lover was hardly loved in return. Now and then I met with a being finer and gentler than others, someone worth hearing talk, and perhaps worth seeing again. Those happy chances were rare, though I may have been to blame. Ordinarily I did no more than appease (or deceive) my hunger. At other times my indifference for such games was like that of an old man.

In my wakeful hours I took to pacing the corridors of the Villa, proceeding from room to room, sometimes disturbing a mason at work as he laid a mosaic. I would examine, in passing, a Satyr of Praxiteles and then would pause before the effigies of the beloved dead. Each room had its own, and each portico. Sheltering the flame of my lamp in one hand, I would lightly touch that breast of stone. Such encounters served to complicate the memory's task; I had to put aside like a curtain the pallor of the marble to go back, in so far as possible, from those motionless contours to the living form, from the hard texture of Paros or Pentelikon to the flesh itself. Again I would resume my round; the statue, once interrogated, would relapse into darkness; a few steps away my lamp would reveal another image; these great white figures differed little from ghosts. I reflected bitterly upon those magic passes whereby the Egyptian priests had drawn the soul of the dead youth into the wooden effigies which they use in their rites; I had done like them; I had cast a spell over stones which, in their turn, had spellbound me; nevermore should I escape from their cold and silence, henceforth closer to me than the warmth and voices of the living; it was with resentment that I gazed upon that dangerous countenance and its elusive smile. Still, a few hours later, once more abed, I would decide to order another statue from Papias of Aphrodisias; I would insist upon a more exact modelling of the cheeks, just where they hollow insensibly under the temples, and a gentler inclination of the head toward the shoulder; I would have the garlands of the vine leaves or the clusters of precious stones give way to the glory of the unadorned hair. I took care to have the weight of these bas-reliefs and these busts reduced by drilling out the inside, thus leaving them easier to transport. The truest likenesses among such portraits have accompanied me everywhere; it no longer matters to me whether they are beautiful or not.

In appearance my life was reasonable: I applied myself more steadily than ever to my task as emperor, exerting more discrimination, perhaps, if less ardour than before. I had somewhat lost my zest for new ideas and new contacts, and that flexibility of mind which used once to help me enter into another's thought, and to learn from it while I judged it. My curiosity, wherein I could formerly trace the mainspring of my thinking and one of the bases of my method, was now aroused only over quite futile details: I opened letters addressed to my friends, to their indignation; such a glimpse into their loves and domestic quarrels amused me for the moment. But an element of suspicion was mingled in this: for a few days I was even prey to the dread of being poisoned, that horrible fear which I had previously beheld in the eyes of the ailing Trajan, and which a ruler dare not avow, since it would seem grotesque so long as unjustified by the event. Such an obsession may seem surprising in one who was already deep in meditation upon death, but I do not pretend to be more consistent than others. When confronted by the least stupidity or the commonest petty contriving I was seized with inward fury and wild impatience (nor did I exempt myself from my own disgust). For example, Juvenal, in one of his *Satires*, was bold enough to attack the actor Paris, whom I liked. I was tired of that pompous, tirading poet; I had little relish for his coarse disdain of the Orient and Greece, or for his affected delight in the so-called simplicity of our forefathers; his mixture of detailed descriptions of vice with virtuous declamation titillates the reader's senses without shaking him from his hypocrisy. As a man of letters, however, he was entitled to certain consideration; I had him summoned to Tibur to tell him myself of his sentence to exile. This scorner of the luxuries and pleasures of Rome would be able hereafter to study provincial life and manners at first hand; his insults to the handsome Paris had drawn the curtain on his own play.

Favorinus, towards that same time, settled into his comfortable exile in Chios (where I should have rather liked to dwell myself), whence his biting voice came no longer to my ears. At about this period, too, I ordered a wisdom vendor to be chased ignominiously from a banquet hall, an ill-washed Cynic who complained of dying of hunger, as if that breed merited anything else. I took great pleasure in seeing the prater packed off, bent double by fear, midst the barking of dogs and the mocking laughter of pages. Literary and philosophical riff-raff no longer impressed me.

The least setback in political affairs exasperated me just as did the slightest inequality in a pavement at the Villa, or the smallest dripping of wax on the marble surface of a table, the merest defect of an object which one would wish to be free of imperfections and stains. A report from Arrian, recently appointed governor of Cappadocia, cautioned me against Pharasmanes, who was continuing in his small kingdom along the Caspian Sea to play that double game which had cost us dear under Trajan. This petty prince was slyly pushing hordes of barbarian Alani toward our frontiers; his quarrels with Armenia endangered peace in the Orient. When summoned to Rome he refused to come, just as he had already refused to attend the conference at Samosata four years before. By way of excuse he sent me a present of three hundred robes of gold, royal garments which I ordered to be worn in the arena by criminals loosed to wild beasts. That rash gesture solaced me like the action of one who scratches himself nearly raw.

I had a secretary, a very mediocre fellow, whom I retained because he knew all the routines of the chancellery, but who provoked me by his stubborn, snarling self-sufficiency, his refusal to try new methods, and his mania for arguing endlessly over trivial details. This fool irritated me one day more than usual; I raised my hand to slap him; unhappily, I was holding a style, which blinded his right eye. I shall never forget that howl of pain, that arm awkwardly bent to ward off the blow, that visage convulsed from which the blood spurted. I had Hermogenes sent for at once, to give the first care, and the oculist Capito was then consulted. But in vain; the eye was gone. Some days later the man resumed his work, a bandage across his face. I sent for him and asked him humbly to fix the amount of compensation which was his due. He replied with a wry smile that he asked of me only one thing, another right eye. He ended, however, by accepting a pension. I have kept him in my service; his presence serves me as a warning, and a punishment, perhaps. I had not wished to injure the wretch. But I had not desired, either, that a boy who loved me should die in his twentieth year.

* * *

Jewish affairs were going from bad to worse. Construction was nearing completion in Jerusalem, in spite of the violent opposition of Zealot groups. A certain number of errors had been committed, not irreparable in themselves but immediately seized upon by fomenters of trouble for their own advantage. The Tenth Legion Fretensis has a wild boar for its emblem; when its standard was placed at the city gates, as is the custom, the populace, unused to painted or sculptured images (deprived as they have been for centuries by a superstition highly unfavourable to the progress of the arts), mistook that symbol for a swine, the meat of which is forbidden them, and read in that insignificant fact an affront to the customs of Israel. The festivals of the Jewish New Year, celebrated with a din of trumpets and rams' horns, gave rise every year to brawling and bloodshed; our authorities accordingly forbade the public reading of a certain legendary account devoted to the exploits of a Jewish heroine who was said to have become, under an assumed name, the concubine of a king of Persia, and to have instigated a savage massacre of the enemies of her despised and persecuted race. The rabbis managed to read at night what the governor Tineus Rufus forbade them to read by day; that barbarous story, wherein Persians and Jews rivalled each other in atrocities, roused the nationalistic fervour of the Zealots to frenzy. Finally, this same Tineus Rufus, a man of good judgement in other respects and not uninterested in Israel's traditions and fables, decided to extend to the Jewish practice of circumcision the same severe penalties of the law which I had recently promulgated against castration (and which was aimed especially at cruelties perpetrated upon young slaves for the sake of exorbitant gain or debauch). He hoped thus to obliterate one of the marks whereby Israel claims to distinguish itself from the rest of human kind. I took the less notice of the danger of that measure, when I received word of it, in that many wealthy and enlightened Jews whom one meets in Alexandria and in Rome have ceased to submit their children to a practice which makes them ridiculous in the public baths and gymnasiums; and they even arrange to conceal the evidence on themselves. I was unaware of the extent to which these banker collectors of myrrhine vases differed from the true Israel.

As I said, nothing in all that was beyond repair, but the hatred, the mutual contempt, and the rancour were so. In principle, Judaism had its place among the religions of the empire; in practice, Israel has refused for centuries to be one people among many others, with one god among the gods. The most primitive Dacians know that their Zalmoxis is called Jupiter in Rome; the Phoenician Baal of Mount Casius has been readily identified with the Father who holds Victory in his hand, and of Whom wisdom is born; the Egyptians, though so proud of their myths some thousands of years old, are willing to see in Osiris a Bacchus with funeral attributes; harsh Mithra admits himself brother to Apollo. No people but Israel has the arrogance to confine truth wholly within the narrow limits of a single conception of the divine, thereby insulting the manifold nature of the Deity, who contains all; no other god has inspired his worshippers with disdain and hatred for those who pray at different

altars. I was only the more anxious to make Jerusalem a city like
the others, where several races and several beliefs could live in
peace; but I was wrong to forget that in any combat between
fanaticism and common sense the latter has rarely the upper
hand. The clergy of the ancient city were scandalized by the
opening of schools where Greek literature was taught; the rabbi
Joshua, a pleasant, learned man with whom I had frequently
conversed in Athens, but who was trying to excuse himself to
his people for his foreign culture and his relations with us, now
ordered his disciples not to take up such profane studies unless
they could find an hour which was neither day nor night, since
Jewish law must be studied night and day. Ismael, an important
member of the Sanhedrin, who supposedly adhered to the side
of Rome, let his nephew Ben-Dama die rather than accept the
services of the Greek surgeon sent to him by Tineus Rufus.
While in Tibur means were still being sought to conciliate differences without appearing to yield to the demands of fanatics,
affairs in the East took a turn for the worse; a Zealot revolt
triumphed in Jerusalem.

An adventurer born of the very dregs of the people, a fellow
named Simon who entitled himself Bar-Kochba, Son of the Star,
played the part of firebrand or incendiary mirror in that revolt.
I could judge this Simon only by hearsay; I have seen him but
once face to face, the day a centurion brought me his severed
head. Yet I am disposed to grant him that degree of genius which
must always be present in one who rises so fast and so high in
human affairs; such ascendancy is not gained without at least
some crude skill. The Jews of the moderate party were the
first to accuse this supposed Son of the Star of deceit and im-
posture; I believe rather that his untrained mind was of the type
which is taken in by its own lies, and that fanaticism in his case
went hand in hand with guile. He paraded as the hero whom the
Jewish people had awaited for centuries in order to gratify their
ambitions and their hate; this demagogue proclaimed himself
Messiah and King of Israel. The aged Akiba, in a foolish state
of exaltation, led the adventurer through the streets of Jerusalem,
holding his horse by the bridle; the high priest Eleazar re-
dedicated the temple, said to be defiled from the time that un-

circumcised visitors had crossed its threshold. Stacks of arms hidden underground for nearly twenty years were distributed to the rebels by agents of the Son of the Star; they also had recourse to weapons formerly rejected for our ordnance as defective (and purposely constructed thus by Jewish workers in our arsenals over a period of years). Zealot groups attacked isolated Roman garrisons and massacred our soldiers with refinements of cruelty which recalled the worst memories of the Jewish revolt under Trajan; Jerusalem finally fell wholly into the hands of the insurgents, and the new quarters of Aelia Capitolina were set burning like a torch. The first detachments of the Twenty-Second Legion Deiotariana, sent from Egypt with utmost speed under the command of the legate of Syria, Publius Marcellus, were routed by bands ten times their number. The revolt had become war, and war to the bitter end.

Two legions, the Twelfth Fulminata and the Sixth Ferrata, came immediately to reinforce the troops already stationed in Judaea; some months later, Julius Severus took charge of the military operations. He had formerly pacified the mountainous regions of Northern Britain, and brought with him some small contingents of British auxiliaries accustomed to fighting on difficult terrain. Our heavily equipped troops and our officers trained to the square or the phalanx formation of pitched battles were hard put to it to adapt themselves to that war of skirmishes and surprise attacks which even in open country retained the techniques of street fighting. Simon, a great man in his way, had divided his followers into hundreds of squadrons posted on mountain ridges or ambushed in caverns and abandoned quarries, or even hidden in houses of the teeming suburbs of the cities. Severus was quick to grasp that such an elusive enemy could be exterminated, but not conquered; he resigned himself to a war of attrition. The peasants, fired by Simon's enthusiasm, or terrorized by him, made common cause with the Zealots from the start, each rock became a bastion, each vineyard a trench; each tiny farm had to be starved out, or taken by assault. Jerusalem was not recaptured until the beginning of the third year, when the last efforts to negotiate proved futile; what little of the Jewish city had been spared by the destruction under Titus was now wiped out. Severus closed his eyes for a long time, voluntarily, to the flagrant complicity of the other large cities, now become the last fortresses of the enemy; they were later attacked and reconquered in their turn, street by street and ruin by ruin.

In those times of trial my place was with the army, and in Judaea. I had utter confidence in my two lieutenants, but it was all the more fitting, therefore, that I should be present to share responsibility for decisions which, however carried out, promised atrocities to come. At the end of a second summer of campaign I made my preparations for travel, but with bitterness; once more Euphorion packed up my toilet kit, made long before by an artisan of Smyrna and somewhat dented by wear, my case of books and maps, and the ivory statuette of the Imperial Genius with his lamp of silver; I landed at Sidon early in autumn.

The army is the first of my callings; I have never gone back into it without feeling repaid for my constraints there by certain inner compensations; I do not regret having passed the last two active years of my existence in sharing with the legion the harshness and desolation of that Palestine campaign. I had become again the man clad in leather and iron, putting aside all that is not immediate, sustained by the routines of a hard life, though somewhat slower than of old to mount my horse, or to dismount, somewhat more taciturn, perhaps more sombre, surrounded as ever (the gods alone know why) by a devotion from the troops which was both religious and fraternal. During this last stay in the army I made an encounter of inestimable value: I took a young tribune named Celer, to whom I was attached, as my aide-de-camp. You know him; he has not left me. I admired that handsome face of a casqued Minerva, but on the whole the senses played as small a part in this affection as they can so long as one is alive. I recommend Celer to you: he has all the qualities to be sought in an officer placed in second rank; his very virtues will always keep him from pushing into first place. Once again, but in circumstances somewhat different from those of yore, I had come upon one of those beings whose destiny is to devote himself, to love, and to serve. Since I have known him Celer has had no thought which was not for my comfort or my security; I lean still upon that firm shoulder.

In the spring of the third year of campaign the army laid siege to the citadel of Bethar, an eagle's nest where Simon and his partisans held out for nearly a year against the slow tortures of hunger, thirst, and despair, and where the Son of the Star saw his faithful perish one by one without consenting to surrender. Our army suffered almost as much as the rebels, for the latter, on retiring, had burned the forests, laid waste the fields, slaughtered the cattle, and polluted the wells by throwing our dead therein; these methods from savage times were hideous in a land naturally arid and already consumed to the bone by centuries of folly and fury. The summer was hot and unhealthy; fever and dysentery decimated our troops, but an admirable discipline continued to rule in those legions, forced to inaction and yet obliged to be constantly on the alert; the army, sick and harassed, was sustained by a kind of silent rage in which I began to share. My body no longer withstood as well as it once did the fatigues of campaigning, the torrid days, the alternately suffocating or chilly nights, the harsh wind, and the gritty dust; I sometimes left the bacon and boiled lentils of the camp mess in my bowl, and went hungry. A bad cough stayed with me well into the summer, nor was I the only one in such case. In my dispatches to the Senate I suppressed the formula which is regulation for the opening of official communications: *The emperor and the army are well.* The emperor and the army were, on the contrary, dangerously weary. At night, after the last conversation with Severus, the last audience with fugitives from the enemy side, the last courier from Rome, the last message from Publius Marcellus, left to clean out the surroundings of Jerusalem, or from Rufus, busy with the reorganization of Gaza, Euphorion would measure my bath water sparingly into a tub of tarred canvas; I would lie down on my bed and try to think.

There is no denying it, that war in Judaea was one of my defeats. The crimes of Simon and the madness of Akiba were not of my making, but I reproached myself for having been blind in Jerusalem, heedless in Alexandria, impatient in Rome. I had not known how to find words which would have prevented, or at least retarded, this outburst of rage in a nation; I had not known in time how to be either supple enough or sufficiently firm. Surely we had no reason to be unduly disturbed, and still less need to despair; the blunder and the reversal had occurred only in our relations with Israel; everywhere else at this critical hour we were reaping the reward of sixteen years of generosity in the Orient. Simon had supposed that he could count on a revolt in the Arab world similar to the uprising which had darkened the last years of Trajan's reign; even more, he had ventured to bank on Parthian aid. He was mistaken, and that error of calculation was causing his slow death in the besieged citadel of Bethar; the Arab tribes were drawing apart from the Jewish communities; the Parthians remained faithful to the treaties. The synagogues of the great Syrian cities proved undecided or lukewarm, the most ardent among them contenting themselves with sending money in secret to the Zealots; the Jewish population in Alexandria, though naturally so turbulent, remained calm; the abscess in Jewish affairs remained local, confined within the arid region which extends from Jordan to the sea; this ailing finger could safely be cauterized, or amputated. And nevertheless, in a sense, the evil days which had immediately preceded my reign seemed to begin over again. In the past Quietus had burned down Cyrene, executed the dignitaries of Laodicea, and recaptured a ruined Edessa. . . . The evening courier had just informed me that we had re-established ourselves on the heap of tumbled stones which I called Aelia Capitolina and which the Jews still called Jerusalem; we had burned Ascalon, and had been forced to mass executions of rebels in Gaza. . . . If sixteen years of rule by a prince so pacifically inclined were to culminate in the Palestine campaign, then the chances for peace in the world looked dim ahead.

I raised myself on my elbow, uneasy on the narrow camp bed. To be sure, there were some Jews who had escaped the Zealot contagion: even in Jerusalem the Pharisees spat on the ground before Akiba, treating that fanatic like an old fool who threw to the wind the solid advantages of the Roman peace, and shouting to him that grass would grow from his mouth before Israel's victory would be seen on this earth. But I preferred even false prophets to those lovers of order who, though despising us, counted on us to protect them from Simon's demands upon their gold, placed with Syrian bankers, and upon their farms in Galilee. I thought of the deserters from the camp who, a few hours back, had been sitting in my tent, humble, conciliatory, servile, but always managing to turn their backs to the image of my Genius. Our best agent, Elias Ben-Abayad, who played the role of informer and spy for Rome, was justly despised by both camps; he was nevertheless the most intelligent man in the group, a liberal mind but a man sick at heart, torn between love for his people and his liking for us and for our culture; he too, however, thought essentially only of Israel. Joshua Ben-Kisma, who preached appeasement, was but a more timid, or more hypocritical Akiba. Even in the rabbi Joshua, who had long been my counsellor in Jewish affairs, I had felt irreconcilable difference under that compliance and desire to please, a point where two opposite kinds of thinking meet only to engage in combat. Our territories extended over hundreds of leagues and thousands of stadia beyond that dry, hilly horizon, but the rock of Bethar was our frontier; we could level to dust the massive walls of that citadel where Simon in his frenzy was consummating his suicide, but we could not prevent that race from answering us 'No'.

A mosquito hummed over me; Euphorion, who was getting on in years, had failed to close exactly the thin curtains of gauze; books and maps left on the ground rattled in the low wind which crept under the tent wall. Sitting up on my bed, I drew on my boots and groped for my tunic and belt with its dagger; I went out to breathe the night air. I walked through the wide straight streets of the camp, empty at that late hour, but lighted like city streets; sentries saluted formally as I passed; alongside the barracks which served for hospital I caught the stale stench of the dysenterics. I proceeded toward the earthwork which separated us from the precipice, and from the enemy. A sentinel, perilously outlined by the moon, was making his round with long, even tread; his passage and return was one part of the movement of that immense machine in which I was the pivot; for a moment I was stirred by the spectacle of that solitary form, that brief flame burning in the breast of a man midst a world of dangers. An arrow whistled by, hardly more irksome than the mosquito which had troubled me in my tent; I leaned to rest against the sandbags of the barricading wall.

For some years people have credited me with strange insight, and with knowledge of divine secrets. But they are mistaken; I have no such power. It is true, however, that during those nights of Bethar some disturbing phantoms passed before my eyes. The perspectives afforded the mind from the height of those barren hills were less majestic than these of the Janiculum, and less golden than those of Cape Sunion; they offered the reverse and the nadir. I admitted that it was indeed vain to hope for an eternity for Athens and for Rome which is accorded neither to objects nor men, and which the wisest among us deny even to the gods. These subtle and complex forms of life, these civilizations comfortably installed in their refinements of ease and of art, the very freedom of mind to seek and to judge, all this depended upon countless rare chances, upon conditions almost impossible to bring about, and none of which could be expected to endure. We would manage to destroy Simon; Arrian would be able to protect Armenia from Alani invasions. But other hordes would come and other false phophets. Our feeble efforts to ameliorate man's estate would be but vaguely continued by our successors; the seeds of error and of ruin contained even in the good would, on the contrary, increase to monstrous proportions in the course of centuries. A world wearied of us would seek other masters; what had seemed to us wise would be pointless for them, what we had found beautiful they would abominate. Like the initiate to Mithraism the human race has need, perhaps, of a periodical blood-bath and descent into the grave. I could see the return of barbaric codes, of implacable gods, of unquestioned despotism of savage chieftains, a world broken up into enemy states and eternally prey to insecurity. Other sentinels menaced by arrows would patrol the walls of future cities; the stupid, cruel, and obscene game would go on, and the human species in growing older would doubtless add new refinements of horror. Our epoch, the faults and limitations of which I knew better than anyone else, would perhaps be considered one day, by contrast, as one of the golden ages of man.

Natura deficit, fortuna, mutatur, deus omnia cernit. Nature

fails us, fortune changes, a god beholds all things from on high:
I fingered the stone of a ring on which, on a day of bitter depres-
sion, I had had those few sad words engraved. I went deeper in
disillusion, and perhaps into blasphemy: I was beginning to
find it natural, if not just, that we should perish. Our literature
is nearing exhaustion, our arts are falling asleep; Pancrates is not
Homer, nor is Arrian a Xenophon; when I have tried to im-
mortalize Antinous in stone no Praxiteles has come to hand. Our
sciences have been at a standstill from the times of Aristotle and
Archimedes; our technical development is inadequate to the
strain of a long war; even our pleasure-lovers grow weary of delight. More civilized ways of living and more liberal thinking in
the course of the last century are the work of a very small minor-
ity of good minds; the masses remain wholly ignorant, fierce and
cruel when they can be so, and in any case limited and selfish; it
is safe to wager that they will never change. Our effort has been
compromised in advance by too many greedy procurators and
publicans, too many suspicious senators, too many brutal cen-
turions. Nor is time granted oftener to empires than to men to
learn from past errors. Although a weaver would wish to mend
his web or a clever calculator would correct his mistakes, and the
artist would try to retouch his masterpiece if still imperfect or
slightly damaged, Nature prefers to start again from the very
clay, from chaos itself, and this horrible waste is what we term
natural order.

I raised my head and moved slightly in order to limber myself. From the top of Simon's citadel vague gleams reddened the
sky, unexplained manifestations of the nocturnal life of the
enemy. The wind was blowing from Egypt; a whirl of dust passed
by like a spectre; the flattened rims of the hills reminded me of
the Arabic range in moonlight. I went slowly back, drawing a
fold of my cloak over my mouth, provoked with myself for
having devoted to hollow meditations upon the future a night
which I could have employed to prepare the work of the next
day, or to sleep. The collapse of Rome, if it were to come about,
would concern my successors; in that eight hundred and forty-
seventh year of the Roman era my task consisted of stifling the
revolt in Judaea and bringing back from the Orient, without too

great loss, an ailing army. In crossing the esplanade I slipped at times on the blood of some rebel executed the evening before. I lay down on my bed without undressing, to be awakened two hours later by the trumpets at dawn.

* * *

All my life long I had been on the best of terms with my body; I had implicitly counted upon its docility, and its strength. That close alliance was beginning to dissolve; my body was no longer at one with my will and my mind, and with what after all, however ineptly, I must call my soul; the ready comrade of other days was only a slave sulking at his task. In fact, my body was afraid of me; continually now I was aware of the obscure presence of fear, of a feeling of constriction in my chest which was not yet pain, but the first step toward it. I had long been used to insomnia, but from this time on sleep was worse than vigil; hardly would I doze off before there were frightful awakenings. I was subject to headaches which Hermogenes attributed to the heat of the climate and the helmet's weight; by evening, after prolonged fatigue, I sank into a chair like one falling; rising to receive Rufus or Severus was an effort for which I had to prepare well in advance; when seated I leaned heavily on the arms of my chair, and my thigh muscles trembled like those of an exhausted runner. The slightest motion became actual labour, and of such labours life was now composed.

An accident almost ridiculous, a mere childish indisposition, brought to light the true malady hidden beneath that appalling fatigue. During a meeting of the general staff I had a nose bleed, but took little notice of it at first; it persisted, however, until the time for the evening meal; I awoke at night to find myself drenched in blood. I called Celer, who slept in the next tent, and he in his turn roused Hermogenes, but the horrid warm flood went on. With careful hands the young officer wiped away the liquid which smirched my face. At dawn I was seized with retching as are the condemned in Rome who open their veins in their bath. They warmed my chilled body the best they could with the aid of blankets and hot packs; to staunch the blood Hermogenes prescribed snow; it was not to be had in camp; coping with innumerable difficulties Celer had it brought from the summit of Mount Hermon. I learned later that they had despaired of my life, and I myself felt attached to it by no more than the merest thread, as imperceptible as the too rapid pulse which now dismayed my physician. But the sudden, inexplicable haemorrhage came to an end; I got up again and strove to live as before, but did not succeed. When, but poorly restored to health, I had imprudently attempted an evening ride, I received a second warning, more serious than the first. For the space of a second I felt my heart-beats quicken, then slow down, falter, and cease; I seemed to fall like a stone into some black well which is doubtless death. If death it was, it is a mistake to call it silent: I was swept down by cataracts, and deafened like a diver by the roaring of waters. I did not reach bottom, but came to the surface again, choking for breath. All my strength in that moment, which I thought my last, had been concentrated into my hand as I clutched at Celer, who was standing beside me; he later showed me the marks of my fingers upon his shoulder. But that brief agony was, like all bodily experiences, indescribable, and remains the secret of him who has lived through it, whether he would tell it or no. Since that time I have passed similar crises, though never identical, and no doubt one does not go twice (and still live) through that terror and that night. Hermogenes finally diagnosed an initial stage of hydropic heart; there was no choice but to accept the orders given me by this illness, which had suddenly become my master, and to consent to a long period of inaction, if not of rest, limiting the perspectives of my life for a time to the frame of a bed. I was almost ashamed of such an ailment, wholly internal and barely visible, without fever, abscess, or intestinal pain, with its only symptom a somewhat hoarser breathing and a livid mark left by the sandal strap across the swollen foot.

An extraordinary silence reigned round my tent; the entire camp of Bethar seemed to have become a sick room. The aromatic oil which burned below my Genius rendered the close air of this canvas cage heavier still; the pounding of my arteries made me think vaguely of the island of the Titans on the edge of night. At other moments the insufferable noise changed to that of galloping horses thudding down on wet earth; the mind so carefully

reined in for nearly fifty years was wandering; the tall body was
floating adrift; I resigned myself to be that tired man who
absently counted the star-and-diamond pattern of his blanket. I
gazed at the white blur of a marble bust in the shadow; a chant
in honour of Epona, goddess of horses, which used to be sung
by my Spanish nurse, a tall, sombre woman who looked like a
Fate, came back to me from the depths of more than half a
century's time. The long days, and then the nights, seemed
measured out not by the clepsydra but by the brown drops which
Hermogenes counted one by one into a cup of glass.

At evening I mustered my strength to listen to Rufus' report:
the war was nearing its end; Akiba, who had ostensibly retired
from public affairs since the outbreak of hostilities, was devoting
himself to the teaching of rabbinic law in the small city of Usfa
in Galilee; his lecture room had become the centre of Zealot
resistance; secret passages were transcribed from one cipher to
another by the hands of this nonagenarian and transmitted to the
partisans of Simon; the fanatic students who surrounded the old
man had to be sent off by force to their homes. After long hesitation Rufus decided to ban the study of Jewish law as seditious; a
few days later Akiba, who had disregarded that decree, was
arrested and put to death. Nine other Doctors of the Law, the
heart and soul of the Zealot faction, perished with him. I had
approved all these measures by nods of assent. Akiba and his
followers died persuaded to the end that they alone were innocent, they alone were just; not one of them dreamed of admitting
his share of responsibility for the evils which weighed down his
people. They would be enviable if one could envy the blind. I
do not deny these ten madmen the titles of heroes, but in no case
were they sages.

Three months later, from the top of a hill on a cold morning
in February, I sat leaning against the trunk of a leafless fig-tree
to watch the assault which preceded by only a few hours the
capitulation of Bethar. I saw the last defenders of the fortress
come out one by one, haggard, emaciated, hideous to view but
nevertheless superb, like all that is indomitable. At the end of
the same month I had myself borne to the place called Abraham's
Well, where the rebels in the urban centres, taken with weapons

in hand, had been assembled to be sold at auction: children
sneering defiance, already turned fierce and deformed by implacable convictions, boasting loudly of having brought death to
dozens of legionaries; old men immured in somnambulistic
dreams; women with fat, heavy bodies and others stern and
stately, like the Great Mother of the Oriental cults; all these filed
by under the cool scrutiny of the slave merchants; that multitude
passed before me like so much dust. Joshua Ben-Kisma, leader
of the so-called moderates, who had lamentably failed in his role
of peacemaker, succumbed at about that time to the last stages
of a prolonged illness; he died calling down upon us foreign
wars and victory for Parthia. On the other hand, the Christianized
Jews, whom we had not disturbed and who harboured resentment against the rest of the Hebrews for having persecuted their
prophet, saw in us the instrument of divine wrath. The long
series of deliriums and misunderstandings was thus continuing.

An inscription placed on the site of Jerusalem forbade the
Jews, under pain of death, to re-establish themselves anew upon
that heap of rubble; it reproduced word for word the sentence
formerly inscribed on the temple door, forbidding entrance to
the uncircumcised. On one day a year, on the ninth of the month
of Ab, the Jews have the right to come to weep in front of a
ruined wall. The most devout refused to leave their native land;
they settled as well as they could in the regions least devastated by
the war. The most fanatical emigrated to Parthian territory;
others went to Antioch, to Alexandria, and to Pergamum; the
clever ones made for Rome, where they prospered. Judaea was
struck from the map and took the name of Palestine by my order.
In those four years of war fifty fortresses and more than nine
hundred villages and towns had been sacked and destroyed; the
enemy had lost nearly six hundred thousand men; battles, en-
demic fevers, and epidemics had taken nearly ninety thousand
of ours. The labours of war were followed immediately by reconstruction in that area; Aelia Capitolina was rebuilt, though
on a more modest scale; one has always to begin over again.

I rested for some time in Sidon, where a Greek merchant lent
me his house and his gardens. In March those inner courts were
already carpeted with roses. I had regained my strength, and was

even discovering surprising resources in this body which at first had been prostrated by the violence of the initial attack. But we have understood nothing about illness so long as we have not recognized its odd resemblance to war and to love, its compromises, its feints, its exactions, that strange and unique amalgam produced by the mixture of a temperament and a malady. I was better, but in order to contrive with my body, to impose my wishes upon it or to cede prudently to its will, I devoted as much art as I had formerly employed in regulating and enlarging my world, in building the being that I am, and in embellishing my life. I resumed the exercises of the gymnasium, but with moderation; although my physician no longer forbade me the use of a horse, riding was now no more than a means of transport; I had to forgo the dangerous jumps of other days. In the course of any work or any pleasure, neither work nor pleasure was now the essential; my first concern was to get through it without fatigue. A recovery which seemed so complete astonished my friends; they tried to believe that the illness had been due merely to excessive efforts in those years of war, and would not recur. I judged otherwise; I thought of the great pines of Bithynia's forests which the woodsman notches in passing, and which he will return next season to fell. Towards the end of spring I embarked for Italy on a large galley of the fleet, taking with me Celer, now become indispensable, and Diotimus of Gadara, a young Greek of slave origin encountered in Sidon, who had beauty.

The route of return crossed the Archipelago; for the last time in my life, doubtless, I was watching the dolphins leap in that blue sea; with no thought henceforth of seeking for omens I followed the long straight flight of the migrating birds, which sometimes alighted in friendly fashion to rest on the deck of the ship; I drank in the odour of salt and sun on the human skin, the perfume of lentisk and terebinth from the isles where each voyager longs to dwell, but knows in advance that he will not pause. Diotimus read me the poets of his country; he has had that perfect instruction in letters which is often given to young slaves endowed with bodily graces in order to increase further their value; as night fell I would lie in the stern, protected by the purple canopy, listening till darkness came to efface both those lines which describe the tragic incertitude of our life, and those which speak of doves and kisses and garlands of roses. The sea was exhaling its moist, warm breath; the stars mounted one by one to their stations; the ship inclining before the wind made straight for the Occident, where showed the last shreds of red; phosphorescence glittered in the wake which stretched out behind us, soon covered by the black masses of the waves. I said to myself that only two things of importance awaited me in Rome: one was the choice of my successor, of interest to the whole empire; the other was my death, of concern to me alone.

*   *   *

Rome had prepared me a triumph, which this time I accepted. I no longer protested against these vain but venerable customs; anything which honours man's effort, even if only for a day, seemed to me salutary in presence of a world so prone to forget. I was celebrating more than the suppression of the Jewish revolt; in a sense more profound, and known to me alone, I had triumphed. I included the name Arrian in these honours. He had just inflicted a series of defeats on the hordes of the Alani which would throw them back for a long time to come into that obscure centre of Asia which they had thought to leave for good; Armenia had been saved; the reader of Xenophon was revealing himself as the emulator of that general, showing that the race of scholars who could also command and fight, if need be, was not extinct. That evening, on returning to my house in Tibur, it was with a weary but tranquil heart that I received from Diotimus' hands the incense and wine of the daily sacrifice to my Genius.

While still a private citizen I had begun to buy up and unite these lands, spread below the Sabine Hills along clear streams, with the patient tenacity of a peasant who parcel by parcel rounds out his vineyard; later on, between two imperial tours, I had camped in these groves then in prey to architects and masons; a youth imbued with all the superstitions of Asia used often to urge devoutly that the trees be spared. On the return from my longest travel in the Orient I had worked in a kind of frenzy to perfect this immense stage-setting for a play then already three-quarters completed. I was coming back to it this time to end my days as reasonably as possible. Everything here was arranged to facilitate work as well as pleasure : the chancellery, the audience halls, and the court where I judged difficult cases in last appeal, all saved me the tiring journeys between Tibur and Rome. I had given each of these edifices names reminiscent of Greece : the Poecile, the Academy, the Prytaneum. I knew very well that this small valley planted with olive trees was not Tempe, but I was reaching the age where each beauteous place recalls another, fairer still, where each delight is weighted with the memory of past joys. I gave way to nostalgia, that melancholy which is born of desire. I had even given the name of Styx to a particularly sombre corner of the park, and the name of Elysian Fields to a meadow strewn with anemones, thus preparing myself for that other world where the torments resemble those of this world, but where joys are nebulous, and inferior to our joys. But most important of all, in the heart of this retreat I had built for myself a refuge more private still, an islet of marble at the centre of a pool surrounded by colonnades; this gave me a room wholly apart, connected with, or rather, separated from the shore by a turning bridge so light that with one hand I could make it slide in its grooves. Into this summer pavilion I had two or three beloved statues moved, and the small bust of Augustus as a child, which Suetonius had given me in the period when we still were friends; I used to go there at the hour of siesta to sleep or to think or to read. My dog would stretch out across the doorway, extending his paws somewhat stiffly now; reflections played on the marble; Diotimus would rest his cheek, to cool himself, against the smooth surface of an urn; my thoughts were on my successor.

I have no children, nor is that a regret. To be sure, in time of weakness and fatigue, when one lacks the courage of one's convictions, I have sometimes reproached myself for not having taken the precaution to engender a son to follow me. But such a vain regret rests upon two hypotheses, equally doubtful : first, that a son necessarily continues us, and second, that the strange mixture of good and evil, that mass of minute and odd particularities which make up a person, deserves continuation. I have put my virtues to use as well as I could, and have profited from my vices likewise, but I have no special concern to bequeath myself to anyone. It is not by blood, anyhow, that man's true continuity is established: Alexander's direct heir is Caesar, and not the frail infant born of a Persian princess in an Asiatic citadel; Epaminondas, dying without issue, was right to boast that he had Victories for daughters. Most men who figure in history have but mediocre offspring, or worse; they seem to exhaust within themselves the resources of a race. A father's affection is almost always in conflict with the interests of a ruler. Were it otherwise, then an emperor's son would still have to suffer the drawbacks of a princely education, the worst possible school for a future prince. Happily, in so far as our State has been able to formulate a rule for imperial succession, that rule has been adoption: I see there the wisdom of Rome. I know the dangers of choice, and its possible errors; I am well aware, too, that blindness is not reserved for paternal affection alone; but any decision in which intelligence presides, or where it at least plays a part, will always seem to me infinitely superior to the vague wishes of chance and unthinking nature. The power to the worthiest! It is good and fitting that a man who has proved his competence in handling the affairs of the world should choose his replacement, and that a decision of such grave consequence should be both his last privilege and his last service rendered to the State. But this important choice seemed to me more difficult than ever to make.

I had bitterly reproached Trajan for having evaded the problem for twenty years before he resolved to adopt me, and for having decided the matter only upon his deathbed. But nearly eighteen years had passed since my accession to power and I in my turn, despite the dangers of an adventurous life, had put off till the last my choice of a successor. Hundreds of rumours were circulating, almost all of them false; countless hypotheses had been built up; but what was supposed my secret decision was only my hesitation and my doubt. All around me good functionaries abounded, but not one of them had the necessary breadth of view. Forty years of integrity made Marcius Turbo a likely candidate, my friend and companion of yore and my

incomparable prefect of the Praetorian Guard; but he was my
age, too old. Julius Severus, an excellent general and a good
administrator for Britain, knew little of the complex affairs of
the Orient; Arrian had given proof of all the qualities expected
of a statesman, but he was Greek, and the time had not yet come
to place a Greek emperor over Rome and its prejudices.

Servianus was living still: such longevity looked like deliberate calculation on his part, an obstinate form of waiting.
He had waited for sixty years. In Nerva's time he had been both
encouraged and disappointed by the adoption of Trajan; he was
hoping for more, but the rise to power of this cousin incessantly
occupied with the army seemed at least to assure him a considerable place in the State, perhaps second place. There, too, he was
mistaken, for he had obtained only a somewhat empty share
of honours. He waited for that time when he had stationed his
slaves to attack me at a turning on the edge of a poplar grove,
above the Moselle; the duel-to-the-death engaged upon on that
morning between the young man and the man of fifty had gone
on for twenty years; he had turned the mind of the sovereign
against me, exaggerating my escapades and making the most of
my slightest error. Such an enemy is an excellent schoolmaster:
Servianus has taught me much, all in all, about prudence. After
my accession to power he had had sufficient subtlety to appear
to accept the inevitable; he disclaimed all connexion with the
plot of the four consular conspirators, and I had preferred not
to remark the stains on those fingers still visibly soiled. On his
side he had limited himself to mere whispered protest, and only
in private pronounced my actions outrageous. With support in
the Senate from that small but powerful faction of life-long conservatives who were hindering my reforms he had comfortably
installed himself in the role of silent critic of my reign. Little
by little he had alienated my sister Paulina from me. Their only
child was a daughter, married to a certain Salinator, a man of
high birth whom I had raised to the consulship, but who had
died young of consumption. My niece did not long survive him;
their one child, Fuscus, was set against me by this pernicious
grandfather.

But the hatred between us kept within certain bounds: I did

not begrudge him his part in public functions, though I took care, nevertheless, not to stand beside him in ceremonies where his advanced age would have given him precedence over the emperor. On each return to Rome I agreed, for appearances' sake, to attend one of those family meals where one keeps on one's guard; we exchanged letters; his were not without wit. In the long run, however, I had become disgusted with such dreary pretence; the possibility of discarding the mask in every respect is one of the rare advantages which I find in growing old; I had refused to be present at the funeral of Paulina. In the camp of Bethar, in the worst hours of physical distress and discouragement, the supreme bitterness had been to tell myself that Servianus was nearing his goal, and nearing it by my fault; that octogenarian so niggardly of his strength would manage to survive an invalid fifty-seven years old; if I should die intestate he would contrive to obtain both the votes of the malcontents and the approval of those who thought that they were remaining faithful to me in electing my brother-in-law; he would profit from our slender kinship to undermine my work. In order to calm my fears I used to say to myself that the empire could find worse masters; Servianus after all was not without qualities; even the dull Fuscus would one day perhaps be worthy to reign. But all the energy which I had left was summoned to refuse this lie, and I wished to live if only to crush that viper.

On coming back to Rome I saw much of Lucius again. In former days I had made commitments to him which ordinarily one hardly troubles to fulfil, but which I had kept. It is not true, however, that I had promised him the imperial purple; such things are not done. But for nearly fifteen years I had paid his debts, hushed up his scandals, and answered his letters without delay; delightful letters they were, but they always ended with requests for money for himself, or for advancement for his friends. He was too much mingled with my life for me to exclude him from it had I wished to do so, but I wished nothing of the sort. His conversation was brilliant: this young man whom people judged superficial had read more, and more intelligently, than the writers who make such works their profession. In everything his taste was exquisite, whether for people, objects, manners, or the most exact fashion of scanning a line of Greek verse. In the Senate, where he was considered able, he had made a reputation as an orator: his speeches were at the same time terse and ornate, and served immediately upon utterance as models for the professors of eloquence. I had had him named praetor, and then consul: he had fulfilled these functions well. Some years earlier I had arranged a marriage for him with the daughter of Nigrinus, one of the consular conspirators executed at the beginning of my reign; that union became the emblem of my policy of conciliation. It was but moderately successful; the young woman complained of being neglected, but she had three children by him, one of whom was a son. To her almost continual repining he would reply with frigid politeness that one marries for one's family's sake and not for oneself, and that so weighty a contract ill accords with the carefree play of love. His complicated system demanded mistresses for display and willing slaves for his pleasure. He was killing himself in pursuit of delights, but was doing so like an artist who destroys himself in completing a masterpiece: it is not for me to reproach him in that.

I watched him live: my opinion of him was constantly changing, a thing which rarely happens except for those persons to whom we are closely attached; we are satisfied to judge others more in general, and once for all. Sometimes a studied insolence and hardness, or a coldly frivolous remark disturbed me; more often, however, I let myself be carried along by his swift and nimble intelligence; an astute comment seemed suddenly to reveal the future statesman. I spoke of all this to Marcius Turbo, who after his tiring day as Praetorian prefect came every evening to talk over current business and play his game of dice with me; together we re-examined in utmost detail Lucius' possibilities for suitably filling the career of emperór. My friends were amazed at my scruples; some of them counselled me, with a shrug of the shoulders, to take whatever decision I liked; such people imagine that one bequeaths half the world as one would leave a country house to a friend. I reflected further about it by night: Lucius had hardly reached thirty; what was Caesar at thirty years but a young patrician submerged in debts and sullied by scandal? As in the bad days of Antioch, before my adoption by Trajan, I thought with a pang that nothing is slower than the true birth of a man: I had myself passed my thirtieth year before the Pannonian campaign had opened my eyes to the responsibilities of power; Lucius seemed to me at times more accomplished than I was at that age. I made up my mind abruptly, after a crisis of suffocation graver than the others, which warned me that I had no more time to lose.

I adopted Lucius, who took the name of Aelius Caesar. He was carefree even in his ambition, and though demanding was not grasping, having always been accustomed to obtain everything; he took my decision with casual ease. I had the imprudence to mention that this fair-haired prince would be admirably handsome clad in the purple; the ill-willed hastened to assert that I was giving an empire in return for a voluptuous intimacy of earlier days. Such a charge shows no understanding of the way that the mind of a ruler functions (provided that in some degree he merits his post and his title). If like considerations had figured, then Lucius would not have been the only one on whom I could have fixed my choice.

My wife had just died in her residence at the Palatine, which she had preferred to the end to Tibur, and where she lived surrounded by a small court of friends and Spanish relations, who were all that she cared about. The polite evasions, the proprieties, the feeble efforts towards understanding, had gradually terminated between us, and had left exposed only antipathy, irritation, and rancour, and, on her part, hatred. I paid her a visit in the last days; sickness had further soured her morose and acid disposition; that interview was occasion for her for violent recrimination; she gained relief thereby, but was indiscreet in speaking thus before witnesses. She congratulated herself in dying without children: my sons would doubtless have resembled me, she said, and she would have had the same aversion for them as for their father. That avowal, in which such bitterness rankled, is the only proof of love which she has ever given me. My Sabina: I searched for the few passably good memories which are left of someone when we take the trouble to look back for them; I recalled a basket of fruit which she had sent me for my birthday, after a quarrel; while passing by litter through the narrow streets of the town of Tibur and before the small summer house which had once belonged to my mother-in-law Matidia, I thought bitterly of some nights of a summer long ago, when I had tried in vain to arouse some amorous feeling for this young bride so harsh and so cold. The death of my wife was less moving for me than the loss of the good Arete, the housekeeper at the Villa, stricken that same winter by fever. Because the illness to which the empress succumbed had been but poorly diagnosed by the physicians, and towards the last caused her cruel intestinal pain, I was accused of having used poison, and that wild rumour was readily believed. It goes without saying that so superfluous a crime had never tempted me.

The death of Sabina perhaps pushed Servianus to risk his all: her influence in Rome had been wholly at his disposal; with her fell one of his most respected supports. And further, he had just entered upon his ninetieth year; like me, he had no more time to lose. For some months now he had tried to draw around him small groups of officers of the Praetorian Guard; sometimes he ventured to exploit the superstitious respect which great age inspires in order to assume imperial authority within his four walls. I had recently reinforced the secret military police, a distasteful institution, I admit, but one which the event proved useful. I knew all about these supposedly secret assemblies, wherein the aged Ursus was teaching the art of conspiracy to his grandson. The nomination of Lucius did not surprise the old man; he had long taken my incertitude on this subject for a well dissimulated decision; but he chose to act at the moment when the legal adoption was still a matter of controversy in Rome. His secretary, Crescens, weary of forty years' faithful service badly repaid, divulged the project, the date and place of attack, and the names of the accomplices. My enemies had not taxed their imagination; they simply copied outright the assault premeditated long before by Quietus and Nigrinus: I was to be struck down during a religious ceremony at the Capitol; my adopted son was to fall with me.

I took my precautions that very night: our enemy had lived only too long; I would leave Lucius a heritage cleansed of dangers. Towards the twelfth hour, on a grey dawn of February, a tribune bearing a sentence of death for Servianus and his grand-son presented himself to my brother-in-law; his instructions were to wait in the vestibule until the order which he brought had been executed. Servianus sent for his physician, and all was decently performed. Before dying he expressed the wish that I should expire in the slow torments of incurable illness, without having like him the privilege of brief agony. His prayer has already been granted.

I had not ordered this double execution light-heartedly, but I felt no regret for it thereafter, and still less remorse. An old score had been paid at last; that was all. Age has never seemed to me an excuse for human malevolence; I should even be in-clined to consider advanced years as the less excuse for such dangerous ill-will. The sentencing of Akiba and his acolytes had cost me longer hesitation; of the two old men I should still prefer the fanatic to the conspirator. As to Fuscus, however mediocre he might be and however completely his odious grandfather might have alienated him from me, he was the grandson of Paulina. But bonds of blood are truly slight (despite assertions to the contrary) when they are not reinforced by affection; this fact is evident in any family where the least matter of inheritance arises. The youth of Fuscus moved me somewhat more to pity, for he had barely reached eighteen. But interests of State re-quired this conclusion, which the aged Ursus had seemed volun-tarily to render inevitable. And from then on I was too near my own death to take time for meditation upon those two endings.

For a few days Marcius Turbo doubled his vigilance; the friends of Servianus could have sought revenge. But nothing came of it, neither attack nor sedition, nor even complaints. I was no longer the newcomer trying to win public opinion after the execution of four men of consular rank; nineteen years of just rule arbitrated in my favour; my enemies were execrated as a group, and the crowd approved me for having rid myself of a traitor. Fuscus was commiserated, but without being judged innocent. The Senate, I well know, would not pardon me for having once more struck down one of its members, but it kept quiet, and would remain quiet until my death. As formerly, also, an admixture of clemency soon mitigated the dose of severity:

not one of the partisans of Servianus was disturbed. The only
exception to this rule was the eminent Apollodorus, the splenetic
depository of my brother-in-law's secrets, who perished with
him. That talented man had been the favourite architect of my
predecessor; he had piled up the great stone blocks of Trajan's
Column with art. We did not care much for each other : he had
of old derided my unskilled amateur paintings, my conscientious
still-lifes of pumpkin and gourd; I had on my side, with a young
man's presumption, critized his works. Later on he had dis-
paraged mine : he knew nothing of the finest periods of Greek
art; that literal mind reproached me for having filled our temples
with colossal statues which, if they were to rise, would batter
their brows against the vaults of their sanctuaries. An inane
criticism that, and one to hurt Phidias even more than me. But
the gods do not rise; they rise neither to warn us nor to protect
us, nor to recompense nor to punish. Nor did they rise on that
night to save Apollodorus.

*   *   *

By spring the health of Lucius began to cause me rather grave
concern. One morning in Tibur we went down from the bath
to the palaestra where Celer was exercising with other youths;
someone proposed one of those contests where each participant
runs bearing his shield and his spear. Lucius managed to excuse
himself from the sport, as he usually did, but finally yielded to
our friendly raillery; in equipping himself he complained of the
weight of the bronze shield; compared with the firm beauty of
Celer that slender body seemed frail. After a few strides he fell
breathless and spat blood. The incident had no sequel, and he
recovered without difficulty; but I had been alarmed. I should
not have been so soon reassured. I resisted these first symptoms
of his illness with the stupid confidence of a man who had long
been robust, and who had implicit faith in the undepleted reserves of youth and in the capacities of bodies to function as
they should. It is true that he was mistaken, too; some light flame
sustained him, and his vivacity created the same illusion for him
as for us. My best years had been passed in travel and in camp,
or on the frontiers; I had known at first hand the values of a

rude life, and the salubrious effect of frozen or desert regions. I decided to name Lucius governor of that same Pannonia where I had had my first experience in rule. The situation on that frontier was less critical than formerly; his task would be limited to the peaceful work of civil administration or to routine military inspections. Such difficult country would rouse him from Rome's easy ways; he would get better acquainted with that immense world which the City governs, and on which she depends. He dreaded those distant climes, and would not understand that life could be enjoyed elsewhere than in Rome. He accepted, however, with the compliance which he always showed when he wished to please me.

Throughout the summer I read with care both his official reports and those more secret communications from Domitius Rogatus, my confidential informant whom I had sent with him as a secretary instructed to watch over him. These accounts satisfied me: Lucius demonstrated in Pannonia that he was capable of the seriousness which I expected of him, but from which he might have relaxed, perhaps, after my death. He even conducted himself rather brilliantly in a series of cavalry skirmishes at the advance posts. In the provinces, as everywhere else, he succeeded in charming everyone around him; his dry and somewhat curt manner did him no disservice; at least this would not be a case of one of those easy-going princes who is governed by a coterie. But with the very beginning of autumn he caught cold. He was thought to be well again soon, but the cough recurred and the fever persisted, setting in for good. A temporary gain was rapidly followed by a dangerous relapse the next spring. The bulletins from the physicians appalled me; the public postal service, which I had just established with its relays of horses and carriages over vast territories, seemed to function only in order to bring me news of the invalid more promptly each morning. I could not pardon myself for having been inhuman towards him in the fear of seeming indulgent. As soon as he was recovered enough for travel I had him brought back to Italy.

In company with the aged Rufus of Ephesus, a specialist in phthisis, I went myself to the port of Baiae to await my fragile

Aelius Caesar. The climate of Tibur, though better than that
of Rome, is nevertheless not mild enough for affected lungs; I
had decided to have him spend the late autumn in that safer
region. The ship anchored in the middle of the bay; a light tender
brought the sick man and his physician ashore. His haggard face
seemed thinner still under the fringe of beard with which he
had let his cheeks be covered, in the hope of resembling me. But
his eyes had kept their hard fire, the gleam of precious stones.
His first words to me were to remind me that he had come back
only at my command; that his administration had incurred no
reproach; that he had obeyed me in everything. He spoke like
a schoolboy who justifies the way that he has spent his day. I
established him in that villa of Cicero where he had formerly
passed a season with me when he was eighteen. He had the
elegance never to speak of those times.

The first few days seemed like a victory over the disease; this
return to Italy was already a remedy in itself; at that time of year
the countryside there was wine-red in hue. But the rains began;
a damp wind blew from the cold sea; the old house built in the
time of the Republic lacked the more modern comforts of the
villa in Tibur; I watched Lucius dispiritedly warming his slender
fingers, laden with rings, over the brazier. Hermogenes had returned but a short time before from the Orient, where I had sent
him to refurnish and augment his provision of medicaments; he
tried on Lucius the effects of a mud impregnated with powerful
mineral salts; these applications were reputed to cure everything.
But they were of no more help to his lungs than to my arteries.

Illness exposed the worst aspects of that hard and frivolous
nature; his wife paid him a visit; as always, their interview ended
in bitter words; she did not come back again. His son was
brought to see him, a beautiful child of seven, laughing and gay,
and just at the toothless age; Lucius beheld him with interest. He asked eagerly for political news from Rome, but more
as a gambler would than a statesman. Such levity, however, was
a form of courage on his part; he would awaken from long after-
noons of pain or of torpor to throw his whole being into one of
those sparkling conversations of former days; that face wet with
sweat still knew how to smile; the emaciated body rose with

grace to receive the physician. He would be to the end the prince formed of ivory and gold.

At night, unable to sleep, I would take up my station in the invalid's room; Celer, who disliked Lucius, but who is too loyal not to serve with care those dear to me, consented to share my vigil; from the covers came rattled breathing. A feeling of bitterness swept over my, deep as the sea; he had never loved me; our relations had quickly become those of the spendthrift son and the indulgent father; that life had run out without ever having known great hopes or serious thoughts and ardent passions; he had squandered his years as a prodigal scatters gold pieces. I had leaned for support on a ruined wall : I thought with anger of the enormous sums expended for his adoption, three hundred million sesterces distributed to the soldiers. In a sense, my good fortune had followed me, though sadly : I had satisfied my old desire to give Lucius all that can be given, but the State would not suffer for it now; I should not risk being dishonoured by that choice. In the very depths of my being I was even fearing that he might get better; if by chance he should drag on some years still, I could not leave the empire to such a shade.

Without ever asking questions he seemed to penetrate my thoughts on this point; his eyes followed anxiously my slightest gesture. I had named him consul for the second time; he worried because he could not fulfil the functions of that office; the dread of displeasing me aggravated his condition. *Tu Marcellus eris.* . . . I repeated to myself Virgil's lines devoted to the nephew of Augustus, likewise designated to rule, and whom death stopped short on the way. *Manibus date lilia plenis.* . . . *Purpureos spargam flores.* . . . The lover of flowers would receive only futile funeral wreaths from me.

He believed that he was better, and wished to return to Rome. The physicians, who no longer disputed among themselves except as to the length of time left him to live, counselled me to do whatever he liked; I took him back by short stages to the Villa. His presentation to the Senate in his capacity as heir to the empire was to take place during the session which would follow almost immediately upon the New Year. According to custom, he was supposed on that occasion to address to me a speech of thanks; this piece of eloquence had preoccupied him for months, and together we had smoothed over its difficult passages. He was working at it on the morning of the first of January, when he was suddenly taken with haemorrhage; he grew faint, and leaned against the back of his chair, closing his eyes. Death was no more than dizziness for this light creature. It was New Year's Day: in order not to interrupt the public and private festivities, I restricted immediate proclamation of the news of his passing; it was not announced officially until the following day. He was buried quietly on his family estate. The evening before that ceremony the Senate sent a delegation to me bearing its condolences, and offering the honours of divinization to Lucius, to which he was entitled as the emperor's adopted son. But I refused: this whole affair had already cost only too much to the State. I confined myself to having some funeral chapels constructed for him, and statues erected here and there in different places where he had lived: this poor Lucius was not a god.

This time, each moment counted. But I had had all the leisure for reflection at the invalid's bedside; my plans were made. I had remarked in the Senate a certain Antoninus, a man of about fifty, of a provincial family distantly related to that of Plotina. He had impressed me by the deferent but tender care with which he surrounded his father-in-law, an old man partially paralyzed, who sat beside him. I read through his records; this honest man had proved himself in every post that he had held an irreproachable official. My choice fell on him. The more I frequent Antoninus the more my esteem for him tends to change into profound respect. This simple man possesses a virtue which I had thought little about up to this time, even when I happened to practise it, namely, kindness. He is not devoid of the modest faults of a wise man: the application of his intelligence to the meticulous accomplishment of daily tasks concerns more the present than the future; his experience of the world is limited by his very virtues; his travel has been confined to certain official missions, though these have been well fulfilled. He is little versed in the arts. He yields only unwillingly to innovation; the provinces, for example, will never represent for him the immense possibilities for development that they have always signified for me; he will continue rather than expand my work, but he will continue it well; in him the State will have an honest servitor and a good master.

But the space of one generation seemed to me but a small thing when the problem was to safeguard the security of the world; I wanted if possible to prolong further this line created by prudent adoption, and to prepare for the empire one more relay on the road of time. Upon each return to Rome I had never failed to visit my old friends, the Verus family, Spanish like me, and among the most liberal members of the upper magistracy. I have known you from your cradle, young Annius Verus, who by my provision now call yourself Marcus Aurelius. During one of the most glorious years of my life, in the period which is marked for me by the erection of the Pantheon, I had you elected, out of friendship for your family, to the sacred college of the Arval Brethren, over which the emperor presides, and which devoutly perpetuates our ancient Roman religious customs. I held you by the hand during the sacrifice which took place that year on the bank of the Tiber, and with tender amusement watched your childish face (you were only five years old at the time), frightened by the cries of the immolated swine, but trying bravely to imitate the dignified demeanour of your elders. I concerned myself with the education of this almost too sober little boy, helping your father to choose the best masters for you. Verus, the Most Veracious: I used so to play on your name; you are perhaps the only being who has never lied to me.

I have seen you read with passion the writings of the philosophers, and clothe yourself in harsh wool, sleeping on the bare floor and forcing your somewhat frail body to all the mortifications of the Stoics. There is some excess in all that, but excess is a virtue at the age of seventeen. I sometimes wonder on what reef that wisdom will founder, for one always founders: will it be a wife, or a son too greatly loved, one of those legitimate snares (to sum it up in a word) where overscrupulous, pure hearts are caught? Or will it be more simply age, illness, fatigue, or the disillusion which says to us that if all is vain, then virtue is too? I can imagine in place of your candid, boyish countenance your weary visage as an older man. I am aware that your severity, so carefully acquired, has beneath it some sweetness, and some weakness perhaps; I divine in you the presence of a kind of genius which is not necessarily that of the statesman; the world will doubtless be for ever the better off, however, for having once seen such a capacity in conjunction with supreme authority. I have arranged the essentials for your adoption by Antoninus; under the new name by which you will one day be designated in the list of emperors you are now and henceforth my grandson. I believe that I may be giving mankind the only chance it will ever have to realize Plato's dream, to see a philosopher pure of heart ruling over his fellow men.

You have accepted these honours only with reluctance; your rank obliges you to live in the palace; Tibur, this place where to the very end I am assembling whatever pleasures life has, disturbs you for your young virtue. I watch you wandering gravely under those rose-covered alleys, and smile to see you drawn towards the fair human objects who cross your path; you hesitate tenderly between Benedicta and Theodotus, but quickly renounce them both in favour of that chaste phantom, austerity. You have not concealed from me your melancholy disdain for these short-lived splendours, nor for this court, which will disperse after my death. You scarcely care for me; your filial affection goes more toward Antoninus; in me you discern a kind of wisdom which is contrary to what your masters teach you, and in my abandonment to the life of the senses you see a mode of life opposed to the severity of your own, but which nevertheless is parallel to it. Never mind: it is not necessary that you should understand me. There is more than one kind of wisdom, and all are essential in the world; it is no bad thing that they should alternate.

Eight days after the death of Lucius, I had myself taken by litter to the Senate; I asked permission to enter thus into the council chamber, and to remain lying against my pile of cushions as I gave my address. Speaking tires me: I requested the senators to form a close circle around me, in order not to be obliged to force my voice. I pronounced Lucius' eulogy; these few lines took the place on that session's programme of the discourse which he was to have given on that same day. Thereafter I announced my decision: I nominated Antoninus, and named you also. I had counted upon completely unanimous adherence, and obtained it. I expressed a last wish, which was acceded to like the others: I asked that Antoninus should adopt Lucius' son, who will in this way become your brother; you two will govern together, and I rely upon you as the elder to look after his welfare. I want the State to conserve something of Lucius.

On returning home, for the first time in many a day, I was tempted to smile. I had played my game singularly well. The followers of Servianus, conservatives hostile to my administration, had not capitulated; all the courtesies which I had paid to this great and ancient, but outworn, senatorial body were no compensation to them for the two or three blows which I had dealt them. They would undoubtedly take advantage of the moment of my death to try to annul my acts. But my worst enemies would not dare to reject their most upright representative, nor the son of one of their most respected members as well. My public duty was done: I could now return to Tibur, going back into that retreat which is called illness, to experiment with my suffering, to taste fully what delights are left to me, and to resume in peace my interrupted dialogue with a shade. My imperial heritage was safe in the hands of the devoted Antoninus and the grave Marcus Aurelius; Lucius himself would survive in his son. All that was not too badly arranged.

PATIENTIA

Aʀʀɪᴀɴ wrote to me thus:

I have completed the circumnavigation of the Black Sea, in conformity with the orders received. We ended the circuit at Sinope, whose inhabitants are still grateful to you for the vast work of enlarging and repairing the port, brought successfully to a conclusion under your supervision some years back. . . . By the way, they have erected a statue in your honour which is not fine enough, nor a good enough likeness; pray send them another, in white marble. . . . At Sinope it was not without emotion that I looked down on that same sea from the hilltops whence our Xenophon first beheld it of old, and whence you yourself contemplated it not so long ago. . . .

I have inspected the coastal garrisons: their commandants merit the highest praise for excellent discipline, for use of latest methods in training, and for the quality of their engineering. . . . Wherever the coasts are wild and still little known I have had new soundings taken, and have rectified, where necessary, the indications of earlier navigators. . . .

We have skirted Colchis. Knowing how interested you are in what the ancient poets recount, I questioned the inhabitants about Medea's enchantments and the exploits of Jason. But they seemed not to know of these stories. . . .

On the northern shore of that inhospitable sea we touched upon a small island of great import in legend, the isle of Achilles. As you know, Thetis is supposed to have brought her son to be reared on this islet shrouded in mist; each evening she would rise from the depths of the sea and would come to talk with her child on the strand. Nowadays the place is uninhabited; only a few goats graze there. It has a temple to Achilles. Terns, gulls, and petrels, all kinds of sea birds frequent this sanctuary, and its porch is cooled by the continual fanning of their wings still moist from the sea. But this isle of Achilles is also, as it should be, the isle of Patroclus, and the innumerable votive offerings which decorate the temple walls are dedicated sometimes to Achilles and sometimes to his friend, for of course whoever loves Achilles cherishes and venerates Patroclus' memory. Achilles himself appears in dream to the navigators who visit these parts: he protects them and warns them of the sea's dangers, as Castor and Pollux do elsewhere. And the shade of Patroclus appears at Achilles' side.

I report these things to you because I think them worthy to be known, and because those who told them to me have experienced them themselves, or have learned them from credible witnesses. . . . Achilles sometimes seems to me the greatest of men in his courage, his fortitude, his learning and intelligence coupled with bodily skill, and his ardent love for his young companion. And nothing in him seems to me nobler than the despair which made him despise life and long for death when he had lost his beloved.

I laid down the voluminous report of the governor of Armenia Minor, admiral of the expeditionary fleet. As always Arrian has worked well. But this time he is doing more than that : he offers me a gift which I need if I am to die in peace; he sends me a picture of my life as I should have wished it to be. Arrian knows that what counts is something which will not figure in official biographies and which is not written on tombs; he knows also that the passing of time only adds one more bewilderment to grief. As seen by him the adventure of my existence takes on meaning and achieves a form, as in a poem; that unique affection frees itself from remorse, impatience, and vain obsessions as from so much smoke, or so much dust; sorrow is decanted and despair runs pure. Arrian opens to me the vast empyrean of heroes and friends, judging me not too unworthy of it. My hidden study built at the centre of a pool in the Villa is not internal enough as a refuge; I drag this body there, grown old, and suffer there. My past life, to be sure, affords me certain retreats where I escape from at least some part of my present afflictions : the snowy plain along the Danube, the gardens of Nicomedia, Claudiopolis turned gold in the harvest of flowering saffron, Athens (no matter what street), an oasis where water lilies ripple above the ooze, the Syrian desert by starlight on the return from Osroës' camp. But these beloved places are too often associated with premisses which have led to some error; some disappointment, some repulse known to me alone: in my bad moments all my roads to success seem only to lead to Egypt, to a sick room in Baiae, or to Palestine. And worse still, the fatigue of my body transmits itself to my memories: recollection of the stairways of the Acropolis is almost insupportable to a man who pants as he mounts the garden steps; the thought of the July sun on the drill-field of Lambaesis overwhelms me as if I were now exposing my head there bare. Arrian offers me something better. Here in Tibur, in the full heat of May, I listen for the waves' slow complaint on the sands of the isle of Achilles; I drink in the cool, pure air; I wander effortlessly over the temple terrace bathed in the fresh sea spray; I catch sight of Patroclus. . . . That place which I shall never see is becoming my secret abode, my innermost haven. I shall doubtless be there at the moment of my death.

In former years I had given the philosopher Euphrates permission for suicide. Nothing seemed simpler: a man has the right to decide how long he may usefully live. I did not then know that death can become an object of blind ardour, of a hunger like that of love. I had not forseen those nights when I should be wrapping my baldric around my dagger in order to force myself to think twice before drawing it. Arrian alone has penetrated the secret of this unsung battle against emptiness, barrenness, fatigue, and the disgust for existing which brings on a craving for death. There is no getting over it: the old fever has prostrated me more than once; I would shudder to feel it coming on, like a sick man aware of an approaching attack. Everything served me as means to postpone the hour of the nightly struggle: work, conversations wildly prolonged until dawn, kisses, my books. An emperor is not supposed to take his own life unless he is forced to do so for reasons of State; even Mark Antony had the excuse of a lost battle. And my strict Arrian would think less highly of this despair brought with me from Egypt had I not triumphed over it. My own legislation forbade soldiers that voluntary death which I accorded to sages; I felt no freer to desert than any other legionary. But I know what it is to caress the harsh fibres of a rope, or to finger the edge of a knife.

Gradually I turned my dread desire into a rampart against itself: the fact that the possibility of suicide was ever present helped me to bear life with less impatience, just as a sedative potion within hand's reach serves to calm a man afflicted with insomnia. By some inner contradiction this obsession with death ceased only after the first symptoms of illness came to distract me from that one thought; I began to interest myself anew in this life which was leaving me; in Sidon's gardens I wanted intensely to enjoy my body for some years more.

One desires to die, but not to suffocate; sickness disgusts us with death, and we wish to get well, which is a way of wishing to live. But weakness and suffering, with manifold bodily woes, soon discourage the invalid from trying to regain ground: he tires of those respites which are but snares, of that faltering strength, those ardours cut short, and that perpetual lying in wait for the next attack. I kept sly watch upon myself: that dull chest pain, was it only a passing discomfort, the result of a meal absorbed too fast, or was I to expect from the enemy an assault which this time would not be repulsed? I no longer entered the Senate without saying to myself that the door had perhaps closed behind me as finally as if I had been awaited, like Caesar, by fifty conspirators armed with knives. During the suppers at Tibur I feared to distress my guests by the discourtesy of a sudden and final departure; I was afraid to die in my bath, or in the embrace of young arms. Functions which formerly were easy to perform or even agreeable, become humiliating now that they have become more laborious; one wearies of the silver vase handed each morning to be examined by the physician. The principal ailment brings with it a whole train of secondary afflictions: my hearing is less acute than before; even yesterday I was forced to ask Phlegon to repeat a whole sentence; no crime would have cost me more shame.

The months which followed the adoption of Antoninus were bad indeed: the stay in Baiae, the return to Rome, with the negotiations accompanying it, had exceeded what strength I had left. The obsession with death again took hold of me, but this time the reasons were plain to see, and could be told; my worst enemy would have had no cause to smile over my despair. There was nothing now to restrain me : people would have understood that the emperor, withdrawn to his country house after having arranged all matters of State, had taken the necessary measures to facilitate his ending. But the solicitude of my friends amounts to constant surveillance : every invalid is a prisoner. I no longer have the force which it would take to drive the dagger in at the exact place, marked at one time with red ink under my left breast; I should only have added to the present ills a repulsive mixture of bandages and bloody sponges, and surgeons discussing at the foot of my bed. To prepare a suicide I needed to take the same precautions as would an assassin to plan his crime.

I thought first of my huntsman, Mastor, the handsome, half-savage Sarmatian who had followed me for years like a devoted wolf-dog. He was sometimes entrusted to keep watch by night at my door. I took advantage of a moment's solitude to call him in and explain what I wanted of him : at first he did not understand. Then my meaning dawned; the barbarian face under the fair shaggy hair contracted with terror. He believes me immortal : morning and evening he sees physicians enter my room and hears me groan at each punction without his faith being shaken thereby; for him it was as if the master of the gods, thinking to tempt him, had descended from Olympus to entreat of him a death-blow. He tore away the sword which I had seized from him, and fled howling. That night he was found in the depths of the park, uttering strange gibberish in his native jargon. They calmed this terrified creature as well as they could; no one spoke to me again of the incident. But the next morning I noticed that Celer had exchanged the metal style on the writing table within reach of my bed for a reed pen.

I sought a better ally. I have complete confidence in Iollas, a young physician from Alexandria whom Hermogenes had chosen last summer as his substitute during his absence. We often talked together, for I liked to build up hypotheses with him on the nature and origin of things, and took pleasure in his intelligence, both daring and dreamy, and in the dark fire of those deep-set eyes. I knew that in Alexandria he had found in the palace archives the formulae for extraordinary subtle poisons com-

pounded long ago by Cleopatra's chemists. An excuse came for
me to get rid of Hermogenes for several hours : he had to
examine candidates for the chair of medicine which I had just
founded at the Odeon; there was thus the chance for a secret talk
with Iollas. He understood me at once; he pitied me; he could
but admit that I was right. But his Hippocratic oath forbade him
to dispense a nocent drug to a patient, under any pretext whatsoever; he refused, standing fast on his professional honour. I insisted; I made absolute demand; I employed every means to try
to draw his pity, or to corrupt him; he will be the last man whom
I shall have implored. Finally won over, he promised me to go
and seek the dose of poison. I awaited him in vain until evening.
Late in the night I learned with horror that he had just been
found dead in his laboratory, with a glass phial in his hands. That
heart clean of all compromise had found this means of abiding
by his oath while denying me nothing.

The next day Antoninus was announced; this true friend could
barely hold back his tears. The idea that a man whom he had
come to love and to venerate as a father suffered enough to seek
out death was to him insupportable; it seemed to him that he
must have failed in his obligations as a good son. He promised
me to add his efforts to those of my entourage in order to nurse
me and relieve my pain, to make my life smooth and easy to the
last, even to cure me perhaps. He depended upon me to continue
the longest time possible in guiding and instructing him; he felt
himself responsible towards the whole empire for the remainder
of my days.

I know what these pathetic protestations and naïve promises
are worth; nevertheless I derive some relief and comfort from
them. Antoninus' simple words have convinced me; I am regain-
ing possession of myself before I die. The death of Iollas, faithful
to his duty as physician, exhorts me to conform, to the end, to
the proprieties of my profession as emperor. *Patientia:* yesterday
I saw Domitius Rogatus, now become procurator of the mint
and entrusted with a new issue of coins; I have given him this
legend, which will be my last watchword. My death had seemed
to me the most personal of my decisions, my supreme redoubt as
a free man; I was mistaken. The faith of millions of Mastors must

not be shaken, nor other Iollases put to so sore a trial. I have realized that suicide would appear to signify indifference, or ingratitude perhaps, to the little group of devoted friends who surround me; I do not wish to bequeath to them the hideous picture of a man racked by pain who cannot endure one torture more.

Other considerations came slowly to mind during the night which followed Iollas' death; life has given me much, or at least I have known how to obtain a great deal from it; in this moment, as in the time of my felicity, and for wholly opposite reasons, it seems to me that existence has nothing more to offer : I am not sure, however, that I have not something more to learn from it. I shall listen for its secret instructions to the end. All my life long I have trusted in the wisdom of my body; I have tried to distinguish between and enjoy the varied sensations which this friend has provided me : I no longer refuse the death agony prepared for me, this ending slowly elaborated within my arteries and inherited perhaps from some ancestor, or born of my temperament formed little by little from each of my actions throughout my life. The time of impatience has passed; at the point where I now am, despair would be in as bad taste as hope itself. I have ceased to hurry my death.

*   *   *

Everything still needs attention. My estates in Africa, inherited from my mother-in-law, Matidia, must be turned into models of agricultural development; the peasants of Borysthenes, the village established in memory of a good horse, are entitled to aid after a severe winter; on the contrary, subsidies should not be granted to the rich cultivators of the Nile Valley, who are ever ready to take advantage of the emperor's solicitude. Julius Vestinus, prefect of Education, sends me his report on the opening of public grammar schools. I have just completed the revision of Palmyra's commercial code : everything there is taken into account, from the entrance fees for caravans to the prices set for prostitutes. At the moment, we are assembling a congress of physicians and magistrates to determine the utmost duration of a pregnancy, thus putting an end to interminable legal squabbles. Cases of bigamy are increasing in number in the veterans' settlements; I am doing my best to persuade these men not to make wrong use of the new laws which permit them to marry, and I council them to abstain prudently from taking more than one wife at a time! In Athens a Pantheon is in process of construction on the model of the Pantheon in Rome; I am composing the inscription to be placed on its walls, and shall enumerate therein (as examples and commitments for the future) my services to the Greek cities and to barbarian peoples; the services rendered to Rome need no such record.

The struggle goes on against brutal misuse of judiciary power: I have had to reprimand the governor of Cilica who took it into his head to execute under torture the cattle thieves in his province, as if simple death were not enough to punish a man and dispose of him. Both the State and the municipalities were abusing their power to condemn men to forced labour in order to procure workers at no cost; I have prohibited that practice not only with regard to free men but for forced labour of slaves as well; it is important, however, to watch sharply lest this detestable system re-establish itself under other names. In certain parts of the territory of ancient Carthage child sacrifice still prevails, so means must be devised to forbid the priests of Baal the pleasure of feeding their fires. In Asia Minor the rights of heirs of the Seleucids have been shamefully disregarded by our civil tribunals, ever prejudiced against the former kings; I have repaired that long-standing injustice. In Greece the trial of Herod Atticus still goes on. Phlegon's dispatch box, with his erasers of pumice stone and his sticks of red wax, will be with me to the end.

As in the days of my felicity, people believe me to be a god; they continue to give me that appellation even though they are offering sacrifices to the heavens for the restoration of the Imperial Health. I have already told you the reasons for which such a belief, salutary for them, seems to me not unwise. A blind old woman has come on foot from Pannonia, having undertaken that exhausting journey in order to ask me to touch her eyes; she has recovered her sight under my hands, as her fervour had led her to expect; her faith in the emperor-god explains this miracle. Other prodigies have occurred, and invalids say that they have seen

me in their dreams, as the pilgrims to Epidauras have visions of
Aesculapius; they claim that they have awakened cured, or at
least improved. I do not smile at the contrast between my powers
as a thaumaturge and my own illness; I accept these new privileges with gravity. The old blind woman who made her way to
the emperor from the depths of a barbarian province has become
for me what the slave of Tarragona had formerly been, namely, a
symbol of the populations of the empire whom I have both ruled
and served. Their immense confidence repays me for twenty
years of work which was itself congenial to me.

Phlegon has recently read me verses of a Jew of Alexandria
who also attributes to me superhuman powers; without irony
I welcomed that description of an elderly prince who is seen
going back and forth over all the roads of the earth, descending
to the treasures of the mines, re-awakening the generative forces
of the soil, and everywhere establishing peace and prosperity;
the initiate who has restored the shrines of all races, the connoisseur in magic arts, the seer who raised a youth to the heavens.
I shall have been better understood by this enthusiastic Jew than
by many a senator and proconsul; this adversary now won over
looks upon me almost as does Arrian; I am amazed to have become for some people just what I sought to be, after all, and I
marvel that this success is made up of so little.

Old age and death, as they approach, begin to add their
majesty to this prestige; men step reverently from my path;
they no longer compare me, as they once did, to serene and
radiant Zeus, but to Mars Gradivus, god of long campaigns and
austere discipline, or to grave Numa, inspired by the gods. Of
late this pale, drawn visage, these fixed eyes; and this tall body
held straight by force of will, suggest to them Pluto, god of
shades. Only a few intimates, a few tried and cherished friends,
escape such dread contagion of respect. The young lawyer
Fronto, this future magistrate who will doubtless be one of the
good servants of your reign, came to discuss with me an address
of mine to be made in the Senate; his voice was trembling, and
I read in his face that same reverence mingled with fear. The
tranquil joys of human friendship are no longer for me; men
adore me and venerate me far too much to love me.

A happy fate not unlike that of certain gardeners has been allotted me: everything that I have tried to implant in the human imagination has taken root there. The cult of Antinous seemed like the wildest of my enterprises, the overflow of a grief which concerned me alone. But our epoch is avid for gods; it prefers the most ardent dieties, and the most sorrowful, those who mingle with the wine of life a bitter honey from beyond the grave. At Delphi the youth has become the Hermes who guards the threshold, master of the dark passages leading to the shades. Eleusis, where his age and status as a stranger formerly prevented him from being initiated with me, now makes of him the young Bacchus of the Mysteries, prince of those border regions which lie between the senses and the soul. His ancestral Arcadia associates him with Pan and Diana, woodland divinities; the peasants of Tibur identify him with the gentle Aristaeus, king of the bees. In Asia his worshippers liken him to their tender gods devoured by summer heat or broken by autumn storms. Far away, on the edge of barbarian lands, the companion of my hunts and travels has assumed the aspect of the Thracian Horseman, that mysterious figure seen riding through the copses by moonlight and carrying away the souls of the dead in the folds of his cloak.

All of that could be no more than an excrescence of the official cult, forms of public flattery or adulation of priests greedy for subsidies. But the young face is escaping from me to respond to the aspirations of simpler hearts: by one of those shifts of balance inherent in the nature of things that sombre but exquisite youth has taken his place in popular devotion as the support of the weak and the poor, and the comforter of dead children. His image on the coins of Bithynia, that profile of the youth of fifteen with floating locks and delighted, wondering smile (which he kept for so short a time), is hung at the neck of new-born infants in the guise of an amulet; it is nailed up likewise in village cemeteries on the small tombs. In recent years, when I used to think of my own death, like a pilot unmindful of himself but trembling for the ship's passengers and cargo, I would tell myself bitterly that this remembrance would founder with me; that young being so carefully embalmed in the depths of my memory seemed obliged thus to perish for a second time. That fear, though justifiable, has been in part allayed; I have compensated for this premature death as well as I could; an image, a reflection, some feeble echo will survive for at least a few centuries. Little more can be done in matters of immortality.

I have again seen Fidus Aquila, governor of Antinoöpolis, as he passed on his way to his new post at Sarmizegethusa. He has described to me the annual rites celebrated now on the banks of the Nile in honour of the dead god, to which pilgrims come by thousands from the regions of the North and the South, with offerings of beer and of grain, and with prayers; every third year anniversary games are held in Antinoöpolis as well as in Alexandria, and in Mantinea and my beloved Athens. These triennial festivities will recur this autumn, but I do not hope to last out until this ninth return of the month of Athyr. It is the more important, therefore, that each detail of such solemnities should be determined in advance. The oracle of the dead youth functions inside the secret chamber of the ancient Egyptian temple restored by my care; its priests distribute daily some hundreds of responses already prepared for all those questions which human hope or anguish may pose. I have incurred reproach for having composed several of these answers myself. I did not intend, in so doing, to be lacking in respect towards my god, or in compassion for the soldier's wife who asks if her husband will come back alive from a garrison in Palestine, for the invalid hungering for comfort, for some merchant whose ships ride the waves of the Red Sea, for a couple who desire a son; at the most I was continuing in this way the games of logogriphs and versified charades at which we used sometimes to play together. Likewise there was comment because here in the Villa, around the chapel of Canopus where his cult is celebrated in Egyptian fashion, I have encouraged the establishment of various pleasure pavilions like those of the suburb of Alexandria which bears that name, and have offered their facilities and distractions to my guests, sometimes participating in them myself. He had grown used to that kind of thing. And then, one does not enclose himself for years in a unique thought without re-introducing into it, little by little, all the mere routines of a life.

I have done all that is supposed to be done. I have waited,

and sometimes I have prayed. *Audivi voces divinas.* ... The light-hearted Julia Balbilla believed that she heard the mysterious voice of Memnon at dawn; I have listened for the night's faintest sounds. I have used the unctions of oil and essence of roses which attract the shades; I have set out the bowl of milk, the handful of salt, the drop of blood, supports of their former existence. I have lain down on the marble pavement of the small sanctuary; the light of the stars made its way through the openings of the wall, producing reflections here and there, strange, pale gleams. I have recalled to myself the orders whispered by the priests in the ear of the dead, and the itinerary written on the tomb: *And he will recognize the way. ... And the guardians of the threshold will let him pass. ... And he will come and go around those who love him for millions of days. ...* Sometimes, after long intervals, I have thought to feel the slight stir of an approach, a touch as light as the contact of eyelashes and warm as the hollow of a hand. *And the shade of Patroclus appears at Achilles' side. ...* I shall never know if that warmth, that sweetness, did not emanate simply from deep within me, like the last efforts of a man struggling against solitude and the cold of night. But the question, which arises also in the presence of our living loves, has ceased to interest me now; it matters little to me whether the phantoms whom I evoke come from the limbo of my memory or from that of another world. My soul, if I possess one, is made of the same substance as are the spectres; this body with the swollen hands and livid nails, this sorry mass almost half dissolved, this sack of ills, of desires and dreams, is hardly more solid or consistent than a shade. I differ from the dead only in my faculty to suffocate some moments longer; in one sense their existence seems to me more assured than my own. Antinous and Plotina are at least as real as myself.

Meditation upon death does not teach one how to die; it does not make the departure more easy, but ease is no longer what I seek. Little face, so wilful and brooding, your sacrifice will have enriched not my life but my death. Death's approach re-establishes between us a kind of close complicity: the living beings who surround me, my devoted if sometimes importunate servitors, will never know how little the world interests the two of us now. I think with disgust of the doleful symbols of the Egyptian tombs: the hard scarab, the rigid mummy, the frog which signifies eternal parturition. To believe the priests, I have left you at the place where the separate elements of a being tear apart like a worn garment under strain, at that sinister crossroads between what was and what will be, and what exists eternally. It is conceivable, after all, that those notions are right, and that death is made up of the same confused, shifting matter as life. But none of these theories of immortality inspire me with confidence; the system of retributions and punishments makes little impression upon a judge well aware of the difficulties of judging. On the other hand, the opposite solution seems to me also too simple, the neat reduction to nothingness, the hollow void where Epicurus' disdainful laughter resounds.

I try now to observe my own ending: this series of experiments conducted upon myself continues the long study begun in Satyrus' clinic. So far the modifications are as external as those to which time and inclement weather subject any edifice, leaving its architecture and basic material unaltered; I sometimes think that through the crevices I see and touch upon the indestructible foundation, the rock eternal. I am what I always was; I am dying without essential change. At first view the robust child of the gardens in Spain and the ambitious officer once more in his tent, shaking the snowflakes from his shoulders, seem as thoroughly obliterated as I shall be when I shall have gone through the funeral fire; but they are still there; I am inseparable from those parts of myself. The man who howled his grief upon a dead body has not ceased to wail in some corner of my being, in spite of the superhuman, or perhaps subhuman calm into which I am entering already; the voyager immured within the ever sedentary invalid is curious about death because it spells departure. That force which once was I seems still capable of actuating several more lives, or of raising up whole worlds. If by a miracle some centuries were suddenly to be added to the few days now left to me I would do the same things over again, even to committing the same errors; I would frequent the same Olympian heights and even the same Infernos. Such a conclusion is an excellent argument in favour of the utility of death, but at the same time it inspires certain doubts as to death's total efficacity.

In certain periods of my life I have noted down my dreams; I have discussed their significance with priests and philosophers, and with astrologers. The faculty for dreaming, though deadened for many years, has been restored to me in the course of these months of agony; the incidents of my waking hours seem less real, and sometimes less irksome, than those of dream. If this larval and spectral world, where the platitudinous and the absurd swarm in even greater abundance than on earth, affords us some notion of the state of the soul when separated from the body, then I shall doubtless pass my eternity in regretting the exquisite control which our senses now provide, and the adjusted perspectives offered by human reason.

And nevertheless I sink back with a certain relief into those insubstantial regions of dream; there I possess for a moment some secrets which soon escape me again; there I drink at the sacred springs. The other day I was in the oasis of Ammon, on the afternoon of the lion hunt. I was in high spirits; everything went as in the time of my former vigour: the wounded lion collapsed to the ground, then rose again; I pressed forward to strike the final blow. But this time my rearing horse threw me; the horrible, bleeding mass of the beast rolled over me, and claws tore at my chest; I came to myself in my room in Tibur, crying out for aid. More recently still I have seen my father, though I think of him rather seldom. He was lying on his sickbed in the room of our house in Italica, where I ceased to dwell soon after his death. On his table he had a phial full of sedative potion which I begged him to give me. I awoke before he had time to reply. It surprises me that most men are so fearful of ghosts when they are so ready to speak of the dead in their dreams.

Presages are also increasing: from now on everything seems like an intimation and a sign. I have just dropped and broken a precious stone set in a ring; my profile had been carved thereon by a Greek artist. The augurs shake their heads gravely, but my regret is for that pure masterpiece. I have come to speak of myself, at times, in the past tense; in the Senate, while discussing certain events which had taken place after the death of Lucius, I have caught myself more than once mentioning those circumstances, by a slip of the tongue, as if they had occurred after my own death. A few months ago, on my birthday, as I was mounting the steps of the Capitol by litter, I found myself face to face with a man in mourning; furthermore, he was weeping, and I saw my good Chabrias turn pale. At that period I still went about and was able to continue performing in person my duties as high pontiff and as Arval Brother, and to celebrate myself the ancient rites of this Roman religion which, in the end, I prefer to most of the foreign cults. I was standing one day before the altar, ready to light the flame; I was offering the gods a sacrifice for Antoninus. Suddenly the fold of my toga covering my brow slipped and fell to my shoulder, leaving me bareheaded; thus I passed from the rank of sacrificer to that of victim. Verily, it is indeed my turn.

My patience is bearing fruit; I suffer less, and life has become almost sweet again. I have ceased to quarrel with physicians; their foolish remedies have killed me, but their presumption and hypocritical pedantry are work of our making: if we were not so afraid of pain they would tell fewer lies. Strength fails me now for the angers of old; I know from a reliable source that Platorius Nepos, for whom I have had great affection, has taken advantage of my confidence; I have not tried to confound him with the evidence, nor have I ordered a punishment. The future of the world no longer disturbs me; I do not try still to calculate, with anguish, how long or how short a time the Roman peace will endure; I leave that to the gods. Not that I have acquired more confidence in their justice, which is not our justice, or more faith in human wisdom; the contrary is true. Life is atrocious, we know. But precisely because I expect little of the human condition, man's periods of felicity, his partial progress, his efforts to begin over again and to continue, all seem to me like so many prodigies which nearly compensate for the monstrous mass of ills and defeats, of indifference and error. Catastrophe and ruin will come; disorder will triumph, but order will too, from time to time. Peace will again establish itself between two periods of war; the words *humanity*, *liberty*, and *justice* will here and there regain the meaning which we have tried to give them. Not all our books will perish, nor our statues, if broken, lie unrepaired; other domes and other pediments will arise from our domes and pediments; some few men will think and work and feel as we have done, and I venture to count upon such continuators, placed irregularly throughout the centuries, and upon this kind of intermittent immortality.

If ever the barbarians gain possession of the world they will be forced to adopt some of our methods; they will end by resembling us. Chabrias fears that the pastophor of Mithra or the bishop of Christ may implant himself one day in Rome, replacing the high pontiff. If by ill fate that day should come, my successor officiating in the vatical fields along the Tiber will already have ceased to be merely the chief of a gang, or a band of sectarians, and will have become in his turn one of the universal figures of authority. He will inherit our palaces and our archives, and will differ from rulers like us less than one might suppose. I accept with calm these vicissitudes of Rome eternal.

The medicaments have no effect on me now; my limbs are more swollen than ever, and I sleep sitting up instead of reclining. One advantage of death will be to lie down again on a bed. It is now my turn to console Antoninus. I remind him that death has long seemed to me the most fitting solution of my own problem; as always, my wishes are finally being fulfilled, but in a slower and more indirect way than I had expected. I can be glad that illness has left me lucid to the end, and I rejoice to have escaped the trials of old age, with its hardening and stiffening, its aridity and cruel absence of desire. If my calculations are exact, my mother died at about the age which I am today; my life has already been half again as long as that of my father, who died at forty. Everything is prepared: the eagle entrusted with bearing the emperor's soul to the gods is held in reserve for the funeral ceremony. My mausoleum, on top of which they are just now planting the cypresses, designed to form a black pyramid high in the sky, will be completed about in time to receive the ashes while yet still warm. I have requested Antoninus to see that Sabina is transported there later on; at her death I did not have divine honours conferred upon her, as was after all her due; it would not be bad to have that neglect repaired. And I would like the remains of Aelius Caesar to be placed at my side.

They have taken me to Baiae; in this July heat the journey has been an ordeal, but I breathe better near the sea. On the shore the waves make their murmur of rustling silk and whispered caress. I can still enjoy the pale rose light of the long evenings. But I hold these tablets now only to occupy my hands, which in spite of me agitate. I have sent for Antoninus; a courier dispatched at full speed has left for Rome. Sound of the hoofs of Borysthenes, gallop of the Thracian Rider. . . .

The little group of intimates presses round my bed. Chabrias moves me to pity: tears ill become the wrinkles of age. Celer's handsome face is, as always, strangely calm; he applies himself steadily to nursing me without letting anything be seen of what might add to a patient's anxiety or fatigue. But Diotimus is sobbing, his head buried in the cushions. I have assured his future; he does not like Italy; he will be able to realize his dream, which is to return to Gadara and open a school of eloquence there with a friend; he has nothing to lose by my death. And nevertheless the slight shoulder moves convulsively under the folds of his tunic; on my fingers I feel those tender tears. To the last, Hadrian will have been loved in human wise.

Little soul, gentle and drifting, guest and companion of my body, now you will dwell below in pallid places, stark and bare; there you will abandon your play of yore. But one moment still, let us gaze together on these familiar shores, on these objects which doubtless we shall not see again. . . . Let us try, if we can, to enter into death with open eyes. . . .

TO THE DEIFIED EMPEROR HADRIAN

SON OF TRAJAN CONQUEROR OF THE PARTHIANS
GRANDSON OF NERVA
HIGH PONTIFF
HONOURED TWENTY-TWO TIMES
WITH THE TRIBUNICIAN POWER
THREE TIMES CONSUL
TWICE HAILED IN TRIUMPH
FATHER OF HIS COUNTRY
AND TO HIS DEIFIED SPOUSE
SABINA
ANTONINUS THEIR SON DEDICATES
THIS MEMORIAL

TO LUCIUS AELIUS CAESAR
SON OF THE DEIFIED HADRIAN
TWICE CONSUL

AUTHOR'S NOTE

A RECONSTRUCTION of a historical figure and of the world of his time written in the first person borders on the domain of fiction, and sometimes of poetry; it can therefore dispense with formal statement of evidence for the historical facts concerned. Its human significance, however, is greatly enriched by close adherence to those facts. Since the main object of the author here has been to approach inner reality, if possible, through careful examination of what the documents themselves afford, it seems advisable to offer the reader some discussion of the principal materials employed, though not to present a complete bibliography, which would extend beyond the scope of the present volume. Some brief indication will also be given of the comparatively few changes, all of secondary importance, which add to, or cautiously modify, what history has told us.

*　　*　　*

The reader who likes to consider sources at first hand will not necessarily know where to find the principal ancient texts relating to Hadrian, or even what they are, since most of them come down to us from writers of the late classical period who are relatively little read, and who are ordinarily familiar only to specialists. Our two chief authorities are the Greek historian Dio Cassius and the Latin chronicler known by the name of Spartianus. Dio's *Roman History,* written about forty years after Hadrian's death but surviving, unfortunately, only in abridged form, devotes a chapter to this emperor. Somewhat more than a century later than Dio, and apparently writing independently of his Greek predecessor, Spartianus composed a *Life of Hadrian,* one of the most substantial texts of the *Historia Augusta,* and a *Life of Aelius Caesar,* a slighter work of that same collection. The latter biography presents a very plausible likeness of Hadrian's adopted son, and is superficial only because, after all, the subject was so himself. These two writers had access to documents no longer extant, among others an autobiography published by Hadrian under the name of his freedman Phlegon, as well as a collection of the emperor's letters assembled by this same secretary. Neither Dio nor Spartianus is great as historian or biographer, but their very lack of

241

art, and, to a certain degree, their lack of system, leave them singularly close to actuality. On the whole, modern research has confirmed their assertions in striking manner, and it is in great part upon their piece-meal accumulation of facts that the present interpretation is based.

Mention may also be made, without attempting a comprehensive listing, of some details gleaned in other lives of the *Historia Augusta*, in particular in the biographies of Antoninus and of Marcus Aurelius by Julius Capitolinus. Some phrases have been taken from Aurelius Victor's *Book of the Caesars* and from the unknown author of the *Epitome*, professedly the work of Aurelius Victor, too. Both these writers, though only some half century later than Spartianus, already conceive of Hadrian's life as almost legendary, but the splendour of their rhetoric puts them in a class apart. The historians Eutropius and Ammianus Marcellinus, also of the latter half of the fourth century, add little to the information given by earlier writers on Hadrian. Likewise the notice on this emperor in the *Lexicon* of the tenth-century Byzantine scholar Suidas, and the few pages devoted to him by the historian Zonaras, of the twelfth century, hardly do more than repeat Dio; but two other notices in Suidas provide each a fact little known about one episode in Hadrian's life, namely that a *Consolation* was addressed to him by the philosopher Numenius, and that Mesomedes, the court musician, composed music for the funeral of Antinous.

From Hadrian himself we have a certain number of works of un-questioned authenticity : from his official life there is administrative correspondence and fragments of discourses or reports, like the noted address to the troops at Lambaesis, conserved for the most part in inscriptions; also his legal decisions, handed down by the jurists. From his personal life we have poems mentioned by authors of his time, such as his celebrated *Animula Vagula Blandula*, or occurring as votive inscriptions, like the poem to Eros and the Uranian Aphrodite on the temple wall at Thespiae (G. Kaibel, *Epigr. Gr.* 811). Three letters supposedly written by Hadrian, and concerning his personal life, are of doubtful authenticity (*Letter to Matidia, Letter to Servianus, Letter addressed by the Dying Emperor to Antoninus*, to be found respectively in the collection of Dositheus, in the *Vita Saturnini* of Vopiscus, and in a fragment of Fayum papyrus, edited by Grenfell and Hunt, *Fayum Towns and Their Papyri*, 1900). All three of these letters, nevertheless, are decidedly characteristic of the man to whom they are attributed, and therefore certain indications which they afford have been used in this book.

References or allusions to Hadrian or to his entourage are to be found scattered through most of the writers of the second and third centuries, and serve to complete suggestions in the chronicles, or fill in lacunae there. Thus, to cite only a few examples, the episode of the hunt in Libya is taken from a fragment of a poem of Pancrates, *The Hunt of Hadrian and Antinous*, found in Egypt and published in 1911 in the collection, *Oxyrhynchus Papyri*, VIII, No. 1085; Athenaeus, Aulus Gellius, and Philostratus have furnished numerous details on the sophists and poets of the imperial court; both the Younger Pliny and Martial add a few touches to the somewhat sketchy information left to us by Apuleius and by Trajan's historians for two of Hadrian's friends, Voconius and Licinius Sura. The description of Hadrian's grief at the death of Antinous is drawn from the historians of the reign, but also from certain passages in the Church Fathers, who though indeed disapproving are sometimes more understanding on this subject, and above all more varied in their approach to it, than the usual blanket references to their opinions would reveal. We have allusions to that grief also in the writings of the emperor's friend Arrian, from whom actual passages have been incorporated in these *Memoirs* (*Letter from Arrian to the Emperor Hadrian on the Occasion of the Circumnavigation of the Black Sea*, a text questioned by some scholars, but accepted by others as genuine except for minor interpolations). For the war in Palestine, certain details known to be authentic have been extracted from the *Talmud*, where they lie imbedded in an immense amount of legendary material; they serve to supplement the principal account of that war as given in Eusebius' *Ecclesiastical History*. Details of the exile of Favorinus come from a fragment of that writer in a manuscript of the Vatican Library published in 1931 (M. Norsa and G. Vitelli, *Il Papiro Vaticano Greco*, II, in *Studi e Testi*, LIII); the horrible episode of the secretary blinded in one eye occurs in a treatise of Galen, who was physician to Marcus Aurelius; the picture of the dying Hadrian is built upon the sombre portrait which Fronto, an intimate of Marcus Aurelius, gives of the emperor in his last years.

Statues, reliefs, inscriptions, and coins have provided factual details not recorded by ancient writers and historians. Certain glimpses into the savagery of the Dacian and Sarmatian wars, such as prisoners burned alive and councillors of King Decebalus poisoning themselves on the day of their capitulation, are afforded by the scenes on Trajan's Column (W. Froehner, *La Colonne Trajane*, 1865); I. A. Richmond, *Trajan's Army on Trajan's Column, Papers of the British School at Rome*, XIII, 1935). Certain inscriptions serve as points of departure for episodes constructed in this work: thus the three poems of Julia

Balbilla carved on the legs of the Colossus of Memnon, and Hadrian's own name carved on that statue as well, help to build the visit to Thebes (J. A. Letronne, *Recueil des inscriptions grecques et latines de l'Égypte*, II, 1848, and R. Cagnat, *Inscr. Graec. ad res Rom. pert.*, I., 1186–7). The day of the year on which Antinous was born is given as it occurs on an inscription left by a fraternity of workmen and slaves in Lanuvium, who chose that new diety for their patron and protector in the year 133 (*Corp. Inscr. Lat.* XIV, 2112). This precision as to the day has been questioned by Mommsen, but has been accepted since his time by less hypercritical scholars. The several phrases presented in these *Memoirs* as if inscribed on the tomb of the favourite are taken from the long text in hieroglyphs on the obelisk of the Pincio in Rome, telling of Antinous' funeral and detailing the ritual of his cult (A. Erman, *Obelisken Römischer Zeit*, in *Mitt. d. deutsch, arch. Inst., Röm. Abt.*, XI, 1896; O. Marucchi, *Gli Obelischi Egiziani di Roma*, 1898). The coins of the reign suggest many details for the voyages described; the legends on some of these coins have furnished titles for the parts of this book (with two exceptions, one drawn from Aurelius Victor), and have often provided the keynotes for Hadrian's meditations themselves.

To discuss briefly the study of Hadrian and his period by modern and contemporary writers it may first be noted that already in the seventeenth and eighteenth centuries all historians of Rome from Tillemont to Gibbon have touched upon this emperor, but their works, substantial as they are (the critical spirit which animates the article on Hadrian in Bayle's *Dictionnaire*, for example, remains unrivalled in its kind), belong henceforth to History's history. Nearer our time even the brilliant sketch of Renan in the first chapter of *L'Église Chrétienne* shows equally the marks of age. Nor is there a complete modern biography, properly speaking, to which the reader can be referred without reservation. The earliest work of the kind, that of Gregorovius, published in 1851, is not without life and colour, but is weak in everything that concerns Hadrian as administrator and prince, and is in great part outdated by researches of the past half century. The more methodical study of O. Th. Schulz, *Leben des Kaisers Hadrian*, 1904, is less rich in humanistic erudition than Gregorovius and is also outdated in part. The more recent biography by B. W. Henderson, *The Life and Principate of the Emperor Hadrian A.D. 76–138*, published in 1923, though lengthy, gives only a superficial idea of Hadrian's thought and of the intellectual currents of his time.

But important specialized studies abound; in many respects modern scholarship has thrown new light upon the history of Hadrian's reign and administration. To cite only a few such studies, recent or at least relatively recent, and easily accessible, there are in English the chapter devoted to Hadrian's social and financial reforms in the masterly work of M. Rostovtzeff, *Social and Economic History of the Roman Empire*, 1926; the valuable studies, respectively, of R. H. Lacey, *The Equestrian Officials of Trajan and Hadrian: Their Careers, with some Notes on Hadrian's Reforms*, Princeton, 1917; of Paul Alexander, *Letters and Speeches of the Emperor Hadrian, Harv. Stud. in Class. Phil.*, XLIX, 1938; of W. D. Gray, *A Study of the Life of Hadrian Prior to his Accession, Smith Coll. Stud. in Hist.*, 1919; of F. Pringsheim, *The Legal Policy and Reforms of Hadrian, Journ. of Rom. Stud.*, XXIV, 1934; of R. G. Collingwood and J. N. L. Myres, *Roman Britain and the English Settlements*, 2nd ed., 1937. Arnold Toynbee offers a wholly modern interpretation of the pacific policy of Hadrian in his essay *Roman Empire and Modern Europe, Dublin Review*, 1945. Among French scholarly studies may be mentioned the chapters devoted to Hadrian in *Le Haut-Empire romain* of Léon Homo, 1933, and in *L'Empire romain* of E. Albertini, 1936; the analysis of Trajan's Parthian campaigns and Hadrian's peace policy in *Histoire de l'Asie* by René Grousset, 1921 (followed closely for the description of the Parthian campaign in these *Memoirs*); the study of the literary productions of Hadrian in *Les Empereurs et les lettres latines* by Henri Bardon, 1944; the respective works of Paul Graindor, *Athènes sous Hadrien*, 1934; of Louis Perret, *La Titulature impériale d'Hadrien*, 1929, and of Bernard d'Orgeval *L'Empereur Hadrien, son œuvre législative et administrative*, 1950. But the most comprehensive studies of the sources for Hadrian and his chronology are still those of the German school, J. Dürr, *Die Reisen des Kaisers Hadrian*, Vienna, 1881; J. Plew, *Quellenuntersuchungen zur Geschichte des Kaisers Hadrian*, Strasbourg, 1890; E. Kornemann, *Kaiser Hadrian und der letzte grosse Historiker von Rom*, Leipzig, 1905; and especially the admirable short work of Wilhelm Weber, *Untersuchungen zur Geschichte des Kaisers Hadrianus*, Leipzig, 1907. By the same Weber is the striking essay *Hadrian*, published in English in the *Cambridge Ancient History*, XI (*The Imperial Peace*), 1936, pp. 294–324. For the study of Hadrian's coins (apart from those of Antinous, to be discussed below) in relation to the events of the reign, consult H. Mattingly and E. A. Sydenham, *The Roman Imperial Coinage*, II, 1926; P. L. Strack *Untersuchungen zur römischen Reichsprägung des zweiten Jahrhunderts*, II, 1933.

Much material about Hadrian is to be found in studies made on his associates, and on problems which led to, or followed, the war in Palestine. For Trajan's reign, and in particular for his wars, see (apart from the text of Grousset mentioned above) R. Paribeni, *Optimus Princeps, Messina*, [1927]; M. Durry, *Le Règne de Trajan d'après les monnaies, Revue Hist.*, LVII, 1932; R. P. Longden, *Nerva and Trajan* and *The Wars of Trajan*, chapters in *Cambridge Ancient History*, XI, 1936; and Wilhelm Weber, *Trajan und Hadrian*, in *Meister der Politik*, I², Stuttgart, 1923. On Aelius Caesar, A. S. L. Farquharson, *On the Names of Aelius Caesar, Class. Quar.*, II, 1908, and J. Carcopino, *L'Hérédité dynastique chez les Antonins*, 1950 (whose hypotheses have been set aside as unconvincing in favour of a more literal interpretation of the texts). On the affair of the four 'consulars', see especially A. von Premerstein, *Das Attentat der Konsulare auf Hadrian in Jahre 188*, in *Klio*, 1908; J. Carcopino, *Lusius Quietus, l'homme de Qwrnyn*, in *Istros*, 1934. On the Greek entourage of Hadrian, see more particularly A. von Premerstein, *C. Julius Quadratus Bassus*, in *Sitz. Bayr. Akad. d. Wiss.*, 1934; P. Graindor, *Un Milliardaire antique: Hérode Atticus et sa famille*, Cairo, 1930; L. Boulanger, *Aelius Aristide et la Sophistique dans la Province d'Asie au IIe siècle de notre ère*, in *Bib. des Ec. Fr. d'Athènes et de Rome*, 1923; K. Horna, *Die Hymnen des Mesomedes*, Leipzig, 1928; Martellotti, *Mesomede*, in *Scuola di Filol. Class.*, Rome, 1929; H. C. Puech, *Numenios d'Apamée*, in *Mélanges Bidez*, Brussels, 1934. On the Jewish war, for studies in English see especially A. L. Sachar, *A History of the Jews*, 1950; S. Lieberman, *Greek in Jewish Palestine*, 1942; and the articles of W. D. Gray, *The Founding of Aelia Capitolina and the Chronology of the Jewish War under Hadrian, Amer. Journ. of Semit. Lang. and Lit.*, 1923; R. Harris, Hadrian's *Decree of Expulsion of the Jews from Jerusalem, Harv. Theol. Rev.* XIX, 1929; W. Stinespring, *Hadrian in Palestine, Amer. Orient. Soc.* LIX, 1939. See also, apart from the German works already cited, A. von Premerstein, *Alexandréinische und jüdische Gesandte vor Kaiser Hadrian*, in *Hermes*, LVII, 1922. In French, Renan's account of Hadrian's war in Palestine, in *L'Église chrétienne*, 1879, is essential still. The archaeologists of Israel, too, are now steadily bringing new contributions to our still limited knowledge of the history and topography of this war.

What we know of Antinous, and of the posthumous cult which was built up around him, is derived from a limited number of ancient texts, both historical, literary and most of them brief, and some of which have been cited already in this *Note*; from a few inscriptions, like that of the very important text on the obelisk of the

Pincio mentioned above; and from the innumerable statues, bas-reliefs, and coins of the Bithynian favourite which have come down to us. That is to say, history, iconography, and aesthetic evaluation are here inseparable. Up to the time of the Renaissance, the very reprobation with which Christian tradition had surrounded the deified youth helped to keep his memory alive; from the sixteenth century on, the statues discovered in Roman vineyards, as well as the counterfeits of forgers, have served to enrich the princely and papal collections with his image. In 1764 Winckelmann, in his *Geschichte der Kunst des Alterthums*, presented with a kind of fervour the first comprehensive study of Antinous portraiture, based on the statues to be seen in the Rome of his time. Such example was soon to be followed in the course of the nineteenth century by numerous essays in the field of scholarship or aesthetics; unequal in value, these studies are chiefly significant for what they reveal of the tastes or the moral conventions of their period. Among them should be noted especially the *Antinous* of L. Dietrichson (Christiania, 1884), a work which though based on somewhat confused idealism, and decidedly outdated from the point of view of iconographic research, nevertheless lists with almost passionate care all the ancient texts and inscriptions known about Antinous at that time. The study of F. Laban, *Der Gemütsausdruck des Antinous*, 1891, enumerates different reactions in German studies of aesthetics from Winckelmann to the end of the nineteenth century which discuss Antinous portraiture, but it hardly touches upon the actual iconography and history of Hadrian's favourite. The essay on Antinous by J. Addington Symonds in his *Sketches in Italy and Greece*, 1900, is singularly penetrating, although the tone is now outmoded and the information on some points is outdated by recent research; unlike Laban, he tries with the help of literary and artistic documentation to approach the young Bithynian as a living reality. The same writer adds a note of value on this same subject to his remarkable essay on inversion in ancient times, *A Problem in Greek Ethics* (privately printed 1883, reimpression 1901). The important study published in 1923 by Piero Marconi, *Antinoo. Saggio sull'arte dell'età adrianea*, (*Mon. Ant. R. Accad. Lincei*, XXIX) provides a very nearly complete catalogue of statues and bas-reliefs of the favourite known at that date; although poor in discussion of aesthetic values, this work marks a great advance over previous studies in its accurate description of the individual statues, and by such close scrutiny adds a few points to our knowledge of the history of Antinous himself. This approach spells an end to the hazy dreaming in which romantic criticism had indulged with regard to that youth. On the contrary, the brief study of E. Holm, *Das Bildnis des Antinous*, Leipzig, 1933, is typical of the narrowly specialized dissertation in which the study of iconography is wholly dissociated from psychology and from history. The second volume of Robert West's *Römishe Porträt-Plastik*, Munich, 1941, contains notices, sometimes too absolute on points still open to question, on the life and portraits of Antinous, information voluntarily subordinated, however, to an admirable photographic presentation of selections from statues and relief figures of Hadrian's favourite. The long essay of G. Blum, *Numismatique d'Antinoos*, *Journ. Int. d'Arch. Numismatique*, XVI, Athens, 1914, is still indispensable for the study of the coins of Antinous, for which it offers the only attempt, so far, at complete cataloguing and analysis. For the coins of Antinous struck in Asia Minor, consult W. H. Waddington, E. Babelon and Th. Reinach, *Recueil général des monnaies grecques d'Asie-mineure*, I–IV, 1904–12, and I, 2nd ed., 1925, for his Alexandrine coins, J. Vogt, *Die Alexandrinischen Münzen*, I–II, 1924; and for some of his coins in Greece, C. Seltman, *Greek Sculpture and Some Festival Coins*, in *Hesperia*, the *Journ. Amer. School of Class. Stud. Athens*, XVII, 1948.

Without mentioning the discussions of portraiture of Antinous in general appraisals of Hadrianic art, which will be referred to below, we should indicate here the great number of books, articles, and archaeological notices containing descriptions of portraits of the young Bithynian newly discovered or identified, or new appreciations of those portrayals; for example, R. Lanciani and C. L. Visconti, *Delle scoperte . . .* in *Bollettino Communale di Roma*, XIV, 1886, pp. 189–90, 208–14; G. Rizzo, *Antinoo-Silvano*, in *Ausonia*, III, 1908; P. Gauckler, *Le Sanctuaire syrien du Janicule*, 1912; R. Bartoccini, *Le Terme di Lepcis (Leptis Magna)*, *Africa Italiana*, 1929; S. Reinach, *Les Têtes des médaillons de l'Arc de Constantin*, in *Rev. Arch.*, Série 4, XV, 1910; H. Bulle, *Ein Jagddenkmal des Kaisers Hadrian*, in *Jahr. d. arch. Inst.*, XXXIV, 1919; E. Buschor, *Die Hadrianischen Jagdbilder*, in *Mitt. d. deutsch. arch. Inst., Röm. Abt.* XXXVIII–IX, 1923–4; H. Kähler, *Hadrian und siene Villa bei Tivoli*, Berlin, 1950, note 151, pp. 177–9; C. Seltman, *Approach to Greek Art*, 1948. Such new research on points of iconography or numismatics has made it possible to ascertain certain aspects of the cult of Antinous and even certain dates in that short life.

As to the religious atmosphere which seems to have surrounded Antinous' death, see especially W. Weber, *Drei Untersuchungen zur aegyptisch-griechischen Religion*, Heidelberg, 1911; likewise P.

Graindor, *Athènes sous Hadrien* (cited above among specialized studies on Hadrian), p. 13. The problem of the exact location of the tomb of Antinous is still unsolved, despite the arguments of C. Hülsen, *Das Grab des Antinous*, in *Mitt. d. deutsch. arch. Inst., Röm. Abt.* XI, 1896, and in *Berl. Philol. Wochenschr.*, 15 Mar., 1919, and opposite view of Kähler on this point (note 158, page 179, of his work already cited). And finally should be noted the valuable chapter of Father A. J. Festugière, *La Valeur religieuse des papyrus magiques* in his book *L'Idéal religieux des Grecs et l'Évangile*, 1932, especially for its analysis of the sacrifice of the *Esies* (death by immersion with consequent attainment of divine status for the victim); though without reference to the story of Hadrian's favourite, this study nevertheless throws light upon practices known to us hitherto only through an outworn literary tradition, and thus allows this legend of voluntary sacrifice to be taken out of the storehouse of operatic episode and fitted again into the very exact framework of a specific occult tradition.

Most books on the general subjects of Graeco-Roman and late Greek art give much space to the art which is termed Hadrianic. Mention is made here only of a few of the more substantial accessible works, all of which could have been also included among the good modern appreciations of Antinous portraiture above: H. B. Walters, *Art of the Romans*, 1911 and 2nd ed. 1928; Eugenie Strong, chapters on *The Golden Age of Hadrian* in *Art in Ancient Rome*, II, 1929; G. Rodenwaldt, *Die Kunst der Antike (Hellas und Rom)*, in *Propyläen-Kunstgeschichte*, III, 2, Berlin, 1930, and *Art from Nero to the Antonines*, in *Cambridge Ancient History*, XI, 1936. The work of Jocelyn Toynbee, *The Hadrianic School, A Chapter in the History of Greek Art*, 1934, is essential for Hadrianic motifs in coins and reliefs, and for their cultural and political implications. For Hadrianic portraiture in general, in addition to the book of West mentioned above, may be noted, among others, the work of P. Graindor, *Bustes et statues-portraits de l'Égypte romaine* (no date), and of F. Poulsen, *Greek and Roman Portraits in English Country Houses*, 1923. This much abridged list may be terminated with reference to only a few studies on Hadrian's architectural constructions: that of P. Graindor, *Athènes sous Hadrian* (mentioned above) for his buildings in Greece; for his military architecture that of J. C. Bruce, *The Handbook to the Roman Wall*, ed. by R. G. Collingwood, 1933, and of the same Collingwood, *Roman Britain*, cited above among the specialized studies on Hadrian. For the Villa Adriana, the works of Gaston Boissier, *Promenades archéologiques*, 1880, and Pierre Gusman, *La Villa impériale de Tibur*, 1904, are still essential; more recent works are those of R. Paribeni, *La Villa dell'Imperatore Adriano a Tivoli* [1930], and H. Kähler, *Hadrian und seine Villa bei Tivoli,* cited above on the subject of Antinous.

We know something of the buildings of Antinoöpolis from the accounts of travellers who visited Egypt in the seventeenth and eighteenth centuries (a sentence from one of them, the Sieur Lucas, who described Antinoöpolis in 1714, has been incorporated in the present work). We know most about them from the admirable drawings of Jomard in the *Description de l'Égypte,* begun at Napoleon's order and containing very moving records of the ruined city, completely destroyed since that time. For, about the year 1860, the ancient materials of the triumphal arch, the colonnades, and the theatre were converted into cement or used otherwise to build factories in a neighbouring Arab town. The French archaeologist Albert Gayet was the first to excavate on the site of Antinoöpolis, at the end of the last century; among his many findings were mummies of officiating attendants in the Antinous cult, together with their funeral equipment, but hardly a vestige was recovered of anything dating from the actual time of the city's founding by Hadrian. Gayet's *Exploration des ruines d'Antinoé,* in *Annales* of the Guimet Museum, XXVI, 3, 1897, and other notes published in those *Annales* on that subject, though rather unmethodical, remain essential for study of the site. The papyri of Antinoöpolis and those of Oxyrhynchus, in the same district, in successive publication since 1901, have afforded no new details about the architecture of the Hadrianic city or the cult of the favourite there, but they provide a very complete list of its religious and administrative divisions, which evidently come down from Hadrian himself and bear witness to the strong influence of Eleusinian ritual on his thought. Weber, *Untersuchungen zur Geschichte des Kaisers Hadrianus,* and Graindor, *Athènes sous Hadrian,* both cited before, give some discussion of this list, as do two other studies: E. Kühn, *Antinoöpolis, Ein Beitrag zur Geschichte des Hellenismus in römischen Aegypten,* Göttingen, 1913, and B. Kübler, *Antonoupolis,* Leipzig, 1914. The brief article of M. J. de Johnson, *Antinoe and its Papyri,* in *Journ. of Egypt. Arch.,* I, 1914, gives an excellent summary of the topography of the ancient city. The Italian archaeologist Evarista Breccia has also studied the site of Antinoöpolis, and has contributed an article on the subject to the *Enciclopedia Italiana* (1928) which includes a useful bibliography.

* * *

History has its rules, though they are not always followed even by professional historians; poetry, too, has its laws. The two are not necessarily irreconcilable. The perspectives chosen for this narrative made necessary some rearrangements of detail, together with certain simplifications or modifications intended to eliminate repetitions, prolixity, or confusion which only didactic explanation would have dispelled. It was important that these adjustments, all relating only to very small points, should in no way change the spirit or the significance of the incident or the fact in question. In other cases, the lack of authentic details for some given episode of Hadrian's life has obliged the writer to prudent filling in of such lacunae from information furnished by contemporary texts treating of analogous experiences or events; these joinings had, of course, to be kept to the indispensable minimum. And last, this work, which tries to evoke Hadrian not only as he was but also as his contemporaries saw him, and sometimes imagined him, could even make some sparing use of legendary material, provided that the material thus chosen corresponded to the conception that the men of his time (and he himself, perhaps) had of his personality. The method of making such changes and additions is best explained by specific examples, with which this Note is hereby concluded.

The character Marullinus is built upon a name, that of an ancestor of Hadrian, and upon a tradition which says that an uncle (and not the grandfather) of the future emperor foretold the boy's fortune; the portrait of the old man and the circumstances of his death are imaginary. The character Gallus is based on an historical Gallus who played the part described here, but the detail of his final discomfiture is created only in order to emphasize one of Hadrian's traits most often mentioned, his capacity for bitter resentment. The episode of Mithraic initiation is invented; that cult was already in vogue in the army at the time, and it is possible, but not proved, that Hadrian desired to be initiated into it while he was still a young officer. Likewise, it is only a possibility that Antinous submitted himself to the ritual blood bath in Palmyra; Turbo, Meles Agrippa, and Castoras are all historical figures, but their participation in the respective initiations is invented. Hadrian's meeting with the Gymnosophist is not given by history; it has been built from first- and second-century texts which describe episodes of the same kind. All details concerning Attianus are authentic, except for one or two allusions to his private life, of which we know nothing. The chapter on the mistresses has been constructed out of two lines of Spartianus (XI, 7–8); on this subject the effort has been to stay within the most plausible general outlines, supplementing by invention where it was essential to do so.

Pompeius Proculus was indeed governor of Bithynia, but was not surely so in 123–4, during the emperor's visit in those years. Strato of Sardis, an erotic poet and compiler of the twelfth book of the *Greek Anthology*, probably lived in Hadrian's time; there is nothing to prove that he saw the emperor in person, but it was tempting to make these two men meet. The visit of Lucius to Alexandria in 130 is deduced (as Gregorovius has already done) from a text often contested, the *Letter to Servianus*, discussed above, nor does the passage of this letter which refers to Lucius require such interpretation. We do not know, therefore, if he was in Egypt at that time, but almost all the details given for him at this period are drawn from his biography by Spartianus. The story of Antinous' sacrifice is traditional (Dio, LXIX, 11; Spartianus, XIV, 7); the detail of the magic operations is suggested by recipes from Egyptian papyri on magic, but the incidents of the evening in Canopus are invented. The episode of the fall of a child from a balcony, during a banquet, placed in these *Memoirs* in the course of Hadrian's stop at Philae, is drawn from a report in the *Oxyrhynchus Papyri* and took place in reality nearly forty years after Hadrian's journey in Egypt. The two examples of miracles reported by Spartianus as supposedly performed by the emperor in his last years have been blended into one. The association of Apollodorus with the Servianus conspiracy is only a hypothesis, but one which can perhaps be defended.

Chabrias, Celer and Diotimus are mentioned several times by Marcus Aurelius, who, however, indicates only their names and their passionate loyalty to Hadrian's memory. They have been introduced into this reconstruction in order to evoke something of the court at Tibur during the last years of the reign; Chabrias represents the circle of Platonist or Stoic philosophers who surrounded the emperor; the military element is represented by Celer (not to be confused with that Celer mentioned by Philostratus and Aristides as secretary for Greek correspondence); Diotimus stands for the group of imperial *erômenoi* (the term long established by tradition for young favourites). These three names of actual associates of the emperor have thus served as a point of departure for those three characters invented only in part. The physician Iollas, on the contrary, is an actual person for whom we lack the true name; nor do we know if he came originally from Alexandria. The freedman Onesimus was in Hadrian's service, but we do not know if his role was that of procurer for Hadrian; the name of Crescens as a secretary of Servianus is authenticated by an inscription, but history does not tell us that he betrayed his master. Opramoas was a great merchant of Hadrian's time who aided Hadrian and his army, but there is nothing to prove that he accompanied Hadrian to the Euphrates. Arrian's wife is known to us by an inscription, but we do not know if she was 'proud and elegant' as Hadrian says here. Only a few minor characters are wholly invented, the slave Euphorion, the actors Olympus and Bathyllus, the physician Leotychides, the young British tribune, and the guide Assar. The two sorceresses, of the Island of Britain and of Canopus respectively, are created to suggest the world of fortune tellers and dealers in occult sciences with whom Hadrian liked to surround himself. The feminine name of *Arete* comes from an authentic poem of Hadrian (*Inscr. Graec.*, XIV, 1089), but is only given arbitrarily here to the housekeeper of the Villa; the name of the courier Menecrates is taken from the *Letter of the King Fermes to the Emperor Hadrian*, a text of wholly legendary content which comes to us from a medieval manuscript and of which history, properly speaking, can make no use; the *Letter* could, however, have borrowed this particular name from other documents now lost.

The brief sketch of the family background of Antinous is not historical, but attempts to take into consideration the social conditions which prevailed at that time in Bithynia. On certain controversial points, such as the cause for enforced retirement of Suetonius, the origin of Antinous, whether slave or free, the active participation of Hadrian in the Palestinian war, the dates of the apotheosis of Sabina and of interment of Aelius Caesar in the Castel Sant' Angelo, it has been necessary to choose between hypotheses of historians, but the effort has been to make that choice only with good reason. In other cases, like that of the adoption of Hadrian by Trajan, or of the death of Antinous, the author has tried to leave that very incertitude which before it existed in history doubtless existed in life itself.

MEMOIRS OF HADRIAN

To G.F.

THE idea for this book and the first writing of it, in whole or in part, and in various forms, date from the period between 1924 and 1929, between my twentieth and twenty-fifth year. All those manuscripts were destroyed, deservedly.

* * *

In turning the pages of a volume of Flaubert's correspondence much read and heavily underscored by me about the year 1927 I came again upon this admirable sentence: 'Just when the gods had ceased to be, and the Christ had not yet come, there was a unique moment in history, between Cicero and Marcus Aurelius, when man stood alone.' A great part of my life was going to be spent in trying to define, and then to portray, that man existing alone and yet closely bound with all being.

* * *

I resumed work on the book in 1934; after prolonged research some fifteen pages were written which seemed to me final in form. Then the project was abandoned, only to be taken up again several times between 1934 and 1937.

* * *

There was a long period in which I thought of the work in the form of a series of dialogues, where all the voices of those times would be heard. But whatever I did, the details seemed to take undue precedence; the parts threatened the balance of the whole; Hadrian's voice was drowned out by all the others. I was not succeeding in my attempt to reconstruct that world as seen and heard by one man.

* * *

From the version of 1934 only one sentence has been retained: 'I begin to discern the profile of my death.' Like a painter who has chosen a landscape, but who constantly shifts his easel now right, now left, I had at last found a point from which to view the book.

* * *

Take a life that is known and completed, recorded and fixed by History (as much as lives ever can be fixed), so that its entire course may be seen at a single glance: more important still, choose the moment when the man who lived that existence weighs and examines it, and is, for the briefest span, capable of judging it. Try to manage so that he stands before his own life in much the same position as we stand when we look at it.

* * *

Mornings spent at the Villa Adriana; innumerable evenings passed in small cafés around the Olympieion; the constant back and forth over Greek seas; roads of Asia Minor. In order to make full use of these memories of mine they had first to recede as far from me as is the Second Century.

* * *

Experiments with time: eighteen days, eighteen months, eighteen years, or eighteen centuries. The motionless survival of statues which, like the head of the *Mondragone Antinous* in the Louvre, are still living in a past time, a *time that has died*. The problem of time foreshortened in terms of human generations: some five and twenty aged men, their withered hands interlinked to form a chain, would be enough to establish an unbroken contact between Hadrian and ourselves.

* * *

In 1937, during a first stay in the United States, I did some reading for this book in the libraries at Yale; I wrote the visit to the physician, and the passage on renunciation of bodily exercise. These fragments, re-worked, are still part of the present version.

In any case, I was too young. There are books which one should not attempt before having passed the age of forty. Earlier than that one may well fail to recognize those great natural boundaries which from person to person, and from century to century, separate the infinite variety of mankind; or, on the contrary, one may attach too much importance to mere administrative barriers, to the customs houses or the sentry boxes erected between man and man. It took me years to learn how to calculate exactly the distances between the emperor and myself.

*   *   *

I ceased to work on the book (except for a few days, in Paris) between 1937 and 1939.

*   *   *

Some mention of T. E. Lawrence reminded me that his tracks in Asia Minor cross and recross those of Hadrian. But the background for Hadrian is not the desert; it is Athens and her hills. The more I thought of these two men, the more the adventure of one who rejects life (and first of all rejects himself) made me desirous of presenting, through Hadrian, the point of view of the man who accepts all experience, or at least who refuses on one score only to accept elsewhere. It goes without saying, of course, that the asceticism of the one and the hedonism of the other are at many points interchangeable.

*   *   *

In October of 1939 the manuscript was left behind in Europe, together with the greater part of the notes; I nevertheless took with me to the United States the several résumés of my former readings at Yale and a map of the Roman Empire at the time of Trajan's death which I had carried about with me for years; also the profile photograph of the *Antinous* of the Archaeological Museum in Florence, purchased there in 1926, the young face gravely sweet.

* * *

From 1939 to 1948 the project was wholly abandoned. I thought of it at times, but with discouragement, and almost with indifference, as one thinks of the impossible. And with something like shame for ever having ventured upon such an undertaking.

* * *

The lapse into despair of a writer who does not write.

* * *

In the worst hours of apathy and dejection I would go for solace to Hartford's fine museum, seeking out a Canaletto painting of Rome, the Pantheon standing brown and gold against the blue sky of a late afternoon in summer; and each time I would come away from it comforted, and once again at peace.

* * *

About the year 1941 I had discovered by chance, in an artists' supply shop in New York, four Piranesi engravings which G— and I bought. One of them, a *View of Hadrian's Villa* which I had not known before, is an interior of the chapel of Canopus, from which were taken in the seventeenth century the *Antinous* in Egyptian style and the accompanying basalt statues of priestesses, all to be seen today in the Vatican. The foreground shows a round structure, burst open like a skull, from which fallen trees and brush hang vaguely down, like strands of hair. The genius of Piranesi, almost mediumistic, has truly caught the element of hallucination here: he has sensed the long-continued rituals of mourning, the tragic architecture of an inner world. For several years I looked at this drawing almost daily, without a thought for my former enterprise, which I supposed that I had given up. Such are the curious detours of what is called oblivion.

* * *

In the spring of 1947, while sorting over some papers, I burned

258

the notes taken at Yale; they seemed to have become by that time completely useless.

* * *

Still, Hadrian's name appears in an essay on Greek myth which I wrote in 1943 and which Roger Caillois published during those war years in *Les Lettres Françaises*, in Buenos Aires. Then in 1945 the figure of the drowned Antinous, borne along somehow on that Lethean current, came again to the surface in an unfinished essay, *Canticle of the Soul and its True Freedom*, written just before the advent of a serious illness.

* * *

Keep in mind that everything recounted here is thrown out of perspective by what is left unsaid: these notes serve only to mark the lacunae. There is nothing, for example, of what I was doing during those difficult years, nor of the thinking, the work, the worries and anxieties, *or* the joys; nor of the tremendous repercussion of external events and the perpetual testing of oneself upon the touchstone of fact. And I pass also in silence over the experiences of illness, and over other, more profound experiences which they bring in their train; and over the perpetual search for, or presence of, love.

* * *

Never mind. That disjunction, that break in continuity, that 'night of the soul' which so many of us experienced at the time, each in his own way (and so often in far more tragic and final form than did I), was essential, perhaps, in order to force me into trying to bridge not only the distance which separated me from Hadrian, but, above all, the distance which separated me from my true self.

* * *

Everything turns out to be valuable that one does for one's self without thought of profit. During those years in an unfamiliar land I had kept on with the reading of authors from classical antiquity: the red or green cloth-bound volumes of

Loeb–Heinemann editions had become a country of my own. Thus, since one of the best ways to reconstruct a man's thinking is to rebuild his library, I had actually been working for years, without knowing it, to refurnish the bookshelves at Tibur in advance. Now I had only to imagine the swollen hands of a sick man holding the half-rolled manuscripts.

*   *   *

Do, from within, the same work of reconstruction which the nineteenth-century archaeologists have done from without.

*   *   *

In December of 1948 I received from Switzerland a trunk which I had stored there during the war, with its contents of family papers and letters some ten years old. I sat down by the fire to work my way through the débris, as if to take some gloomy inventory after a death. I passed several evenings alone at the task, undoing the separate packets and running through them before destroying that accumulation of correspondence with people whom I had forgotten, and who had forgotten me, some of them still alive, others dead. A few of the pages bore dates of a generation ago, and even the names had quite gone from my mind. As I unfolded and threw mechanically into the fire that exchange of dead thoughts between a Marie and a François or a Paul, long since disappeared, I came upon four or five typewritten sheets, the paper of which had turned yellow. The salutation told me nothing: 'My dear Mark . . .' *Mark* . . . What friend or love, what distant relative was this? I could not recall the name at all. It was several minutes before I remembered that *Mark* stood here for *Marcus Aurelius*, and that I had in hand a fragment of the lost manuscript. From that moment there was no question but that this book must be taken up again, whatever the cost.

*   *   *

That same night I re-opened two of the volumes which had also just been returned to me, remnants of a library in large part lost. One was Dio Cassius in Henri Estienne's beautiful printing, and the other a volume of an ordinary edition of *Historia Augusta*, the two principal sources for Hadrian's life, purchased at the time that I was intending to write this book. Everything that the world, and I, had gone through in the interval now served to enrich these chronicles of an earlier age, and threw upon that imperial existence certain other lights and other shades. Once I had thought chiefly of the man of letters, the traveller, the poet, the lover; none of that had faded, to be sure, but now for the first time I could see among all those figures, standing out with great clarity of line, the most official and yet the most hidden form of all, that of the emperor. The fact of having lived in a world which is toppling around us had taught me the importance of the Prince.

* * *

I fell to making, and then remaking, this portrait of a man who was *almost* wise.

* * *

Only one other figure in history has tempted me with nearly the same insistence: Omar Khayyám, the poet-astronomer. But the life of Khayyám is that of the pure contemplator, and of the sombre sceptic, too; the world of action meant little to him. Furthermore, I do not know Persia, nor do I know its language.

* * *

Another thing virtually impossible, to take a feminine character as a central figure, to make Plotina, for example, rather than Hadrian, the axis of my narrative. Women's lives are much too limited, or else too secret. If a woman does recount her own life she is promptly reproached for being no longer truly feminine. It is already hard enough to give some element of truth to the utterances of a man.

* * *

I left for Taos, in New Mexico, taking with me the blank sheets for a fresh start on the book (the swimmer who plunges into the water with no assurance that he will reach the other shore).

Closed inside my compartment as if in a cubicle of some Egyptian tomb, I worked late into the night between New York and Chicago; then all the next day, in the restaurant of a Chicago station where I awaited a train blocked by storms and snow; then again until dawn, alone in the observation car of a Santa Fé limited, surrounded by black spurs of the Colorado mountains, and by the eternal pattern of the stars. Thus were written at a single impulsion the passages on food, love, sleep, and the knowledge of men. I can hardly recall a day spent with more ardour, or more lucid nights.

* * *

I pass as rapidly as possible over three years of research, of interest to specialists alone, and over the development of a method akin to controlled delirium, of interest, probably, to none but madmen. And yet this term *delirium* smacks too much of romanticism; let us say, rather, a constant participation, as intensely aware as possible, in *that which has been*.

* * *

One foot in scholarship, the other in magic arts, or, more accurately and without metaphor, absorption in that *sympathetic magic* which operates when one transports oneself, in thought, into another's body and soul.

* * *

Portrait of a voice. If I have chosen to write these *Memoirs of Hadrian* in the first person it is in order to dispense with any intermediary, in so far as possible, even were that intermediary myself. Surely Hadrian could speak more forcibly and more subtly of his life than could I.

* * *

Those who put the historical novel in a category apart are forgetting that what every novelist does is only to interpret, by means of the techniques which his period affords, a certain number of past events; his memories, whether consciously or unconsciously recalled, whether personal or impersonal, are all

262

woven of the same stuff as History itself. The work of Proust is a reconstruction of a lost past quite as much as is *War and Peace*. The historical novel of the 1830s, it is true, tends toward melodrama, and to cloak-and-dagger romance; but not more than does Balzac's magnificent *Duchess of Langeais*, or his startling *Girl with the Golden Eyes*, both of wholly contemporary setting. Flaubert painstakingly rebuilds a Carthaginian palace by charging his description with hundreds of minute details, thus employing essentially the same method as for his picture of Yonville, a village of his own time and of his own Normandy. In our day, when introspection tends to dominate literary forms, the historical novel, or what may for convenience's sake be called by that name, must take the plunge into time recaptured, and must fully establish itself within some inner world.

* * *

Time itself has nothing to do with the matter. It is always surprising to me that my contemporaries, masters as they consider themselves to be over space, apparently remain unaware that one can contract the distance between centuries at will.

* * *

We lose track of everything, and of everyone, even ourselves. The facts of my father's life are less known to me than those of the life of Hadrian. My own existence, if I had to write of it, would be reconstructed by me from externals, laboriously, as if it were the life of someone else; I should have to turn to letters, and to the recollections of others, in order to clarify such uncertain memories. What is ever left but crumbled walls, or masses of shade? Here, where Hadrian's life is concerned, try to manage so that the lacunae of our texts coincide with what he himself might have forgotten.

* * *

Which is not to suggest, as is too often done, that historical truth is never to be attained, in any of its aspects. With this kind of truth, as with all others, the problem is the same: one errs *more* or *less*.

* * *

The rules of the game: learn everything, read everything, inquire into everything, while at the same time adapting to one's ends the *Spiritual Exercises* of Ignatius of Loyola, or the method of Hindu ascetics, who for years, and to the point of exhaustion, try to visualize ever more exactly the images which they create beneath their closed eyelids. Through hundreds of card notes pursue each incident to the very moment that it occurred; endeavour to restore the mobility and suppleness of life to those visages known to us only in stone. When two texts, or two assertions, or perhaps two ideas, are in contradiction, be ready to reconcile them rather than cancel one by the other; regard them as two different facets, or two successive stages, of the same reality, a reality convincingly human just because it is complex. Strive to read a text of the second century with the eyes, soul, and feelings of the second century; let it steep in that mother solution which the facts of its own time provide; set aside, if possible, all beliefs and sentiments which have accumulated in successive strata between those persons and us. And nevertheless take advantage (though prudently, and solely by way of preparatory study) of all possibilities for comparison and cross-checking, and of new perspectives slowly developed by the many centuries and events separating us from a given text, a fact, a man; make use of such aids more or less as guide-marks along the road of return towards one particular point in time. Keep one's own shadow out of the picture; leave the mirror clean of the mist of one's own breath; take only what is most essential and durable in us, in the emotions aroused by the senses or in the operations of the mind, as our point of contact with those men who, like us, nibbled olives and drank wine, or gummed their fingers with honey, who fought bitter winds and blinding rain, or in summer sought the plane tree's shade; who took their pleasures, thought their own thoughts, grew old, and died.

* * *

Several times I have had physicians 'diagnose' the brief passages in the chronicles which deal with Hadrian's illness. Indications not so different, after all, from the clinical descriptions of Balzac's last days.

* * *

Make good use, the better to understand Hadrian's malady, of the first symptoms of a heart ailment.

* * *

'What's Hecuba to him?' Hamlet asks when a strolling player weeps over that tragic queen. Thus the Prince of Denmark is forced to admit that this actor who sheds genuine tears has managed to establish with a woman dead for three thousand years a more profound relationship than he himself has with his own father, so recently buried, and whose wrongs he does not feel fully enough to seek swift revenge.

* * *

The human substance and structure hardly change; nothing is more stable than the curve of a heel, the position of a tendon, or the form of a toe. But there are periods when the shoe is less deforming than in others. In the century of which I speak we are still very close to the undisguised freedom of the bare foot.

* * *

In crediting Hadrian with prophetic insight I was keeping within the realm of plausibility as long as such prognostics remained vague and general. The impartial analyst of human affairs ordinarily makes few mistakes as to the ultimate course of events, but he begins to err seriously when he tries to foresee the exact way that events will work out, their turning points and details. Napoleon on Saint Helena predicted that a century after his death Europe would have turned either revolutionary or Cossack; he stated the two terms of the problem extremely well, but could not imagine one superposed upon the other.

On the whole, however, it is only out of pride or gross ignorance, or cowardice, that we refuse to see in the present the lineaments of times to come. Those sages of the ancient world, unbound by dogma of any kind, thought as we do in terms of physics, or rather, of physiology, as applied to the whole universe: they envisaged the end of man and the dying out of this sphere. Both Plutarch and Marcus Aurelius knew full well that gods, and civilizations, pass and die. We are not the first to look upon an inexorable future.

*   *   *

My attribution of clairvoyance to the emperor was, in any case, only a means of bringing into play the almost Faustian element of his character, as it appears, for example, in the *Sibylline Verses* and in the writings of Aelius Aristides, or in the portrait of Hadrian grown old, as sketched by Fronto. Rightly or not, the contemporaries of this dying man ascribed to him something more than human powers.

*   *   *

If this man had not maintained peace in the world, and revived the economy of the empire, his personal fortunes and misfortunes would have moved me less.

*   *   *

One can never give enough time to the absorbing study of relationships between texts. The poem on the hunting trophy consecrated by Hadrian at Thespiae to the God of Love and to the Uranian Venus, 'on the hills of Helicon, beside Narcissus' spring', can be dated as of the autumn of the year 124; at about that same time the emperor passed through Mantinea, where, according to Pausanius, he had the tomb of Epaminondas rebuilt, and wrote a poem to be inscribed upon it. The Mantinean inscription is now lost, but Hadrian's act of homage is to be fully understood, perhaps, only if we view it in relation to a passage of Plutarch's *Morals* which tells us that Epaminondas was buried in that place between two young friends struck down at his side. If for date of the meeting of the emperor and

Antinous we accept the stay in Asia Minor of 123–124, which is in any case the most plausible date and the best supported by iconographical evidence, these two poems then would form a part of what might be called the Antinous cycle; both are inspired by that same Greece of heroic lovers which Arrian evoked later on, after the death of the favourite, when he compared the youth to Patroclus.

*   *   *

A certain number of persons whose portraits one would wish to develop: Plotina, Sabina, Arrian, Suetonius. But Hadrian could see them only in part, from the point of view at which he was standing. Antinous himself has to be presented by refraction, through the emperor's memories, that is to say, in passionately meticulous detail, not devoid of a few errors.

*   *   *

All that can be said of the temperament of Antinous is inscribed in any one of his likenesses. 'Eager and impassioned tenderness, sullen effeminacy': Shelley, with a poet's admirable candour, says the essential in six words, while most of the nineteenth-century art critics and historians could only expatiate upon the subject with righteous declamation, or else idealize about it, vaguely and hypocritically.

*   *   *

We are rich in portraits of Antinous; they range in quality from the mediocre to the incomparable. Despite variations due to the skill of the respective sculptors or to the age of the model, or to differences between portraits made from life and those executed to commemorate the youth after death, all are striking and deeply moving because of the incredible realism of the face, always immediately recognizable and nevertheless so diversely interpreted, and because they are examples, unique in classical antiquity, of survival and repetition in stone of a countenance which was neither that of a statesman nor of a philosopher, but simply of one who was loved. Among these portraits the two most beautiful are the least known: they are also the only ones which transmit to us the name of the sculptor. One is the bas-relief signed by Antonianos of Aphrodisias and found some fifty years ago on the property of an agronomic institute, the Fundi Rustici, in the Committee Room of which it is now placed. Since no guidebook of Rome indicates its existence in that city already so crowded with statues, tourists do not know about it. This work of Antonianos has been carved in Italian marble, so it was certainly executed in Italy, and doubtless in Rome, either because that artist was already established in the capital, or because he had been brought back by Hadrian on one of the emperor's travels. It has exquisite delicacy. The young head, pensively inclined, is framed by the tendrils of a vine twined in supple arabesque; the brevity of life comes inevitably to mind, the sacrificial grape and the fruit-scented air of an evening in autumn. Unhappily, the marble has suffered from storage in a cellar during the recent war-years: its whiteness is temporarily obscured and earth-stained, and three fingers of the figure's left hand have been broken. Thus do gods pay for the follies of men.

*[*The preceding paragraph appeared for the first time six years ago; meanwhile this bas-relief was acquired by a Roman banker, Arturo Osio, a whimsical man who probably would have stirred the imagination of Stendhal or of Balzac. Signor Osio has lavished upon this fair object the same solicitous attention that he gives to the animals on his property at the edge of Rome, where they run free in their natural state, and to the trees which he has planted by the thousand on his shore estate at Orbetello. A rare virtue, this last, for Stendhal was writing as early as 1828, 'The Italians loathe trees'; and what would he say today when real estate speculators, trying to pack more and more colossal apartment houses into Rome, are circumventing the city's laws to protect its handsome umbrella pines. Their method is simply to kill the trees by injections of hot water. A rare luxury, too, though one which many a man of wealth could enjoy, is this landowner's animation of woods and fields with creatures at full liberty, and that not for the pleasure of hunting them down, but for reconstituting a veritable Eden. The love for*

* Addition of 1958.

statues of classical antiquity, those great peaceful objects which seem so solid and yet are so easily destroyed, is an uncommon taste among private collectors in these agitated times, cut off from both past and future. The new possessor of the bas-relief of Antonianos, acting on the advice of experts, has just had it cleaned by a specialist whose light, slow rubbing by hand has removed the rust and moisture stains from the marble and restored its soft gleam, like that of alabaster or of ivory.]

*   *   *

The second of these masterpieces is the famous sardonyx known as the Marlborough Gem, because it once belonged to that family collection, now dispersed. For more than thirty years this fine intaglio seemed to have been lost, or hidden away, but in January of 1952 it came to light in a public sale in London; the informed taste of the great collector Giorgio Sangiorgi has brought it back to Rome. I am indebted to him for the chance to see and to handle this unique gem. A signature, though no longer complete, can be read around the edge; it is thought, and doubtless correctly, to be that of the sculptor of the bas-relief, Antonianos of Aphrodisias. So skilfully has the master-carver enclosed that perfect profile within the narrow compass of a sardonyx that this bit of stone stands as testimony to a great lost art quite as much as does any statue or any relief. The proportions of the work make us forget the dimensions of the object. At some time during the Byzantine period the gem was set in a nugget of solid gold, and in this form passed from collector to collector, none of whose names we know, until it reached Venice; it is mentioned as part of a great seventeenth-century collection there. In the next century it was purchased by the celebrated dealer in antiques, Gavin Hamilton, and brought to England, whence it now returns to Rome, its starting-point. Of all objects still above ground today it is the one of which we can assume with some assurance that it has often been held in Hadrian's hands.

*   *   *

One has to go into the most remote corners of a subject in

order to discover the simplest things, and things of most general literary interest. It is only in studying Phlegon, secretary to Hadrian, that I learned that we owe to this forgotten personage the first, and one of the finest, of the great ghost stories, that sombre, sensuous *Bride of Corinth* which inspired Goethe's ballad, and likewise the *Corinthian Wedding* of Anatole France. It must be said, however, that Phlegon also took down, with the same avid and uncritical curiosity for everything beyond ordinary experience, some absurd stories of two-headed monsters, and of hermaphrodites got with child. Such was the stuff of the conversations, on some days, at least, at the imperial table.

* * *

Those who would have preferred a *Journal* of Hadrian to his *Memoirs* forget that a man of action rarely keeps a journal; it is almost always later on, and in a period of prolonged inactivity, that he does his recollecting, makes his notations, and, very often, has cause for wonder at the course his life has taken.

* * *

If all other documents were lacking, the *Letter of Arrian to the Emperor Hadrian on the Circumnavigation of the Black Sea* would suffice to recreate in broad outline that great imperial figure: the scrupulous exactitude of the chief-of-state who would know all details; his interest in the work both of war and of peace; his concern for good likenesses in statues, and that these should be finely wrought; his passion for the poetry and legend of an earlier day. And that society, rare in any period, but destined to vanish completely after the time of Marcus Aurelius, wherein the scholarly administrator can still address his prince as a friend, however subtly shaded his deference and his respect. Everything is there: the nostalgia for ancient Greece and its ideals, discreet allusion to a lost love and to mystical consolation sought by the bereaved survivor, the haunting appeal of unknown lands and barbarous climes. The evocation of desert wastes peopled only by sea-birds, so profoundly romantic in spirit, calls to mind the exquisite vase found in Villa Hadriana, to be seen today in the Museum of the Terme in Rome; there on a field of marble snow a flock of wild heron are spreading their wings to fly away, in utter solitude.

*   *   *

Note of 1949: the more I strive for an exact portrait the farther I diverge from the kind of book, and of man, who would please the public. Only a few students of human destiny will understand.

*   *   *

In our time the novel devours all other forms; one is almost forced to use it as the medium of expression. This study of the destiny of a man called Hadrian would have been cast in the form of a tragedy in the seventeenth century, or of an essay, perhaps, in the period of the Renaissance.

*   *   *

This book is the condensation of a vast work composed for myself alone. I had taken the habit of writing each night, in almost automatic fashion, the result of those long, self-induced visions whereby I could place myself intimately within another period of time. The merest word, the slightest gesture, the least perceptible implications were noted down; scenes now summed up in a line or two, in the book as it is, passed before me in fullest detail, and as if in slow motion. Added all together, these accounts would have afforded material for a volume of several thousand pages, but each morning I would burn the work of the night before. In such fashion I wrote a great number of decidedly abstruse meditations, and several descriptions bordering on the obscene.

*   *   *

He who seeks passionately for truth, or at least for accuracy, is frequently the one best able to perceive, like Pilate, that truth is not absolute or pure. Hence, mingled with his most direct assertions we find hesitations, deviousness, and reservations which a more conventional mind would not evince. At certain moments, though very seldom, it has even occurred to me that the emperor was lying. In such cases I had to let him lie, like the rest of us.

* * *

The utter fatuity of those who say to you, 'By "Hadrian" you mean yourself!' Almost as unsubtle as those who wonder why one should choose a subject so remote in time and in space. The sorcerer who pricks his thumb before he evokes the shades knows well that they will heed his call only because they can lap his blood. He knows, too, or ought to know, that the voices who speak to him are wiser and more worthy of attention than are his own clamorous outcries.

* * *

It did not take me long to realize that I had embarked upon the life of a very great man. From that time on, still more respect for truth, closer attention, and, on my part, ever more silence.

* * *

In a sense, every life that is recounted is offered as an example; we write in order to attack or to defend a view of the universe, and to set forth a system of conduct which is our own. It is none the less true, however, that nearly every biographer disqualifies himself by over-idealizing his subject or by deliberate disparagement, by exaggerated stress on certain details or by cautious omission of others. Thus a character is arbitrarily constructed, taking the place of the man to be understood and explained. A human life cannot be graphed, whatever people may say, by two virtual perpendiculars, representing what a man believed himself to be and what he wished to be, plus a flat horizontal for what he actually was; rather, the diagram has to be composed of three curving lines, extended to infinity, ever meeting and ever diverging.

* * *

Whatever one does, one always rebuilds the monument in his

own way. But it is already something gained to have used only the original stones.

★   ★   ★

Every being who has gone through the adventure of living *is* myself.

★   ★   ★

This second century appeals to me because it was the last century, for a very long period of time, in which men could think and express themselves with full freedom. As for us, we are perhaps already very far from such times as that.

★   ★   ★

On the 26 December 1950, on an evening of freezing cold and in the almost polar silence of Mount Desert Island, off the Atlantic shore, I was striving to live again through the smothering heat of a day in July, in the year 138 in Baiae, to feel the weight of a sheet on weary, heavy limbs, and to catch the barely perceptible sound of that tideless sea as from time to time it reached a man whose whole attention was concentrated upon other murmurs, those of his approaching death. I tried to go as far as the last sip of water, the last spasm of pain, the last image in his mind. Now the emperor had but to die.

★   ★   ★

This book bears no dedication. It ought to have been dedicated to G.F—, and would have been, were there not a kind of impropriety in putting a personal inscription at the opening of a work where, precisely, I was trying to efface the personal. But even the longest dedication is too short and too common-place to honour a friendship so uncommon. When I try to define this asset which has been mine now for years, I tell myself that such a privilege, however rare it may be, is surely not unique; that in the whole adventure of bringing a book successfully to its conclusion, or even in the entire life of some fortunate writers, there must have been sometimes, in the background, perhaps, someone who will not let pass the weak

273

or inaccurate sentence which we ourselves would retain, out of fatigue; someone who would reread with us for the twentieth time, if need be, a questionable page; someone who takes down for us from the library shelves the heavy tomes in which we may find a helpful suggestion, and who persists in continuing to peruse them long after weariness has made us give up; someone who bolsters our courage and approves, or sometimes disputes, our ideas; who shares with us, and with equal fervour, the joys of art and of living, the endless work which both require, never easy but never dull; someone who is neither our shadow nor our reflection, nor even our complement, but simply himself; someone who leaves us ideally free, but who nevertheless obliges us to be fully what we are. *Hospes Comesque.*

* * *

In December 1951 learned of the fairly recent death of the German historian Wilhelm Weber, and in April 1952 of the death of the scholar Paul Graindor, both of whose works I have so much used. A few days ago talked with G.B— and J.F—, who had known the engraver Pierre Gusman in Rome at the time that he was drawing, with passion, all the different parts of the Villa. The feeling of belonging to a kind of *Gens Aelia*, of being, as it were, one of the throng of secretaries who had served the great man, of participating in the change of that imperial guard which poets and humanists mount in relay around any great memory. Thus (and it is doubtless the same for specialists in the study of Napoleon, or for lovers of Dante), over the ages is formed a circle of kindred spirits, moved by the same interests and sympathies, or concerned with the same problems.

* * *

The pedants of comedy, Vadius and Blazius still exist, and their fat cousin Basil is ever about. Once and once only have I happened to be confronted with that mixture of insults and coarse jokes; with extracts truncated or skilfully deformed, so as to make our sentences say some absurdity which they do not say; with captious arguments built up by assertions both vague and peremptory enough to win ready credence from the reader respectful of academic trappings and lacking the time, or the desire, to look up the sources for himself. Characteristic, all of it, of a certain species which, fortunately, is rare. On the contrary, what genuine good will have so many scholars shown who could just as readily, in these times of excessive specialization, have disdained outright any literary effort at reconstruction of the past which might seem to them to trespass on their domain . . . Too many of them have graciously, and of their own accord, taken trouble to rectify some error already in print, or to confirm a detail, support a hypothesis, expedite new research, for me not to express here a word of gratitude to such well-disposed readers. Each book which sees a new edition owes something to the discriminating people who have read it.

*   *   *

Do the best one can. Do it over again. Then still improve, even if ever so slightly, those retouches. 'It is myself that I remake,' said the poet Yeats in speaking of his revisions.

*   *   *

Yesterday, at the Villa, I thought of the thousands of lives, silent and furtive as those of wild beasts, unthinking as those of plants, who have followed in succession here between Hadrian's time and ours: gypsies of Piranesi's day, pillagers of the ruins, beggars, goatherds, and peasants lodged as best they could in some corner of the rubble. At the end of an olive grove, in an ancient corridor partly cleared, G— and I came upon a shepherd's bed of rushes, with his improvised clothespeg stuck between two blocks of Roman cement, and the ashes of his fire not yet cold. A sense of intimacy with humble, ordinary things, a little like what one feels at the Louvre when, after closing hour, the cots of the guardians appear in among the statues.

*[*Nothing need be changed in 1958 in the preceding paragraph;*
* Addition of 1958.

275

*the clothes-peg of the shepherd is still there, though not his bed. G—
and I have again sat resting on the grass of the Vale of Tempe,
among the violets, at that sacred moment of the year when everything
begins anew, in spite of the threats which man today is everywhere
raising overhead. But nevertheless the Villa has suffered pernicious
change. Not all of it, to be sure: a whole which the centuries have
slowly destroyed, but have also formed, is not so quickly altered. By
an error seldom committed in Italy certain dubious 'embellishments'
have followed in the wake of excavations and necessary repairs.
Olive groves have been cut down to make way for a highly
conspicuous parking lot, complete with shop and counter service of
the type prevalent at exposition grounds, thus transforming the
Poecilium's noble solitude into a city square; visitors may drink from
a cement fountain which offers water through an absurd plaster
mask, a would-be imitation of the antique; another mask, even
more pointless, decorates the wall of the great pool, where a flotilla
of ducks now holds forth. Still more plaster graces the Canal: casts
of the garden statues found here in recent diggings have been placed
on pedestals and lined up somewhat arbitrarily along its banks; the
originals, fairly average Greco-Roman work, do not deserve the
honour of so conspicuous a position, but neither do they merit the
indignity of being copied in such hideous material, both swollen and
unsubstantial. This new décor gives to the once melancholy Canopus
something of the air of a studio set, ready for a film version of 'life
in Imperial Rome'.*

*There is nothing more easily destroyed than the equilibrium of the
fairest places. A text remains intact regardless of our whims of
interpretation, and survives our commentaries; but the slightest
imprudence inflicted upon stone, the shortest macadamized road cut
through a field where grass has peacefully grown for centuries, does
something irreparable, and for ever. The beauty goes, and the
authenticity likewise.]*

* * *

There are places where one has chosen to live, invisible abodes
which one makes for oneself quite outside the current of time.
I have lived in Tibur, and shall die there, perhaps, as Hadrian
did on Achilles' Isle.

No. Once more I have gone back to the Villa, to its garden pavilions built for privacy and for repose, to the vestiges of a luxury free of pomp, and as little imperial as possible, conceived of rather for the wealthy connoisseur who tries to combine the pleasures of art with the charms of rural life. In the Pantheon I have watched for the exact spot where sunlight would fall on a morning of 21 April, and along the Mausoleum's halls have retraced that funeral path so often walked by the friends of the emperor's last days, Chabrias, Diotimus, and Celer. But I have ceased to feel the immediate presence of those beings, the living reality of those events; they are near me still, but of the past, neither more nor less now than the memories of my own life. Our commerce with others does not long endure; it ceases once satisfaction is obtained, the lesson learned, the service rendered, the book complete. What I could say has been said; what I could learn has been learned. Let us turn, for the time that is left to us, to other work.

FIND OUT MORE ABOUT
PENGUIN BOOKS

We publish the largest range of titles of any English language paperback publisher. As well as novels, crime and science fiction, humour, biography and large-format illustrated books, Penguin series include *Pelican Books* (on the arts, sciences and current affairs), *Penguin Reference Books*, *Penguin Classics*, *Penguin Modern Classics*, *Penguin English Library* and *Penguin Handbooks* (on subjects from cookery and gardening to sport), as well as *Puffin Books* for children. Other series cover a wide variety of interests from poetry to crosswords, and there are also several newly formed series—*King Penguin*, *Penguin American Library*, *Penguin Diaries and Letters* and *Penguin Travel Library*.

We are an international publishing house, but for copyright reasons not every Penguin title is available in every country. To find out more about the Penguins available in your country please write to our U.K. office – Dept EP, Penguin Books Ltd, Harmondsworth, Middlesex UB7 0DA – unless you live in one of the following areas:

In the U.S.A.: Dept DG, Penguin Books, 299 Murray Hill Parkway, East Rutherford, New Jersey 07073.

In Canada: Penguin Books Canada Ltd, 2801 John Street, Markham, Ontario L3R 1B4.

In Australia: Marketing Department, Penguin Books Australia Ltd, P.O. Box 257, Ringwood, Victoria 3134.

In New Zealand: Marketing Department, Penguin Books (N.Z.) Ltd, P.O. Box 4019, Auckland 10.

In India: Penguin Overseas Ltd, 706 Eros Apartments, 56 Nehru Place, New Delhi 110019.

A selection

THE BOOK OF LAUGHTER AND FORGETTING
Milan Kundera

'No question about it. The most important novel published in Britain this year was Milan Kundera's *The Book of Laughter and Forgetting*, a whirling dance of a book by a Czech novelist who is fully the equal of the great satirist Joroslav Hasek, creator of *The Good Soldier Švejk*. Kundera is a self-confessed hedonist in a world beset by politics, and his marvellous novel mingles a hedonist's love of eroticism, fantasy and fun with knife-sharp political satire (it recounts, for example, the case of a Communist leader who is so thoroughly erased from history that nothing is left of him but his hat). A masterpiece, full of angels, terror, ostriches and love' – Salman Rushdie in the *Sunday Times*

NIGHT THOUGHTS OF A CLASSICAL PHYSICIST
Russell McCormach

This brilliant and unorthodox novel draws us into the mind of a scientist: Victor Jakob, an old professor of physics living in Germany, September 1918. Story and history, Jakob's approaching death and Germany's impending destruction give the novel an extraordinary urgency as, speaking his night thoughts, Jakob summons up the classical past of German physics and confronts the future – his ordered world disturbed by the genius of Einstein, and fragmented into chaos by the raw vitality of modernism . . .

'A wonderful book' – *The Times Higher Education Supplement*

'Part history, part science lesson, part philosophical treatise, *Night Thoughts* is a brilliant piece of scholarship and a profoundly moving portrait of a man and his time' – *Time*

KING PENGUIN

A selection

FIRE ON THE MOUNTAIN
Anita Desai

Nanda Kaul has chosen to spend her last years high up in the mountains. There, free from the demands of a busy life, she could arrange her thoughts into tranquillity.

Her great-grandchild comes to join her. A thin, fragile, secretive girl whose intrusion Nanda Kaul deeply resents. But this child has a capacity to change things, and Nanda Kaul discovers new needs deep within herself. When the violence explodes she faces the truth.

'Beautifully accomplished and memorable by any standards . . . I admired it unreservedly' – Susan Hill in *The Times*

'Written in cool, clear prose, beautifully shaped, infinitely moving' – Paul Scott in *Country Life*

'The most original person I've come across in fiction for a long time' – Anthony Thwaite in the *Observer*

BIRTHSTONE
D. H. Thomas

'Fantasy as Freud envisaged it, powerful enough to counter reality, working like free association and allowing the unconscious to take over' – *London Review of Books*

The magical properties of the birthstone Men-an-Tol are legendary. When Jo and the Bolithos crawl through it, the world on the other side looks very different. As they settle into their holiday cottage on the Cornish coast, Lola begins to grow younger, behaving with all the abandon of her volatile ancestor Lola Montez. Her son races towards senility, though not too fast to prevent him from responding to the sexual enticements of both women. But this is nothing compared to the behaviour of Jo, whose demonic alter egos interrupt her life with absurd, erotic and often violent results.

With a logic of its own, *Birthstone*, revised by the author for this edition, is as assured and resourceful as the comic turns – and U-turns – are fast and furious.

A selection

THE REBEL ANGELS
Robertson Davies

The University of St John and the Holy Ghost (Spook) is jolted out of its crabbed and scholarly pursuits by the return of the evil, brilliant Brother Parlabane, and by the discovery of an unpublished manuscript by Rabelais.

Coincidentally, beautiful, sexy Maria Magdelena Theotky is doing postgraduate work on Rabelais (provoking not entirely academic responses in the breasts of her colleagues) . . . and when the manuscript disappears all the unbridled furies of sex, vanity and violence are let loose.

A glittering extravaganza of wit, scatology, saturnalia, mysticism, and erudite vaudeville, *The Rebel Angels* places Robertson Davies in the forefront of contemporary writers.

BEDBUGS
Clive Sinclair

'Disconcerting brilliance, crazy humour and perfect control . . . He threads together West Coast, argot, psychiatrists' newspeak, Yiddish, Hebrew, and can casually pop in an overheard exchange in a Cambridge pub so that it sounds just as outlandish' – *Observer*

'Wildly erotic and weirdly plotted, the subconscious erupting violently into everyday life . . . His stories work you hard; tease and torment and shock you' – *Financial Times*

'Words come flying up at you from all angles . . . marvellously funny . . . he will make you laugh aloud' – *Punch*

KING PENGUIN

A selection

THE VENDOR OF SWEETS
R. K. Narayan

A widower of firm Ghandian principles, Jagan nonetheless harbours a warmly embarrassed affection for his wastrel son Mali. But even Jagan's patience begins to fray when Mali descends on the sleepy city of Malgudi full of modern notions, with a new half-American wife and a grand plan for selling novel-writing machines . . .

Different generations and different cultures, father and son confront each other and are taken by surprise as this beautifully-worked novel unfolds, and as Narayan brings all his delightful genius for comedy into play.

'Narayan wakes in me a spring of gratitude, for he has offered me a second home. Without him I could never have known what it is like to be an Indian' – Graham Greene

A CONFEDERACY OF DUNCES
John Kennedy Toole

A monument to sloth, rant and contempt, a behemoth of fat, flatulence and furious suspicion of anything modern – this is Ignatius J. Reilly of New Orleans, noble crusader against a world of dunces. Propelling his monstrous bulk amongst the flesh-pots of a fallen city, he documents life on his Big Chief tablets as he goes; until his maroon-haired mother decrees that he must work.

'I succumbed, stunned and seduced, page after page . . . it is a masterwork of comedy' – *The New York Times*

Winner of the Pulitzer Prize

A selection

THE IMAGE OF A DRAWN SWORD
Jocelyn Brooke

The Image of a Drawn Sword is Jocelyn Brooke's only true novel. Yet in this exploration of friendship, sexuality, guilt, alienation and power, he reveals an underlying autobiographical element in which his own physical experiences in the army are translated into a Kafkaesque vision where fantasy and reality are disturbingly blurred.

'The skill and intensity of the writing make peculiarly haunting this cry of complaint on behalf of bewildered Man' – Pamela Hansford Johnson

'Seldom have naturalism and fantasy been more strangely merged. Mr Brooke is a great writer' – Elizabeth Bowen

BLACK LIST: SECTION H
Francis Stuart

Opening with his marriage to Maud Gonne's daughter, and concluding with his arrival in Hitler's Germany, Francis Stuart calls his magnificent and disorientating book: 'an imaginative fiction in which only real people appear and under their actual names where possible.'

'Answers to Yeats's favourite epithets of commendation – cold, strange, detonating' – *Guardian*

'A preposterous, dissimulating, macho-machiavellian novelist, but he has a rare streak of genius' – *London Magazine*

KING PENGUIN

A selection

BULLET PARK
John Cheever

Linked by the mysterious binding power of nomenclature, Paul Hammer and Eliot Nailles are nonetheless violently opposite.

Nailles, a chemist dedicated to the elimination of bad breath, is strictly monogamous and, apparently, an exemplary father to his teenage son Tony. Hammer is the illegitimate son of a socialist kleptomaniac, and certainly not the scrubbed and decent citizen he seems . . . When the two men are viewed together as halves of the overburdened American psyche, John Cheever's satirical etching of small-town American life begins to take on a lethal new dimension.

'Very funny indeed . . . Cheever formulated the great American unease almost before anyone else had noticed it' – *The Times*

THE BEGGAR MAID
Alice Munro

'Wonderful! Whether *The Beggar Maid* is a collection of stories or a new kind of novel I'm not quite sure, but whatever it is, it's wonderful' – John Gardner, author of *Grendel*

As a child Rose had a hard life. Born into the back streets of a small Canadian town, she battled incessantly with her practical and shrewd stepmother, who cowed her with tales of her own past and warnings of the dangerous world outside. But Rose was ambitious – she won a scholarship and left for Toronto where she married Patrick; for him she was his Beggar Maid, 'meek and voluptuous, with her shy white feet', and he was her knight, content to sit and adore her . . .

'A work of great brilliance and depth . . . Munro's power of analysis, of sensations and thoughts, is almost Proustian in its sureness' – Alan Hollinghurst in the *New Statesman*

KING PENGUIN

A selection

THE SAILOR WHO FELL FROM GRACE WITH THE SEA
Yukio Mishima

After five years of celibate widowhood, Fusako consummates her two-day relationship with Ryuji, a naval officer self-convinced of his glorious destiny . . . and they are spied on by Fusako's son, Noboru, a self-possessed thirteen-year-old, 'No. 3' in a sinister élite of precocious schoolboys.

'Here, within the compass of 150 pages, are love, violence, lyrical dreams of glory, superb plotting and gruesome pay-off. This may sound a lurid hotch-potch but in fact it is a work of exquisite balance and beauty' – *Sunday Telegraph*

THE STORIES OF WILLIAM TREVOR

At an Irish wedding, a wife-swapping party or a boarding school; with a gesture or a deceptively casual observation, William Trevor can open up secret lives. Drawing us into other people's worlds – and into their seedy, comic underworlds – here he proves himself an enthralling interpreter of the human heart, and a master storyteller.

This volume contains all the stories published in *Lovers of Their Time*, *The Ballroom of Romance*, *Angels at the Ritz*, *The Day We Got Drunk On Cake*, and *Beyond the Pale*.

'William Trevor's admirably comic universe, his world of stilted speech and dark repressed feeling . . . all these are *tour de force* stories' – Malcolm Bradbury in the *Observer*

A selection

A PALE VIEW OF HILLS
Kazuo Ishiguro

After her daughter's suicide, Etsuko, a Japanese widow living in England, is left to face her memories. As they crowd in, shifting perspectives, Etsuko is transported back to a hot, insect-ridden summer in Nagasaki, when her family and friends were struggling to rebuild their lives after the war. Her memories turn to her strange friendship with Sachiko – a wealthy woman reduced to vagrancy – and her little girl, Mariko . . . and then past and present become fused in a narrative of macabre and haunting poignancy.

'Elegiac, beautifully written, deceptively gentle . . . marked by a rare generosity of spirit' – Angela Carter

AT THE JERUSALEM
Paul Bailey

The road to Jerusalem – a 'home' for old ladies – was the road which led to silent obliteration. Its cheerless walls offered widowed Mrs Gudny little sanctuary and its impersonal monotony was worse than pain. She was going to need all her gentle stubbornness to survive.

'It gave me a pleasure I've been missing for quite a while, the discovery of a new fictional talent' – Mary McCarthy in the *Observer*